continued . . .

Demon Night

"Meljean is now officially one of my favorite authors. And this book's hero? . . . I just went weak at the knees. And the love scenes—wow, just wow."
—Nalini Singh

"This is the book for paranormal lovers. It is a phenomenal book by an author who knows how to give her readers exactly what they want. What Brook's readers want is a story that is dangerous, sexy, scary, and smart. *Demon Night* delivers all that and more! . . . [It] is the epitome of what a paranormal romance should be! I didn't want to put it down."
—*Romance Reader at Heart*

"Poignant and compelling with lots of action, and it's very sensual. You'll fall in love with Charlie, and Ethan will cause your thermometer to blow its top. An excellent plot, wonderful dialogue . . . Don't miss reading it or any of Meljean Brook's other novels in this series."
—*Fresh Fiction*

"An intense romance that will leave you breathless . . . I was drawn in from the first page."
—*Romance Junkies*

Demon Moon

"The fourth book in Meljean Brook's Guardian series turns up the heat without losing any of the danger."
—*Entertainment Weekly*

"A read that goes down hot and sweet—utterly unique—and one hell of a ride."
—Marjorie M. Liu, *New York Times* bestselling author

"Sensual and intriguing, *Demon Moon* is a simply wonderful book. I was enthralled from the first page!"
—Nalini Singh

"Brings a unique freshness to the romantic fantasy realm . . . Action-packed from the onset."
—*Midwest Book Review*

"I loved every moment of it."
—*All About Romance*

"Fantastically drawn characters . . . and their passion for each other is palpable in each scene they share. It stews beneath the surface and when it finally reaches boiling point . . . OH WOW!"
—*Vampire Romance Books*

Demon Angel

"I've never read anything like this book. *Demon Angel* is brilliant, heartbreaking, genre-bending—even, I dare say, epic. Simply put, I love it."
—Marjorie M. Liu

"Brook has crafted a complex, interesting world that goes far beyond your usual . . . paranormal romance. *Demon Angel* truly soars."
—Jennifer Estep, author of *Jinx*

"I can honestly say I haven't read many books lately that have kept me guessing and wondering 'what's next,' but this is one of them. [Brook has] created a unique and different world . . . Gritty and realistic . . . Incredibly inventive . . . This is a book which makes me think and think about it even days after finishing it."
—*Dear Author*

"Enthralling . . . [A] delightful saga."
—*The Best Reviews*

"Extremely engaging . . . A fiendishly good book. *Demon Angel* is outstanding."
—*The Romance Reader*

"A surefire winner. This book will captivate you and leave you yearning for more. Don't miss *Demon Angel*."
—*Romance Reviews Today*

"A fascinating romantic fantasy with . . . a delightful pairing of star-crossed lovers."
—*Midwest Book Review*

"Complex and compelling . . . A fabulous story."
—*Joyfully Reviewed*

continued . . .

The Iron Duke

MELJEAN BROOK

BERKLEY SENSATION, NEW YORK

THE BERKLEY PUBLISHING GROUP
Published by the Penguin Group
Penguin Group (USA) Inc.
375 Hudson Street, New York, New York 10014, USA
Penguin Group (Canada), 90 Eglinton Avenue East, Suite 700, Toronto, Ontario M4P 2Y3, Canada
(a division of Pearson Penguin Canada Inc.)
Penguin Books Ltd., 80 Strand, London WC2R 0RL, England
Penguin Group Ireland, 25 St. Stephen's Green, Dublin 2, Ireland (a division of Penguin Books Ltd.)
Penguin Group (Australia), 250 Camberwell Road, Camberwell, Victoria 3124, Australia
(a division of Pearson Australia Group Pty. Ltd.)
Penguin Books India Pvt. Ltd., 11 Community Centre, Panchsheel Park, New Delhi—110 017, India
Penguin Group (NZ), 67 Apollo Drive, Rosedale, North Shore 0632, New Zealand
(a division of Pearson New Zealand Ltd.)
Penguin Books (South Africa) (Pty.) Ltd., 24 Sturdee Avenue, Rosebank, Johannesburg 2196,
South Africa
Penguin Books Ltd., Registered Offices: 80 Strand, London WC2R 0RL, England

This book is an original publication of The Berkley Publishing Group.

Copyright © 2010 by Melissa Khan.
Cover illustration by Chad Michael Ward.
Cover design by Rita Frangie.
Interior text design by Kristin del Rosario.

PRINTING HISTORY
Berkley Sensation trade paperback edition / October 2010

Library of Congress Cataloging-in-Publication Data

Brook, Meljean.
    The iron duke / Meljean Brook.—Berkley Sensation trade pbk. ed.
      p. cm.
    ISBN 978-0-425-23667-3 (trade pbk.)
    I. Title.
    PS3602.R64274I76 2010
    813'.6—dc22

                                                    2010028988

PRINTED IN THE UNITED STATES OF AMERICA

10 9 8 7 6 5 4 3

Chapter One

Mina hadn't predicted that sugar would wreck the Marchioness of Hartington's ball; she'd thought the dancing would. Their hostess's good humor had weathered them through the discovery that fewer than forty of her guests knew the steps, however, and they'd survived the first quadrilles. But as the room grew warmer, the laughter louder, and the gossiping more vigorous, the refreshment table set the First Annual Victory Ball on a course for disaster.

Which meant Mina was enjoying the event far more than she'd expected to.

Not that it wasn't as grand as everyone had said it would be; the restoration of Devonshire House had cost Hartington, and it showed. Candle-studded chandeliers displayed everyone in the great ballroom to their best advantage. Discreet gas lamps highlighted the enormous paintings gracing the room but their smoke had not yet smudged the silk-papered walls. Human musicians played in the gallery, and their violins did sound sweeter than the mechanical instruments Mina was accustomed to—and *much* sweeter than the hacking coughs from forty of the guests, all of them bounders.

Two hundred years ago, when most of Europe was fleeing from the Horde's war machines, some of the English had gone with them. But an ocean passage over the Atlantic hadn't come cheaply, and although the families who'd abandoned England for the New World hadn't all been aristocrats, they'd almost all been moneyed. After the Iron Duke had freed England from Horde control, many of them had returned to London, flaunting their titles and their gold. Now, nine years after England's victory over the Horde, the aristocratic bounders had decided to hold a ball celebrating the country's new-found freedom, though they had shed no blood to gain it. They'd charitably included all of the peers who had little to their names but their titles.

At first glance, Mina could detect little distinction between the guests. The bounders spoke with flatter accents, and their women's dresses exposed less skin at the neck and arms, but everyone's togs were at the height of New World fashion. Mina suspected, however, that forty of the guests could not begin to guess how dear those new togs were to the rest of the company.

And they probably could not anticipate how stubborn the rest of the company could be, despite their thirst and hunger.

Near the southern wall of the ballroom, Mina sat with her friend and waited for the entertainment to begin. Considering Felicity's condition, she might be the one to provide it. Pale blue satin covered her friend's hugely pregnant abdomen. With such a belly to feed, Mina couldn't see how Felicity wasn't constantly ravenous, consuming everything in her path. If no sugarless cakes were available, she might start with the bounders.

"If it has taken Richmond this long, he hasn't found anything." Beneath intricately curled blond hair that had made Mina burst into laughter when she had first seen it that evening, Felicity's gaze searched the crowd for her husband. With a sigh, she turned to regard her friend. "Oh, Mina. You are too amused. I doubt anyone will break into fisticuffs."

"They should."

"You think it's an insult to supply sweet and strong lemonade? To stack cakes like towers?" Felicity rubbed her belly and looked longingly toward the towers. Mina guessed that the cakes were sup-posed to have been demolished by now, symbolic of England's victory over the Horde, but they still stood tall. "Surely, they did not realize how strongly we felt about it."

"Or they realized, but thought we must be shown like children that we can eat imported sugar without being enslaved."

Two hundred years ago, the Horde had hidden their nanoagents in tea and sugar like invisible bugs, and traded it on the cheap. The Horde had no navy, and even though Europe had fled before the Horde, Britain was protected by water and a strong fleet of ships. And so for years, they'd traded tea and sugar, and England had thought itself safe.

Until the Horde had activated the bugs.

Now, no one born in England trusted sugar unless it came from beets grown in British soil and processed in one of the recently built refineries—and after two hundred years of the Horde's crippling taxes, no one had enough money to pay for the luxury, anyway. New to England, beet sugar was as precious as gold was to the French, and as Horde technology was to the smugglers in the Indian Ocean and South Seas.

"You judge them too harshly, Mina. This ball itself is goodwill. And it must have been a great expense." Felicity looked around almost despairingly, as if it pained her to think of how much had been spent.

"Hartington can obviously afford it. Look how many candles." Mina lifted her chin, gesturing at the chandelier.

"Even your mother uses candles."

That wasn't the same. Gas cost almost nothing; candles, especially wax tapers of good quality, rivaled sugar as a luxury. Her mother used candles during her League meetings, but only so the dim light would conceal the worst of the wear. Repeated scouring of the walls removed the smoke that penetrated every home in London, but had worn the paper down to the plaster. Rugs had been walked threadbare at the center. The sofa hadn't been replaced since the Horde had invaded England. But at Devonshire House, there was no need for candles to forgive what brighter gas lamps revealed.

"My mother will also make certain that each of her guests is comfortable." Physically comfortable, at any rate. Mina supposed her mother could not help the discomforting effect that they both had on visitors. "Goodwill should not stab at scars, Felicity. Goodwill would have been desserts made with beet sugar or honey."

"Perhaps," Felicity said, obviously unwilling to think so little of the bounders, but acknowledging that they could have been done better. She cast another glance at the towers of cake. "Mine would have mousse."

"Your *what* would have mousse?"

"My table, if I gave a ball. Do not laugh, Mina. I might one day."

Even if her friend's purse was full, Mina could not imagine Felicity loosening the strings enough to pay for anything resembling a ball. But her friend's wistful expression caught Mina off guard. She swallowed her laugh and nodded.

Taking that as an invitation to continue, Felicity said, "I've heard that in the Antilles, they have a mousse of Liberé chocolate so light that it floats away like an airship, and éclairs filled with cream. In Lusitania, they bake *massa sovada* so—"

Mina shook away a vision of mousse envelopes floating about with éclairs tethered beneath. "*Massa* what?"

"Portuguese sweet bread." Felicity's eyes widened innocently. "*The Lamplighter Gazette* has a new section featuring New World desserts. It follows their adventure serials. Surely you looked to the recipes after reading the last Archimedes Fox story?"

Mina flushed and hoped the candlelight would hide it. Her family managed—barely—to employ two maids *and* a cook. Other families tended to their own homes; if left to Mina or her parents, they'd likely starve while their townhouse fell down around them.

To cover her embarrassment, she said, "And so you would lay your table out like the northern American continent. Islands of mousse for the Antilles, a peninsula of Lusitanian bread topped by . . . ?" What did they eat in the Castilian wilderness? Mina had no idea—and she couldn't ask a bounder. After losing almost all of their territory and the native trade routes to the Spanish, the bounders spoke as if the Castilians dined on human hearts.

"Flan," Felicity replied. She rubbed her belly again. "Lemon ices from Manhattan City, and Dutch pastries from Johannesland."

And blubber from the natives who lived farther north. Mina stared at her friend in astonishment. "I'm beginning to think that you aren't with child. You've simply become fat after reading too many recipes."

"If one could become fat just from reading them, I would be." She slanted a narrow look at Mina. "Don't pretend they don't tempt you."

Mina could pretend very well. She had plenty of practice. "At least now I know why bounders all have such horrible teeth. And why I can differentiate a foreigner from a bugger just by opening his mouth."

Felicity's hand flew to her lips, and Mina was suddenly thankful that buggers didn't suffer from pregnancy sickness. Her friend had a weak stomach even when she wasn't with child.

"Mina, you swore! For one night, we were to have no talk of corpses."

"I did not say a corpse." Though she had meant one. But it hardly mattered; there was little difference. "The teeth are rotting out of the heads of the living, too."

"Shhh." Felicity smothered her laugh and glanced around to make sure no one had overheard. "You look to find the worst in everyone, Mina."

"I would not be very good at my job if I didn't." The worst in everyone was what led them to murder.

"You *like* to look for the worst in bounders. But they cannot be blamed for their ancestors abandoning us, just as we cannot be blamed for buying the Horde's sugar and teas. It seems to me, the fault can be laid on both sides of the ocean . . . and laid to rest."

No, the bounders hadn't abandoned England—and if that were the only grievance Mina had against them, she *could* have laid her resentment to rest. But neither could she explain her resentment; Felicity thought too well of them, and she was too fascinated by the New World.

The bounders were part of that fascination—and they were part of the New World, no matter that they referred to themselves as Englishmen, and were called Brits by everyone except those born on the British Isles.

Damn them all, they probably didn't even realize there was a difference between England and Britain.

No matter what the bounders thought they were, they weren't like Mina's family or Felicity's—or like those in the lower classes who'd been altered and enslaved for labor. Bounders hadn't been born under Horde rule. And Mina resented that when they'd returned, they'd carried with them the assumption that they better knew how to live than the buggers did. This ball, for all that it celebrated victory over the Horde, reflected everything bounders thought society should be: They'd had their Season in Manhattan City and were determined for the tradition to continue in London, though most of the peers born here couldn't dream of holding their own ball. And although the ball provided a pleasant diversion, buggers had more important things to occupy their minds and their time—such as whether they could afford their next meal, and working to earn it.

The bounders had no such worries. They'd returned, their heads filled only with grand ideas and good intentions, and they meant to force them onto the rest of England.

But their intentions did not mean they'd returned for the benefit of their former countrymen. Not at all. A good situation within Manhattan City was impossible to find, they'd run out of room on the long Prince George Island, and the Dutch would not relinquish any territory in the mainland. So the aristocrats returned to claim their estates and their Parliament seats, the merchants to buy what the aristocrats didn't own, and all of them to look down their noses at the poor buggers who'd been raised beneath the heel of the Horde.

Or to be horrified by them. Mina's gaze sought her mother.

Even in a crowd, she was easy to locate—a small woman with white-blond hair, wearing crimson satin. Spectacles with smoked lenses dominated her narrow face. Wide brass bracelets shaped like kraken circled her gloved arms, and she was demonstrating the clockwork release mechanism to three other ladies—all bounders. When her mother twisted the kraken's bulbous head, the tentacles wrapped around her wrist sprang open. The ladies clapped, obviously delighted, and though Mina couldn't hear what they said, she guessed they were asking her mother where she'd purchased the unique bracelets. Such clockwork devices were prized as both novelties and jewelry—and expensive. Mina doubted her mother told them the bracelets were of her own design and made in their freezing attic workshop.

In any case, the novelty of the bracelets didn't divert the ladies from their real interest. Even as they spoke, they cast surreptitious glances at her mother's eyes. One lady leaned forward, as if to gain a better angle to see the bracelets—and gained a better angle to see behind her mother's spectacles. Her mouth fell open.

Rarely did anyone hide their surprise when they glimpsed the shiny orbs concealed by the lenses. Some stared openly, as if the prosthetic eyes were blind, rather than as keen as a telescope and a microscope combined. This particular lady was no different. She continued to look, her expression a mixture of fascination and revulsion. She'd probably expected modification on a coal miner—not on the Countess of Rockingham.

But if mirrored eyes still horrified the woman, chances were she'd never actually seen a miner. And if she'd heard the story behind her mother's eyes, the lady's gaze would soon be seeking Mina.

Felicity must have looked to see what had caught Mina's attention. She asked, "And what is your mother's goal tonight? A husband for you, or new recruits for her Ladies Reformation League?"

Mina's friend underestimated her mother's efficiency. "Both."

As efficient as her mother was, however, finding new recruits for her League had greater possibility for success. Finding a husband for Mina was as likely as King Edward writing his own name legibly. Mina was approaching thirty years of age without once attracting the attention of a worthy man. Only bounders searching for a taste of the forbidden, or Englishmen seeking revenge for the horrors of the Mongol occupation—and Mina resembled the people they wanted to exact their vengeance on.

A loud, hacking cough from beside Mina turned her head. A bounder, red in the face, lowered his handkerchief from his mouth. His gaze touched Mina and darted away.

She arched her brows at Felicity, inviting comment.

Felicity watched the man walk away. "I suppose it does not matter, anyway. They will all soon retreat to the countryside or back to the New World."

Yes, they'd soon run. They'd been made too confident by their success in America. They'd built a new life out of a wild land, taming it to suit their needs. Now, they thought they could return and reshape London—but London reshaped them, instead. The only way to stay alive in the city was to infect themselves with the tiny machines that their ancestors had run from two hundred years before. Without the bugs, the insides of their lungs would become as black as a chimney.

Some bounders eventually relented and took an injection of infected blood. But even with the same nanoagents in their bodies, they still weren't anything like those buggers born in England. They still thought like bounders, talked like bounders, and had a bounder's interests. The bugs didn't change that.

From directly beside Mina came the sound of a throat clearing. She turned. A ginger-haired maid in a black uniform bobbed a curtsy. Though Mina had noted that the servants from the New World usually lowered their gazes, this girl couldn't seem to help herself. The maid studied Mina's face, fascinated and wary. The Horde trade routes didn't cross the Atlantic to the New World, and only a few of the Horde were left in England. Perhaps the maid had never seen a Mongol before—or, as in Mina's case, a mongrel.

Mina raised her brows.

The maid blushed and bowed her head. "A gentleman asks to see you, my lady."

"Oh, she is not a lady," Felicity said airily. "She is a detective *inspector.*"

The mock gravity weighing down the last word seemed to confound the maid. She colored and fidgeted. Perhaps she worried that *inspector* was a bugger's insult?

Mina said, "What man?"

"A Constable Newberry, my lady. He's brought with him a message to you."

Mina frowned and stood, but was brought around by Felicity's exasperated, "Mina, you didn't!"

Mina could determine the motives of opium-addled criminals, yet she couldn't follow every jump of Felicity's mind. "I didn't what?"

"Send a gram to your assistant so that you could escape."

Oh, she *should* have. It would be a simple thing; all of the bounders' restored houses had wiregram lines installed.

"You mistrustful cow! Of course I didn't." She lowered her voice and added, "I will at the next ball, however, now that you've given me the idea." As Felicity smothered a laugh into her hand, Mina continued, "Will you inform my father and mother that I've gone?"

"Gone? It is only a message."

Newberry wouldn't have come in person if it was only a message. "No."

"Oh." Realization swept over her friend's expression, brushing away her amusement. "Do not keep the poor bastard waiting, then."

The maid's eyes widened before she turned to lead Mina out of the ballroom. She could imagine what the girl thought, but Newberry was not the poor bastard.

Whoever had been murdered was.

They'd put Newberry in a study in the east wing—probably so the guests weren't made nervous by his size or his constable's overcoat. He stood in the middle of the room, his bowler hat in his large-knuckled hands. Mina had to admire his fortitude. Small automata lined the study's bookshelves. If given more than a few seconds to wait, she couldn't have resisted winding them and seeing how they performed. She recognized a few of her mother's more mundane creations that had been sold through the Blacksmith's shop—a dog that would wag his tail and flip; a singing mechanical nightingale—and felt more charitable toward her hosts. They might not have provided dessert, but they'd unknowingly put food on her table.

Newberry's eyes widened briefly when he saw her. She'd never worn a skirt in his presence, let alone a yellow satin gown that exposed her collarbone and the few inches of skin between her cap sleeves and her long white gloves.

But he must have known she wouldn't be in her usual attire, and had apparently stopped at her home. Her overcoat, weapons, and armor were draped over his left forearm. She could have no doubt they were leaving now, and he'd come in such a hurry he hadn't taken time to shave. Evening stubble flanked the red mustache that drooped over the corners of his mouth and swept up the sides of his jaw to meet his sideburns with his ears. The beard made him appear much older than his twenty-two years, and offered the impression of a large, protective dog—an accurate impression. Newberry resembled a wolfhound: friendly and loyal, until someone threatened. Then he was all teeth.

Not every bounder who returned had a title and a bulging purse. Newberry had come so that his young wife, suffering a consumptive lung condition, could be infected by the bugs and live.

"Report, Newberry." She accepted the sleeveless, close-fitting black tunic whose wire mesh protected her from throat to hips. Usually she wore the armor beneath her clothing, but she did not have that option now. She pulled it on and began fastening the buckles lining the front.

"We're to go to the Isle of Dogs, sir. Superintendent Hale assigned you specifically."

"Oh?" Perhaps this murder touched another she had investigated. The docks east of London weren't as rough as they'd once been, but she still visited often enough. "Who is it this time?"

"The Duke of Anglesey, sir."

What? Her gaze skidded from a buckle up to Newberry's earnest face. "The Iron Duke's been killed?"

She had never met the man or seen him in person, and yet her heart kicked painfully against her ribs. Rhys Trahaearn, former pirate captain, recently titled Duke of Anglesey—and, after he'd destroyed the Horde's tower, England's most celebrated hero.

"No, inspector. It isn't His Grace. He only reported the murder."

Newberry sounded apologetic. Perhaps he hadn't expected her to feel the same reverence for the Iron Duke that most of England did. Mina didn't, though her racing pulse told her that she'd taken some of the stories about him to heart. The newssheets painted him as a dashing figure, romanticizing his past, but Mina suspected he was simply an opportunist who'd been in the right place at the right moment.

"So he's killed someone, then?" It wouldn't be the first time.

"I don't know, sir. Only that a body has been found near his home."

Mina frowned. Given the size of his park, that could mean anything.

When she finished fastening the tight armor, the gown's lacings pressed uncomfortably against her spine. She slung her gun belt around her hips; one of the weapons had been loaded with bullets, the other with opium darts, which had greater effect on a rampaging bugger. She paused after Newberry passed her the knife sheath. Typically, Mina wore trousers and strapped the weapon around her thigh. If she bound the knife beneath her skirts in the same location, the blade would be impossible to draw. Driving through east London at night without as many weapons as possible would be foolish, however. Her calf would have to do.

She sank down on one knee and hoisted her skirts. Newberry

spun around—his cheeks on fire, no doubt. Good man, her Newberry. Always proper. Sometimes, Mina felt sorry for him; he'd been
assigned to her almost as soon as he'd stepped off the airship from
Manhattan City.

Other times, she thought it must be good for him. In two centuries, the Brits who'd fled to the New World had devolved into
prudes. Probably because Cromwell and his Separatists had settled
there decades before the others had begun leaving England, and
everyone living in Manhattan City hadn't had the Horde scrub away
all but the vestiges of religion. A few curses and traditions remained
in England. Not much else did.

Mina tightened the knife sheath below her knee and grimaced
at the sight of her slippers. Newberry hadn't brought her boots—or
her hat, but it was probably for the best. She wasn't certain she
could shove it down over the knot of hair the maid had teased into
black curls. She took her heavy overcoat from him and turned for
the door, stifling a groan as her every step kicked her yellow skirts
forward.

A detective inspector turned inside out on top, and a lady below.
She hoped Felicity did not see her this way. Never would Mina hear
the end of it.

Newberry's two-seater cart waited at the bottom of the front
steps, rattling and hissing steam from the boot, and drawing appalled
glances from the attending servants. Judging by the other vehicles in
the drive, the attendants were accustomed to larger, shinier coaches,
with brass appointments and velvet seats. The police cart had four
wheels and an engine that hadn't exploded, and that was the best
that could be said for it.

As it wasn't raining, the canvas top had been folded back, leaving
the cab open. The coal bin sat on the passenger's side of the bench,
as if Newberry had dumped in the fuel on the run.

Newberry colored and mumbled, heaving the bin to the floorboards. Mina battled her skirts past the cart's tin frame as he
rounded the front. She resorted to hiking them up to her knees, and

the constable's cheeks were aflame again as he swung into his seat. The cart tilted and the bench protested under his weight. His stomach, though solid, almost touched the steering shaft.

Newberry closed the steam vent. The hissing stopped and the cart slowly pulled forward. Mina sighed. Though the sounds of the city were never ending, courtesy dictated that one didn't blast the occupants of a private house with engine noise. Always polite, Newberry intended to wait until after they'd passed out of the drive before fully engaging the engine.

"We are in a hurry, constable," she reminded him.

"Yes, sir."

He hauled the drive lever back. Mina's teeth rattled as the cart jerked forward. Smoke erupted from the back in a thick black cloud, obscuring everything behind them. *Too bad, that.* She'd wanted to see the attendants' expressions when the engine belched in their faces, but she and Newberry were through the gate before the air cleared.

Wide and smooth, Piccadilly Street held little traffic. The ride became bumpier as they passed Haymarket. Blocks of flats crowded closer together and nearer to the street, their windows shuttered against the noise. The night hid the sooty gray that covered all the buildings in London, and concealed the smoke that created a haze during the day—a haze thickened by the fire that had raged through the Southwark slums the previous week. Though the worst of the blaze across the Thames had burned out, it still smoldered in patches. If the fog came tonight, the gas lamps lining the streets would be all but useless. So would the lanterns hanging above either side of the two-seater's front wheels.

The rattling of the cart and the noise of the engine made hearing difficult, and conversation became near impossible when Newberry steered onto Viktrey Road, the commercial route the Horde had built from the tower to the docks. The road had once been named after London's *darga*—but nine years ago, as revolutionaries marched along this route, the road signs bearing the Horde

governor's name had been destroyed. Someone had scratched "Viktrey" in its place, and the route had kept the name. In the past few
years, those defaced signs had been replaced with official placards,
and the misspelling had remained.

Though not the pandemonium of the day, traffic still choked
the roadway. Newberry slowed as a spider-rickshaw cut in front of
them. The driver's feet rapidly pumped the hydraulic pistons that
cranked the vehicle's segmented legs, scuttling over the pocked road
like a crab. His passengers kept a white-knuckled grip on the sides
of the wheeled cart as the rickshaw darted left, narrowly avoiding
a collision with two women riding a pedal buggy. On Newberry's
right, a huge vehicle muscled down the center lane, the back pens
full of bleating sheep.

"That lorry has just passed us!" Mina shouted over the noise.

"And no wonder—it has a vent the size of the Castilian queen's
backside!" The louder Newberry became, the less proper he was.
Mina enjoyed driving with him. "With enough space between him
and the engine that he won't roast the faster he goes!"

Mina could stand to roast a little more. Her satin dress was
fine for a ballroom. But even with the wool overcoat, the moist
cold night seeped in. Her dress—purchased at her mother's insis-
tence, with money that could have been put to a thousand better
uses elsewhere—was just like the candles in her mother's parlor: all
show. Beneath it, Mina's underclothes were patched and threadbare.

"At least it'd be warmer."

Newberry glanced at her, a question in his eyes. He must have
seen her speak, but hadn't heard her reply.

She shouted, "I've a draft up to my pants!"

Even in the dark, Newberry's blush shone bright.

Farther east, traffic slowed to a crawl. At the edge of Whitecha-
pel, children sold clothes and trinkets along the walks. Deep within
the borough, surrounded by thick stone walls, many children still
lived within the Crèche, forming their own hierarchy, manufac-
turing their own goods for sale—and better off than many of the

families outside. Mina watched two of the teenaged children, each carrying a length of pipe, stop to chat with the smaller ones selling the wares. The children patrolled their own territory, and human predators didn't last long near the Crèche. Mina had come to recognize the bludgeon marks left on an adult body when the children exacted their form of justice.

Unsurprisingly, when she questioned the children, no one ever reported seeing anything.

"Have you met His Grace?"

Mina glanced over as Newberry shouted the question. He often looked for impressions of character before arriving at a scene, but Mina had no solid ones to give. "No."

She'd eaten rice noodles at Trahaearn's feet, however. Near the Whitehall police station, an iron statue of the duke had been erected at the center of Anglesey Square. Standing twenty feet tall, that statue did not offer a good angle to judge his features. But Mina knew from the caricatures in the newssheets that he had a square jaw, hawkish nose, and heavy brows that darkened his piercing stare into a glower. The effect was altogether strong and handsome, but Mina suspected that the artists were trying to dress up England's Savior like her mother lighting candles in the parlor.

Perhaps all of him had been dressed up. The newssheets speculated that his parents had been Welsh landowners and that he'd been taken from them as a baby, but nothing was truly known of his family. Quite possibly, his father had pulverizing hammers for legs, his mother fitted with drills instead of arms, and he'd been born in a coal mine nine months after a Frenzy, squatted out in a dusty bin before his mother returned to work.

Twenty years ago, however, his name had first been recorded in Captain Baxter's log on HMS *Indomitable*. Trahaearn, aged sixteen, had been aboard a slaver ship bound for the New World, and was pressed with the crew into the navy. Within two years he'd transferred from *Indomitable* to another English ship, *Unity*, a fifth-rate frigate patrolling the trade routes in the South Seas.

Before they'd reached Australia, Trahaearn had led a mutiny, taken over the ship as its captain, and renamed the frigate *Marco's Terror*. With the *Terror*, he'd embarked on an eight-year run of piracy—no trade route, no nation, no merchant had been safe from him. Even in London, where the Horde suppressed any news that suggested a weakness in their defenses, word of Trahaearn's piracy had seeped into conversations. Several times, the newssheets claimed the Horde had captured him. He'd been declared dead twice.

Perhaps that was why the Horde hadn't anticipated him sailing *Marco's Terror* up the Thames and blowing up their tower.

"Is he enhanced?"

Mina almost smiled. Even shouting, Newberry didn't unbend enough to use *bugger*. *Enhanced* had become the polite term for living with millions of microscopic machines in each of their bodies. *Bugger* had been an insult once—and still was in Manhattan City. Only the bounders seemed to care about that, however. Not a single bugger that Mina knew took offense at the name.

Of course, if Newberry called her by the name the Horde had used for them—*zum bi*, the soulless—she'd knock his enhanced teeth out.

"He is," she confirmed.

"How did he do it?" When Mina frowned, certain she'd missed part of the question, Newberry clarified in a shout, "The tower!"

He wasn't the first to ask. The Horde had created a short-range radio signal around their tower, preventing buggers from approaching it. Trahaearn *had* been infected, but he hadn't been paralyzed when he'd entered the broadcast area. Mina's father theorized that the frequency had changed from the time that Trahaearn had lived in Wales as a child, and so he hadn't been affected on his return. She'd heard the same theory echoed by other buggers, but bounders preferred to think he hadn't been infected with nanoagents—despite Trahaearn himself confirming that he'd carried the bugs since he was a boy.

Her father's theory seemed as sound as any. "Frequencies!"

Newberry looked doubtful, but nodded.

Frequencies or not, it didn't matter to Mina or to any other bugger. Thanks to the Iron Duke, the nanoagents no longer controlled them, but assisted them. The Horde no longer suppressed their emotions—violence, lust, ambition—or, when the *darga* wanted them to breed, whipped them into a rutting frenzy.

After nine years, many who'd been raised under Horde rule were still learning to control strong emotions, to fight violent impulses. Not everyone succeeded, and that was when Mina stepped in.

With luck, this murder would be the same: an unchecked impulse, easily traceable—and the murderer easy to hold accountable.

And with more luck, the murderer wouldn't be the Iron Duke. No one would be held accountable then. He was too beloved—beloved enough that all of England ignored his history of raping, thieving, and murdering. Beloved enough that they tried to rewrite that history. And even if the evidence pointed to Trahaearn, he wouldn't be ruined.

But as the investigating officer who arrested him, Mina *would* be.

Chapter Two

By the time she and Newberry reached the Isle of Dogs, the nip of the evening air had become a bite. Not a true island, the isle was surrounded on three sides by a bend in the river. The Horde had drained the marshland and built part of it into their commercial and trading center—all looted and burned during the revolution. Afterward, the Crown had granted Trahaearn tracts of land on the island along with his title, and he'd rebuilt the docks that now serviced his trading company's ships and the merchants who paid for the space. At the center of the island, near the Marshwall dock, he'd razed the remains of the Horde's holdings and built his fortress on the ashes.

The high, wrought-iron fence that surrounded his park had earned him the nickname the Iron Duke—the iron kept the rest of London out, and whatever riches he hid inside, in. The spikes topping the fence prevented anyone in the surrounding slums from scaling it, and no one was invited to his house. At least, no one in Mina's circle, or her mother's.

She was never certain if their circle was too high, or too low.

Newberry stopped in front of the gate. When a face appeared at the small gatehouse window, he shouted, "Detective Inspector Wentworth, on police business! Open her up!"

The gatekeeper appeared, a grizzled man with a long gray beard and a heavy clanking step that marked a prosthetic leg. A former pirate, Mina guessed. Though the Crown insisted that Trahaearn and his men had all been privateers, acting with the permission of the king, only a few children who didn't know any better believed it. The rest of them knew the story was designed to bolster faith in the king and his ministers after the revolution. Bestowing a title on Trahaearn had been one of King Edward's last cogent acts. The crew had been given naval commissions, and *Marco's Terror* pressed into the service of the Royal Navy . . . where the ship had supposedly been all along.

The Iron Duke had traded the *Terror* and the seas for a title and a fortress in the middle of a slum. Mina wondered if he felt that exchange had been worth it.

The gatekeeper glanced at her. "And the jade?"

At Mina's side, Newberry bristled. "*She* is Lady Wilhelmina Wentworth, the detective inspector."

Oh, Newberry. In Manhattan City, a title still meant something. In England, it only meant that Mina's family hadn't been subjected to the same horrors that the lower classes had suffered under the Horde. And when the gatekeeper looked at her again, she knew what he saw—and it wasn't a lady. Nor was it the epaulettes declaring her rank, or the red band sewed into her sleeve, boasting that she'd spilled Horde blood in the revolution.

No, he saw her face, calculated her age, and understood that she'd been conceived during a Frenzy. And that, because of her family's status, her mother and father had been allowed to keep her rather than being taken by the Horde to be raised in a crèche.

The gatekeeper looked at her assistant. "Then who are you?"

"Constable Newberry."

Scratching his beard, the old man clanked back toward the gatehouse. "All right. I'll be sending a gram up to the captain, then."

He still called the Iron Duke "captain"? Mina could not decide if that said more about Trahaearn's opinion of his new rank, or the gatekeeper's. But whatever his staff thought of his title, Trahaearn apparently didn't force them to address him by it.

The gatekeeper didn't return—and former pirate or not, he must be literate if he could write a gram and read the answer from the main house. That answer came quickly. She and Newberry hadn't waited more than a minute before the gates opened on well-oiled hinges.

The park was enormous, with green lawns stretching into the dark. Dogs sniffed along the fence, their handlers bundled up against the cold. If someone had invaded the property, he wouldn't find many hiding places on the grounds. All of the shrubs and trees were still young, planted after Trahaearn had been granted the property.

The house rivaled Chesterfield before that great building had been burned during the revolution. Of gray stone, two rectangular wings jutted forward to form a large courtyard. Unadorned casements decorated the many windows, and the blocky stone front was relieved only by the window glass and the balustrade along the edge of the roof. A fountain tinkled at the center of the courtyard. Behind it, the main steps created semicircles leading to the entrance.

On the center of the steps, a white sheet concealed a body-shaped lump. No blood soaked through the sheet. A man waited on the top step, his slight form in a poker-straight posture that Mina couldn't place for a moment. Then it struck her: navy. Probably another pirate, though this one had been a sailor—or an officer—first.

A house of this size would require an army of staff, and she and Newberry would have to question each one. Soon, she'd know how many of Trahaearn's pirates had come to dry land with him.

As they reached the fountain, she turned to Newberry. "Stop here. Set up your camera by the body. Take photographs of everything before we move it."

Newberry parked and climbed out. Mina didn't wait for him to gather his equipment. She strode toward the house. The man descended the steps to greet her, and she was forced to revise her opinion. His posture wasn't rigid discipline, but a cover for wiry, contained energy. His dark hair slicked back from a flushed, narrow face. Unlike the man at the gate, he was neat, and almost bursting with the need to help.

"Inspector Wentworth." With ink-stained fingers, he gestured to the body, inviting her to look.

She wasn't in a rush. The body wouldn't go anywhere. "Mr—?"

"St. John." He said it like a bounder, rather than the two abbreviated syllables of someone born in England. "Steward to His Grace's estate."

"This estate or his property in Wales?" Which, as far as Mina was aware, Trahaearn didn't often visit.

"His estate on Anglesey, inspector."

Newberry passed them, carrying the heavy photographic equipment. St. John half turned, as if to offer his assistance, then glanced back as Mina asked, "When did you arrive here from Wales, Mr. St. John?"

"Yesterday."

"Did you witness what happened here?"

He shook his head. "I was in the study when I heard the footman—Chesley—inform the housekeeper that someone had fallen. Mrs. Lavery then told His Grace."

Mina frowned. She hadn't been called out here because someone had been a clumsy oaf, had she? "Someone tripped on the stairs?"

"No, inspector. Fallen." His hand made a sharp dive from his shoulder to his hip.

Mina glanced at the body again, then at the balustrade lining the roof. "Do you know who it was?"

"No."

She was not surprised. If he managed the Welsh estate, he wouldn't know the London staff well. "Who covered him with the sheet?"

"I did, after His Grace sent the staff back into the house."

So they'd all come out to gawk. "Did anyone identify him while they were outside?"

"No."

Or maybe they just hadn't spoken up. "Where is the staff now?"

"They are gathered in the main parlor."

Where they'd pass the story around until they were each convinced they'd witnessed it personally. *Blast*. Mina firmed her lips.

As if interpreting her frustration, St. John added, "The footman is alone in the study, however. His Grace told him to remain there. He hasn't spoken with anyone else since Mrs. Lavery told His Grace."

The footman had been taken into the study and asked nothing? "But he has talked to the duke?"

The answer came from behind her, from a voice that could carry his commands across a ship. "He has, inspector."

She turned to find a man as big as his voice. Oh, damn the newssheets. They hadn't been kind to *him*—they'd been kind to their readers, protecting them from the effect of this man. A hollow fear shivered within her, much like the first time she'd run into a razor-clawed ratcatcher in an alley—the instinctive knowledge that she faced something dangerous and that she didn't wholly understand.

Not that he looked strange, or mutated as those ratcatchers were. He was just as hard and as handsome as the caricatures had portrayed—altogether dark and forbidding, with a gaze as pointed and as guarded as the fence that was his namesake. The Iron Duke wasn't as tall as his statue, but still taller than any man had a right to be, and as broad through the shoulders as Newberry, but without the spare flesh.

But it was not his size that made her wary. And for the first time, she could see why his crew might follow him through kraken-infested waters or into Horde territory, then follow him back onto shore and remain with him. When he leveled that cold, detached gaze at them, as if he couldn't care less whether they dropped dead in front of him, they would be too terrified to do anything else. He leveled it at Mina now, and the message in his eyes was clear.

He didn't want her here.

Because of her bloodline or her occupation? Mina couldn't decide. It hardly mattered, anyway—she was here now.

She glanced at the man standing beside him: tall, brown-haired,

his expression bored. Mina didn't recognize him. Like the Iron
Duke, he wore a fashionable black overcoat, breeches, and boots.
A red waistcoat buckled like armor over a white shirt with a simple
collar reminiscent of the Horde's tunic collar. Perhaps a bounder
and, if so, probably an aristocrat—and he likely expected to be
treated as one.

Bully for him.

She looked to the duke again. Though she'd never been introduced to someone of his standing before, she'd seen Superintendent
Hale meet a marquess without a single gesture to acknowledge that
he ranked above her. Mina followed that example and offered a
short nod before addressing him.

"Your Grace, I understand that you did not witness this man die."

"No."

"And your companion . . . ?"

"Also saw nothing," the other man answered.

She'd been right; his accent marked him as a bounder. Yet she
had to revise her opinion of him. He wasn't bored by death—just
too familiar with it to be excited by yet another. She couldn't understand that. The more death she saw, the more the injustice of each
one touched her. "Your name, sir?"

His smile seemed just at the edge of a laugh. "Mr. Smith."

A joker. How fun.

She thought a flicker of irritation crossed the duke's expression.
But when he didn't offer his companion's true name, she let it go.
One of the staff would know.

"Mr. St. John has told me that no one has identified the body,
and only your footman saw his fall."

"Yes."

"Did your footman relate anything else to you?"

"Only that he didn't scream."

No scream? Either the man had been drunk, asleep, or already
dead. She would soon find out which it was.

"If you'll pardon me." With a nod, she turned toward the steps, where Newberry adjusted the camera's thermite flash. She heard the Iron Duke and his companion follow her. As long as they did not touch the body or try to help her examine it, she did not care.

Mina looked down at her hands. *She* would touch the body, and Newberry hadn't brought her serviceable wool gloves to exchange for her white evening gloves. They were only satin—neither her mother's tinkering nor her own salary could afford kid—but they were still too dear to ruin.

She tugged at the tips of her fingers, but the fastenings at her wrist prevented them from sliding off. Futilely, she tried to push the small buttons through equally small satin loops. The seams at the tips of her fingers made them too bulky, and the fabric was too slippery. She looked round for Newberry, and saw that the black powder from the ferrotype camera already dusted his hands. *Blast it.* She would bite them through, if she had to. Even the despised task of sewing the buttons back on would be easier than—

"Give your hand over, inspector."

Mina's hackles rose at the command. She looked up into Trahaearn's face and heard a noise from his companion, a snorted half laugh—as if Trahaearn had failed an easy test.

The duke's expression didn't soften, though his words did. "You'll finish more quickly if I assist you. Will you allow me?"

No, she thought. *Do not touch me, do not come close.* But the body on the steps would not allow her that reply.

"Yes. Thank you."

She held out her hand and watched as he removed his own gloves. Kid, lined with sable. Just imagining the luxurious softness warmed her.

Mina wouldn't have been surprised if his presence had, as well. With his great size, Trahaearn seemed to surround her with heat just by standing so near. His hands were large, his fingers long and nails square. As he took her wrist in his left palm, calluses audibly scraped the satin. His face darkened. She could not tell if it was in anger or embarrassment.

However rough his skin was, his fingers were nimble. He deftly unfastened the first button, and the next. "This was not the evening you had planned."

"No."

She did not say this was preferable to the Victory Ball, but perhaps he read it in her voice. To her surprise, his teeth flashed in a smile—then his face quickly hardened again, as if his smile had surprised him, as well. He bent his head over her hand again and Mina found herself staring at his short eyelashes, so thick and black that his eyelids seemed lined with kohl. She looked away, but gold glinting through the thickness of his dark hair drew her gaze again.

Three tiny rings pierced the top curve of each ear. His earlobes had been pierced, too, though he wore no jewelry in them.

And so the newssheets *had* dressed him up. In a drawing, his thickly lashed eyes and jewelry would have appeared feminine. But not up close, not in person. Instead, the effect was . . . primitive.

Unsettled, she focused on her wrist. Only two buttons left, and then she could work.

She should be working now. "Were the dogs patrolling the grounds before the body was discovered?"

"No. They search for the point of entry now."

Mina pictured the iron fence. Perhaps a child could slip through the bars; a man could not. But if someone had let him through . . . ? "Have you spoken with your man at the front gate?"

"Wills?"

She had not asked the gatekeeper his name. "If Wills has a prosthetic left leg, and often saves a portion of his supper in his beard for his breakfast, then we are speaking of the same man."

"That is Wills." He studied her with unreadable eyes. "He wouldn't let anyone through."

Without my leave, Mina finished for him. And perhaps he was correct, though of course she would verify it with the gatekeeper, and ask the housekeeper about deliveries. Someone might have hidden themselves in one.

His gaze fell to her glove again. "There we are," Trahaearn said. "Now to . . ."

She pulled her hand away at the same time Trahaearn gripped the satin fingertips. He tugged. Satin slid in a warm caress over her elbow, her forearm.

Flames lit her cheeks. "Sir—"

His expression changed as he continued to pull. First registering surprise, as if he hadn't realized the glove extended past her wrist. Then an emotion hard and sharp as the long glove slowly gave way. Its white length finally dangled from his fingers, and to Mina seemed as intimate as if he held her stocking.

Her sleeve still covered her arm, but she felt exposed. Stripped. With as much dignity as she could, Mina claimed the glove.

"Thank you. I can manage the other." She stuffed the glove into her pocket. With her bare fingers, she made quick work of the buttons at her left wrist.

Mina looked up to find him staring at her. His cheekbones blazed with color, his gaze hot.

She'd seen lust before. This marked the first time that she hadn't seen any disgust or hatred beneath it.

"Thank you," she said again, amazed by the evenness of her voice when everything inside her trembled.

"Inspector." He inclined his head, then looked beyond her to the stairs.

And as she turned, the trembling stopped. Her legs were steady as she walked to the steps, her mind focused.

"Tell me, captain: Did you plan to assist her, or undress her?" she heard his companion ask. Trahaearn didn't reply, and Mina didn't look back at him.

Even the pull of the Iron Duke was not stronger than death.

Mina had come to recognize patterns to death—when calculation or passion drove violence, when it was accidental or deliberate.

But as she bent over the body on the stairs of Trahaearn's mansion, she could make no sense of this pattern.

Naked, the brown-haired male lay facedown, his left arm trapped beneath him, his legs splayed. No markings or wounds marred his flesh.

But this was not a freshly dead body. The skin had blackened, and was shockingly cold—much colder than the surrounding air. The tissues hadn't swollen, but the impact against the stairs might have deflated the gases like a burst balloon. Only a small amount of blood, thick and congealed, had splattered the stairs.

Mina turned the head. The face was completely smashed. Identification would be difficult. She opened the broken jaw. The teeth shattered, and the tongue . . . Frowning, she slipped her fingers into his mouth. The thick muscle at the back of his tongue felt as solid and as cold as ice. Though he was thawing now, at some point this man's body had been frozen.

She glanced over her shoulder at Newberry. "Have you finished with the photographs? I need to turn him."

When the constable nodded, she slid her hands beneath the shoulder and hip and rolled him. The torso remained a solid block. The leg flopped over like a half-cooked pudding stuffed into a sausage casing.

From behind Mina came the sound of Newberry retching, though he held it in. St. John didn't. The Iron Duke's companion muttered something before turning away.

Mina had to swallow hard, but she continued her examination. The bones had apparently been pulverized when he'd landed, but she couldn't see any wounds aside from the smashing. Perhaps he'd been beaten around the face and the evidence had been erased by the fall.

When she lifted his left arm, it remained stiff, as if still in full rigor. How strange. Unlike the legs and his right arm, the bones hadn't shattered. She scratched lightly at the gray skin, and her nails didn't leave a mark—probably a prosthetic constructed of mechanical flesh.

If so, someone would be looking for this man. Mechanical flesh didn't come cheaply.

But she would have to finish her examination at the station. She pulled the cloth back over the body as the house's front door opened.

A stout, curly-haired woman came out, keys jangling at her ample waist. "Begging your pardon, Your Grace, but a gram from Mr. Wills has just arrived. A police wagon has come for the body."

The housekeeper sounded uncertain. Mina wondered if she expected the duke to deny the wagon entrance to the estate. And Trahaearn did appear as if he resented the idea of them taking away the body—his lips had thinned, as if he struggled against an automatic response.

Trahaearn met her eyes. Another moment passed before he said, "Let them through."

Behind him, his companion shook his head, looking ill. He started up the stairs. "And I intend to drink until I can imagine that leg is stiff again."

Mina stood before the duke could join him. "With your permission, I would like to see the roof."

St. John stepped forward. "Certainly, inspector. I will—"

"Remain with the constable while I show her the roof," Trahaearn said.

St. John flushed. Mina glanced at Newberry, and he nodded. She didn't need to give him an instruction out loud. Newberry knew to stay with the body until they loaded it onto the wagon.

She followed the duke into the house. Though the foyer was enormous and gas lamps lighted the entrance, dark paneling on the walls gave the impression of a cave. She had little opportunity to look farther. Trahaearn turned left into the first shadowed parlor and strode toward the far wall, where a metal grating formed a gate. He slid the grating aside, revealing a small lift, and stepped into the cage.

As soon as she crowded in next to him, he threw the lever. With a sharp rattle, the lift began to rise. Mina pushed her back to the side of the car. The Iron Duke stared down at her like another man might examine a worm. Only inches separated them, and her imagination—so useful when determining a murderer's motive—was not so helpful when she shared a confined space with a pirate. The newssheets might spread rumors that he'd never raped anyone, but they'd also called him a privateer.

She tamped down her nervousness and forced herself to focus. "Does anyone else use this lift?"

"No."

"Is there stair access?"

"Yes."

She would ask the staff members if they'd seen anyone use the stairs. Mina suspected that the dead man hadn't fallen from the roof, however, but from something higher.

To her relief, the lift rattled to a stop a moment later. Even before Trahaearn opened the grating, she could see that the roof had been designed with defense in mind. Cannons and rail guns lined the balustrade like a ship's hull. The great lawns provided no cover for anyone attempting to cross the park. Past the fence lay the docks and the warehouses, the buildings crowding the riverside, and beyond them, the lanterns of the ships and barges on the Thames.

With no traffic and no nearby residences, the night was quiet. Shockingly so.

She almost said as much, until she glanced at the Iron Duke and found him watching her.

Unsettled by that penetrating gaze, she looked up. Airships weren't permitted to fly over the city unless they'd been granted special permission. Cloud cover and haze could conceal one, however. As long as the crew didn't fire its engines, an airship could sail silently over London without drawing notice.

She turned to the duke. "Were you outside when the incident took place?"

"No. I was at dinner."

If he'd been interrupted, a peek into the dining rooms would confirm that. "Do you recall any unusual noises while you were dining? An engine, perhaps?"

"No."

"And after the body was discovered?"

She saw the speculation in his gaze before he said, "No."

"Have you received any threats?" That question would be of the utmost importance to Superintendent Hale, and everyone else Mina answered to. The Iron Duke must be kept safe.

"Yes." A brief smile accompanied his answer.

Of course he had. "Threats from anyone who would dare act on them?"

"No."

And if someone had, Mina suspected that she'd never have been called. A law unto himself, he'd have concealed the evidence. Indeed, she was surprised he hadn't hidden this—or handled it on his own. Which begged the question, "Why did you contact police headquarters?"

When he didn't answer, she realized, "You didn't. Who did?"

His gaze sharpened, as if she'd surprised him in return. Still, he offered her nothing else. Protecting his people? She could not decide.

"Tell me, sir—how long has Mr. St. John been a member of your staff?"

This time, he said, "Three days."

So the new steward hadn't known better, and contacted the police rather than letting Trahaearn deal with the corpse in his own way. "And if I have questions to ask of him in three more days' time, will I find him still in your employ?"

"That depends, inspector. If you discover that he knew the man under the sheet, then you will not find him."

Had he just promised to kill St. John if the steward was connected to the dead man? Anger began a slow burn in her chest.

"And if he doesn't know him?"

"Then St. John will be here."

But less eager to talk to her, Mina suspected. So it would have to be now. "I've finished here. If you'll arrange for my use of a room, I would like to speak with your staff."

His gaze ran over her before he nodded. She preceded him into that tiny lift again—though it would not have seemed so small and crowded if the Iron Duke had not taken up so much room. With so little space between them, she was aware of his every breath and movement, the faint scent of smoke and cedar that clung to his overcoat. Pressing back against the side of the cage, she focused at a point beyond his shoulder and ignored the uneasiness gnawing at her nerves.

Trahaearn pushed the lever forward, and the lift began a smooth, slow descent. "So he was thrown from an airship."

"That conclusion is premature. We've seen no concrete evidence of an airship, only the suggestion of one."

He frowned. "His bones are shattered, yet you must *see* an airship to know what happened to him?"

"I must see *evidence* of an airship," Mina repeated, controlling her irritation. "Most likely, the body will give that evidence to me. But it requires further examination before I will say definitively that he was thrown from an airship, because I have seen other bodies similarly damaged by pulverizing hammers. And if I draw conclusions too hastily, I risk overlooking information that points to his murderer—or making assumptions that will lead to the wrong man. I will accept neither of those outcomes."

His gaze searched her features. Finally, he gave a short nod—as if she needed his permission to proceed. He certainly had a high opinion of himself. Unfortunately, everyone else in England shared that view.

But aside from his arrogance, Mina could not pin him at all. Meeting his eyes, she said, "I was called away from a ball that was partly in your honor."

He smiled slightly. "Yes."

And that was all he had to say? It told her almost nothing. She tried again, this time hoping to get a rise from him. "Did you choose not to attend, Your Grace? Or perhaps you did not receive an invitation."

"I received several."

Humor had touched his eyes. And so he was amused rather than offended—but she could not determine if he laughed at the question or at *her*.

The lift reached the main floor, stopping with a clang and a jolt. The duke looked down at her for another moment before sliding open the gate. She swept past him into the parlor, thinking aloud.

"You are well-loved in this town, yet a corpse falls on your steps." She turned to face him. "Perhaps it is not a threat, but someone trying to get your attention."

"They should have chosen another method."

Not even amusement now—just detachment again. Mina frowned at him.

"Do you care that a man is dead, sir? Beyond the possible threat to you, or the insult, or whatever motive his murderer had—do you care that a *man* is dead?"

He met her gaze squarely. "I don't know him from a Castilian trapping for furs through American forests or a Hindustani enslaved by the Horde in India. Do you weep over the fate of every man you don't know?"

She wasn't weeping over this one, but she did feel the injustice of it. "I don't know his name, but he isn't a stranger to me now, some hypothetical individual who lives across the globe. Nor is he to you—and odds are, he is here because of some connection to you."

His eyes narrowed, and although humor glinted within them again, it was a cold and dangerous light. Mina suppressed the urge to step back and draw her weapon.

"Then find out who he is and why he's on my doorstep . . . and I will make whoever did it sorry they caught my attention."

She had no doubt he would. And although Mina had every

intention of solving both the mystery of the man's identity and his death, now she had even more reason not to fail.

She didn't want to be the one who attracted the Iron Duke's notice.

Rhys could think of many reasons to kill a man—but only fear kept someone from owning up to what he'd done. Whoever had dropped that body onto his steps was a bloody coward.

He had no use for cowards, especially those who turned and ran. Did they think he wouldn't chase after them?

The inspector had best be quick about finding the direction to go. He hadn't intended to let her investigate the man's death, but Rhys wouldn't have allowed her to take the body if he hadn't believed she'd be successful. Hell, if not for her examination of the corpse, he might not have realized it had fallen from an airship.

An airship. Idiots. If the coward had been just one man—or several men—sneaking onto his grounds, he'd have dealt with them quietly. But they'd come after him in an airship . . . and so his response would be in kind.

As soon as he learned who they were.

Holding his frustration in a tight grip, Rhys left the house and stalked the grounds until his temper cooled. Almost an hour passed before he returned and found Scarsdale in the library, already soused. Rhys poured a brandy for himself, his gaze searching the corners of the large room. He hated the size of it. When he'd built the house, he'd filled it with giant chambers, thinking he would enjoy the space after years of sleeping in cramped quarters and ducking beneath low decks. Instead, he was always on edge.

Scarsdale wasn't. Sprawled on the sofa, the bounder lay with his eyes closed. "Cyclops Cushing swore revenge after you stole *Cerberus* out from under him, but he didn't strike me as stupid enough to throw a man on your house."

His words slurred. Even with a gun pointed at him, Scarsdale wouldn't climb higher than the first yard arm of a mainmast. If he'd guessed the dead man been dropped from an airship, Rhys was surprised he was still coherent.

But though liquor loosened the navigator's tongue, it never impaired his sense. Rhys couldn't claim the same. He set the brandy on his desk, untouched.

Scarsdale struggled into a half-sitting position. He covered his left eye with his empty glass and opened his right. "Then again, I've heard that Cyclops caught the pox from a Dutch whore, and he wasn't smart enough to bug up. Once a pox crawls from your jewels to your brains, it might make a man stupid enough."

"Even with a pox, Cushing wouldn't have dared this." And most of Rhys's enemies wouldn't have murdered someone he didn't know—they'd make it personal. Not tossed a stranger off an airship like disposing a piece of garbage.

"Then what of the Black Guard?" Scarsdale suggested. "Maybe they've caught on to how you've cut off their smuggling route out of Wales."

Perhaps. But even if the Black Guard had realized he'd paid for the submersible that terrorized the slaver ships in those waters, until all but the most desperate mercenaries refused to sail along the coast, Rhys didn't think they'd retaliate. Whoever the members of the Black Guard were, they'd remained secretive about their activities and their purpose—and threatening him would be akin to waving a red flag in front of a bull. Unless they'd changed tactics, they wouldn't draw attention to themselves. No, they'd simply find another smuggling route, and continue selling the slaves to fund their society.

"Of course, Mad Machen has killed fourteen of their slavers, and they've never gunned for him—or dropped a dead body on his ship." Scarsdale weaved before he rested his head against the sofa arm again. "Maybe the threat wasn't aimed at you. Someone might have heard I was here."

Yes. Most of his crew had made enemies, somewhere. The inspector might be finding that out now. But even if they didn't tell her, she had a blasted quick mind. Detective Inspector Wilhelmina Wentworth would fill in the missing pieces on her own.

Damn St. John for bringing her here.

And damn Rhys's own arrogance, that he hadn't booted both the inspector and her constable back through the gates the moment they'd arrived. But he'd been certain how their visit would proceed: The inspector would be an ass-sniffing dog, eager to serve. Rhys would decide whether she could be of use to him, at present or in the future. Then he would send the inspector on her way and continue searching for the coward who'd trespassed in his home.

He still couldn't determine at which point she'd blown him off course. Perhaps the moment she'd first turned to face him, wearing her intelligence and determination like a mask. Or perhaps when he'd seen a flicker of heat as he'd stripped off her glove.

He damn well hadn't expected the flare of desire he'd felt in return—not for a detective inspector with cold, inscrutable eyes . . . and a glove that belonged to a lady.

Wentworth. He didn't recognize the family name. He rarely interacted with the peers who'd been born under the Horde; they had no money to invest or goods to trade. If she was the daughter of a peer, chances were that her mother had been a Horde whore. Most of them had left for the Americas after the revolution, however. So had most of the mongrel children they'd borne. Why had the inspector stayed?

"Who is she?"

Scarsdale lifted his head. After one glance at Rhys's face, he closed his eyes again. "I know that look. A fine ship comes over the horizon, and you want what it's carrying. Let this one sail on, captain."

Rhys shook his head. Scarsdale had mistaken his intentions. He didn't intend to steal her. He'd met few officers of any sort who weren't for sale, and he doubted that Wilhelmina Wentworth would be any different. He simply wanted to know her price.

A scratch at the door stopped his response. A moment later, Mrs. Lavery announced the inspector.

She swept in, her back straight, her shoulders squared. A small thing, but not weak. Her dark eyes seemed to take him in all at once, her gaze cool and assessing. He couldn't detect the spark of heat she'd shown earlier—but he knew it was there. What would it take for her to reveal it again?

In the hall, the red giant stood watching her. Protective, but not as a man was toward his woman.

That shouldn't have pleased Rhys as much as it did. He didn't intend to have her. Yet just by looking at her, desire twisted in his gut—not sexual hunger, but an urgent need to possess. Perhaps Scarsdale had read him better than he'd thought.

But no matter the effect she had on him, Rhys wouldn't let her push him off course again.

"Have you finished?"

"Yes. No one saw his fall or recognized him," she said. For a woman of small size and clipped words, she had a low, full voice. No breathiness, no softness. "When we establish his identity, however, we may of course have more questions—and perhaps the motive will become clear."

"You'll send updates to me."

Her soft mouth tightened before she nodded. "I'll inform Superintendent Hale of your request."

They both knew it hadn't been a request—and they both knew those updates would be sent. He allowed her the small victory of not reporting to him personally.

Looking away from him, she glanced at Scarsdale before allowing her gaze to skim the library, and Rhys realized it was the first time she'd taken her eyes off him since she'd entered the room.

Wariness or curiosity? Either satisfied him.

Her searching gaze halted on the replica of his ship displayed beside the desk. "Is that *Marco's Terror*?"

Long ago, at the request of the Great Khan of the Golden Horde, a Roman pope had sent a handful of scholars, missionaries, and scientists along the Silk Road to the Horde's capital in Xanadu, guided by Venetian explorers: the Polo brothers, and the young Marco Polo. After two decades, Marco had returned alone, raving like a madman about missionaries who'd been put to death, and the workshops where scientists were forced to invent machines of war. His rantings and night terrors had become a legendary joke, but two hundred years later, when the Horde's war machines rolled in from Asia, everyone in Europe learned that they should have listened. With *Marco's Terror*, Rhys had made certain that the Horde, merchants, and slavers had listened to him.

But he didn't have much worth saying now.

His answer was simply, "Yes."

Scarsdale sat up and reached for the absinthe bottle on the sofa table. "The terror of the seven seas! The nautical nightmare!" He poured a small amount of green liquor into his glass and lay back again. "Now you are His Bastard Grace."

Rhys should have curbed his drinking until after the inspector had gone.

A faint smile curved her mouth as she moved closer to study the replica. "My youngest brother is aboard," she said.

"Training in the diplomatic corps?" One of the pampered brats who used the *Terror* as a pleasure cruise between England and the Caribbean.

"No. Andrew is a midshipman."

Not pampered, then. Even on a diplomatic ship, that boy would be working, learning an officer's role from the ground up. "Not an easy position."

"No." It was a quiet response, tinted with resignation and worry—and told him that she missed the boy. Then it was gone, replaced by another faint smile as she looked sideways at him. "You inspired him. He's determined to captain his own ship one day—preferably *Marco's Terror*."

If the boy was lucky, he wouldn't take the same route that Rhys had. But rather than answering, Rhys pointed to the level of the orlop deck, where the midshipman's berth housed their trunks and their hammocks. "Unless he's on watch, he'll be sleeping here."

The inspector peered closely, as if imagining, then glanced up at him. "Thank you."

She did seem grateful. No wonder Scarsdale had been quiet during this exchange. Rhys relied on him to manage the aristocracy and to soften his blunt responses, but the bounder must have thought Rhys was doing well enough on his own.

She looked to his friend. "If I need to include you in those follow-up questions, Lord Scarsdale, will I find you here?"

The bounder lifted his glass to her. "The game is up! She is obviously quite adept at discovering identities, and so our liquefied friend is in good hands, captain."

Rhys lowered his gaze to her hands. Small and finely wrought, her fingers were twisting nervously. They suddenly stilled. When he looked at her face again, faint color had spread over her cheeks.

Scarsdale tossed back his drink and reached for another. "Yes, yes. Well done, Lady Wilhelmina, daughter of the Earl of Rockingham."

She observed him with wry amusement. "You have the advantage, sir."

"Because everyone has heard of your unique beauty? I'm crushed. I thought everyone had heard that I was so handsome."

Was Scarsdale flirting with her? Rhys couldn't tell, but he didn't like it. And he didn't know many English-born aristocrats—but Rockingham, he knew. Like clockwork, the countess sent him a letter every week asking for his support. "Your mother leads the Ladies Reformation League?"

The inspector's brows lifted in surprise. "Yes."

He looked her over. The League lobbied to remove women from the factories and the mines and place them back in their homes, in order to repair the damage the Horde had done to English families. The Reformation League wanted the Crown to reward marriages in the underclass, and for raising children at home rather than delivering them to the crèches. Yet here was the daughter of the lady who worked the hardest to keep women out of any profession, the detective inspector in her overcoat and armor.

He almost laughed. "She must hate the sight of you."

Ice swept over her face, settling in her eyes and her brittle smile. "Not for many years. Good evening to you, Your Grace."

She left the room in a swirl of yellow skirts. He stared after her, wondering what he'd said to piss her off. Blast it all. He *should* have left the inspector to Scarsdale. He glanced at his friend, and found Scarsdale watching him with a frown darkening his face.

"Bad sport, captain?"

Rhys clenched his jaw. *Bad sport* was terrorizing a woman. *Bad sport* included taking slaves from the Welsh shores and selling them overseas. Rhys had never indulged in bad sport.

Scarsdale's expression lightened with disbelief. "You don't know who she is?" When Rhys didn't reply, he said, "You knew her mother is Lady Rockingham."

"Yes."

"So you know who the countess is, but you don't know what she did? Good Christ, Trahaearn. Everyone knows this."

Rhys didn't. Unlike Scarsdale, he didn't care for the aristocrats' gossip, whether in conversation or printed in the newssheets. "Tell me."

"Thirty years ago, the Horde *darga* held a state function. All of the peers were required to attend, of course. Not a single one knew that the Horde planned a Frenzy for that evening."

All of the buggers would have been affected. Not so the Horde. "Her mother rutted with one of them?"

"Or several. Who can tell? But the countess didn't—or wouldn't—remember what had happened. Not until they showed her the baby girl." Scarsdale's mouth twisted. "Lady Rockingham took one look at her daughter—and gouged her own eyes out."

Chapter Three

Mina received insults too often to dwell on them—and even His Bastard Grace seemed insignificant when she had a man's chest opened on an examination table in the small, third-floor laboratory at police headquarters in Whitehall. She poked through the slushy frozen innards, where the remaining ice crystals appeared sharply detailed through the lenses of her magnifying goggles.

Every winter in London, hundreds of people too poor or too unlucky to find shelter were found frozen in the streets. But autumn had only just come to England, and the nights were too warm to kill a bugger, let alone freeze him solid. And so unless she discovered that this man had been on an expedition in the far north, Mina could assume that he hadn't frozen to death.

Standing on the opposite side of the table, Newberry stopped breathing through his mouth for a long second—which told Mina that he'd held back a comment for fear of disturbing her concentration. One day, she hoped, he'd come to understand that a woman could manage both an examination and a conversation simultaneously.

Without looking up, she asked, "What is it, constable?"

He cleared his throat. "Begging your pardon, sir—I wondered if you can determine how long he's been frozen."

Ah, good. He'd finally asked. From the first, Newberry had disliked participating in these morbid exams. Mina had assumed squeamishness on his part, until she'd learned that almost every bounder—along with many others in the New World—viewed mortuary science with distaste, claiming that the examinations showed disrespect toward the dead. In Mina's mind, *disrespect* was failing to scrutinize every detail that might lead her to apprehending this man's murderer.

For a short time after he'd been assigned to her, she'd thought ill of Newberry for his reluctance—until she realized that his determination to solve a murder was as strong as hers. Now, she supposed that her upbringing gave her an advantage over the constable. Necessity had forced her father to become both physician and surgeon, and with no money to hire an assistant, Mina had often performed in that capacity. And although operating on a living being differed greatly from opening up a corpse, the methods of deduction were not so different. Her father observed the body's symptoms to root out the cause of an illness, and so it seemed only natural for Mina to examine the evidence left on a body to determine the cause of death.

She'd hoped it would eventually become natural for Newberry to think so, too—and hoped his question indicated that he'd begun to recognize the value of the morbid exams, even if his distaste hadn't yet faded.

"I can't be certain how long he remained frozen," she told him, "but the decomposition suggests that he wasn't immediately put on ice."

"So he was frozen as an afterthought?"

"It would seem so. Or they hadn't intended to kill him, and it took time to procure the ice." Had dropping him on the Iron Duke's steps been an afterthought, as well?

"To what purpose?"

"The smell, perhaps." Mina slipped her hand beneath the man's right lung. Her fingers ached from the icy cold, but she held her scalpel steady. "If his murderer had to wait for an opportunity to drop the body, he'd have needed to keep it concealed until the right time arrived."

"And if the wait became too long, someone might have reported the odor," Newberry said.

"Yes. Or they wanted to stop decomposition, to make sure that he'd be recognized." Which might have been possible before the impact with the steps had destroyed his face. Mina finished with the lung, and moved upward to examine the nasal cavity. "All that we know for certain is that this man didn't die in London."

Newberry leaned in, staring into the open chest. "How can you be certain of that?"

"The lungs are clean, and there's no trace of smoke in his nasal passages." Mina straightened and pushed her goggles to the top of her head, surveying the body grimly. Even though the bugs continually cleaned the soot from the respiratory organs, residue always remained. This man had either lived outside London, or he'd been away for a while. He certainly hadn't drawn his last breath here.

And although his mechanical arm meant that he must possess nanoagents, it didn't mean that he was English. He could be a bounder who'd come to England to be infected and his severed arm restored, or from any of the European nations in the New World.

"He's lucky that he landed on the Iron Duke's doorstep," she said.

Newberry's gaze shot to hers. "Lucky?"

"If he'd landed anywhere else, he'd be destined for a pauper's grave." He hadn't died in London, and so Superintendent Hale wouldn't have authorized the expense of having him identified. A notice would have been put in the newssheets on the slim hope that someone would come forward with information, but someone rarely did. "If knowing who he is will help us determine whether the Iron Duke has been threatened, however, Hale will pay for a visit to the Blacksmith."

Newberry swallowed audibly. "*The* Blacksmith?"

"Yes." There were many blacksmiths who tended to machines that ranged from steamcarts to locomotives, clockwork devices and artificial limbs. But only one could create mechanical flesh—and there was only one Blacksmith. "Even if he can't identify whose arm this was, he can examine the brain's nanoagents and see the images that this man last saw. So we'll take both to his shop."

"Both of what, sir?"

Mina picked up a bone saw. "Brain and arm."

The constable's face blanched, then seemed to melt with relief when a scratch sounded at the laboratory door. When he scrambled to answer it, Mina had to laugh.

So there *was* a bit of squeamishness, too.

He returned a moment later, his eyes averted away from the body. "That was the night secretary. The superintendent awaits you in her office."

Where Mina would deliver her report. She set her saw blade against the man's forehead and noticed the color drain from her assistant's face again. "I'll be with her shortly. Newberry?"

"Yes, sir?"

"I need you to fetch more ice."

The constable backed toward the door, quick as a shot. "Right away, inspector."

Mina removed her blood-spattered apron before leaving the laboratory. She donned her armor over her dress again, fastening the buckles as she trotted down the narrow creaking stairs to the second floor, emerging into a dim hallway. Her fingers were slower than her feet. She paused outside of Hale's office to finish buckling the armor, and glanced to her left, where a paneled casement window overlooked the Thames . . . and farther down the river, almost obscured by smoke, the Horde's tower.

Her breath hitched and her fingers stumbled. Even after nine years, a glimpse of the tower's silhouette caused a painful twist in her chest—followed by fierce pleasure when that half-seen shadow condensed into its jagged, crumbling shape. The Iron Duke's explosives had been a fist that shattered a giant's teeth, and now the tower leaned brokenly next to the Thames, now and again spitting another stone to the river's north bank. Bounders often suggested tearing it down and building a monument to victory in its place—and for several months following the revolution, Mina would have gladly ripped out each stone with her bare hands. But now, the sight of the ruins themselves felt like a victory over fear and the Horde's control, and she would rather see the crumbling blocks than a monument.

The king's regency council must have thought the same. So far, they'd let the ruins stand. Perhaps Edward's heir would demolish the tower when he came of age and took the council's place as regent. Like Mina's brother Andrew, the prince had only been five years old when the Horde's radio signal had abruptly ended. To someone so young, the Horde's occupation and the sudden, unexpected freedom was more of a story than a memory. When he took the throne, perhaps he'd rather see a plaque repeating that tale than the reality of the broken tower.

Perhaps by then, Mina would be ready to accept a glossy monument in its place.

She clicked the last buckle home and glanced away from the tower, across the river. The haze over Southwark glowed faintly orange, lit from below by the remains of the fire that had blazed through the rookeries.

Those poor bastards. No one would have welcomed a return of the Horde's tower, but not everyone could bear the onslaught of emotion that freedom had brought. Pleasure, hatred, and fear no longer skimmed along the surface—and neither did pain. When the depth of feeling became unbearable, many buggers sought oblivion in the dens, uncaring that they'd exchanged one slave master for another when they traded the Horde for an opium pipe. No one yet knew how many of those pipelayers had died in the fires. Even if they'd been aware their room was ablaze, they'd probably been too disoriented to make their way outside. Mina hoped they hadn't felt anything when they'd burned—and that those who survived would shed their addiction and learn to cope. Pain and strong emotions were inescapable, but they could just . . . try not to feel them.

That was what Mina did. She assumed that was what most buggers who'd been raised under the Horde did.

And at this moment, she needed to push away her pity and focus. Mina turned from the window and rapped on Hale's door. When the superintendent's response came, Mina straightened her shoulders and tried to forget that she wore an absurdity of a dress with tiny yellow sleeves and bare arms. From Mina's first day of training the superintendent had impressed upon her the importance of an inspector—particularly a woman—maintaining a proper appearance, one that inspired confidence and conveyed authority. What Mina's clothing couldn't suggest now, her manner would have to.

When she entered, a single gas lamp lit the small office, casting a warm glow on the maps of London pinned to the walls. A tall woman with narrow, pale features, Superintendent Hale sat behind her desk, sorting through a stack of wiregram messages. Despite the late hour, Hale looked as if she'd never left for the evening: her graying auburn hair scraped back into a bun, her jacket smartly buckled.

Mina wasn't surprised that Douglas Sheffield sat slumped in the chair facing Hale; she'd heard that he had recently returned from Manhattan City. With his clothing rumpled and his waistcoat buttoned crookedly, he appeared as if he'd rolled from bed and dressed hurriedly in order to accompany her. Even a police superintendent wouldn't travel through London alone at night, and the industrialist took care to look after his interests. Mina didn't know which interest he rated more important, the widow Hale or the airships that had made his family a fortune in Manhattan City, but his dedication to both was unquestionable.

He half rose when Mina came in, then sat heavily again, coughing a greeting into his handkerchief.

Hale looked Mina over, pausing briefly on the yellow skirts. "I see that you understood the urgency of the matter."

"Yes, sir. We traveled from Devonshire House directly to the island."

Hale gestured to the wiregram machine occupying the surface of a long table against the wall. "I've already received grams from the commissioner and the mayor. I expect to find more from the king's council in the morning. Give me something to tell them that won't have them coming here in person—or having me summoned."

And they wouldn't want to hear about the dead man. Neither did Sheffield. His eyes were bright with curiosity, and although Mina would have preferred to deliver her report solely to Hale, the superintendent had made it clear more than a year and a half ago that Mina could speak freely in front of him. Mina supposed that Hale had been fortunate to find a man whom she could trust to share her bed—but Sheffield's trade concerns figuratively put him in more beds than just hers.

Mina had only pointed that out once, however. She valued her job too much to bring it up again.

"The Iron Duke is unharmed," Mina said. "I don't believe he's under imminent threat."

"I'll leave out 'imminent' when I send my grams, or risk being bombarded with questions of what threat is delayed." With a wry twist of her lips, Hale leaned back in her chair. "You've brought the body here? Who is it?"

"I haven't yet been able to identify him, sir."

"Then tell me what you do know."

Pitifully little, which became all the more apparent as Mina reported her findings, including her suspicions about the airship and the need to consult with the Blacksmith.

Hale grimaced over the expense, but approved the visit. She watched Mina closely as she asked, "And what is your feeling regarding Anglesey's involvement?"

Mina considered her response. Suggesting that the Iron Duke murdered a man had to be handled delicately. Fortunately, she could say in all honesty, "At this time, the only connection I've found between the duke and the corpse is the body's location. I've seen nothing to suggest his personal involvement in the man's death."

"Is he *involved*?" Sheffield broke in with a disbelieving laugh. "Of course he is. Perhaps Anglesey didn't kill the man, but that blaggard will have been involved at some point. Most likely, he'd sent this man to tangle with one of his enemies, or to put pressure on another merchant, and this was the result."

Mina had wondered the same. Whoever had thrown the man from the airship had been making a statement, but perhaps the Iron Duke had delivered the first threat.

She didn't think Trahaearn would have concealed that, however—not after openly warning her that St. John's life would be forfeit if the steward was connected, and promising to make the murderer regret catching his attention. If Trahaearn had known who the man was, he wouldn't have let Mina through the gates and allowed her to question the staff. No, he'd already be moving to retaliate.

"A man like that, given a duke's title." Sheffield lowered his handkerchief from his mouth, revealing a disgusted frown. "It's an insult to the rank. He knows nothing of honor or duty. Only the idolatry heaped on his head keeps it out of a hangman's noose—and even this murder will be pardoned."

Mina bristled. Though she held a similar opinion of Trahaearn, a bounder didn't get to determine the Iron Duke's worth, or judge the buggers who valued him over any other man *or* title.

Hale cast Sheffield a severe look. "If all he's done is made an enemy, then he hasn't done anything that needs pardoned."

That wasn't the response Mina would have given, but she appreciated Hale's. Though Hale was also a bounder, the destruction of the tower had given her a measure of freedom, as well—and so perhaps she understood better why the Iron Duke was so revered. In Manhattan City, Hale had been an assistant to her late husband, a chief inspector. When he'd died, the Manhattan City police hadn't let her step into his place or continue in the same occupation, though she'd been well-qualified for it. She'd been one of the first who'd returned from the New World following the revolution, and had joined London's newly formed and critically understaffed Metropolitan Police Force.

Sheffield coughed again. Hale's expression softened and her

brow furrowed, perhaps wondering if he would relent and visit a blacksmith or physician who could infect him with the nanoagents. With his every cough, Mina wondered the same. Sheffield would have to gain special permissions to return to Manhattan City after being infected, but he had money enough for bribes, and enough power that even a New Worlder's fear of the bugs wouldn't affect his business or his status.

But perhaps Sheffield was the one who needed to overcome his fear of the bugs.

Hale's gaze returned to Mina's. "I'll inform the commissioner that we are confirming identity and motive—and that we anticipate *imminent* apprehension."

Mina suppressed her smile. "Yes, sir."

"Mr. Sheffield, would you please wind the machine?" Hale selected letter-specific punch cards from the stack on her desk, arranging their order and forming her message. At the wiregram, Sheffield began spinning the influence machine's handle, building up static stored in the battery of Kleistian jars. As if suddenly remembering Mina's presence, Hale glanced up again, and raised her voice over the whir of the influence machine. "You're dismissed, inspector. Send me a wiregram detailing your progress at every step, starting after your meeting with the Blacksmith in the morning."

So that Hale could update their superiors. Mina nodded. "I will. Good night, sir." She looked to the gentleman. "Mr. Sheffield."

He bowed his head, never pausing in his spinning. "My lady."

Inspector, Mina almost corrected him, but held her tongue.

As she turned, she saw Hale's mouth tighten and the sharp glance she gave Sheffield. The superintendent didn't hold with privileging the title over the occupation.

And Sheffield wasn't a bad sort, but he would have to figure out a few things before Hale changed one of her titles to his missus.

Chapter Four

When Mina came down for breakfast, her parents were already seated at one end of the dining table, wearing enough layers to ward off the chill in the room. The gray early-morning sunshine trickling in through the windows seemed more like a drizzle, so that everything the pale light touched appeared damp.

Even her mother's white hair seemed muted by it. Without glancing up from the newssheets spread across her father's reading apparatus, she observed, "You forgot to wind your clock, Mina."

Mina hadn't thought she would need to. The night had been a sleepless one . . . except during the hour she was supposed to have risen. "Yes."

"Are you in a hurry, then?"

"Not yet." Newberry wouldn't bring his cart around for another quarter hour.

From the sideboard, Mina selected a boiled egg and thinly sliced toast. Simple fare, perhaps, but Cook's toast was unequaled anywhere—even her mother had not yet devised a machine that could replicate it. To Mina's surprise, a length of sausage was leftover, given as payment after her father had infected the butcher's newborn with nanoagents. If her brothers Henry and Andrew had still lived here, not even a smear of grease would have remained. Suddenly missing them acutely, she slid the sausage onto her plate and took the chair across from her mother.

She poured the cheap Liberé coffee and pretended not to notice as, on her left, her father looked up from the newssheets and subjected her to a quiet scrutiny—looking for bruises or stiffness in her movements, she knew. In the first years following the revolution, she'd tried to hide them, scuffling with her brothers as cover. Stupid, perhaps, because her father hadn't been fooled. But she couldn't bear the helpless anger in her father's eyes every time she returned home with a puffy lip or a bruised cheek. At least the fights with her brothers let him *do* something, even if it was only a reprimand.

Fortunately, she hadn't needed to cover any bruises of late—not since Newberry had been assigned to her. A giant hulk of a man following her about dissuaded anyone from striking her, no matter how much they hated the Horde.

And if not for Newberry, her brothers might never have felt they could leave—first the practical Henry, gone to Northampton to see if he could wrestle order and prosperity from an estate that no one in their family had seen for two hundred years, followed by Andrew, embarking on the first steps toward a career at sea. Her gaze fell on Andrew's empty seat. *Marco's Terror* should have reached the Caribbean by now, and so his letters would be arriving from the French Antilles within a few weeks. She wondered if he'd write of how much he hated the ship, or how much he loved it.

Strange, that she couldn't guess. Unlike Henry, whose steely good sense rivaled their father's, Andrew's and Mina's characters had been assembled from both parents—though neither were as high-strung as their mother, whose emotions even the Horde hadn't been able to suppress. Typically, Andrew's opinions and reactions mirrored Mina's, but she couldn't predict how he would find life aboard the ship. Would he chafe against the rigid order on the *Terror*, or revel in the freedom of the open seas and every new sight that his journey presented? And if it were both, which would win out over the other?

Whatever his response, she was certain of one thing: that he would be grateful for the opportunity to *know* whether it suited him, rather than forever wondering. Mina would always be similarly grateful to Hale—and for finding a job that so perfectly suited her.

Dead people of all sorts were more tolerable than most of those living.

Her father finished his silent examination and returned to his newssheets, clicking the page turner. Though faster by hand, anyone living with her mother soon learned the simple pleasure of watching a well-designed machine at work. A stylus with a rubber ball at its tip slowly pushed the paper over, treating Mina to a sideways view of the caricature of a Horde magistrate: rat-faced, his eyes nothing more than slits drawn with heavy slashes of a pen, and a wispy mustache drooped over loose, bulbous lips.

She looked down at her plate. Reading the story that accompanied the drawing was unnecessary; it had played out several times over the past months. The few Horde officials who hadn't fled or been killed during the revolution had been imprisoned at Newgate for the past nine years. Now, they underwent trials for the horrors committed during the occupation. Thus far, all had been found guilty and sentenced to hang. No doubt this magistrate would, too.

When the page finished turning over, Mina looked up again. Her mother read along with her father, the newssheet a tiny upside-down reflection in her silver eyes; Mina couldn't have hoped to discern the small print from the same distance, even reading right-side up. Not long after the Blacksmith had grafted the mechanical eyes, her mother had tried to explain how everything appeared through them. She'd mentioned telescopes, magnifying goggles, and the glow of a fire before giving up, frustrated by her inability to describe what she saw. The gist had been clear enough, however: Not only was her mother's vision more acute, it was *different*. She saw not just in color and shapes, but temperatures. She'd stumbled around for almost a year—stumbled far more than she had while completely blind—before finally learning to interpret the images the new eyes gave her.

Mina had never asked what price the Blacksmith had put on her mother's eyes, but after six years, the debt hadn't yet been paid off.

Her mother's automata sold at his shops for enormous amounts, yet she received a pittance after the Blacksmith took his portion.

Her dead man's arm had cost someone. Perhaps he or his family had money—but if he was still indebted, the Blacksmith would have information regarding the dead man's recent whereabouts. Rumor was, if anyone missed a payment, the Blacksmith always found them.

Information about where the man had been might prove useful. All Mina *needed*, however, was a name.

The reading apparatus clicked again. As the stylus slowly turned the paper over, her father said, "Until your mother saw the blood on your dress, she'd thought that you'd bribed young Newberry to help you escape the Victory Ball."

Mina laughed and saw her mother's quick smile. No one could accuse her father of inefficiency. He could poke fun at them both with one statement.

His brown beard hid most of her father's smile, but the corners of his mustache twitched as he continued, "Whereas I suspected that you put the blood there simply to convince your mother. It wasn't fresh."

Her father had probably examined the stains to make certain the blood wasn't Mina's. "It wasn't. He'd been frozen for some time." She glanced across the table at her mother. "Is the dress ruined?"

"Quite." No censure filled her voice, only acceptance. She seemed downtrodden this morning. "We will see what Sally can salvage of the fabric."

"Unfortunately, Newberry did not think to bring my wardrobe." Mina looked down at her black trousers tucked into sturdy boots. She should have worn this to the ball. People might as well meet her as she truly was . . . though it hardly mattered. She could parade naked down Oxford Street, and no one would notice anything but her Horde features. She glanced to her father. "Were you able to speak with Mr. Moutten?"

The patients her father tended were often worse off than Mina's family, and payment rarely came as money. Her father accepted anything—chickens, food, repairs—but asked for broken machines above all else, which her mother used to build the automata sold in the Blacksmith's shops. Mina's salary covered the bare necessities. After paying the taxes, which were hardly lower than the Horde had demanded, and wages for the cook and two maids—far fewer than the town house needed, even with most of the rooms closed up—all together Mina's family earned just enough to scrape by.

But her father had heard that a bounder's personal physician had fled back to the New World. To bring in more ready cash, he'd intended to recommend his services to the gentleman.

"I am," he said, puffing himself up in parody and adopting a bounder's flat accent, "a jolly good man to offer such a favor."

A favor? That didn't sound promising. "In exchange for what?"

"His good esteem? A reference?" He shook his head, his chest deflating to normal size. "I couldn't say. But clearly, payment did not enter Moutten's mind."

Did they assume her father's work was a hobby? *Blast those thickheaded bounders.* What in the blazes did they eat in Manhattan City? *Air?* Maybe the food fell from the trees and rolled onto golden plates.

Or maybe they thought the services of a Horde-trained physician weren't worth anything. Arrogant bigots, those bounders were—the whole lot of them.

"Perhaps it's for the best, however," he continued evenly, and Mina didn't know how he could remain so calm when steam all but spouted from her ears. "I would advise them all to infect themselves, and none of them want to hear that."

Her mother lifted her chin, gesturing at the newssheets. "They'll not be able to anyway, once the Free Party has their way."

Unlike every nation in the New World, England hadn't outlawed the practice of injecting someone with blood infected by the nano-agents. Any physician or blacksmith could perform the injection. The process posed no risk; some people contracted low-grade bug fever in the first hours, but Mina had never heard of anyone dying from the injection—and her father had infected thousands, most of them children.

But the health risks concerned the Free Party less than the nano-agents themselves, and had become the most divisive issue in the upcoming general election. And it shouldn't have been so, but with the bounders reclaiming their seats and the influence of merchants on pocket boroughs, the Free Party had the buggers themselves arguing against their own interests. Political opponents debated whether a bugger should be able to hold office or inherit, citing the danger of a judge or a lawmaker whose decisions could be influenced by a radio signal. Pointing out that the Horde hadn't controlled their thoughts did little to help, because the Horde *had* made King Edward a puppet, yanking on his strings so hard and so often that they'd ruined his mind.

Fear of control had become the Horde's legacy, and the Free Party did little to dispel it. The paranoia had become so prevalent that Mina had even heard tales of a Black Guard—silent agents of the Horde who stole into buggers' homes during the night, freezing their nanoagents and leaving them helpless, or taking others away to enslave.

Mina didn't know how many letters her father had written to aristocrats and the influential merchants, asserting the need for common sense over fear, but he spent almost every evening composing them. When Parliament came into session again, he'd be occupied by matters in the White Chamber during the daytime hours—and tend to fewer patients.

So they'd tighten their belts again.

"I will do my best, dear. Perhaps we will win more over before the election."

Her mother sighed and nodded. "And despite my efforts, I do not expect any new ladies at this evening's League meeting. Mina, please tell us that you were more successful than we proved to be."

She hadn't been; she didn't even know *who* had been murdered. But she was determined to change that.

"I met the Iron Duke and spent several hours at his home," she told them, and although Mina didn't look up from her plate, she felt the sudden intensity of their regard. "He knew who you were, Mother. He mentioned your League."

Her mother gasped, hand flying to cover her heart. Her mouth opened and closed several times before she whispered, "You are not lying."

Her mother could recognize when someone lied to her, detected through a change of skin temperature and the involuntary movements of facial muscles. Perhaps that was another reason for her melancholy. How many lies had been spoken to her face last night?

Now, a smile warmed her delicate features. Mina's father said, "Look there, love. You've touched more people than you know."

"It is the letter duplicating machine. I would never have time to write so many if it couldn't record the movement of my pen." She laughed suddenly. "If I continue sending the letters every week, perhaps he will join the League just to halt them."

Mina grinned. Most likely, her mother would do exactly that. Glancing up, she found those silver eyes focused on her.

"And so what was your impression of him?"

"He is a formidable figure—very large, physically—but also intimidating in manner." And he'd made her burn with both embarrassment and anger. "It is easy to see why so many captains surrendered their ships to him without a single shot fired. I would have."

"No, Mina," her father said. "You'd have fired back."

The Iron Duke had taken a shot with his remark about her mother, but Mina hadn't returned fire. She'd retreated. His statement had been either thoughtless or cruel, and Trahaearn didn't strike her as a man who spoke without thinking.

So it had been cruelty, then—and she'd had enough of that in her lifetime. But unleashing her temper on him would have been foolish;

retreat had been her smartest option. He'd had his fun, and now that she was out of his sight, he'd forget about her.

"I wouldn't fire back if I were outgunned," she said.

Her parents exchanged an odd glance. Her mother's lips curved. "Yes, I imagine that he possesses a rather large cannon," she said, spearing her sausage with a fork.

Her father's cough sounded like a laugh.

Oh, blast. What had Mina started by mentioning the duke? But she could only blame herself, since she'd been the one to restore her mother's good humor. "Perhaps. But after he looked at the cargo, I'm certain he'd lose interest."

Her mother persisted. "Is he as handsome as the caricatures in the newssheets?"

Mina gave up. "Yes. Handsome *and* obliging. He rescued my glove from certain ruin."

"Thank the blue heavens for him." Not a trace of sarcasm tinted her mother's response.

Her father's mustache twitched. "He is still very much the hero."

Mina frowned. Yes, he was.

But who didn't think so?

The Blacksmith's property in the Narrow stood as close to the Thames as possible without falling into it—and pieces of the buildings near the smithy often did. Situated at Limehouse's south edge, the Narrow had once been a street. Now, it only resembled one, forming a twisting path between deteriorating buildings, with rubble spilling out over the cobblestone walks.

Mina instructed Newberry to drive as close to the Blacksmith's as the piles of debris allowed, stopping the cart in front of a burned-out brewery and behind a steamcoach whose driver looked rough enough to scare away any thieves . . . if he didn't steal the cart himself.

While Newberry locked the tires, she climbed out and looked down the Narrow, breathing through her mouth. The scent of the slaughterhouses across the river and the tanneries to the east lay heavy in the air, overwhelming even the smoke and the Thames itself. Small groups of laborers who hadn't found work at one of the foundries or repairing a ship at the dry docks gathered along the walks, hoping that they'd be hired onto a day crew. A message runner darted past her—probably a child from the Crèche. Clean and bright-cheeked, he looked as out of place as Mina did.

The laborers didn't eye him with the same suspicion and hatred. Mina gave them hardly a second glance as she passed their groups. They wouldn't bother her—though not out of respect for her uniform or fear of Newberry trailing in her wake. The Blacksmith held the only authority here. But anyone coming to the Narrow likely had business with the Blacksmith, and no one dared interfere with that.

She looked back at the constable, recognizing his tension as he realized that his presence wasn't what held the laborers back. Anticipating his unease, she'd made certain his hands would be occupied carrying the wooden chest full of ice, a mechanical arm, and a brain. If a Manhattan City constable walked into the Narrow with his hands on his guns, he might not even have the protection of the Blacksmith.

Newberry's gaze searched the buildings. "Which one is it, sir?"

Mina pointed to a three-storied brick warehouse. Though weathered and dingy, the structure was well kept, the window glass intact. Tall chimneys released steam and smoke in a steady cloud.

"There's no sign over the entrance. How do people find it?"

Mina assumed that by "people," Newberry meant bounders. Everyone else knew where to go. The smithy had once housed the Horde's modification shops, the only location in London more terrifying than the tower. "If they want what the Blacksmith offers badly enough, they'll find it."

Though some who found it weren't always ready to go in. For those, the Hammer & Chain lay only thirty paces down the street, and they often found their courage at the bottom of a pint. Others went for the cheap food—or a fight. No matter what its patrons were looking for when they went into the Hammer & Chain, they were as likely to be tossed out as walk out.

But no one would have dared toss out the dark-haired giant who pushed through the doors and stepped into her path.

Trahaearn.

Mina's gut clenched with the same split-second punch of fear that hit her when she glimpsed the tower. She forced her step not to falter, her hands not to fly to her weapons.

By the starry sky, she would *not* feel this.

She breathed deep, gathering her calm. Surely what she'd felt wasn't fear, no matter how imposing he was, and despite her certainty that to have timed his exit so perfectly, he must have been lying in wait for her.

Surely it wasn't fear. Dislike seemed far more probable.

As Mina halted, the bright-cheeked boy she'd seen earlier ducked from behind Trahaearn's long overcoat, gold winking in his small fingers before disappearing into his pocket. Not a message runner, then, but a little spy. And the duke *had* been waiting for her. Now he stared down from his great height, his dark gaze searching her face. She didn't give him anything to find but an enquiring arch of her right brow.

His eyes narrowed, as if she'd displeased him. Had he expected her to curtsy? To faint? His silence continued. Perhaps he'd forgotten that his rank and his actions demanded that he speak first. Almost amused now, she arched her left brow.

"Inspector Wentworth," he finally said, and although his deep voice didn't seem loud, it carried. Heads turned in his direction. Every laborer in a nearby group looked toward him, their expressions both wary and hopeful, as if they thought he might be here with work for the day. But they didn't appear surprised, which told Mina that Trahaearn's was a familiar face in the Narrow.

She inclined her head. "Your Grace."

"You haven't yet identified him."

It wasn't a question, and she had no doubt that he'd been updated with everyone else—and would continue to be updated. After Trahaearn learned the man's identity, staying a step ahead of him would pose a problem. Perhaps it was best that he was here, then, so that Mina could see where he stepped.

"I have not," she said. "Have you?"

"No."

"And do you intend to dog my steps until we determine who he is?"

He smiled briefly, and she was reminded not of a dog, but the drawing of a timber wolf she'd seen in one of her father's books, lean and hungry.

"Yes," he said.

Sudden frustration ate at her amusement. "You know I can't stop you."

"Yes." No gloating. Just fact.

"Then I ask that you don't interfere."

He glanced over his shoulder toward the Blacksmith's. "My interference will keep you from waiting—and from overpaying."

Did he know the Blacksmith? Or did Trahaearn assume his reputation would earn him special treatment?

Not that it mattered. That hadn't been what she'd meant. She shook her head. "If I discover something that you don't like—"

"You're asking me not to kill him. I won't promise that."

She gritted her teeth. Should she try to convince a pirate of the importance of law and order? She might as well beat her head against the cobblestones.

"Very well." She stepped around him, continuing on toward the Blacksmith's. "Then we will race to see who will reach him first: me to arrest him, or you to carry out your brand of justice."

"Not justice. I've no interest in that." Trahaearn fell into step beside her, leaving Newberry to trail behind. "But I always protect what's mine."

And didn't hesitate to destroy what wasn't. "And if this man isn't yours?"

"Then he'll still be yours."

Though his reply was exactly what she'd wanted to hear, Mina

frowned. The determination in his tone bothered her—as if Trahaearn intended to follow this investigation through to the end, even
if the dead man had no connection to him. Warily, she glanced over
and found the duke watching her again.

"But I haven't come just to learn his identity, inspector. Scarsdale told me that my final comment to you last night was . . .
ill-considered." His pause said that *ill-considered* was indeed Scarsdale's word. "It pained you. I apologize."

Perhaps *all* of that statement had been at Scarsdale's prompt-
ing. Trahaearn didn't strike her as a man who apologized often. She
looked at him with suspicion. "You're sorry?"

His jaw clenched before he said, "Yes."

That had come with effort. Mina didn't intend to make it any
easier.

"You trampled on my mother's honor, not mine. Her response
when I was born was not about me, but what the Horde had done
to her. If you are truly sorry, you will make it up to her—and you'll
give your support to her Reformation League."

He frowned. "Her League will solve few problems."

"I agree," Mina said, and saw his surprise. "But it doesn't hurt
anyone, either. She advocates for responsibility and stability, and
those who find it through marriage probably *want* to marry."

"And you don't?"

"My situation has never been the same as theirs." Mina's gaze
sought out a group of laborers, a good portion of them women.
Chances were, several of them lived together—and at their home,
another woman watched over the children they'd borne. Women rarely
left their babies at the crèches now, but few could work to support
a family *and* raise it alone. Fewer even considered matrimony—the
Horde had all but destroyed the institution among the lower classes
by forbidding them to marry for two centuries. In the years since the
Horde had left, communal families consisting mostly of females had
become more common than a man and woman living together.

"My mother wants to reintroduce an option that the Horde took away, but unlike the Horde, she won't force it upon anyone. If you simply mention the League to the right people—your Scarsdale will know who they are—your support will go further than a thousand letters. Or you could attend one of her meetings. She's holding one tonight, if you wish to come."

Perhaps she only imagined the fleeting expression that suggested the wolf had his foot caught in a trap, but having sat through more of her mother's meetings than she cared to count, it buoyed her spirits immeasurably.

They reached the Blacksmith's warehouse. Mina passed by the storefront entrance, where clerks sold automata to those who could afford it. Few in the Narrow could. The Blacksmith's shop on the Strand was much larger, and one of the most popular destinations for bounders in the city. Curious, Mina slowed, watching the duke. He didn't pause at the shop, but continued smoothly on toward the smithy entrance, out of sight around the corner.

All right. She would assume that he was familiar with the Blacksmith—which begged the question of why he'd waited.

"Why did you bother?"

He glanced down at her, brows drawing together. "With what?"

"Apologizing," she said. "Have you apologized to the families of men you've killed, the women you've violated? To every merchant and government you've ever stolen from? Yet now you are sorry for a mere insult. To what purpose? You can obtain the information you want without it."

The Iron Duke pivoted into her path and faced her. Mina spun toward the brick wall to avoid crashing into him, stumbling over debris. *What in blue blazes?* Her temper leapt. She opened her mouth, looked up—and froze with her back against the building, her eyes locked on his, certain that if she glanced away, he'd cross the distance between them.

He didn't appear angry. His expression remained detached, unreadable. Yet she could almost *feel* the control he wielded over himself—and over her, under threat of it being unleashed.

Perhaps she ought not to have recounted his crimes. Softening accusations of murder and rape by calling them *killing* and *violation* probably wasn't a distinction he recognized.

She heard Newberry's heavy approach—and his concern. "Inspector?"

The look Trahaearn sent to Newberry halted the constable midstride, the box of ice secure against his chest. Uncertain, the constable looked to Mina. She shook her head, telling him to remain where he was, and met Trahaearn's detached gaze again.

In a low voice, he asked, "Do you have a man, inspector?"

"A man?" she echoed, fearing that she understood him. He'd laid in wait and apologized for *this*? A laugh bubbled up, dissipating her fear. Did he truly imagine that an insult and a lover would be her only objections? Oh, but Mina hoped she was wrong. "A man like Constable Newberry?"

"No. A man in your bed."

She *had* understood. Damn his arrogance. "The only man who interests me is the one whose brain and arm Newberry is carrying. I will not waste your time by pretending otherwise, Your Grace. I ask that you do not waste mine."

"I wouldn't. So tell me whether you have a man."

As if it would matter to someone like him. "And if I do?"

"I'll discover what he gives you. Then I'll offer more."

Ah, she should have realized; this was a business transaction. Last night, when he'd removed her glove, she'd seen his lust. It wasn't here now—and that made rejecting him surprisingly easy, despite his power and the trouble he could make for her.

"I don't have a man." When she saw his triumph, Mina added, "But you have nothing to offer me, sir. I answer to no one. I must make time only for myself. Can you offer better than absolute freedom?"

"The daughter of a bugger earl would never have anything of the sort."

Well, that was true enough. But she came closer to freedom now than she could ever hope to after sharing his bed. "And you're a duke, so you have even less freedom to offer, no matter how deep your pockets."

His expression hardened, like heated steel plunged into an ice bath. But even as she tensed, wondering if she'd finally gone too far, he looked away from her.

It was as if a cage door had been opened. Mina exhaled softly and continued along the walk. Reaching the smithy entrance, she stepped through a solid wall of heat and noise. No smell of the tanneries and slaughterhouses here—only smoke, sweat, and oil. Stokers wearing leather aprons and gloves shoveled coal into the furnaces squatting along the wall. Enormous boilers hissed steam, and the ring of metal hammering against metal came from every direction of the smithy.

Mina started for the stairs at the other end of the warehouse, passing the repair and refitting stations. Standing between two brick columns, a blacksmith gestured for the woman in front of him to walk. With her threadbare skirts hiked up to reveal skeletal prosthetic legs, she took a step. The metal ball of her right heel dragged, scraping loudly over the stone floor. In the next station, a tinker concentrated over pneumatic cylinders protruding from a man's shoulders like a stunted pair of tubed wings—routine maintenance for a dockworker that cost less than waiting until something broke. Beside him, a female blacksmith tested the fingers of an elderly woman's new prosthetic. Tears glistened on her wrinkled cheeks; she clutched to her breast a rusted forearm, with the Horde's sewing apparatus and pincers still attached. Though they could trade the old limbs in, most took their prosthetics home. Even knowing what the Horde had done, it was difficult letting part of themselves go—and that woman had probably worn an awl and pincers longer than Mina had been alive.

The blacksmith working on the old woman's hand looked up. She shouted to the tinker watching over her shoulder, then jerked her head in Mina's direction.

The girl jogged toward her, pushing back her welding goggles as she drew close. Her mouth dropped open when she spotted Mina; Mina's lips parted in surprise. The girl had Horde blood in her. The tinker looked Mina up and down, then up again.

Mina stared back. Grease streaked the girl's hands, but her black hair and clothes were clean. Probably from the Crèche, the girl couldn't have been more than ten years old, but she already wore a tinker's chain tattooed around her wrist. When she became a blacksmith, a hammer would be tattooed below the chain, completing the guild's mark.

The girl looked away from Mina, focusing on the man behind her. "The Blacksmith said to go up soon as you arrived, captain."

Captain. Even here? Mina didn't glance back at him. She turned toward the stairs, but the girl shook her head.

"The quick way," she said, gesturing to the back of the warehouse. Mina walked alongside the tinker, noting how the girl watched her from the corner of her eye. Mina was little better at hiding her interest than the girl was.

"What do they mean?" The girl nodded at the epaulettes decorating Mina's shoulders.

"Detective Inspector."

A thoughtful expression came over her small face. "Is that what they call you?"

"Just 'inspector.'" Which was better than most of the names Mina was called. This girl probably heard them, too. "It's almost as good as 'blacksmith.'"

"Oh?"

"A blacksmith can go anywhere. A detective inspector only goes where the dead bodies are."

"But there aren't any dead people here today."

Mina glanced over her shoulder at the chest Newberry carried. "That's why I brought my own."

They reached the lift. The shaft rose between two enormous exhaust fans installed near the high ceiling before disappearing into the next level of the warehouse. The girl slid aside the grating and turned, holding the gate open.

"The Blacksmith is on the third level, then all the way to the east wall!" she called over the noise of the fans.

Mina nodded, but didn't board the lift. "What's your name, tinker?"

The girl's eyes widened. "Anne."

"So it will be Anne Blacksmith. That name will treat you well." And the Blacksmith's guild tattoo would keep her safe. "But if it doesn't, I'm at police headquarters in Whitehall. Ask for Wentworth."

Anne nodded, her round cheeks dimpling with a huge smile. Mina stepped into the lift, standing to the side to make room for Trahaearn and Newberry. The Iron Duke boarded and closed the cage behind him. Newberry abruptly stopped, staring at them through the grating.

Trahaearn locked the gate. "It will be too crowded and over its weight capacity, constable. I'll send it back down for you."

Mina looked at him in disbelief. Though it'd be a tight fit, the lift could accommodate her assistant. Then the duke glanced down at her, wearing that cold detachment she'd begun to hate, and Mina understood.

She'd rejected his offer outside and put an end to the matter. But the Iron Duke wasn't done.

Anger balled tight and high in her throat. Swallowing it down, she looked through the grating at Newberry. "We'll meet you on the third level, constable. Anne, will you show Constable Newberry to the stairs?"

As soon as they turned to go, Trahaearn started the lift. Metal scraped as he threw the lever forward. Mina stared at the gate's flat steel panel, almost blind with rage.

So this is how it would be? When pirates took over a ship, they usually gave the crew a choice between keeping their positions under a new captain, abandonment, or death. What choice would he give to her? She accepted his offer, or he ruined her family? Or would he simply rape her here?

The noise of the fans assaulted her ears, then was muffled as they rose past the second level floor. Unlike the smithy below, this level had been partitioned. An empty corridor led from the lift to the rooms where the Blacksmith grafted his mechanical flesh to living tissue, and where those undergoing the excruciating process waited while the flesh grew. Mina's mother had waited in one of these rooms, but had forbidden Mina and her brothers from accompanying her. Instead, her father had held her hand through each step, carried her home each night—and every morning, he'd had to convince her mother to return to the Blacksmith's and finish it. By the end of the week, he'd been as pale and haggard as her mother.

Remembering that, Mina's anger built into resolution. What could Trahaearn do to her family that the Horde hadn't already done? *Nothing.* And her family had always fought back, always survived. The only danger he posed was to Mina's person and her career—but no matter the damage he caused, she would survive that, too.

She looked up. The roof of the lift had almost reached the next floor. The duke still hadn't spoken. Her tension began to loosen its grip. Had she mistaken his intentions, then? Perhaps he just hadn't wanted to be crowded.

Metal scraped, and the lift jolted to a halt. Mina stumbled forward before catching her balance—and realized that he'd timed it perfectly. They'd stopped halfway between the floors. The lift's roof concealed them from above, and if anyone entered the corridor below, the gate blocked the view of the lift's interior.

Damn him. *Damn* him.

Mina wouldn't make it out of the Narrow alive if she shot him, but he couldn't know she wouldn't be crazy enough to do it. She pushed back the sides of her overcoat to expose her weapons.

He remained silent, staring at her from the opposite side of the lift, his dark gaze searching her face. Was he waiting for her to protest, or just trying to intimidate her?

She *was* afraid. Not of him, or what he could do to her body. Her bugs could heal bruises and tears, inside and out. But by forcing her, by taking her choice, he'd rip away everything that he'd given when he'd destroyed the Horde's broadcasting tower.

Never would Mina allow that. And on second thought, maybe she *was* crazy enough. Her hands slid from her hips to her holstered weapons. His gaze fell and lingered on her weapons—or her thighs. She repressed the urge to let her overcoat fall closed. He looked up again, meeting her eyes. Mina arched a brow.

His slow smile didn't soften his hawkish features. "You'll come to my bed. And you won't think it a waste of time."

"You're wasting it now. Start the lift."

"A blacksmith earns more than an inspector, yet you didn't say that to the girl. You placed the ability to go anywhere ahead of money." As he spoke, his detachment turned to speculation, but his gaze never wavered from her face. "I can offer you enough that you'd be able to go anywhere you'd like, too."

Anger and unease mixed with surprise. He'd listened to her conversation with Anne? She'd have to be careful never to reveal anything of herself in his vicinity again, not if he'd use it against her.

"I'm happy where I am," she said. "Except I'd rather be ascending."

His short laugh made her stomach drop, her fingers tighten on her weapons. He crossed the lift in two strides, each step rattling the cage around them. Mina held her ground. He stopped with only a few inches between them—and blast his monstrous height, the top of her head barely reached his shoulder.

What did he mean to prove by stopping so close? Did he intend for Mina to tilt her head back, making it appear as if she lifted herself to his kiss? Resolutely, she stared ahead at the small brass buckles that fastened his waistcoat—and suddenly realized that her refusal to look up made her seem afraid.

No matter what her response was, she couldn't win.

She stiffened as his palm cupped her nape. Hard fingers tilted her chin up; he lowered his head. Mina jerked her face to the side. She felt his rough laughter against her neck, the gentle touch of his lips to her throat. His hand tightened in her hair, holding her still as he inhaled, as if drawing in her scent.

Tremors started low in her belly. Fear, she recognized. Anger, she welcomed. But not the burn beneath her skin, so similar to when he'd taken her glove.

He lifted his head, but didn't release her. His thumb brushed her bottom lip. "You will accept me. And now I will know you, even if you come to me in the dark."

Know her? Arrogant, insufferable knacker. He knew *nothing* about her.

And she didn't need her weapons to get him away from her. Not when he was so stupid as to come this close.

Her hand shot to the front of his breeches, making claws of her fingers and trapping his genitals in a tight grip. He froze. As if testing, she hefted the firm weight she found. Heavy, but so very delicate.

She bared her teeth. "And even in the dark, now I'll know that I'm ripping off the right cods."

His eyes narrowed, and the hot interest she saw in his gaze sent shivers skittering down her spine. That wasn't just business now. She tightened her grip.

"Back away from me, Your Grace."

He suddenly grinned. The thick flesh beneath his breeches stirred, hardening against her palm. Mina snatched her hand away.

The duke stepped back—but not, Mina thought, in retreat. He looked too amused and too self-satisfied for that. Wary, she watched him return to the opposite side of the lift and throw the lever forward.

"I'd have offered you a job."

Mina blinked. "What?"

"Make no mistake, inspector: I intend to have you under me, in one way or another. It didn't need to be in my bed, though that was my preference. But if you refused me, I planned to offer you a position on my staff, with a salary only a fool would turn down."

As much as Mina loved her work, she wasn't a fool. And she could tolerate five years of employment by an insufferable knacker—time

enough for her mother to pay off the Blacksmith, for Henry to make
a go of their Northampton estate, for Andrew to buy a lieutenant's
commission. When she and her family had a comfortable cushion
and no longer pinched every penny, the dead would still be waiting
at the end of it, and she could return to the police force.

"What position?"

"My interests span six continents. We'd have found something
that suited your talents." He shrugged. "But it no longer matters,
inspector. Only your bed will do now."

Damn and blast. Jaw set, Mina faced forward, staring blindly
out over the gate. Why did he still intend to pursue her? Somehow,
she'd made a critical error. She wouldn't have thought that threatening a man's privates would encourage him, but—*Oh, blue heavens.*

She'd fired back. Though she'd been outgunned, she'd challenged
the Iron Duke.

So she *was* a fool. And now she would stay out of his way—she'd
run, if necessary—until he forgot about it.

She was already unlocking the gate when Trahaearn stopped the
lift on the third level. His hand clamped over the steel before she
could slide it open.

His voice was low. "I warn you, inspector. The next time I have you
alone, I'll *have* you. Your mouth, at the least—and more, if you offer it."

She wouldn't. "We've both lived many years in London, and our
paths never crossed. After today, I cannot imagine we'll meet again
or have reason to be alone."

"You'll go wherever there are dead bodies." He released the gate.
"I can arrange for several to be found."

Mina choked on a laugh. He would be like her mother, sending
out letters until the recipients gave in. She hoped he did use bodies,
then. With every one, her resolve would harden against him.

Pushing aside the grating, she abandoned the lift and came upon
Newberry standing in the middle of a large room, blushing a fiery
red and unable to meet her eyes. Frowning, Mina looked round and
saw why.

The devices in this room weren't sold in the public shops, but by special arrangement. A low chair supported a rubber phallus attached to a piston, which would pump when the user pushed on a pedal. A similar device sat next to it, designed to function with the woman in a standing position. Various others obviously took two people to operate, with suction cups and pistons driven by complicated gear mechanisms.

Trahaearn stopped beside her, his gaze once again cold and disinterested as it skimmed the equipment. She truly, truly hated that look.

"That one might serve your needs, Your Grace," she said, and Newberry made a noise like a skewered eel when she gestured to a life-sized automaton featuring a rubber vagina and hips that swiveled. Though Mina felt sorry for the poor man, she could not resist pointing to another device. "But I suggest you do not try *that* one. A man hung himself on a similar machine last year. His mother suspected his wife of murder, but he'd simply been too eager, and strapped himself in before she returned from the market. Before the wife returned, that is. Not the mother."

Without expression, Trahaearn turned away from her. "The Blacksmith's laboratories are in this direction."

Could a man who boldly propositioned a woman in a lift so quickly become a prude? She frowned, looking after him, but another wretched sound had her swinging around to check on her assistant.

"*Breathe*, Newberry. If you faint in the Blacksmith's laboratory, only the stars above know what might be grafted to your body when you wake up."

Mina didn't know when the Blacksmith had come to England. Years before the revolution, rumors had begun to circulate that a man in London could manipulate the advanced Horde technology that had created the nanoagents, creating mechanical flesh from it—advanced technology, which was forbidden outside of Xanadu, the Horde capital. But perhaps those rumors had just been wishful thinking, like the tales of a Horde rebellion that would destroy the empire from within.

The rumors of a Horde resistance had proven false—but the Blacksmith might very well have been the source of the other tales. Before the fires of the revolution had cooled, he'd already carved out his territory in the Narrow, and defended it fiercely.

But he rarely had to fight for it. Instead, his weapons included the incredible amounts of money from his shops—much of which he poured into the Crèche and the industrial guilds—and the unwavering loyalty he earned by offering prosthetic repairs and replacement parts for less than most blacksmiths could. For those laborers who couldn't afford even his rates, he traded on favors. There were few people who had passed through the Blacksmith's shop who didn't feel as if they still owed him, even if they'd paid their debt in full or completed the task he'd asked of them.

And for those who didn't feel loyalty, and those who weren't indebted, there were always those who feared him.

From behind her, she heard Newberry's step falter when the Blacksmith emerged from a laboratory into the corridor. Mina had tried to prepare the constable by describing the Blacksmith's appearance, but she supposed preparation was impossible—just as most people who'd been told about her mother's eyes still reacted with shock when they saw her.

The Blacksmith had the same silver eyes, but the modification hadn't stopped there. Every inch of skin not covered by his shirtsleeves and brown trousers was the pale gray of mechanical flesh, shaped to mimic human features. The effect, Mina had to admit, was uncanny. With steel prosthetics, the difference between the human parts and the machine was obvious. Even prosthetics made of mechanical flesh, sculpted to match the person's natural limbs in everything but color, didn't generate a shiver of unease on the first glance. But when it was the face—the *whole* face—something beyond the hairless gray skin seemed wrong, even if Mina couldn't have pointed to a feature that didn't look and move as it should. Perhaps it was simply not knowing whether the face that the Blacksmith owned was his. Had he modeled the broad forehead and high cheekbones on his natural features, or did they serve a different function?

That unsettling effect was compounded by his appearance denying any attempt to place him—and Mina thought that most disturbed anyone first meeting him. He could have been an American native or the Horde, or from the islands in the South Seas. He could have had Liberé blood, descended from the Africans who'd managed to flee the Horde on French ships, mixed with European or the few Russians who'd escaped to the New World, instead of running north to the Scandinavian countries.

But although the Blacksmith's lineage was impossible to guess, his origins weren't. Mina had once met a man from Australia—the Japanese districts in the north, rather than the southern territories that teemed with smugglers—and she thought the Blacksmith's accent resembled his.

To her surprise, he and the duke clasped forearms in greeting, as if no formality existed between them. That impression was strengthened when the Blacksmith simply said, "Trahaearn."

"Blacksmith," the duke replied, dashing Mina's hope that she might learn his real name.

Maybe he didn't have one, however. Many children raised in the Horde's crèches weren't given family names. Most named themselves, as Trahaearn probably had, or made their occupation a surname. Perhaps "blacksmith" *was* his only identity.

"Inspector." The Blacksmith looked to Mina before his mirrored gaze settled on Newberry. "You share the same nanoagents."

"My father's," Mina said. "He infected us both."

"Yes, I recognize them. He assisted me during your mother's operation. He's a skilled physician."

Mina would make a point to repeat that to her father later. "Yes."

The Blacksmith nodded and approached Newberry, taking the

heavy ice box from him. The bugs made everyone strong; even Mina could have carried it braced against her chest. The Blacksmith tucked it under his arm like a pillow.

To Mina's disappointment, he led them into an office, not a laboratory. Still, she had plenty to look at while he set the chest on a desk. A tall armored suit stood in the corner, less clunky than the Royal Marines' steelcoats, too small for the Blacksmith to wear—and probably far too heavy for anyone to walk in without a boiler to operate the limbs. A curious device sat on a shelf: a smooth, foot-long spike atop a solid cube. It didn't seem to have any moveable parts, but it might have been a puzzle bank, which unfolded and reshaped itself when the right combination was dialed in. Next to it lay a half-constructed model of a kraken, its tentacles made of mechanical flesh—and a dull gray, obviously lacking electrical input.

In humans, that input came from the nervous system and was delivered by the bugs. Without electrical impulses to power it, however, the mechanical flesh remained as immovable as a metal slab.

At the desk, the Blacksmith lifted the arm from the ice chest. His frown creased the smooth gray skin around his mouth. "The nanoagents are dead."

"So is he," Trahaearn said.

"Yes. But there should be residual activity." He reached for a battery of Kleistian jars and connected the nodes to the ragged end of the shoulder, where wires blended into flesh. A spark arced between the contact points. The Blacksmith's frown deepened. "How long was he dead?"

"I don't know," Mina told him. "He was frozen."

He scooped the brain out of the ice, holding it cupped in his palms. The intense focus of his silvery eyes reminded Mina of her mother's—looking at the brain on a scale few humans would ever see. So small were the nanoagents that Mina couldn't hope to observe them, even with a microscope.

But the Blacksmith saw more than her mother did. He could

detect and interpret the last electrical signals the nanoagents had received from the visual regions of the brain, seeing the final images that the dead man had seen.

Mina didn't think that he was seeing them now, however. A line had formed between his brows, as if he were baffled.

He glanced at her. "What was the state of the body?"

"Frozen, but mostly uninjured. Some trauma from the fall from the airship. If he'd been injured before his death, the impact destroyed the evidence."

Shaking his head, the Blacksmith slid the brain back into the box. "The nanoagents are dead," he repeated.

Mina didn't understand. "Like a battery will fail?"

"No. Even completely drained, they should have responded to the electrical impulse. They didn't."

"Have they been utterly destroyed?" She didn't even know what the bugs *looked* like; she could hardly imagine them broken. "Did they shatter in the fall?"

"They haven't been physically destroyed. All of their components are in order, but they've stopped functioning. They're inert."

All right. She'd accept that, and move on. "Would that kill a man?"

"Yes. Immediately, if they were all deactivated. If only some were destroyed, he might recover, but the dead nanoagents would act as poison in his system. He'd probably contract bug fever as the remaining nanoagents tried to heal him—and possibly die of the fever." The Blacksmith paused, examining the arm and brain again. "All of this man's are dead."

"What could kill the bugs? A signal that could turn them off—like disconnecting a wire?" Mina gestured to his battery of Kleistian jars.

The Blacksmith looked at her, and she saw her uneasiness mirrored in his eyes. "No. There is no 'off.' Not as long as the host is alive."

Trahaearn stepped closer to the desk. "Do you know what could do this?"

"No."

Then they desperately needed to know where this man had come from. "Do you know who it is?"

"Yes." The Blacksmith looked to Trahaearn, who seemed to still—as if a message had passed between them.

Trahaearn's face hardened. "Who?"

The Blacksmith glanced at Mina.

Interpreting that look as well, Trahaearn said, "You can tell her."

You'll damn well tell me. Mina held her tongue with difficulty.

"It's Baxter's grandson."

Baxter? Mina looked at him blankly. The name meant something. But *what?*

It meant something to the Iron Duke, too. After a moment of absolute stillness, he turned and strode for the door.

Oh, blast. Whoever it was, he was going after them.

Mina hurried into the corridor, calling behind, "Newberry, please collect the parts and find us!"

Trahaearn hadn't slowed. Running, Mina finally caught up at the stairs. "Your Grace? What does the name mean to you?"

Without even looking at her, he started down the stairs. Cursing, Mina followed, jogging to keep up with his long stride as he reached the ground floor and strode into the street, trying desperately to recall why the name seemed so familiar. *Baxter, Baxter . . .*

Oh, blue heavens. The captain who had conscripted the Iron Duke from a slave ship's crew into the navy had been a Baxter. He was an admiral now . . . whose grandson, Roger Haynes, captained the most famous ship in the Royal Navy: *Marco's Terror.*

Mina's heart almost lurched out of her chest. Her head swam, and she slowed, dizzy.

Andrew was on that ship.

And her only hope of knowing what had happened to him was still walking away. She caught up to Trahaearn again as he passed the Hammer & Chain.

"Was that Roger Haynes? Did that man come off of *Marco's Terror?*"

He didn't stop. Damn him. Mina tugged at his coat sleeve, then pulled harder when he didn't acknowledge her.

"Trahaearn! *Was that Haynes?*"

The duke paused, looked down at her. Deliberately, he gripped her shoulders and steered her back against the pub's brick wall, holding her there for a long second. As if satisfied, he let her go and walked away.

Mina shook her head in disbelief. Did he think she would remain here, as if magnetized to the building?

Farther along the Narrow, the steamcoach driver left his bench and opened the carriage door. Newberry's cart would never catch up to that vehicle, but Mina would leap onto the back and hang on through the streets, if necessary. She waited for a drunk leaving the pub to stagger past her, preparing to sprint for the coach.

She ignored the drunk's muttered "jade whore"—but the rough hawking noise warned her. Mina spun to the side just in time. The glob of spit flew past her cheek and splattered against the bricks.

Almost sick with anger, Mina balled her fists, turning to stare at the drunk. Cheeks ruddy, he returned her glare through bleary, hate-filled eyes. A dockworker, his prosthetic arms and shoulders had been reinforced with pneumatic tubes. Strong, but slow—and probably why he hadn't hit her.

And she'd have loved to thrash him, but had no time. Trahaearn's steamcoach engine had started up—

A dark figure suddenly blocked her view, then whipped around. The drunk slammed into the bricks beside her, Trahaearn's hands fisted in his jacket. The man's feet dangled six inches above the ground.

Gone was the maddening detachment. Fury paled the duke's skin and sharpened the angles of his face, as if an icy lathe had passed over his features.

The drunk shouted before abruptly falling silent, recognizing Trahaearn—or just recognizing the danger he was in.

Trahaearn said quietly, "Pay for it."

The command sent unease shivering down her spine. Despite her own anger, Mina couldn't let him do anything to this man. And they had more pressing problems, anyway.

This drunk didn't matter. Andrew did.

"An apology is enough," she said.

The drunk's eyes widened as he looked from her to Trahaearn. "Is she your woman?"

The duke's gaze raked over her, settling on her face. "Yes."

No, Mina thought, her heart sinking. How fast would his answer get around? But it wasn't worth fighting over now. *Only Andrew.*

"I'm sorry, sir. I didn't realize." The man's lips trembled before widening into a grin. He chuckled. "I see. You're still giving it to the Horde, eh—"

The drunken laugh cut off when Trahaearn faced him again, his expression darkening.

"Apologize to *her*."

The humor drained from the man's face. "You'll have to strike me dead, sir."

Smoking hells. Would he? Mina grabbed Trahaearn's arm, her fingers wrapping around biceps of steel. She couldn't pull him away.

And she could see Newberry coming, making his way down the Narrow with the ice chest in his hands, but she couldn't ask the constable to wrestle the duke back. She had to stop this *now*.

"Trahaearn. Please." She felt him tense, and hoped that meant he'd heard her, or was reacting to her holding on to him—not that he was preparing to kill the man. "We've more important matters to attend to."

His jaw clenched. The drunk's prosthetics scraped over brick as he lowered the man to his feet. "Get gone."

He didn't wait to see if the man listened. He turned to Mina. His hand lifted to her face, tilting her chin as if searching for bruises.

"Baxter," she reminded him. "Will he be at the Admiralty in town, or the shipyards at Chatham?"

"Chatham." He let go of her chin and started for the steamcoach.

"You're headed there now?"

"Yes."

All right, then. She glanced over at Newberry as he drew even with her. "Give that chest to the duke's driver, then return to the Blacksmith's. Use his wiregram to let Hale know that we've identified the body as Roger Haynes off *Marco's Terror.* I'm leaving for Chatham to speak with Admiral Baxter."

A flicker of shame and disappointment crossed the constable's face, but his "Yes, sir" was as steady as always.

She turned for the steamcoach. Trahaearn was already seated inside the carriage, but the driver was at the door, holding it open—clearly waiting for her.

Tagging along next to her, Newberry said, "I'm sorry I wasn't at your side, sir, when that cur turned on you—"

"You followed my orders, Newberry. You've nothing to be sorry for." She paused at the steamcoach door and looked back at him. An ill-fed puppy looked less mournful than Newberry did. "Hurry along, constable—and catch up with us at Charing Cross station. Chances are, the train will depart late, and you'll be able to accompany us."

He brightened. "Yes, sir." Looking into the carriage, he added, "Thank you, sir."

The duke gave a short nod. Mina clambered into the coach and took the bench across from him—then immediately wished she hadn't when his gaze settled on her, and didn't move away.

He smiled slightly. His focus shifted to her lips.

"We're alone, inspector," he said softly.

The bench seemed to fall out from under her bottom. Somehow, she'd walked right into this—but she wouldn't let him make good on his threat to kiss her. "Your driver is just outside, sir."

"Outside, yes. So we're alone."

Damn him. "If you make a move toward me, I'll shoot you with enough opium to lay out an ox."

"Would you wake me up when we reached Chatham?"

THE IRON DUKE   79

"I'd leave you in the gutter by the station."

"Then I'll wait until we've boarded the locomotive." He grinned. "I always hire a private car."

"And I always wear my weapons."

His laugh was low and deep. As if making himself comfortable, he stretched his legs out and crossed his booted feet at the ankles. His breeches pulled tight over his thighs. His gaze still didn't leave her face.

She forced herself not to avert her eyes, and not to fidget under that piercing stare.

They only had a drive across town to Charing Cross, then a journey east to Chatham. Not far, measured in miles . . . but Mina suspected that this was going to be a very long trip.

Chapter Five

Rhys wasn't sorry that Newberry caught up to them, though it meant he wouldn't be alone with the inspector—and might not be again for a good length of time. Someone had taken *Marco's Terror*. Where Rhys went next depended on what Baxter had to tell them. If that destination wasn't London and Rhys didn't return with her, Newberry could watch over the inspector until she reached home.

And he wished to hell that he'd realized earlier why the red giant always followed her. Never again would Rhys leave her without protection—and very soon, she'd have more than a constable looking out for her. When he made it common knowledge that Wilhelmina Wentworth was *his* woman, that connection would protect her better than fifteen constables could. No one would dare touch her.

No one but him.

He sat in the chair across from her as the locomotive gave a loud hollow whistle. The car rattled around them before slowly pulling out of the station. He hated traveling this way. There was no escaping the clacking, the great puffing engine, the vibration of the floors, the sickening rush as the landscape raced past the windows.

He focused on the inspector, instead, though she didn't want him watching her. But Rhys liked the way she looked, particularly when her expression suggested that she'd prefer to have a gun aimed at his head rather than sit across from him in a private railcar. He liked the severe roll of black hair at her nape, and how the style didn't conceal any of her face. He liked the line that formed between her black brows when she frowned at him. He liked the angry pinch of her lips, and the anticipation of watching them soften. He liked her small hands, and that she hadn't hesitated to use them to defend herself in the lift—and he'd liked the feel of her fingers squeezing his cock even more. He liked the snug fit of her trousers when she sat, the way they clung to slender legs that could wrap around his back, holding him tight inside her.

So Rhys watched her, and imagined her riding him all the way to Chatham.

Or he would have, if she hadn't interrupted his imaginings with her questions, as if she still had a role in this, as if her investigation still mattered.

It didn't. Someone had taken the *Terror*. Whoever had killed Haynes belonged to Rhys now. But he answered her questions anyway, because he liked her voice, the full strength of it.

Had he met Haynes? *Yes.* Why hadn't Rhys recognized him? *The man's face had been smashed.* Where was his ship? *It was supposed to be in the Caribbean.* What will happen to the crew? *That depended on who took the ship.*

At that point, Rhys had to force his thoughts back to shagging her—hard and rough. If he dwelt on the *Terror* being taken and a good captain tossed like rubbish onto his house, he wouldn't be able to stop his fury from boiling over; it was too hot and too new. But his need to possess the inspector was hot and new, too, so he used it ruthlessly to combat his rage.

They were almost to Chatham when he recalled that her brother was aboard.

Thoughts of the *Terror* and of shagging receded. For the first time since the Blacksmith had told him who'd landed on his front steps, Rhys *looked* at her—and he didn't see anything. No anxiety, no panic. But he remembered her voice when she'd spoken of the boy . . . Andrew. He remembered the softness, the worry, and how he'd been certain that she missed her brother.

She must be terrified. Desperate. But she concealed every bit of it, just as he held back his rage.

Except it didn't burn so hotly now, and suddenly his anger wasn't all that drove him. A part of him began to focus on easing her fear. Not just taking the *Terror* back, not just making someone pay. The inspector needed something, too—to find out what had happened to her brother. Rhys could give her that.

So she still did have a role in this—and he had reason to keep her close.

With a shriek of brakes and another bone-shaking rattle, they drew into the Chatham station. Rhys watched her face as she stepped down from the car, and saw that her first glance was in the same direction as everyone else who journeyed from London—up, where the sun hung high in the brilliant blue sky, rather than shining like a dull coin embedded in a shark's belly. Her lips parted and her face softened, and Rhys vowed that he would see that expression again.

Preferably when she looked at him, and preferably when she was under him.

Then her focus shifted, and he followed her gaze to the airships tethered over the river. Nearly fifty, and most of them the navy's rigid dreadnoughts—too slow and too heavily armed to be maneuverable, and with their engines, too loud to have sailed over London unnoticed. But there were others who might have, skyrunners that carried a few passengers or light cargo over short distances.

Rhys knew all of the skyrunners' captains, however, and all of them would have refused to take on a job that might bring the Iron Duke to their ships. All but one.

Lady Corsair hovered across the Medway. Yasmeen had some balls, tethering her airship at a naval dock. And if the price was right and the gold paid in advance, she'd have dropped a dead man onto Rhys's house.

But then she'd have climbed down a ladder, shared a drink with Scarsdale, and told them both who'd been fool enough to pay her upfront.

Not Yasmeen, then. But she might have heard something useful. "Do you recognize any of them?"

He glanced at the inspector, who was still looking over the array of airships. "All of them. But there's only one that interests me. We'll talk with her captain after we see Baxter."

The inspector's mouth twisted, as if she didn't want to smile, but couldn't completely stop herself. "I suspect that you're a useful man to have around a port, Your Grace."

He was. "Have you visited Chatham before?"

"I've never been farther from London than Dartford before, and that only the once." A faint blush stole under her skin when Rhys narrowed his eyes at her, when Newberry's mouth dropped open. She turned toward the platform exit. "And so I'll let you lead the way."

Christ. No farther than Dartford. Not that unusual for buggers living in London, Rhys knew. Most never left town, not even the once. But the knowledge put heavier weight on her conversation with the tinker girl. A blacksmith could go anywhere . . . and the inspector never had.

So he'd renew his offer. When she accepted it, he'd take her a hell of a lot farther than a shipyard town in Kent.

Chatham wasn't a bad start, however. The town had grown in the past five years, since the Royal Navy had begun rebuilding its shipyards in England, and the boom had spilled over almost at their feet. Between the busy railway station and the cabstands, a tent city had sprung up—part market, part carnival. Started by locals taking advantage of sailors passing through, and their numbers increased by Londoners who'd run as far from town as their money would take them, they sold music and sexual favors, clockworks and grilled meats. The inspector would have seen better—and worse—in London, but she hadn't seen it under blue skies, hadn't heard it without the noise of engines and traffic. Every color appeared deeper, brighter. Every sound clear and true. Hell, Rhys enjoyed it, too, and so he took the long way around.

Blacksmiths repaired singing birds and steamcarts next to a stall selling live chickens. An old woman in a ragged shawl balanced on a tree stump, proclaiming that the end of the world neared, and their doom rode on the backs of steam-powered horses. Behind her, a miner danced on the pulverizing hammers grafted to his legs. His audience laughed and threw pennies when he activated the pneumatics, juddering and singing through the steps.

The tent barkers pitched their attractions, yelling invitations to look inside tents to see the Human Ape, a result of the Horde's breeding experiments, to see an old man open up his chest and reveal his clockwork heart, to see the lost sketches from the great Leonardo da Vinci's pen. Even the stoic Newberry laughed at the last—anyone in possession of a genuine da Vinci sketch wouldn't be displaying that treasure beneath a tent in Chatham and charging pennies.

He turned to catch the inspector's reaction, and saw that she'd paused along the path beside the next tent, her head cocked to listen. A crude drawing of a human with misshapen teeth and taloned hands illustrated the sign out front. Rhys drew closer. A garbled hiss from behind the striped walls lifted the hairs at the back of his neck.

He knew that sound too well.

She rubbed her hands against her sleeves, as if she'd suddenly been struck with gooseflesh. "It's an eerie noise."

And damned close to the real thing. "Let's look inside."

Tired-looking and thin, the blond barker at the tent entrance brightened as he turned her way. When the inspector and the constable came with him, nervousness ticked over the barker's features before she firmed them with bravado. She widened her eyes and dipped into the exaggerated pose of someone frozen in fear.

"They hunger," she whispered hoarsely. "They eat the flesh from your bones and drink your marrow. The soulless zombies hunt even the Horde, and you won't see another anywhere in England or the New World . . . *if* you're lucky."

Rhys hadn't been. "How much?"

The blond straightened. "A denier each."

Not English money, but the French currency that ruled the trade routes in the Old and New Worlds. The inspector hesitated and looked to the constable, who shook his head. Probably neither carried anything but pennies. Anything more in London would be an invitation for a pickpocket.

Fortunately, Rhys hadn't had a purse lifted in years. He paid the barker, who waved the curtain aside with a flourish.

Her dramatic whisper followed him inside. "If you value your life, stay behind the lamps."

He had to duck beneath the low canvas roof. Two gas lamps sat on the dirt floor, more than an arm's length from the small cage at the back of the tent, throwing bright light through the iron bars and onto the thing crouched on filthy straw. Nude, its tangled and matted hair ripped out in chunks, it wasn't as dirty as most zombies he'd seen. Perhaps the barker threw a bucket of water at it every week.

The zombie's hissing gurgle became a low growl. Ruined lips drew back from sharp teeth. Spit and gore crusted its mouth.

He heard Newberry choke back an oath. The inspector said, "Avert your eyes, constable," before stopping beside Rhys.

"It was a woman," she murmured.

Rhys couldn't read her reaction to it. *Fascination? Disgust?* His own response was familiar, though: *Kill it.*

He'd have to use her weapons. While in England, Rhys only carried a dagger in his boot—which was useless against a zombie unless he sawed off its head with the blade. But he wouldn't risk stepping that near to the thing, anyway.

The zombie threw its shoulder against the bars. The cage rattled. Growling, it clawed the air between them, black eyes fixed hungrily across the short distance.

The inspector turned, looking to the tent barker waiting at the entrance. "It's illegal to bring them into England."

"I didn't bring it in, did I? It was a fat salvage trader who brought that thing in from Europe on his boat."

The inspector appeared unmoved by that argument. The barker's defiance vanished. She lifted her hands. "Me and my sisters, we've got seven little ones between us. The deniers we earn here barely keep us off the streets . . . and out of them other workhouses."

With a sigh, the inspector faced the cage again. She tilted her head, as if trying to see better through the bars. "I've often wondered if the person is still in there."

A living hell, if it was. Most of the zombies in Europe were originally the humans who'd been left behind after each nation fled to the Americas, escaping the Horde's advancing war machines. But the Horde didn't want to occupy the land; they wanted the resources. Their harvesting machines gathered those, and the Horde infected the remaining humans with nanoagents to prevent the nations who'd fled from returning and fighting for their territory.

But the zombie's nanoagents weren't like those infecting the buggers, and weren't controlled by a tower. They acted like a disease, spread through a bite. The bodies they inhabited only hungered and hunted, never dying unless their brain was destroyed. This zombie could be two hundred and fifty years old, a woman's mind trapped by the diseased bugs.

"Even during the Frenzies, or when the Horde locked us down and paralyzed our bodies . . . we were aware. We *knew* we were being controlled." She paused. "But I suppose you remember how it was."

Scarsdale had suggested that her mother hadn't remembered. But Rhys wouldn't mention that now. He simply said, "No."

She glanced up at him. "Weren't you from a crèche?"

"Yes. Caerwys." When she looked at him blankly, he said, "County Clwyd. There until I was smuggled out of Wales at eight years of age."

Smuggled out and sold to the Ivory Market, where he'd seen his first zombie in a cage, selling for a few gold sous. But there wasn't much that couldn't be bought and sold along that stretch of West African coast. Both a zombie and a boy were on the lowest end of the scale.

"Oh." The inspector blinked. Her gaze searched his face, as if trying to find pieces of him to put together. *Good*. He wanted her curious. "Then I suppose you would have been too young to be affected by a Frenzy."

He wouldn't have been affected, anyway. He'd never been controlled by his bugs. But he knew what it was to be controlled, and he'd never liked it.

She stepped closer to the cage, standing between the two lamps. Rhys stopped himself from yanking her back. The zombie battered itself against the cage, hissing, growling, biting the bars in fury.

Bending slightly, as if she wanted to look into its eyes, she said, "Some believe that the nanoagents kill the person and use the body. That a zombie is like a steamcoach driven by the diseased bugs. Not thinking, not feeling."

"If she's lucky."

"Yes. And I've heard that New World scientists are trying to concoct a cure."

"Some of them. Some scientists are hoping to concoct immortality—and to sell it."

She threw him a glance over her shoulder. "Are you familiar with them?"

"I've funded research and expeditions."

"Have they discovered anything? A cure?"

"Not yet."

"Then I'm sorry for this one."

Stepping back, she drew her gun and aimed it into the cage. Surprise rammed through him. Only a moment ago, Rhys had been certain she'd soon begin weeping over the zombie's plight, and wondering if he should return later to kill it and save her the distress of witnessing the thing's death. *Confounding woman*. He wanted to drag her close and kiss her senseless. He moved aside to give her room, instead.

"No!" The barker shoved past him, rushing in front of the gun. She spread her hands wide, as if to prevent the inspector from shooting around her. "No!"

"Stand aside," the inspector said. "With one mistake—if some-one comes too close, or the cage fails—then your sisters and your children will be dead. *All of England* will be."

Panic widened the woman's eyes. "We're careful."

"Stand aside."

"She's not real! It's a feeble-minded woman we found on the street. She pisses on herself. We earn our money."

"Then step closer to the cage."

The woman hesitated.

"Step back to the cage, close enough that she can bite you. Or step aside."

Tears welled up, spilled over. "We've got nothing else. If I don't earn our money here, I don't bring anything home."

"I'll count to three."

"Please, don't—"

"One."

"You can't—"

"Back to the cage," the inspector repeated, "or step to the side. Two."

"—please we need—"

"Three."

With a shriek, the barker flung herself to the side, falling to her knees beside the gas lamp. The inspector fired. A dark hole exploded open between sunken breasts.

Convulsing against the bars, the zombie raged, spitting blood. Rhys stepped forward. Folding his hand over the inspector's, he adjusted her aim.

"The head," he said. "Always the head."

With a nod, she finished it off.

"And what now, you Horde cunt?" The woman screamed from the floor, pulling at her hair. "We earned the right to that thing, you bloody fucking jade whore! That fat old trader had me and my sisters on our backs. And we *earned* it."

The inspector holstered her gun. "Then find that trader and put him in the cage. You'll make money enough—fat old men in England are almost as rare as zombies." She looked to Newberry. "See that the body is burned. Then find us at Baxter's."

Newberry glanced with some anxiety to Rhys, who reassured the constable with a look before following the inspector outside. Oh, yes, he'd watch over her.

And he wouldn't let her away from him.

By the starry skies, that *thing* could not have been a human.

Mina emerged from the tent, lifting her hand against the blinding sun. The air seemed thin and tasteless. A deep breath left her light-headed, sick.

The barker's screams from inside the tent rose to a higher pitch, driving like a nail into Mina's head. She started down the path, leaving them behind. Trahaearn would catch up any moment, probably with just two of his absurdly long strides, and she damned well wouldn't let him see how that thing and that woman's pleas had shaken her to the core.

And no more of this tarrying about. A cabstand lay beyond all of these tents and stalls, and any driver worth a penny would know how to find the admiral.

Not relishing the thought of being crowded into a tiny seat with the duke, she passed a cheap spider-rickshaw and stopped at a steamcoach with the top folded back. A youngish man with a flop of ginger hair perched on the driver's bench.

Mina withdrew her purse. "Will you take me to Admiral Baxter's residence, sir?"

The driver's eyes narrowed on her, lips curling back in a sneer. For a moment, she thought he'd refuse to let her hire him. Then his gaze shifted beyond her, something like awe passed over his face, and he nodded.

There were days when she found it difficult not to hate everyone in bloody England. Mina choked out her thank-you and clambered into the coach, wishing she could cosh the driver upside the head with her billy club.

And she wished Andrew were here. He'd always had a knack for making her laugh herself out of these moods. But only the stars above knew where Andrew was, and instead she had the damned Iron Duke, and a ramshackle coach that dipped and creaked alarmingly as he stepped inside, as if four men had boarded rather than just one. He seated himself beside her and began watching her again, lord of all he bleeding surveyed—and taking up more room than any man had a right to. Even Newberry didn't push into her space, and he outweighed the duke by two stone.

Well, he could peer at her all he wanted. She'd stare ahead at the ginger skull she'd like to bash in.

His voice sounded low and alarmingly near her ear. "Thank you, inspector, for saving me the trouble of killing the zombie with my knife."

She glanced at him sharply. With the sun behind him, his face was all in shadow, but he was smiling. Maybe laughing. Who could tell over the engine's racket? She lifted her voice. "What would you have used?"

"Your guns. A machete, if I'd thought to carry one to the Blacksmith's this morning." His smile faded. "I need something to call you other than 'inspector.'"

"No, sir. You don't."

When he shook his head, the tiny gold hoops through the upper curves of his ears glinted through his dark hair. Such a peculiar place for jewelry. But she supposed there were many odd places that a person could pierce their body, if they wished to.

The Iron Duke probably had. *Primitive scoundrel.*

"I do," he countered. "And I know your names: Wilhelmina Elizabeth Wentworth. They don't fit. What do your friends call you?"

"Stubborn." She glanced away from him when his laughing smile returned. "You may continue to call me inspector."

"And you may call me Rhys."

"I won't."

"Even when I'm in your bed?"

Mina dropped her hand to her gun.

"I agree. That was too brazen." He leaned in toward her, taking up so much space she could hardly draw a breath. "I should have said *my* bed, yes?"

Shaking her head, she looked forward again. Not quite so blood-thirsty, this time. She'd still have liked to give the driver a good whack, but bludgeoning him didn't seem as necessary now.

On to other things, then—such as whether there would be bludgeoning when they reached the admiral's house. "How well do you get on with Baxter?"

"He's been a friend to me for years."

"No." Disbelieving, she searched his expression for a lie, and didn't find one. "But he forcibly conscripted you."

"Not forcibly. I was on a slave ship bound for the Lusitanian coal mines. Even the Royal Navy is better than a mine shaft."

"As a slave? No. The newssheets have said you were on that slave ship's *crew*. Words quoted from your mouth."

"Those rags took my words as they saw fit. And they didn't want a story of a boy enslaved. So they suggest that I was a slaver."

Mina gaped at him. "And you don't care?"

He shrugged. "It's a useful lie. The alternative is giving those who want to destroy me a picture of a weak young boy, chained in a hold."

"A lie for your enemies." She shook her head. "I can think of many people who aren't your enemies, and who would be inspired, picturing you as a weak young boy who rose out of his chains to save us."

"To save you?" His face hardened. "*That* is a lie that will never come from me, inspector."

She looked blindly away from him. Something had grabbed hold of her innards and twisted, hurting from her stomach to her throat. And she'd forgotten why they'd begun speaking of these . . . lies.

"Why do you tell me the truth now?"

"Because you asked me."

Mina wasn't certain if she wanted to again. "All right. And so Baxter is your friend. What kind of man is he?"

"A good one, inspector."

And so she'd be telling a good man that his grandson was dead. "There are many types of good men. Is he soft and kind, a man who easily gives into his emotions? Generous? Strongly principled? I need to know what I can expect."

The duke nodded and seemed to think it over, as if he didn't make a habit of nailing his friends down with words. "He doesn't make rash decisions. Quick, but not rash. And he won't hold his men to a higher standard than himself, won't expect more effort from them than he puts in. And he'll give a man a second chance. But not a third."

Was this Trahaearn's idea of a good man, or a good *captain*?

Perhaps to him, they were the same thing. "So he's different from the captain you mutinied against when you first took the *Terror*?"

"Adams wasn't worth the shit I left him bleeding in. But I wouldn't have known that if I hadn't served under Baxter first."

Mina doubted that. According to every account of the mutiny she'd read, Adams had been a brutal, murderous despot. Mutiny had been inevitable. If not Trahaearn, then it would have been someone else who'd led the crew against him.

She smiled slightly. "And so that is my answer. Baxter is the type of man who can inspire a young sailor to mutiny on another man's ship."

Trahaearn grinned. "Yes, hold Baxter responsible for it. I still do."

No, he wouldn't. Not truly. Mina couldn't admire what the duke had done, but she'd never seen him shift blame to someone else. He owned up to the decisions he'd made, and their consequences.

And why not? He'd got a dukedom out of them.

"Have you been in contact with the admiral recently?"

"Not recently, no."

"So Haynes's death probably wasn't about your connection to Baxter, but the connection to your ship."

"Most likely."

"Why not strike at you personally, then? Why use *Marco's Terror*? You've given her over to the navy. She's not yours anymore."

He tensed beside her. "Make no mistake, inspector. She's *mine*."

Fierce possession loaded his voice. Mina hadn't expected that. "Why give her over to the navy, then?"

He didn't answer.

All right. Perhaps that was the wrong question, anyway. Anyone who didn't know him well would have probably thought the same as she did: Giving the *Terror* up suggested that he didn't have a strong attachment to it. "Who else would know that you still think of *Marco's Terror* as your ship?"

He stared at her before slowly nodding. "Not many. That will narrow it."

Good. She took a long breath, feeling the need to steady herself, and wound up light-headed instead. The steamcoach jolted through a rut, jarring her into warm muscles as hard as steel. Quickly, she scooted over again, and though she didn't see him follow, Mina was certain the duke took up more space than he had before.

She confirmed that an inch of empty seat still lay between them. Unfortunately, she didn't know how much farther they had to go before they reached Baxter's. It felt as if they'd driven through these streets for miles.

But if she had a few more minutes, then she had a few more questions.

"Of those who it can be narrowed to, how would they treat the crew? They've killed the captain. But what of the rest?"

"Inspector." Though his response was soft, she heard him over the engine. When she lifted her gaze to his, he said, "Do you want to hear all of the possibilities, or only those that leave your brother alive?"

She hadn't thought he'd remember. "Dead is dead. So tell me what might bring him home."

"Most would keep the ship rather than sink her—and if they don't have a crew, then they don't have the *Terror*. They'll kill the lieutenants and the marines, but not the others, so long as they fall in line. So he would just have to remain aboard until I find him."

A terrible constriction around her chest eased. Andrew was an intelligent boy. He'd stay alive, keep his head down and follow orders.

"And the *Terror* is carrying eight men—not much older than boys—all training in the diplomatic corps. Every one of them comes from a merchant family in Manhattan City or London."

Her heart leapt. "Do you believe the boys will be ransomed?"

"Whoever took the ship would be fools to pass up the money. They'll ransom anyone with connections—including the younger son of an earl."

Slowly, her heart fell back into place. Even if her family sold everything they had, would it be enough? "How much would they ask?"

"It doesn't matter. I'd pay it for you."

Her laugh was short and hollow. Of course he would. "At what price?"

His eyes narrowed. "Wouldn't your brother be worth it?"

A man raised in a crèche might not understand how much Mina valued her family. And so she'd forgive him that question, just this once.

But she couldn't prevent the bitterness from claiming her voice. "Yes, Your Grace, he is. Which means that I would be in your service for a very long time, because Andrew's worth is a hundred thousand times greater than any man who uses a threat on his life to strong-arm me into bed."

Amusement touched his hard mouth. "I take my opportunities where I find them, inspector."

A bitter knot was still lodged in Mina's chest when they arrived at the admiral's residence. Newly built in a less ostentatious version of the Gothic-style that the bounders favored in both their homes and their churches, the admiral's house featured steeply pitched gables and narrow windows that rose into pointed arches. Mina expected a dark and forbidding interior, but a butler led them past light, airy rooms to a study that looked out over a small garden and the river.

At first glance, the man who'd made such an impact on the Iron Duke didn't appear even half as formidable. He waited at the window with hands clasped behind his back, a thin gray-haired figure in a somber jacket who stood not much taller than Mina. He turned as they entered. A short beard softened his austere features, but couldn't soften the impression of steel and solid good sense when Mina met his eyes, or the quiet regret that lay behind them.

"Anglesey." The admiral's troubled gaze sought the duke. "I've just received the gram, yet you are already here. So you must have heard that she is lost—and that I have failed to keep her safe, as I promised you."

Received the gram? Mina bit back her dismay. Apparently, Hale's updates had beaten them to Chatham—forwarded to the admiral by some unthinking fool. A wiregram was the poorest way to deliver this sort of news.

Trahaearn frowned. "And you must know that I wouldn't come to blame you."

"Only because you have not yet heard the worst." With a grim smile, the admiral strode to his desk and poured a finger of amber liquid into a snifter. "I not only failed to keep her safe, I *sent* her into danger. And my grandson with her. God help him, wherever he might be."

The duke's brows drew together. He glanced at Mina, and his puzzlement mirrored hers. *Wherever he might be?* Had the wiregram not told Baxter how they'd known the *Terror* was lost?

Realization crossed the duke's expression, and he looked to the admiral again. But he didn't speak. Perhaps having trouble finding the words to tell him.

Mina could make that easier for him—and more importantly, for the admiral.

"Sir." Mina stepped forward. "It is my sad duty to inform you that your grandson, Roger Haynes, was found dead in London this past evening."

"In *London*?" Mouth open, he glanced to Trahaearn, as if for confirmation. When the duke nodded, he dropped heavily into the chair behind his desk.

Mina sensed that not much shocked the man—and that being informed of Haynes's death hadn't surprised him. But the *location* had. She took a seat facing him.

"Sir, your grandson was supposed to be en route to the Caribbean. Last night, however, his body was delivered to His Grace's estate. Do you have any idea why?"

He looked to Trahaearn as the duke sat next to Mina. "Delivered?"

"Dropped."

Trahaearn didn't soften it—and perhaps he didn't need to. The admiral appeared to be recovering from his shock.

Baxter's eyes narrowed. "From *Bontemps*?"

Bontemps. That infamous airship had been captained by Dame Sawtooth, a pirate with a reputation almost as notorious as the duke's. The newssheets speculated that she was either dead or in hiding—she hadn't preyed on any merchant or passenger ships in almost a decade. Not since the Iron Duke had destroyed the tower.

Trahaearn frowned. "The Dame hates me well enough, but she hasn't flown in years. Why would you think that she took the *Terror*?"

"This arrived from the Admiralty." He pushed a half-sheet wiregram message across the desk. Trahaearn leaned forward to retrieve it. "Roger's name wasn't listed among the others', and so I knew."

A list of ransomed hostages. Her breath locking in her throat, Mina came out of her chair and looked over Trahaearn's shoulder. She didn't read the opening message, but scanned the wiregram machine's heavy type, searching for a name. Then scanned the message again, hoping that she'd simply missed it, but she couldn't force the words to appear.

No Rockingham. No Wentworth. No Andrew.

Chest aching, she returned to the head of the message and read slowly. By the end of it, her panic had become a dull pain that she shoved to the rear of her mind. She *would* learn what had become of Andrew and make certain that he was safe. But she couldn't know now, however much she wished it. Haynes's murder, however, still lay in front of her, and she *could* pursue that.

She returned to her seat. According to the message Baxter had received, the ransom demands had been sent from a wiregram station in Dover to the Admiralty building in London at almost the same time that Mina had been boarding the train for Chatham. The ransom payments were to be collected and sailed across the Channel to Calais in two days' time, and the money left on the beach. When payment had been verified, the boys would be returned to England.

Trahaearn returned the half sheet to Baxter. "An idiot wrote those demands."

"Why an idiot?" Mina looked from the duke to the admiral. "They seem rather straightforward."

"They would be, if not for the Dame having lived in Calais for the past eight years. She'd never bring the navy to her doorstep." Trahaearn shook his head. "She isn't this foolish."

"The gram confirmed that *Bontemps* had been seen near Dover," Mina pointed out.

"With someone else at the helm, most likely. And if someone botched that ransom demand, she won't be staying in Calais much longer." He caught Mina's gaze and smiled slightly. "So we'll go and ask her where the *Terror* is now."

To Calais? Zombies roamed all of Europe—and what had once been the French coast was no exception.

Mina's heart thudded and fear worked along her spine, but she nodded. From across the desk, Baxter regarded her with a quiet curiosity, as if he'd just realized that she was in the room, and didn't know what to make of her presence in the midst of all this. Even as he watched her, however, his gaze seemed to lose focus and the few lines on his face deepened with grief or worry—or guilt.

She recalled his earlier confession about sending the ship into danger. But an admiral did not answer to a detective inspector, and wouldn't justify or explain to her any commands that he'd given to his ships.

And so she directed her question to the duke, instead. "I'd also like to know where the *Terror* was supposed to have been."

With a nod, Trahaearn looked to Baxter. "Tell me."

The admiral poured another drink first, and offered the same to Trahaearn and Mina. When they refused, he sighed and sank deeper into his chair. "I sent her to join the Gold Coast fleet."

Though his expression didn't change, Trahaearn's fingers clenched. "To the Ivory Market? Why?"

Baxter regarded him for a long moment before turning to Mina. "Inspector—Rockingham's girl, are you?"

Mina's heart sank. Whatever the admiral's reasons, she wouldn't be hearing them in person. He wasn't looking at her as an officer of the law now, but a lady. "Yes, sir. Are you acquainted with my father?"

"Only by reputation. He writes a formidable letter."

Baxter stood. Left with little other choice, Mina rose to her feet with him. Trahaearn's chair creaked, and a moment later, the duke towered beside her.

"She hasn't eaten since this morning," he said.

"We'll remedy that." The admiral smiled as he escorted her to the door. "And I promise we will not leave you alone for long."

Not long after the revolution, when Mina had been still struggling with the emotions that forever seemed to be rising up and exploding out, Mina's mother had advised her not to waste her anger on things that she couldn't change. Mina *tried*, certainly. The problem, however, lay in knowing exactly which things couldn't be changed. Two hundred years ago, an Englishwoman couldn't have hoped to become a detective inspector—if such a thing had existed then. Mina had once read that no one escaped the Black Death, and yet when plague had swept through the Horde territories fifty years ago, decimating the Horde military forces occupying England, not a single bugger had succumbed to it. Even death wasn't certain, though there had to be a better alternative than becoming a zombie.

And so Mina thought that railing against immutable situations could prove more productive than her mother believed. But since she couldn't imagine a way to change an admiral's reluctance to speak of naval matters in front of a mere inspector, she took her mother's advice and let her dismay and frustration go.

The abundant tray of food that the admiral's staff provided further improved her mood.

Baxter kept his promise not to leave her alone for long. Only a short time passed before Trahaearn appeared at the parlor entrance, wearing his cold detachment like a mask.

Lovely. That was exactly what she'd wanted to see. She would remember to thank the admiral later.

With a sigh, Mina pushed the orange she had saved for Newberry into her overcoat pocket—an *orange* served as part of an everyday meal; she could hardly comprehend it—and joined the duke in the hallway.

He didn't appear quite so cold by the time she reached him, and less so the longer his gaze remained on her face. She wished he'd look away from her, but she sensed that if there was one thing on Earth that wouldn't change, no matter how she railed against him, it was the Iron Duke.

"All set, then?" he said, and she forced herself not to interrogate him there. What had the admiral told him? But she resisted and started for the front door.

A maid was leading another man back to the admiral's study, a gentle-looking fellow with sandy hair and soft blue eyes. He carried a physician's bag, which made Mina immediately like him a little better—until they passed each other, and he offered her a smile that said, *I accept you*, the kind that often accompanied a short bow and a greeting in the Horde language.

She despised that smile even more than she despised the blatant hatred. Condescending yellow-toothed lackwit *bounder*. She'd lived in this blasted country longer than *he* had.

Patience suddenly gone, she only waited until the door closed behind them. Spinning to face Trahaearn, she demanded, "What did he—"

Her tongue froze into place. Panic and terror ripped though her mind, spiked through her heart. Blood pounded in her ears, but she couldn't move, couldn't scream. Her muscles locked up, and she almost toppled down the stairs and would have if the duke had not leapt forward and caught her rigid body, calling *Inspector!* and shouting at her to tell him what was wrong but all that Mina could think was *The tower has come back, by the starry skies please no no no, not the Horde not the tower again.*

From inside the house, a gunshot cracked.

Trahaearn's head whipped around. For an instant, he stared at the admiral's door, before gently laying Mina at the top of the stairs. Then he was up, charging through the entrance. She heard his boots pounding down the length of the hallway, a shout—not the duke's—followed by a crash.

The hold on Mina's body vanished.

Gasping, she surged to her feet. Beyond the open door, the butler was slowly climbing to his knees. The maid lay sobbing in the hall. Mina sprinted past them, drawing her weapon and bursting into the study.

Baxter lay on the floor, eyes open and unseeing. Blood pooled over the wooden boards beneath his head. Next to him lay the physician's bag, and a metal box topped by a foot-long spike. Recognition spit through her, cold and sick, but she couldn't stop to examine it. The window overlooking the garden had been shattered, as if someone had crashed through. Mina rushed to look, and caught a glimpse of

Trahaearn's long overcoat as he disappeared over the garden wall—chasing after the shooter.

Oh, blue heavens. Chasing after a man armed with a gun . . . and the stupid pirate only had a *dagger.*

She turned and ran, almost barreling into the white-faced butler in the hall. Mina stumbled, recovered, and shouted, "Don't let anyone into that room!" before racing outside.

Another shot gave her a direction and almost made her heart explode through her ribs. *Don't be dead, Trahaearn, don't be dead.* Leaping over a low stone wall, she skidded on wet grass, then sped around the side of the house. A second gunshot rent the air.

Twenty feet away, the bounder collapsed to the ground, the hand holding his gun falling away from his head. In front of him, still in a dead run, Trahaearn shouted, a roar of frustration and fury. He hauled the dead man up by his jacket, slammed him back to the ground. His fist drew back.

"Trahaearn!" Mina caught his wrist in both hands. He turned on her, eyes blazing with rage. Chest heaving, she managed—"Not the face. Not until he's identified."

She let him go and stepped back to catch her breath. Insanity. The man had killed himself rather than be caught.

Trahaearn's fist fell to his side. Though he still knelt beside the body, battering the dead murderer had apparently lost its appeal.

His breath was as labored as hers, his voice rough as he asked, "Baxter?"

"No," Mina said quietly. "I'm sorry."

He nodded and faced her. Mina's stomach dropped through to her knees. He *had* been shot. Blood poured down the left side of his head. The bullet had dug a furrow beside his temple, deep enough that a flap of skin and dark hair hung loose over his ear.

Oh, smoking hells. Mina steadied herself. "Your head, sir. Are you all right?"

"Yes." He touched the wound, looked at the blood on his fingers. "I have a hard skull."

She didn't doubt it, but he didn't seem in a hurry to stand up, either. A noise from behind her brought Mina around. A maid stood near the corner of the house, eyes wide.

"You there!" Mina called. "Bring bandages for the Duke of Anglesey. Be quick about it!"

The maid darted back to the house. Mina yanked a handkerchief from her pocket, bent closer to him. His eyes were closed, hands fisted at his thighs.

"Keep still for a minute, now." She wiped at a little blood, and when he didn't draw away, asked quietly, "Do you recognize him?"

"No."

Damn. "Did he say anything before he killed himself?"

"No." He slammed his fist against his thigh. "He walked past me. Right past me."

"Right by me, too."

His head lifted slightly, as if he'd tried to look up at her. She continued cleaning, wincing as slight pressure parted the wound, exposing his gray skull—

Mina stilled. *Gray.* Not white bone, but dark gray.

Iron gray.

Swallowing, she pressed the cloth against his scalp, holding the flap of skin in place over the furrow. The bleeding had already begun to slow, thanks to his bugs. He'd be completely healed by the time they returned to London.

She heard running steps behind her, heavy enough that she guessed they were Newberry's. A moment later, the constable appeared beside her, huffing like an engine.

His face paled when he saw Trahaearn. Not the blood, she knew. The Iron Duke had been shot on Mina's watch. She'd be lucky to walk away with just a reprimand.

"Go into the house, Newberry. Secure the study. If the staff hasn't notified the locals already, send one of them to locate a constable."

"Yes, sir." Newberry immediately turned to go, but halted when

Trahaearn said, "Collect the freezing device. We're not leaving it for the locals."

So he'd recognized the device, too. Mina stared at him for a moment before nodding. She said to Newberry, "There's a physician's bag and a metal block with a spike." *A small tower.* Shriveling fear scurried up her spine. She forced it away. "Take care in how you handle it, constable. As soon as you've secured the room, bring them here."

"Yes, sir."

He trotted off. The admiral's staff had begun to gather on the lawn, watching from a distance.

Armed with bandages, the maid pushed through the group and ran up. Mina selected a length of linen and turned to the duke. "Hold this handkerchief here. The bleeding has almost stopped, but we'll wrap a bandage around to keep the skin in place until it heals."

His hand came up over the handkerchief. Mina sent the maid off for towels, hot water, and a clean shirt, though the chances of her finding the right size were nil.

She began winding the cloth around his head. Around *flesh*, over an iron skull. In all of her years assisting her father and opening up corpses, she'd never seen that before. Steel prosthetics, yes. Mechanical flesh. But not human flesh and skin that grew over metal as if it were bone.

And that wasn't all that was different about him. The evidence that he possessed nanoagents lay in that quickly healing gash. But he hadn't been affected by that device.

"I was frozen," she said quietly. "So was the butler, the maid— and since we didn't hear Baxter yell or fight, he probably had been, too. Why weren't you?"

He glanced up at her. "The device used the wrong frequency."

Mina was doubtful, but said nothing.

The intensity of his gaze deepened. "Are *you* all right, inspector?"

"Yes." Still shaken, but as long as she didn't think about how the device had stolen her will and her control, she would function. "I'm sorry that the admiral is dead."

"Me, too." His voice was grim. "But I'm damned if I know why he is."

"Perhaps someone in Chatham will identify him." She looked over his head at the dead man, and a thought struck her. "Could he be one of the Dame's men?"

"No. This is something else."

"What?"

"I don't know yet." He stood when she tied off the bandage. "But we'll ask the Dame about him, too, just to be certain. How long will you be needed here?"

She'd probably have time for a quick examination of the bounder before the local police arrived, followed by the naval authorities. Both would boot her out, and she didn't want to fight them over this. When they discovered his identity, and if this murder connected to her investigation, she'd step back in then—with the full power of the London force and the Iron Duke behind her, if necessary.

"An hour," she said. "We'll have to answer their questions."

"Only for an hour." His tone said that if the locals weren't done with them by that time, he'd leave anyway.

"Yes." She looked to Newberry as the constable returned, carrying the physician's bag. She traded him the orange for the bag, feeling the weight of the device inside, and hushed his exclamation of gratitude. "Find the town's wiregram station and update Hale. The admiral has been murdered. We don't yet know if it's connected. We're pursuing Dame Sawtooth, who likely possesses information regarding Captain Haynes's murder."

"Yes, sir—"

Trahaearn cut in. "While you're at it, send a runner to *Lady Corsair*. Tell her to expect us in an hour, and to ready for departure."

The infamous mercenary airship? Mina frowned at him. "Can't we use another? Surely when the *Terror* has been taken, the navy can—"

"She's the fastest of them all, and there's no better flyer than her captain."

All right. If he paid for it, then she didn't care. She turned to Newberry again. "Meet us at the airship in an hour. Inform Hale that we are crossing the Channel on *Lady Corsair,* but don't wait for a response."

Newberry's brows rose. "Sir?"

"She'll order us not to board the airship," Mina said. "But if we never receive a response, we won't have disobeyed orders."

"Yes, sir."

Mina sighed as he left. The poor man. "He looked rather faint, didn't he?"

"Yes."

Was that amusement in the duke's voice? She couldn't tell. But she felt the need to defend her assistant. "He's a brave man."

"Yes."

Still no mocking note, though in Mina's experience, immoral scoundrels like the Iron Duke held good men like the admiral and Newberry in great contempt. She didn't know what to make of it.

Disconcerted, she left him for the dead bounder lying on the grass. Hopefully, she would soon know who he was and where he'd come from. But even if she didn't learn any of those things from his body, she already knew something about him: He hadn't been a brave man.

This one had been a coward.

Chapter Six

Unlike the enormous bullet-shaped dreadnoughts that Sheffield made for the aerocorps, *Lady Corsair* sported a long, cloud-white balloon over a wooden ship that resembled a brown seal—ridiculous and awkward if stranded on its belly, but sleek and maneuverable in its element. At the sides of the ship, the yardarms that should have been extended like oars in preparation for their journey were still tucked against the hull, the sails furled. The propellers at the tail of the ship twirled slowly in the breeze, and Mina couldn't detect the quiet rumble that always accompanied an idling engine. Despite the duke's message, *Lady Corsair* hadn't been readied for departure.

Beneath the bloodied bandage that still wrapped his head, Trahaearn's expression didn't appear either surprised or angry. He glanced at Mina, who was watching him warily and waiting for an explosion.

"She's never liked being told what to do," he said, and before Mina could ask *Who?* a rope ladder swung past her face. Startled, Mina stepped back, looked up.

Her heart caught in her throat. A woman was sliding down the ladder, too fast, as if she couldn't find her grip and couldn't stop herself on one of the rungs. Mina's fingers clenched, urging the woman to hold on, waiting for the inevitable horrifying drop to the ground.

Then the woman kicked her legs, twisting her body around. Flipping like an acrobat at a Horde pony festival, she rolled twice in the air and landed in a crouch at Trahaearn's feet.

Mina wasn't certain whether to applaud or to draw her weapon. No doubt this woman was the airship's mercenary captain, who went by the same name as her ship: Lady Corsair. She rose from her crouch, a head taller than Mina and armed with a cutlass across her back, pistols at her hips, and daggers tucked into the tops of her long leather boots. She wore a ruby kerchief over her black hair, the silk knotted at her nape, its trailing ends twisting around her braids. Wide cheekbones tapered to a pointed chin. With her cat-green eyes narrowed to slits, she was obviously spitting mad—fury she directed straight at Trahaearn.

" 'Be ready for me?' " Even tight with anger, her voice was husky, with an accent Mina couldn't place. Lady Corsair flung her arms wide, and her short aviator's jacket opened to reveal two more knives tucked into a wide crimson belt. "Look around us, Trahaearn. There are plenty of asslickers here, all of them with airships. You go and find one."

Unfazed, Trahaearn simply said, "I want *Lady Corsair*."

"And so I'm to take you on, just like that?" Her lips curled into a snarl, exposing teeth that seemed too sharp. "Too late, captain. I'm already under contract to sail out tomorrow, half paid up front. I won't break it."

"We'll return by tonight. We only have to cross the Channel to Calais."

Curiosity flashed through the woman's expression. Her gaze flicked to his bandages before she sized up Mina and Newberry. "With a cargo of London coppers? That's not worth my time. Find another ship, Trahaearn."

She reached for the rope ladder.

"Twenty-five livre," the duke said.

Mina's mouth fell open. The equivalent in English pounds would cover all of her family's expenses for five years: the servants' wages, food, taxes—with enough leftover to refurnish the town house.

Lady Corsair turned back to Trahaearn, smiling. "Welcome aboard, captain."

* * *

Mina hadn't realized how cold the open deck of an airship became after it started moving. Shivering, she buckled her overcoat, trying to remain out of the aviators' way as they ran forward and aft, hauling on the sail lines. Near the ship's bow, she finally found a seat on a wooden chest that no one seemed to be using, and high enough that she could look over the side. Below, the Medway ran like a sparkling ribbon through the yellow fields. The sun dazzled her eyes, but she looked up and out, amazed by the blueness of the sky. Even the clouds were a surprise, a faint wisp across the heavens and so incredibly white. She'd never seen anything so white, not even bone.

A vibration started up her legs, beneath her bottom. Glancing back, she saw the propellers begin to pick up momentum, felt the thrust of the engines as the airship gained speed. Lady Corsair stood on the quarterdeck, strapping on her goggles. Mina faced forward again. The icy wind whipped tears from her eyes, its roar almost deafening. She hunkered down in her overcoat, pushing up her collar—but she wouldn't be able to stay up here long. She'd have to join Newberry in the forecastle below, and be content with the view from the portholes.

A pair of aviator's goggles suddenly dangled in front of her face. Mina glanced up. Trahaearn stood beside her, carrying a second pair of goggles and a brown woolen scarf. Gratefully, Mina took both, buckling on the goggles and covering her ears with the scarf.

The wooden chest she'd chosen unfortunately proved wide enough for two—though barely. When Trahaearn sat, his hard thigh pressed against hers. He'd removed the bandages and washed away the blood, leaving his dark hair wet and slicked behind his ears, those small gold rings on full display.

They drew her gaze like a magnet almost as strong as the sky. She wished he'd cover them.

Her stomach tightened as he leaned in to speak, his mouth only an inch from her cheek. Though the only alternative was shouting against the wind, a raw throat and ringing ears seemed preferable to his disquieting proximity.

"Baxter sent Haynes to the Gold Coast as a messenger boy."

Mina pulled back, frowning. "Why?"

He gestured her close again. "Keep still. I'll tell you all that he said to me."

His breath heated the air between them, and she wanted to pull away again, but it would be over more quickly if he relayed the admiral's reasons all at once. She nodded.

"Six months ago, Baxter was asked to meet with a friend—he didn't give me a name—in Port Fallow. You know of the city?"

Only by reputation. The notorious walled city had been built on Amsterdam's remains, and provided a safe haven for anyone on the run—including many criminals and pirates. Whoever he'd met with probably had a reason not to come to England, and Baxter probably hadn't sailed into the port under an admiral's flag.

She tilted her head so that their cheeks were almost aligned, the better for him to hear her. "So you were not the only unsavory type he'd befriended."

His startled laugh reverberated against her skin. "No. No, I wasn't."

She heard the grief that suddenly deepened the last word, as if his amusement had been a crack that let other emotions spill through. Jaw tightening, Trahaearn turned his head. Cold air rushed between them.

Only a moment later, he angled his head to hers again and continued, "He told Baxter that he'd received an invitation from Jean-Pierre Colbert to attend an auction on the Gold Coast. And the only reason for an exclusive auction in the Ivory Market is so that word doesn't reach the wrong ears."

Like the ears of a Royal Navy admiral, Mina guessed. And the Frenchman's name sounded familiar. "Colbert?"

"Brimstone Island," he said.

That Colbert? Mina shook her head in disbelief. Situated in the Antilles, Brimstone Island had another, official name, but after the French and Liberé war, during which a military camp on the island had been used to hold prisoners of war, the island was only known by the name given to it by the thousands of prisoners who'd suffered there. Colbert, a pipelayer, the camp's commandant—and an illegitimate relation of the French monarch—had hired mercenaries to oversee the prisoners. The mercenaries had taken the money for food and medicine, and left the men nothing to live on. The accounts of starvation and sickness from the surviving prisoners had been beyond horrifying.

"I thought Colbert had been hanged?"

"No. He was quietly pardoned and shipped over to the Ivory Market. Now, he runs an auction house—and when truly rare items come into his possession, he makes certain that his family knows of them, and holds exclusive auctions like these . . . usually with invitations issued to parties who won't have the funds to outbid the French Crown."

Fixing the auctions in favor of his family—probably to regain *their* favor. "Did the invitation indicate what kind of item was up for auction, then?"

"A weapon. One-time use, powerful, but no other details were given. No one would lay out that much money on an untested weapon, though—so Colbert scheduled a demonstration, during which the interested buyers would settle on a date for the auction."

A demonstration of a weapon that could be used once? Mina frowned, but as if anticipating her question, Trahaearn shook his head. "Baxter didn't know what they'd planned to use for the demonstration. But his friend intended to view it—and was to pass along a description of the weapon to Haynes, along with the date the auction would take place."

"So the *Terror* was supposed to have sailed to the Gold Coast and collected this message?"

"Yes."

"And while there, join the Gold Coast fleet."

"Yes. The fleet is scheduled to return to England shortly, and would have escorted the *Terror* home."

"So either Haynes didn't locate the fleet, or Dame Sawtooth took the ship before the *Terror* reached the Gold Coast." Another thought struck her. "Or after Haynes received the message, he couldn't wait for the fleet, and tried to return alone. When was the demonstration supposed to be?"

"Six days ago. But if he received information that demanded immediate response, he'd have gone to the fleet commander."

Immediate response . . . such as if the weapon posed an imminent threat to England. "Has there been word from the fleet?"

"No. But Baxter doesn't expect any for another week."

Something tightened in Mina's chest. Baxter *didn't* expect any. Trahaearn seemed to notice his slip, too. He fell silent.

Mina sat back, looked out over the airship's bow. A hundred questions took their places at the tip of her tongue, like lemmings preparing to leap. But the Iron Duke was at the forefront of them, not a captain dead by unknown means, not a ship lost, not the woman who had taken it.

She chose another instead. Turning back, she glanced at his face and wished she hadn't. Some men looked ridiculous in goggles. Some were dashing. With his gold hoops and a half-day's growth of stubble darkening his lean jaw, the Iron Duke simply looked the rogue.

And he watched her, even now. The train, the steamcoach, and the bow of an airship. She couldn't escape him.

With a sigh, she gestured him closer and leaned in to speak. He dipped his head, his cheek brushing hers. Deliberately, she was certain. Her fingers curled against her thighs and she tilted her face away from him, looking directly at the top of his ear—and was struck by a sudden and powerful need to lick him there, to feel the gold rings against her lips, to learn whether the wind chilled the metal or if his body heated them. To bite him, gently. To draw in the scent of his warmth and to bury her fingers in his hair while she flicked her tongue over the hoops.

Insanity.

Appalled by the strange compulsion, Mina shook herself. What had she meant to ask him?

A moment later, she remembered. "I saw something that looked exactly like the freezing device in the Blacksmith's office this morning. *Surely* he doesn't make them?"

Mina could imagine the Blacksmith capable of many things, but not that—and not because devices that emitted radio signals had been outlawed in England. She simply couldn't believe that any man would build and sell a device that might be used to control him.

"He doesn't," Trahaearn confirmed. "That device came from one of my men, Mad Machen, who took it from a slaver ship near Anglesey. He sent it to London, hoping that the Blacksmith might recognize where it came from."

"It's obviously a Horde device," she said.

"Yes, but these men aren't part of the Horde. On the slaver ship, the man carrying the device called himself a member of the Black Guard."

Mina drew back to frown at him. *The Black Guard?* Those rumors fell into the same category as the stories of a kraken off the Welsh coast, the fears that a bugger magistrate could be mind-controlled, or a New Worlder's certainty that every infected person became a zombie after death. Fueled by paranoia, the whispers about the Black Guard had begun in the slums, and flourished whenever someone disappeared unexpectedly. But Mina had seen too many unidentified corpses collected off the streets to put any stock in tales of buggers who were frozen in their beds at night and taken away by the Black Guard.

Frozen in their beds. *Oh, blue heavens.*

Trahaearn must have seen the realization on her face. Nodding, he tugged her forward again. "Mad Machen has run into fourteen

Black Guard members on these slaver ships. They always kill themselves rather than be captured—or he has to kill them—and so we still don't know what they want."

"Or why they would murder your friend."

"Yes. That wasn't like anything we've seen them do before. They run, they hide, and they abduct their slaves under cover of night—not assassinate a man in broad daylight."

"That doesn't mean it hasn't happened before. The murderer just wasn't caught—or cornered against a garden wall."

"The rutting coward." His voice hardened. "There's no use in the world for men who can't face the consequences of what they've done."

Mina almost snorted. That, from a pirate turned duke? But since she agreed with him, and because that coward had just murdered his friend, she let it pass without comment.

"What of Dame Sawtooth?" Mina wondered. "Would she be part of the Black Guard?"

He suddenly grinned, shaking his head. "The Dame has never done anything quietly—and she'd never join any organization that expected her to kill herself rather than make a scene."

"You know her well?"

"From the day I took the *Terror* from Adams until the year after I blew the tower, there wasn't a moment when the Dame wasn't trying to kill me. After almost a decade of keeping an eye out for her, I know her well enough."

A full decade dedicated to chasing after him? Even the Horde hadn't expended that much effort to catch him, and Mina could only imagine one reason to pursue a man for that long: revenge. "Why does she hate you so much?"

"She was Adams's woman."

And Trahaearn had said he'd left Adams bleeding in dung. "Did she witness the mutiny?"

"No. She was on the stage in Port-au-Prince."

"An actress?"

He nodded. "After she heard what happened, she purchased *Bontemps* and came after me."

"Just to kill you? Then why take the *Terror* now? Why not drop a firebomb on your house instead of a man?"

"It's always been about the *Terror*. If she killed me, if she returned the ship to Manhattan City, she thought Adams's reputation would be restored."

But his reputation hadn't been destroyed because he'd lost the ship; it had been destroyed because a quarter of his crew had starved, been hanged, or whipped to death.

He must have read Mina's disbelief. "I deserted the lieutenants and the crew who didn't want to join with me. When they were returned to Manhattan City for the court-martial, half of them spoke the truth about what had happened under Adams—and the Dame believed the others. She still wants to clear his name."

Mina shook her head. "So to restore his reputation, she took to piracy, and became a thief and murderer?"

"To finance her pursuit. She had to pay her crew."

Unbelievable. "And you never killed her?"

"Why would I? She surprised me now and again, but never had me on the straights."

After destroying the tower, however, he hadn't been continually on the move. He'd begun building his house on the Isle of Dogs. The Dame could have easily killed him then—*Oh*.

"You gave up the *Terror*, and you cut her off at the knees," Mina said quietly. "But that meant you wouldn't have to kill her."

Trahaearn tensed beside her, and she realized he hadn't expected her to make that leap. Perhaps he hadn't *wanted* her to make that leap.

Had he felt sorry for the woman? Mina couldn't. "And if she *is* the one who murdered Haynes?"

Iron determination hardened his response. "Then she'll pay for it."

Mina sighed. She didn't suppose he intended for the Dame to pay with an arrest and trial. So when the time came, Mina would have to go around him . . . or end up arresting the Iron Duke for murder, instead.

But since she didn't want to spend the rest of this flight contemplating the destruction of her career, she asked, "What has the Dame been doing since?"

"She took up with Jasper Evans—"

"The steelcoat inventor?" And the bounder who'd been cheated out of a fortune fifteen years earlier, when Cornelius Morgan stole his patent to build the armored suits. When the navy didn't support Evans's claim—Morgan's bid came in at half the price—he'd gone mad. "I'd heard he was dead. That he drowned himself in one of the suits, jumping off a ship taking him out of Manhattan City."

"No better way to stop the navy from searching for you."

"So he's not insane?"

"He is." Trahaearn's grin flashed. "And angry enough that he holed himself up in Calais, so that no one could steal his work again. The Dame's there with him now, though—has been for the past eight years."

Probably stewing in her resentment and hate. "If he's holed up, how do you know this?"

"They sail to Port Fallow regularly for supplies and to spend a few nights at the taverns. They both drink too much, and talk even more."

Mina laughed softly, shaking her head.

A bell rang behind them, a sharp chime audible over the engines and the rushing wind. Trahaearn looked round and stood. "Yasmeen has something for us."

Lady Corsair's name was Yasmeen? That narrowed her accent, then. Either she'd escaped from the territories that the Horde still occupied in the Orient, or she'd grown up in one of the Arab tribes who'd settled along the southern coast of the South American continent.

They joined her on the quarterdeck, where she stood behind a thick, curved sheet of glass that formed a windbreak around the helm. Cigarillo in hand, she'd pushed her goggles up, and exhaled a mouthful of tobacco smoke past the windbreak.

The aviator captain had expensive tastes—but if she earned twenty-five livre in one day, Mina supposed the woman could afford them.

"The wind is in our favor, captain. I'll have you to the Dame's fort in less than an hour." Though it was quieter behind the glass, Lady Corsair still had to raise her voice over the engines. "Where's the windup boy? Scarsdale won't thank you for having to miss a reunion with the Dame—and I'm sorry that I won't see you knock him unconscious again in order to get him up here."

Mina couldn't read the expression that passed over the duke's face. Part concern, part irritation.

"He was still abed," he said.

"Hungover?" Yasmeen gave her head a little shake before looking Mina over. "You're keeping strange company in his place, captain. I'm not sure what's worse—that you've taken up with the Horde, or that you've taken up with a London copper."

Mina's jaw clenched.

"Yasmeen." Trahaearn's voice held a warning.

The woman grinned, her green eyes keen and suddenly full of humor. "I don't hold it against *you*," she told Mina. "I am only surprised that Trahaearn doesn't. I remember a time when his only purpose was to destroy the Horde, along with every New World government and institution therein—including the police forces. And look at him now: a duke who conducts most of his business legally and pays *taxes* to the Crown. God's truth, it's heartbreaking. Smoke?"

After the barrage aimed at Trahaearn, the offer Yasmeen tacked on took a moment to sink in. Curious, Mina nodded. Yasmeen withdrew a silver case and a small spark lighter from her belt, and passed her cigarillo to Mina to hold while she lighted it. They traded, and Mina observed how the other woman drew another mouthful before putting the cigarillo to her lips.

"The Lusitanians make a fortune on this stuff," Yasmeen said, then glanced at Trahaearn. "You have, too?"

"Shipping it, yes."

His gaze had settled on Mina's mouth as she sucked in a long breath. Yasmeen burst into a deep and throaty laugh, accompanied by a shake of her head.

"I should have warned you—inspector, is it? Shallow inhalations. You'll feel that one."

Mina already was feeling it—dizzy, light-headed.

"And you'll want more," Trahaearn added, not as amused as Yasmeen, but smiling.

Mina wasn't sure if she would. The taste wasn't unpleasant, but it wasn't good, either. It most certainly wasn't worth the price. "Why will I?"

He shrugged. "Ask Yasmeen to make this her last, and to never smoke another again. She won't be able to. Perhaps she'd last until tomorrow, but no longer."

"I *could*," Yasmeen said. "I don't *want* to."

Mina glanced at the cigarillo between her fingers and thought of the opium pipelayers in their dens. She looked to Trahaearn. "How do you know?"

"When I realized how much I needed it, I meant to quit them. But I only managed to stop after I ran out when I was still six weeks from any port."

"You stopped because you needed it?" Yasmeen shook her head, laughing. "Did you stop eating, too?"

That decided her. Mina liked to eat—but if her tastes began to run toward these cigarillos, she wouldn't be able to afford any food afterward. Carefully pinching out the burning end, she gave the remainder back to Yasmeen. "Thank you."

The other woman tucked it into her case. "Such manners. And you don't speak like a crèche baby."

"No, I don't."

Yasmeen narrowed her eyes, then looked around when a bell

chimed. One of the crew pointed out over the bow, to a faint blue line across the horizon. Mina's heart leapt. She gripped the side of the windbreak, peering through the thick glass. That had to be the Channel—her very first glimpse of the sea.

Turning back to them, Yasmeen said, "We're almost to Dover, then. Are you heading into Evans's fort, just the two of you?"

"And the constable," Trahaearn said.

"That red giant?" The other woman pursed her lips. "Yes, yes, that will make all the difference, I'm sure. I want payment upfront, captain."

With a laugh, the duke shook his head.

Mina frowned at him before looking to Yasmeen. "Why don't you think we'll return? The Dame is hoping for a ransom. Won't she wait to see whether it will be paid?"

"She'll honor a ransom payment, but getting Trahaearn out again is another matter." Her gaze ran over Mina from head to toe. "*You* obviously can't pay me, and your employer *won't.*"

No, Mina couldn't pay her—or a ransom. She asked Trahaearn, "What if the boys are there? Will you pay for their release?"

Yasmeen snorted. "And play the hero again? If you do, this reward won't compare to the last you received. Dukedoms only come with towers."

Trahaearn's mouth tightened, and that awful detached expression came over his features. "No."

Mina stared at him. "No?"

"They aren't in danger. Their families will pay, and the Dame won't risk harming them before they return home."

"Yes, but if she's the one who killed Haynes, then I'm going there to *arrest* her. If those boys aren't at the fort, how will we find them? But if we pay the ransom first and verify their location, then bringing Haynes's murderer to justice won't come at the expense of the boys' lives."

Aghast, Yasmeen gaped at her before looking to the duke. "It's worse than I thought. Not just the Horde, not just the police—you're keeping company with someone who has *principles*."

"Unfortunately," Trahaearn said.

Very well, then. Mina could think of several other reasons not to leave the boys to rot. "If the Dame lies about the *Terror*'s location, those boys can probably tell you who has it now and where it was headed. At the very least, they can tell you where it was taken. If their lives aren't worth the money, surely the information they have is?"

He frowned at her, and Mina supposed she ought to have quivered or cowered. She turned to the airship captain, instead.

"What can we expect at the fort, Captain Corsair?"

"Zombies, the Dame's crew walking about in Evans's steelcoats, and whatever mad inventions he's spent the past fifteen years creating. Then there's the Dame herself. *Sawtooth* isn't just a name, but a role she's determined to play to the very, *very* end." Yasmeen waved her cigarillo in a dramatic flourish before glancing over at Trahaearn. "I truly think you should pay me upfront."

Chapter Seven

Mina returned to the bow as the airship passed the Dover cliffs and flew out over a breathtaking expanse of dark blue water. The clouds weren't wisps now, but small puffs crowding the sky like sheep huddled together. Dozens of ships sailed the lanes, their white canvases full, the rigging standing tall and proud against the water. Her heart hurt, it was all so beautiful. Andrew would have loved this.

By the starry sky, she hoped he was well.

In the distance, the shores of France waited, a flat band of dark green that separated the sapphire water and the azure sky.

The crew's activity near the rail caught her attention, and a moment later she was forced to abandon her wooden chest when a red-faced aviator told Mina that she was sitting on his gun. Unlike a sailing ship, the airship didn't carry heavy artillery, but rail cannons—electric-powered weapons that fired smaller ammunitions at greater velocity than a traditional cannon. Though more destructive and accurate, only the most desperate of sea captains ever fired up a rail cannon on the water; the electricity required demanded the use of steam engines, whose vibrations drew the monstrous sea creatures the Horde had altered and bred for their own unimaginable purposes. Fortunately, no megalodons or kraken inhabited the Channel, but there swam sharks big enough to damage rudders, and giant eels who generated electrical discharges strong enough to kill a swimmer or burn holes in a wooden hull. But an airship had nothing similar to fear, and could fire its engines for both propulsion and defense.

She watched in trepidation as they readied the gunports and mounted the rapid-fire rifles, whose multiple spinning barrels could shoot almost two hundred rounds per minute. When Trahaearn came up beside her, he swept an exacting gaze over each weapons station, but must have found little to criticize. With a nod, he looked down at her.

His lips quirked, and he bent to her ear. "Even a fast airship isn't worth twenty-five livre," he said. "But no navy in the world could boast of a ship this tight, or a crew as loyal. And so *Lady Corsair* is worth every denier."

Mina had to take his word for it. She'd never stepped foot on another airship, let alone a sailing ship. She gestured to the guns. "Do you believe we'll need those?"

"I believe we'll need to be ready to use them."

Said by a man who only carried a dagger. Uncertainty trembled in her stomach. Despite hearing of zombies and insane inventions, Mina realized that his presence had prevented fear from rattling her as hard as it should have. Almost a decade of reading his praise in the newssheets must have seeped into her, down to her bones—and she'd felt safe all the while she'd been with him, knowing that no one in England would dare touch the Iron Duke.

But it was different, here. They'd passed out of England . . . and were on course to confront enemies who *would* dare.

His gaze sharpened. "What is it? What's frightened you?"

She shook her head. His expression darkened and he caught her chin, forcing her to look up at him.

"Tell me now, inspector, or—"

A bell chimed, followed by Yasmeen's shout from the quarterdeck. Trahaearn looked round. He took Mina's hand, and though she tugged, he didn't release her until they'd reached the windbreak.

Yasmeen passed him a telescoping spyglass. "Somebody's father yanked on the navy's leash. Idiots."

The duke looked. His face settled into grim lines as he passed the spyglass to Mina. He pointed to the right of the bow. "There, do you see? Five ships under full sail, including two ships of the line."

The navy's largest and most heavily gunned warships. Mina found them more easily than she'd expected. Most of the ships passed through the Channel, heading for the mouth of the Thames or having just come from the river. Only one flotilla of five ships was headed south, straight crossing the Channel—and was already halfway there.

Mina lowered the spyglass. "Will we reach the fort ahead of them?"

"Yes. Yasmeen will put the engines at full bore, and with this wind, she'll run at sixty knots to their fifteen."

Even as Trahaearn spoke, Yasmeen gave orders that an aviator relayed by shouting into metal tubes running through the deck floor. Bells rang up and down the rails.

"And we'll fly directly over the fort," he said. "They'll have to anchor offshore and row their boats in. Altogether, we should have an hour on them after we've arrived."

Mina nodded. "Why did she call them idiots?"

Keeping his mouth still near to her left ear, Trahaearn moved around behind her until he shared her line of sight. His right palm flattened against her side, and she felt the huge size of his hand through her jacket and armor. "Raise that glass up again, and look to the first ship of the line."

Swallowing, Mina did. She searched, and finally found the ship's squared-off stern and tall rigging through the lens, the image shaking from the vibrations in the airship and the unsteadiness of her hands.

"There's smoke coming from the main deck. Do you see it?"

Barely. If he hadn't told her to look for it, she wouldn't have detected the dark smudge. "Yes."

"Those are the steelcoats. They're firing up the suits' mobility engines, and waiting in formation on the decks."

Oh, smoking hells. That couldn't bode well for the boys. As harrowing as the kidnapping was, as long as the ransom was paid, very few men or women held hostage came to harm. The practice had become so common among pirates that being taken for ransom was almost to be expected by the upper classes and the wealthy traveling on the high seas—and treated as an everyday business transaction.

But when relations refused to pay the ransom and instead attacked the pirates, everyone usually ended up dead.

"Are they readying the steelcoats as a threat? Or do they intend to storm the fort?"

"Does it matter? Either way, the Dame will know that a ransom won't be part of any deal they make. So if she sees them coming, she'll cut and run—and we'll have no information on the *Terror*, no arrest for you, no boys left alive." He took the spyglass. "Some idiot merchant threw his weight around, demanded his boy be rescued, and now the navy's charging in. Two hundred years with no nation to protect, just the trade routes, and the navy got used to bending over for them—but it's everyone else who's fucked."

The bitterness in his voice startled her. *He'd been angry about this once*, she thought. But now there was more resignation than fury.

And he probably had it exactly right. While the Horde had occupied England, the navy had become the merchants' muscle in Manhattan City. But it didn't have to stay that way.

"That should change now that the Crown is funding naval operations again." At least she hoped so. The taxes squeezed out of her had to be doing some good—and right or wrong, loyalty very often followed money. Even if she felt the pinch of it, Mina preferred that the navy took money from the Crown's purse than from the merchants. "And England's interests will be put ahead of the merchants' again—and already must be. Not every commander is the merchants' tool."

"No, not all of them. But there's one fewer now."

Baxter, Mina realized. "There will soon be more like him."

"That won't help us today." Trahaearn lowered the spyglass. His fingers curled around the side of her waist. "You've got armor. And your constable?"

She remembered to breathe. "He does, too."

"All right." His voice lowered against her ear, though no one could possibly have heard him before. "I'll keep you safe, inspector."

How? He was a danger to her, just by being who he was. Moving away from his hand, she said, "I'll do that myself, sir."

The captain cut *Lady Corsair*'s engines a mile from the shore and let the sails take them in. In the sudden quiet, Mina stared out over bow, entranced by the thin ribbon of yellow sand, and the tangled marsh surrounding Calais's ruins, now little more than stone rubble. Beyond it, a forest stretched to the horizon. Never had she seen so many trees, gnarled and twisted near the sand, becoming fuller and greener farther away from the beach.

Zombies could hide between those trees. But how could an airship?

She looked to Trahaearn, standing beside her. "Where is *Bontemps*?"

He pointed to the west of Calais's ruins, near the edge of the marsh, where the growth of trees didn't seem so dense. "The old fort is there. They maintain the walls to keep out the zombies."

Using the spyglass, she could just make out the stone remains—worn and weathered, but not rubble. Gray stone walls surrounded the ruins of long structures supported by crumbling arches. Aqueducts, maybe. As they drew closer, she spotted a few sheep grazing in the yards, and small wooden shacks that probably housed chickens, but nothing inhabitable by humans.

"Where do they live?"

"Underground," Trahaearn said. "Evans settled here because he wanted to dig a tunnel under the Channel from the fort to Dover—"

A laugh burst from her. She couldn't have heard that correctly. "A *what*?"

He grinned. "A tunnel under the Channel."

"Did he actually try?"

"Yes. But it filled with water even before he reached the shore. He blamed the marshes."

No. Shoulders shaking, Mina steepled her hands in front of her mouth, laughing silently. When her stomach hurt and she couldn't take another breath, she pushed up her goggles and wiped her eyes. "Oh, he *is* insane."

"But brilliant," Trahaearn said. "When his tunnel failed, he kept digging. This area is a maze of underground chambers now. His generators power electric lights and continually pump the water seepage into the steam engines, so that all he has to do is keep the furnace stoked."

Mina looked out over the fort again, eyes wide. "Are you certain that's not just a drunk's tale?"

"Three years ago, one of the Dame's aviators went in to the Blacksmith's for a new leg. Scarsdale found out, and chatted him up at the Hammer & Chain."

More drunken stories then, but from a different source. "But where would Evans find enough fuel? That much coal would—*Oh,*" she realized. "The trees. But how does he avoid the zombies?"

"Evans built a harvester—an armored tank that saws down the trees and drags them back to the fort."

Just like the Horde was rumored to do in other parts of Europe. Giant machines harvested their crops, and stored the food within walled settlements until it was shipped east.

"Inspector." Trahaearn's eyes were narrowed as he looked toward the fort. "The spyglass."

She passed it to him, and watched his face as he peered through the telescope. Whatever he saw didn't please him. "What is it?"

"I'm not sure." He shook his head. "No one is manning the walls. There should be at least two lookouts—one for the forest, one for the sea."

Uneasy, Mina watched the fort for any signs of humans—or zombies—but not a single one appeared as they flew closer.

They were passing over the fort walls when Newberry came up on the main deck, carrying two machetes, a gun belt with holsters, and a fat-barreled blunderbuss. He offered them to Trahaearn.

"Captain Corsair said that these were for you."

Trahaearn nodded and shrugged out of his long overcoat—and then his short one, followed by his waistcoat. A white lawn shirt stretched over his broad back, doing little to hide the heavy muscles beneath . . . yet she would have liked to see them, anyway. Mina turned away, gripping the rail. Newberry joined her, his face red as a plum.

He cleared his throat. "I don't see the airship, sir."

Buckling the holsters around his hips, Trahaearn glanced over the side and nodded. "It's there. The main yard."

Puzzled, Mina stared at the ground before realizing that a fence surrounded a long, rectangular section of the yard, preventing the sheep from straying into that area. The oddly mottled ground surface in that section was sunken . . . as if a painted canvas had been stretched across a large hole.

Unbelievable. If the airship was anchored beneath that, she could hardly imagine the size of the underground chamber.

"Yasmeen will wait for us near the fort's south wall," Trahaearn said, pushing the machetes through leather loops on each side of the gun belt. "We'll ride *Lady Corsair*'s cargo platform down into the compound rather than taking the ladder one at a time. The walls should keep out the zombies, but if one comes over, shoot it on sight. Aim for the head. We run straight for the cover over *Bontemps*, and drop in on the Dame from there."

He hefted a coil of rope over his shoulder. Mina looked back toward the sea. The fort only sat five hundred yards from the beach, and the navy ships were drawing quickly nearer. "How long?"

"The wind picked up," Trahaearn said. "They'll be ready to anchor in twenty minutes, but it'll take them longer to row into shore and to cross the marsh. So we need to be done in forty. Ready, then?"

With a nod, Mina followed him amidships, where two aviators waited at the platform's control lever. With a rattle of chains, the cargo platform rose even with the decks. Bracing his hand on the gunwale, Trahaearn vaulted over the side onto the platform, and turned to help Mina while Newberry clambered over.

She looked back at the airship and blinked. All along the wooden sides, small gunports had opened. At each one, an aviator stood with a rifle, watching the ground below.

Trahaearn must have noted her surprise. "Worth every denier," he said.

Apparently. Mina braced her feet as the platform began lowering. Trahaearn held the blunderbuss loosely in his left hand, barrel pointed toward the ground. Behind her, she heard Newberry draw in a deep, steadying breath.

The platform touched the ground, and she felt the vibration under her feet. She glanced at Trahaearn. "The generators?"

"Yes."

"Then someone must be here." A furnace didn't stoke itself.

He nodded. "Let's go."

A sheep bleated as they raced across the yard. Mina's heart pounded, but there were no shouts, no gunshots. Trahaearn reached the fence and lifted Mina over before she could protest. Three feet away from the fence, the painted canvas cover had been fastened to a metal frame with hook-and-eye loops. Mina quickly freed one corner, folding back a triangle of heavy canvas. She peered down into the chamber.

Bontemps's white balloon almost reached the chamber's canvas roof, and obscured most everything below. Squinting, Mina made out a few large crates stacked on the floor near the corner. No movement, no lights.

Trahaearn crouched beside her, the coil of rope in hand, and Mina saw that he'd tied the other end around the thick fence post. He tossed the rope into the chamber. "I'm down first. I'll wave you in when it's secure."

Her heart leapt into her throat as he backed up and jumped in—not using the rope to climb down, but to slow his fall. On her knees, she braced her hands at the edge, looked over, and saw him land near the crates. The tension on the rope slackened. She tracked him by his white shirt as he walked along the wall of the chamber, until he disappeared from view beneath the sides of the balloon.

Glancing back, she checked on Newberry. The constable had apparently shed his nervousness. Weapons ready, he stood near the fence, quietly scanning the yard. *Good man.*

She looked into the chamber again as Trahaearn walked into view again. Mina took hold of the rope when he waved her down.

"Follow as soon as I'm at the bottom, Newberry."

He nodded, and Mina eased herself over the side. Though her bugs made her strong enough to support her weight, they couldn't guard against a friction burn. She clamped the rope between the sole of her boot and her leather-covered ankle, and eased down slowly. Dim light spilled into the chamber at the opposite end, and once Mina could see past *Bontemps*'s balloon, she saw that it came from a corridor leading east. Trahaearn stood near an unlit corridor at the near end.

As she reached bottom, he told her quietly, "I don't hear any noises from this direction."

They'd go the opposite way, then. She looked around the chamber while Newberry descended. Though damp, its stone walls faintly wet, the air didn't smell of must or mildew. The chamber was warm, as if heated—but if so, the heat had to have been coming from the opposite corridor.

Newberry dropped the last few feet to the stone floor. Mina looked to Trahaearn, and gestured toward the lighted corridor. He nodded and led the way.

Unlike the straight rectangular walls in the chamber, the passageways were rounded at the top and sides, as if an enormous drill had passed through the stone, and the floor squared off later. A wire ran along the ceiling, connecting small bulbs that glowed with yellow light that flickered and buzzed. *Incredible*. She'd seen electric lamps before, but always used as novelties, and never put to practical use—that was, if burning a few trees every day in order to light an underground compound could be considered *practical*.

Halfway down the corridor, she noticed the smell. Sweet, pungent—and as familiar as an opium den. Someone had stopped here to smoke.

"Is Evans a pipelayer?" she whispered.

Trahaearn shook his head. "The Dame isn't, either—and she'd be damned before allowing her crew to smoke. They can't work if they're blissed."

The scent dissipated as they emerged into another large chamber—this one with a ceiling. Either a workspace or for storing Evans's inventions, the chamber had been packed full of machinery. Steelcoats stood among piles of scrap metal. Flying autogyros lay against the wall, their bladed rotors propped beside them like steel daisies. A two-seater balloon with a flat envelope had been parked atop a hulking cylindrical vehicle that might have been a submersible. Two more lighted passageways led from the chamber: one directly across, and the other to the right. Mina followed Trahaearn across the chamber, picking her way through the machines. Accustomed to her mother's meticulously organized attic, the place seemed a disastrous—and dangerous—mess.

A faint yell sounded from the passageway in front of them. Trahaearn paused. Mina did the same, listening as the yelling continued. Male, young, but not angry or panicked—the shouts had an unmistakably bored and insolent tone.

"That's the yell of someone looking to make his jailer's life hell, sir," Newberry said behind her. "But he doesn't truly think he's getting out."

Her pulse racing, Mina nodded. Andrew hadn't been named among the boys held for ransom . . . but maybe he'd been left off the list.

She had to hope.

Trahaearn slowed at the mouth of the passageway. Turning, he tossed the blunderbuss to Newberry and drew a machete. "Walk backward, constable," he said softly. "Watch this end of the corridor, and blow the head off anything that enters."

The muscles in the back of Mina's neck tightened. Another scent greeted her as she entered the passageway, more familiar than an opium den—and becoming stronger as they approached the next chamber.

There were dead here.

Trahaearn paused at the end of the corridor. "Inspector."

She joined him, breathing through her mouth as the odor became overwhelming, and looked into the chamber. *Oh . . . blue heavens.* What had once been a chapel had become a morgue. Four wooden pews had been pushed to the walls, and on the floor lay three rows of sheet-wrapped bodies—fifteen in all.

"Cover me," she said softly. She crouched next to the first body. Her fingers found the edge of the sheet beneath stiff hair and pulled the linen back from his face. He hadn't been dead for more than a few days. She pushed aside his collar. Round pustules ringed with crimson had formed a rash beneath his jaw. His swollen tongue was dark red, the vessels in his eyes shot like scarlet starbursts. Unusual, but she'd seen it before.

She covered him and looked to Trahaearn. "Bug fever."

"And the others?"

Probably not the fever. It wasn't contagious—and usually only occurred when a severe injury forced the nanoagents to overextend their healing capabilities and to replicate too quickly, burning the body up from the inside.

She pulled the sheet back from the next. Ice slid down her spine. "This one, too."

"How?"

"I don't know. Maybe they were all caught in an explosion, or all injured at the same time."

Ripping the rest of the sheet away, she looked for blood, bruising, anything out of the ordinary. There was nothing to account for the fever—and nothing on the next body.

"I couldn't find any evidence of injury on Haynes's body, either," she realized.

"Haynes died of bug fever?"

"No. Absolutely no." She shook her head, looked up at him. "Even frozen, the fever would have left its mark on him."

Mouth set in a grim line, Trahaearn nodded. Pulling back sheets from faces, he checked each body. A few looked as if they'd only been dead for hours.

"Evans and the Dame aren't here," he said. "Fifteen men and women . . . this must be her entire crew."

And there was nothing to be done for them now. Mina stood. "Let's keep going."

Through another chamber that had served as a dining room and parlor, Trahaearn found a short corridor that terminated at a wooden door inset with a barred window. A face peered between the bars. A moment later, cheers and whoops sounded. Mina gestured for them to quiet, to no avail.

Damn and blast. With Newberry guarding the head of the corridor, Mina approached the cell door and glanced through the bars. Though they appeared tired and hungry, the boys were yanking on boots and shirts, hugging each other—and still yelling. None looked injured. None were young enough to be Andrew.

Three boys crowded the window, fingers wrapped around the bars as they peered through. She tried the door. *Locked.*

"Who has the key?"

"The Dame," one said. "Around her neck."

Lovely. Mina gripped the bars and pulled. The door creaked but didn't give, and earned her a disbelieving snort from one of the boys.

"Do you imagine we didn't try that?"

Ungrateful toe-rag. She resisted the urge to bare her teeth at him and to point out that as bounders, they probably weren't infected—which meant that her strength doubled theirs.

"Inspector." She felt Trahaearn's hand against her waist, gently guiding her to the side. He spared a glance for boys. "You'd best stand back."

Mina waited, heart pounding. Bracing his feet, Trahaearn lowered his shoulder and shoved his weight into the door. Wood cracked like a shot, splintering the jamb. Trahaearn drew back. His great booted foot slammed beneath the lock. The door crashed open to more cheers. Eight boys boiled out, grabbing the duke's hand to shake, whooping.

She hissed for them to quiet. Half did. She gritted her teeth and looked to Trahaearn.

"Pipe down!" His quiet command snapped like a whip. Silence immediately fell. Some looked to him wide-eyed, and others with dawning realization. Mina stepped forward before they could begin fawning at the Iron Duke—or sneering at His Bastard Grace. With bounders, one never knew.

"Are the Dame and Jasper Evans still alive?"

Nods all around. *All right.* Then she and Trahaearn weren't leaving yet, but these young men were.

She gestured to Newberry and spoke loud enough for him to hear. "The constable will lead you to our airship. You will not make noise. You will follow his directions without hesitation. Your way out is via a rope. I'm ordering him to climb up first, so that he can haul you up—he's *not* leaving you down here. Understood?"

More nods. *Good enough.*

She led them to the end of the corridor. Still holding the blunderbuss at ready, Newberry looked down at her. She read his reluctance—not to lead the boys out, but to leave her. She reassured him with a glance.

"All set, constable?"

"Yes, sir."

"We'll see you on *Lady Corsair*, then. I recommend that you move at a trot."

She watched his back until the last boy disappeared into the chapel chamber, then looked round. The long dining table at this end of the chamber could have served the Dame's entire crew. At the opposite end, two striped sofas sat at right angles to each other, facing a playing table surrounded by chairs. The scent of opium was faint here, but had been smoked recently—probably as a restive for those struck by the fever.

Trahaearn listened at one of the adjacent corridors, his head cocked. The smell of opium and sickness thickened as she joined him. Like the cell corridor, this one didn't open into another chamber, but ended at a door, with several others set off on the sides.

He said softly, "Bedchambers this way."

They'd hardly taken a step when a side door creaked open. Trahaearn shoved Mina behind him. She barely breathed as they waited, weapons aimed down the corridor.

A woman staggered out, a pistol loosely gripped in her limp hand. Mina's eyes widened. Wearing only a nightgown, brown hair tangled over her face, she had to be Dame Sawtooth. Serrated blades filled the grin she aimed toward them.

"Trahaearn, finally." His name emerged as a triumphant whisper from between the blades. "This must be Heaven."

She tried to lift her gun—and wavered. Stumbling against the opposite wall, she braced herself. A rash of pustules had spread beneath her jaw and underarms. A hoarse laugh burst from her. With bloodshot eyes, she stared at Mina.

"Heaven. So why is a jade here?"

She collapsed in a heap.

"Christ," Trahaearn said. Striding forward, he kicked the Dame's gun away from her hand, knelt. He glanced back up at Mina. "Take her feet. And watch her teeth."

The opium scent surrounded the woman like a cloud. Her skin

burned with fever against Mina's palms. They headed to the sofa, the Dame's heavy bulk sagging between them.

"Marguerite?"

Mina dropped the Dame's ankles, whipping around and taking aim. A tall, wiry man stared back at her, a bucket of ice in his hand, his face lined with exhaustion. His shiny bald scalp and the black tufts of hair over his ears made his head seem enormous in comparison to his thin neck.

"Jasper Evans?" she guessed.

"Yes." His eyes were bright blue, and quick as a bird's. They darted to Trahaearn, to the corridor where the boys had been held, and back to Mina. "You've come to arrest her, then?"

"We have to keep her alive for that. Bring the ice." Mina turned to the sofa, where Trahaearn laid the Dame lengthwise over the striped pillows. "We have an airship. If we keep her temperature down, she'll make it across the Channel. We'll find a physician—or the Blacksmith."

With a shallow breath, the Dame opened her eyes. Each word was an effort. "That bastard . . . will kill . . . me."

Trahaearn or the Blacksmith? Mina didn't ask. Evans knelt next to the sofa, gently stroking the Dame's face. She smiled weakly up at him.

Mina reached for the ice. "What happened to you and your men?"

"Big performance," the Dame whispered. Her eyes rolled back. "Last call."

Evans put his forehead to hers. "A *brilliant* performance, Marguerite."

And they were playing out a scene that had Mina's throat aching. She wrapped ice in a handkerchief, leaned forward to place it against the Dame's neck.

The Dame jerked her head, snapping her bladed teeth an inch from Mina's fingers. Yanking her hand back, Mina stared. The Dame laughed hoarsely. Her eyes closed and she rested her head against the pillows again.

Mina gave the handkerchief to Evans to use, instead.

"What happened to your men, then?" Trahaearn repeated Mina's question. "What happened to the *Terror*?"

When the Dame didn't—or couldn't—answer, Evans glanced up at him, eyes shimmering with tears. Mina couldn't read any malice in that look. Either he didn't hate the duke as the Dame did, or her condition had rendered him unable to care about anything else.

"Colbert told her that if the ship remained at a distance, the explosion wouldn't affect them."

Trahaearn's expression turned dangerously cold. "An explosion on *my* ship?"

"No. *We* were on the *Terror*, watching the explosion." Evans wiped his cheeks, leaving streaks of grease and oil. "It was a demonstration. Showing the buyers. Colbert had a little one, and it just needed a generator. The trigger requires an electric current."

A little what? "A little weapon?"

"Nothing like I've seen before. Nothing like I've dreamed of." Evans's hands shook. "They rowed Haynes out in a launch, all of the oarsmen without bugs. And they took that little one with them. A mile, they said, was that safe distance, so the men rowed a mile and a half. They started up that generator, the sharks came at them, and then they put the little one into the water and—" He flung his hands up and out, mimicking an explosion. "On the *Terror*, we felt it—*thump!*—against our chests. It didn't blow up big. Only like a cannon, shot into the water. But everything around that launch was dead. They had those giant sharks floating around that little boat. And the oarsmen rowed back—but the captain, he was dead. Without a mark on him."

Trahaearn lowered to his heels next to Mina. "So you boarded the *Terror* and took her over. You sent Haynes out on a boat with a bomb. And it killed him, but everyone on the *Terror* who felt that thump got bug fever. Except you."

Those quick blue eyes stared steadily back at him. "I'm not infected, captain. I run machines. They don't run me."

Mina began wetting the Dame's nightgown with ice water, trying to swallow down the sick lump in her throat. Andrew was infected with nanoagents, and he'd been on the *Terror*. But if he came down with the fever, he knew to stay cold . . . if there was anywhere cold to go on the west coast of Africa. He'd find something. She closed her eyes. Wishing couldn't make it true, but she'd try.

Trahaearn flattened his palm against the small of her back, as if to reassure her. Mina gathered herself. She looked up again as he asked, "The weapon kills any bugs within one mile?"

"The little one did. The one they're selling at the auction, they say it'll kill all the zombies and all the Horde in a two-hundred-mile radius."

Mina's mouth dropped open. *Sweet blue heavens.* Who *wouldn't* want that? It could be a devastating attack against the Horde, and a strong first step toward taking back Europe or Africa.

"Someone smuggled this out of Horde territory?" Trahaearn asked.

"Yes, from what I know. Whoever did, the risk will pay off. Starting bid is twenty-five thousand livre."

Twenty-five thousand? Astonished, she stared at Evans. Who could possibly pay that much? Certainly no individual person. Perhaps the Lusitanians. The French—though they'd nearly gone bankrupt in their war with the Liberé. The Arabian tribes, if they pooled their resources.

Even the duke appeared taken aback. His mouth opened, but he remained speechless.

Mina finally found her voice. "Why the *Terror*?"

"Colbert owed Marguerite. When he heard *Marco's Terror* was sailing to the Gold Coast, he made her an offer: He'd give her *Marco's Terror*, and she'd give him a man for the demonstration."

Haynes. "How did he know the *Terror* was coming?"

Evans shook his head. "I don't know."

"When you took the ship, how many besides Haynes were killed?"

"Three of our men. All of their steelcoats and lieutenants."

All of the marines and officers executed. "Any young boys, four-teen years of age?"

"No." Evans gave an emphatic shake of his head. "No. A couple of the crew were injured in the fight. But none of those we threw over were that young. Marguerite won't hold for that."

Mina looked to Trahaearn for confirmation. He nodded.

The knot around her chest eased. Knowing about the bug fever, she couldn't be truly relieved. But knowing that they hadn't killed any boys helped.

"So who has the *Terror* now?"

As if Trahaearn's voice stirred her, the Dame smiled. "Hunt," she said dreamily. "Hunt has her."

Whoever Hunt was, the Dame apparently couldn't have hit Tra-haearn harder. The duke's face whitened with cold fury. His fingers found the machete's handle.

Oh, no. Grabbing his wrist, Mina tried to head him off, to distract him. "Who dropped Haynes in London?"

"I did, for her. She was already sick and wanted it done." Evans's face seemed to crumple. "We used almost all of our ice on him."

"We'll get more," she promised. "We'll take her back—"

A deafening boom cut Mina off, knocked her sprawling to the stone floor. Pain shot up her elbows. She couldn't draw breath, as if someone had punched her in the chest. The lights flickered.

Smoke billowed through the room, hot and acrid. She felt Tra-haearn's hand, and turned her head, searching.

He kneeled next to her, and through the ringing in her ears, she realized he was shouting *Inspector!* again. Faintly, she recognized his other words: *a firebomb.*

Shot from one of the navy ships? She struggled to understand. Why would the navy bomb them?

She saw Evans looking wildly around, his body covering the Dame's. Mina got her boots under her, but apparently not quick enough. The duke hauled her up. Her hearing cleared, the ringing fading to a buzz.

". . . all right?" he was saying.

Dizzy, but not hurt. She nodded. Then her heart stilled. "Newberry!"

She sprinted for the corridor. The duke caught her in the chapel, amid the smell of rot and smoke and death. She fought him off.

Grabbing hold of her overcoat, he whipped her around, pushing her back up against the wall. "You can't!" he shouted. "If a firebomb hits *Bontemps*, the hydrogen envelope will blow! And you can't make him haul those boys up any faster!"

No. But she could order him to leave the boys and run.

As if he'd read her face, Trahaearn gave her a shake. "He wouldn't run. Because that means he'd leave you down here. His only chance is if he's already up in *Lady Corsair*. We have to go back. Evans will tell us another way out that won't take us past a hydrogen—"

Another boom shook the chamber. Trahaearn flattened his body against hers as rubble rained around them. *That one hadn't been as bad*, Mina thought, but then her ears popped and the air thinned, as if sucked through the corridor by a giant lifting bellows.

Trahaearn's face stilled. "Fuck me," he whispered hoarsely.

In a powerful surge, he dived with her to the corner of the chamber, tearing her overcoat down her arms. Shoving her bottom to the floor, he crouched over Mina's form and flung the wool over their heads like a tent.

The fireball exploded from the corridor, visible around the loose edge of the overcoat. Gasping, Mina flattened it against the wall, sealing them in. Orange light and heat radiated through the thick wool, charring with a rancid stink. Flames roiled and flicked between their legs, hot against her boots. Over the roar, she heard the hiss of Trahaearn's indrawn breath, knew the overcoat was burning against his back, and so didn't scream that her feet felt boiled in leather.

Then it passed, and Trahaearn whipped the overcoat away. Mina had expected cool air to hit her face but it was hot, thin. She blinked, adjusting to the dim light. The electric bulbs had blown out, but fires burned in patches on the wooden benches and the sheets covering the bodies.

His gaze searched her face. "Are you all right?"

She nodded. "You?"

"I'll live. Come with me."

He pulled her up. They ran back to the parlor, her feet shrieking with every step. Though the fireball had burned itself out before reaching the chamber, the lights were off. The sound of the generators had vanished.

Mina called out, didn't receive an answer. Still holding on to Trahaearn, she felt her way to the sofa. Evans and the Dame had gone.

Stunned, she stared into the dark. The duke gave a short bark of laughter, gruff and amused, and she almost liked him for it, but then another explosion rocked the chamber and she was on her knees, coughing, with Trahaearn coughing beside her. Crashing sounds came from the chapel, wood splintering against stone, the shriek of metal. Not the bomb. The underground chambers were being shaken apart.

"All right," he said a moment later. "Evans isn't a bugger. He's carrying a woman twice his size. He's not gone too far."

"He's carrying a woman who needs more ice," Mina added. "He brought some from the passageway nearest the table."

"We'll go that way, then."

He helped her up. Within a minute, they found the passage entrance and hurried along its length, using the curving sides as a guide.

At the end of it, Trahaearn paused before tugging her to the left. "There's faint light there, do you see?"

Faint light and the familiar sound of a steam engine. They ran toward it. The quick pace beat tears of pain from her eyes, but by the time they emerged into a new chamber lit by a single gas lamp, the agony in her feet had reached excruciating, and so she didn't need to feel it anymore, *wouldn't* feel it anymore.

And then she stopped running anyway, her jaw dropping at the sight of the rattling, hissing machine in front of her. The enormous armored vehicle had to be the tree harvester. Twice Mina's height and half as long as a locomotive car, it resembled a giant black scorpion with two sawing pincers, and a long chute lined with shredding blades at the tail.

Trahaearn shouted, "*Evans!*"

She spotted the horizontal slits at the vehicle's front and back, the flickering light that shone through. Evans looked at them and shook his head. The machine lurched into motion, rolling on a track of segmented steel plates.

"Goddammit!" Trahaearn roared and started for him, then staggered as another explosion came from deep within the compound. A long spar of shale shaved off from the ceiling. Mina screamed a warning. Trahaearn covered his head and the stone crashed to the floor less than two yards from where he stood, shattering into thousands of razor-edged pieces.

Mina's hands flew to her mouth. He stared at it, shocked, before looking toward her.

"We have to get out of here," she said.

He nodded. "We'll follow him out on foot."

Mina snatched up the gas lamp. The harvester was already far ahead of them, rolling at speed down a long passageway dug out to the machine's dimensions.

Trahaearn took the lamp and pulled her into a jog. "The generator's off, but the furnace is probably still burning. If that boiler blows, it'll be worse than any bomb."

Oh, blue heavens. Mina ran faster. Her thighs began to burn as the passageway sloped uphill. Ahead, she could see daylight, and that was . . . *terrible.*

"That harvester doesn't break through the fort's walls every time they use it!" she shouted over their pounding feet. "This passageway will probably take us outside the fort!"

Trahaearn laughed again, shaking his head. She realized it wasn't a denial, but a *What next?* But he knew what to do. He dropped the lamp, let go of her hand, and drew his machetes.

They slowed as they neared the exit—a steel door that probably remained closed except for when the harvester came and went. Now it stood wide open, facing the forest. Birds chirped and twittered merrily among the branches, as if zombies didn't prowl the earth below them.

Ridiculous little animals.

Mina checked her weapons. "Please tell me that fire and explosions will frighten the zombies away."

He cast her a look that she couldn't interpret—almost as if he was deciding whether to lie. Finally, he shook his head. "No. The noise draws them."

"Lovely," she said, and sighed. "We're past the south wall of the fort. Do you think *Lady Corsair* will still be waiting for us there?"

"No. Not within range of the firebombs."

Mina frowned. "They seem to have stopped."

"Because they've sent in the steelcoats. Listen."

She strained to hear, beyond the birds and the distant rumble of the collapsing compound. There was a regular rhythm, like heavy footsteps all moving in sync. The sound sent unease trembling through her belly.

Trahaearn rolled his shoulders, as if loosening stiff muscles. "I'm going to see where Yasmeen's gone. Stay put."

Moving quietly for such a big man, he vanished around the steel door. He returned a moment later, his jaw tight.

"She's over the forest. Not far. A two-hundred-yard run."

Through the forest. She swallowed hard before nodding.

"And inspector . . ." He strode forward and stared down at her, his gaze fierce. "You *run*. Because I am not taking a zombie into my bed."

Mina's mouth dropped open, and he bent his head as if to kiss her. She jammed her gun barrel under his chin. He grinned.

And stepped back. "I'll be behind you. Don't stop for anything."

No stopping. She drew a deep breath. Another. With her hand, she verified the direction, saw his nod. And she took off.

She immediately spotted the balloon, so bright and white through the leaves. Racing toward it, she dodged trees that blended together, imagining every one a zombie with clawing hands until their shapes resolved into trunks and branches. Everything was loud, her heartbeat, the airship engines, the crash of her feet though the grass and the brambles, and the Iron Duke behind her. Would the zombies hiss and growl? Would she even hear them before their teeth were tearing pieces from her? Lungs burning, she sprinted through a small tree-less glade, where the knee-high dried grass wanted to wrap around her ankles, and though her feet burned she was glad of her boots, because after the Horde had turned so many creatures of the sea into monsters, the stars alone knew what they might have done to the animals on land. Unless the zombies had eaten them all. With no people left to kill, they must be consuming something.

Hopefully they'd started eating each other.

Another cluster of trees, and then she burst through into another glade, and there was the cargo platform, waiting ten feet above the grass. She heard a shout from above and the platform fell to the ground with a clank. She leapt aboard, heart racing, chest heaving.

The airship's engines huffed and hissed. The platform lifted from the ground. Her scream *Not yet!* was lost in the noise. She spun to look for Trahaearn.

Terror gripped her in an icy claw. He was crossing the glen at a dead run, two zombies racing in from the sides, streaked with gore and their hungry visages too terrible to believe. Trahaearn met her eyes—and dropped his machetes.

Through her shock and horror, she understood. He couldn't jump and catch on to the platform with weapons in his hands. And if he stopped to kill the zombies, to wait for the platform to lower again, more would come. She could see them through the trees now, running, so *fast*.

Mina braced her feet. He couldn't stop them.

So she would.

Rhys saw the inspector's weapon come up, and hoped she had decent aim, or she'd soon be putting a bullet into his brain, too.

Her gun cracked once, twice. The cargo lift had almost raised her over his head.

Leaping up, he snagged the chain. His stomach slammed into the edge of the platform, half his body still dangling over the side. Fighting the hot pain that threatened to swamp his vision, he swung his leg up and hauled himself aboard. He looked down. The zombies were twitching on the ground.

He collapsed onto his back and laughed, which pulled like hell at his gut—but at least he wasn't going to end up in a zombie's.

The inspector stared down at him. "You've gone mad!"

Maybe he had. He'd never tossed away his weapons before, and rarely put his life in someone else's hands. "I weighed chances that you'd miss against the odds that Yasmeen would leave me here. I chose the right one . . . and I'm glad you didn't miss."

She smiled a little, and he liked watching that sweet curve form on her lips. If he wasn't tasting her mouth, then looking at it was the next best thing.

"But if she left you, you couldn't pay her," the inspector said.

He got to his feet. "She doesn't need me now. She has eight boys aboard that she could hold for ransom."

That surprised a laugh out of her. Rhys's gut twisted again, but with possession and need and a deep emotion that had formed in the dark chambers of the fort. Admiration made up some of it. She had balls of steel, this woman. But there was more, too—and he wanted all of it. *Needed* all of it, all of her. But what he had now was looking, and so he took in his fill.

The black roll of hair at her nape had lost its pins somewhere between the first explosion and the third, and fell in a tangle to her waist. Without her long wool overcoat, he could see the modest layers of lace sewn to the back of her trousers, as if the ruffles could conceal the perfect shape of her ass. Her short coat fastened to her throat and nipped in at her narrow waist, and suggested that she had no tits to speak of under those buckles and her armor, but a little mouthful would be enough, her nipples against his tongue—as soon as he got those buckles open.

The first opportunity he got, Rhys was going to shag her blind.

That wouldn't be now. The platform rose into place beside the weather deck. Rhys helped the inspector over the rail—she was still shaking a little. Christ Jesus, he was amazed she didn't scream and cry. He could only see a few bruises and cuts, but Rhys felt like he'd been beaten all over; she probably felt just as ragged.

Yasmeen had already picked up speed, flying west—keeping out of range of the navy ships. They'd gone far enough that the forest obscured the fort from view, though the smoke rising above it marked the location.

He held on to the inspector's hand and pulled her along to the quarterdeck. Unwilling to let her go just yet, he ignored her tugging—but he couldn't ignore how she was looking around, her gaze panicked and searching.

He needed to take that fear away for her, then.

Yasmeen turned to him. Before she could vent the fury he saw in her eyes, he had to know, "Did her constable make it aboard?"

His inspector stilled, waiting, and closed her eyes with relief when Yasmeen snapped, "What? Yes—they're all below decks. And those bluecoat bilgewater trouts *fired on me* without a single fucking flag!"

Rhys frowned and looked toward the ships. Ten years ago, they wouldn't have given Rhys on the *Terror* any warning, either—but even though Yasmeen was well-known as a mercenary and had a deadly reputation, she wasn't a pirate. She hadn't broken English law. Unless she'd fired on them or posed an immediate threat, *Lady Corsair* should have been treated the same as a civilian or merchant vessel: signaled and given an opportunity to surrender.

Brow furrowed, the inspector shook her head. "Why would they fire on the airship or the fort? They had to have known about the ransom demand and the possibility that the boys were here."

Rhys could only imagine one reason for such a response. "Unless they knew about the auctioned weapon, too," he said. "If they had enough information to link the *Terror* to the auction, and the Dame to the *Terror*, they might have come up with a weapon that can kill every bugger within two hundred miles sitting just thirty miles from English shores."

"Even if the Dame didn't have it?"

"They wouldn't have taken the risk of finding out. But now they'll be wishing they had."

Against such a threat, the lives of eight young men would have been an acceptable cost. To placate the merchant families, their deaths would be painted as a noble sacrifice, the blame laid at the Dame's feet—and no one would have known that the weapon hadn't actually been at the fort.

But the boys' rescue had changed that. And both the merchants and the public wouldn't just see their rescue as an escape from the Dame, but a narrow escape from an overreaction by the Royal Navy.

The inspector seemed to be coming to the same realization. "Whatever their intentions, this will not reflect kindly on them. They fired on that fort knowing the boys might be there—and that *you* were there. There are few people in England who will accept that they intended to sacrifice the Iron Duke, no matter the size of the threat."

Yasmeen's brows arched. She looked to him for an explanation, and he returned the look with a gesture that said he'd catch her up to speed soon—particularly as he'd be needing her services again.

She nodded and asked the inspector, "How could they have known he was on my ship?"

"Newberry sent an update to Hale from Chatham. She'd have passed that on to the Admiralty."

"They might have launched the ships from Dover before receiving it."

Yasmeen was right: The timing would have been close. But with such a cock-up, the navy might be looking to cover it up—and he didn't want to be thrown under when they did. Especially as his inspector and *Lady Corsair* would be thrown under with him.

He said to Yasmeen, "Keep a wide berth around the ships, then fly north into London."

"And let them shoot me down over town? We can't know that they've received the message that you're on board . . . and now they might believe I'm carrying some kind of weapon from the fort into London."

Even if they didn't believe it, that would be the perfect method of concealing their blunder. "Stop over Ashford's wiregram station. We'll send grams to the parents, police headquarters, and the news-sheets that *Lady Corsair* has their children aboard."

"And you," the inspector added.

He nodded. "You'll tether the ship over the Embankment near Westminster Palace, and we'll tell them to meet with us there."

A bell from the stern chimed. Even as he and Yasmeen looked around, the airship shuddered, and a deep rumble sounded over the roar of the engines.

He looked to the inspector, whose lips had parted as she stared at the enormous black cloud rising over the fort, tall enough that it would be seen from Dover.

She swallowed and appeared slightly faint. "The boiler?"

"Yes." He sure as hell wouldn't have made her run through a forest full of zombies for any other reason. "So will you tell me what to call you now?"

She blinked in confusion, but her gaze quickly sharpened and her lips curved. "How does 'grateful' sound, sir?"

Her smile took a good hold of him, wrapped Rhys right up into her fingers. It wasn't comfortable, but tight and constricting. He'd accept that—but only if he got a hold on her in return.

"Not good enough," he said.

"Then you will have to keep making do with 'inspector.' "

He wouldn't, but he pushed aside his frustration. He'd know more of her soon. He'd know *all* of her soon. With a sharp nod, he turned to the ladders leading below decks. "Let us go find your constable, then."

* * *

Newberry waited outside the door to the wardroom, as if standing guard over the boys taking their meal inside—which meant that he didn't think much of them. If he'd liked their company, he'd have been standing inside the cabin, instead.

His composure slipped when he spotted Mina. Last night a dress, today her hair down and stripped of her overcoat. His whole world must seem to be falling apart.

She stopped in front of him. A faint bruise darkened his cheekbone and his bottom lip was swollen. Those weren't from any explosion. Those were from fists . . . and the reason he didn't wait inside the wardroom?

If so, she'd toss those boys to the zombies herself. But she'd find out what had caused those bruises before she gave her temper free rein.

"You made it all right, then?"

"Yes, sir." With a nod, Newberry regained his stiff upper lip. "The aviators must have been watching from the airship. After I pulled the first boy up, Lady Corsair sent down a man with a rope ladder. It speeded the process, and we were aboard before the navy fired the first bomb."

"Then why is your mouth swollen, constable?"

He stared straight ahead—which was well over Mina's head. "After I had the boys aboard, I tried to return to the compound, sir. Lady Corsair prevented me."

After the firebombing started? He'd have been blown to pieces. Though it was difficult to get into the face of a man who stood a foot taller than Mina, she did it. When his stoic gaze lowered to meet hers, she snapped, "You tried to return against my orders, constable? *I said to await me here.*"

"Yes, sir. You did. I apologize for my insubordination, sir."

That apology was bunk. She narrowed her eyes, but backed down. "Your apology is noted and will be taken under consideration."

"Yes, sir." He paused. "It took six of her men to stop me, sir."

Pride filled her chest. *Good man*. She turned away to conceal her reaction, and found herself meeting Trahaearn's steady dark eyes. *Damn him*. Why did he always seem to be trying to see into her, down to her bones?

She would not let him see how that unsettled her. She knew his intentions. He wanted to bed her. But if she valued her family, if she valued *herself*, then his bed could never be an option.

Mina looked to the wardroom door. "And how do the young gentlemen fare, constable?"

"Mostly hungry, sir. Evans apparently neglected them in favor of the sick crew and the Dame."

"And your impressions of them, Newberry?" When his gaze flickered to the Iron Duke, she said, "Speak freely, please. I doubt that His Grace will run to tell their fathers."

"They don't seem long out of the schoolyard, sir. Not just their age, but that they look to Mr. Wright as their leader. They take their cues from him." He paused, as if giving it another thought. "Three of them aren't so bad."

So over half of them were brats. At least that solved the mystery of why Newberry stood outside—and unless they had something worth telling her about Andrew or the *Terror*, she would not be long, either. All that she wanted was something to drink, and a place to remove her boots while she let the burns and blisters heal.

"Thank you, constable. You may go above decks, if you wish. We're returning to London. The two hours between here and there are your own."

She opened the door and immediately saw the group formation Newberry had noted. When she entered, each boy at the table looked up at her—and then four glanced to the face of the handsome, dark-haired boy sitting nearest to her. Mr. Wright, she presumed. The three at the opposite end of the table shifted their focus behind her, instead—which told her that Trahaearn must have stepped through the door. He came to her side, and she felt him there, big and imposing, but she didn't look over at him.

"Gentlemen," she said. "I am Detective Inspector Wentworth of the Metropolitan Police Force. I see that you've been given something to eat. Is there anything else that you need? Have any of you injuries that need to be seen to?"

"We're fine," Wright spoke for them all, and looked to Trahaearn. "Are those bastards dead?"

"Most of them succumbed to bug fever," Mina answered. No need to mention now that Evans had escaped with the Dame in his harvester. "We believe Dame Sawtooth will, too."

Wright's jaw clenched. That answer wasn't good enough for him—and Mina supposed she couldn't blame him. In his place, she'd have probably wished to hear that her kidnappers had been shot or killed in the bombing, rather than succumbing to an illness.

Maybe he'd be satisfied if she told him that bug fever was a far worse way to die.

A boy from the end of the table spoke up. "Was the Royal Navy firing on us?"

"We believe they had misinformation regarding the events surrounding your kidnapping. Will you tell me what you remember of the incident?"

They told her—but there was little she hadn't already heard. The pirates from *Bontemps* had boarded *Marco's Terror* before dawn six days ago, and most of the boys had slept through the ensuing fight. Afterward, the pirates had taken them up to *Bontemps*, and they'd been locked in a cabin during the demonstration. Haynes hadn't met with the English fleet, they didn't know the exact location of the *Terror* when she'd been taken, and they didn't know where she was headed.

Mina held back her sigh, and shared a look of frustration with Trahaearn. This wasn't the boys' fault, but she'd hoped for more.

"Evans said that he felt a thump against his chest during the explosion," she said. "Did any of you feel it?"

They all nodded.

She couldn't quite contain her surprise. "Are any of you infected?"

A few looked mildly horrified by her question. They all shook their heads. She tried not to feel disappointed. She hadn't expected otherwise.

"Were there any other sailors or officers from the *Terror* with you? Perhaps someone who developed bug fever on the way?"

Again, the answer was no. *Damn it.* But perhaps one of them knew *something*.

"There was a boy on the *Terror*—the Earl of Rockingham's son, Andrew Wentworth. Did any of you know him?"

They looked to each other, their surprise obvious.

"No," Wright said.

"Fourteen years of age, blond hair." She pointed to the boy across from Wright. "As tall as you. He was a midshipman."

There was a shocked silence—then hoots of laughter from all around.

Wright shook his head. "An earl's son, a midshipman? You're codding us."

"No, no! You!" Another boy slapped the table, then pointed to Mina, wide-eyed. "She's the one I told you all about. Her mother's the blind countess who bent Oedipal when—"

"She saw her Horde bastard! So this midshipman is the son of the cuckold earl?" Wright crowed, laughing and shaking his head. With his fingers at the corners of his eyes, he stretched them into slits. "We didn't know anyone who looked like—"

He broke off suddenly, his face paling. The other boys weren't looking to Mina anymore, laughing, but to the man beside her.

"Leave the cabin, inspector."

Trahaearn's soft command sent crackles of ice down her spine. Sudden bursts of noise ricocheted through the room. Pleas of "No!" and "Wait!" Chairs scraped the floor as half the boys jumped to their feet, their hands out—in apology or surrender.

"I'm not finished here, Your Grace." Still, she didn't look at him. Her face was hot. Her heart beat with sickening thuds. "Did *any* of you see my brother? Fourteen. Blond." She focused on the closest boy. "You?"

His skin flushed a dull red. "No. Or if I did, I didn't notice."

"Anyone else?"

Petrified with their eyes on the duke, only half responded with a shake of their head.

Trahaearn barked, "Anyone?"

This time there was a chorus of *Nos* and heads whipping back and forth like monkey drums.

Mina nodded. "Thank you, gentlemen."

She tried to escape quickly, but he caught her in the corridor, slamming his hand against the bulkhead in front of her and blocking her way. She stared over the gate of his left arm. Her feet hurt. She wanted to sit. She didn't want to do *this*.

But there was one thing she needed to say.

"Thank you for defending my family's honor, Your Grace."

With light fingers, he brushed hair away from her face. She heard his deep sigh. "What do you need, inspector?"

Would he care for a list? But she couldn't even drum that up. A better question: What could she have now?

"A cabin where I can be alone," she said. "A washbasin, cold water, and hairpins."

"I'll see that you get them." But he didn't yet leave her. "Why wasn't your brother taken to *Bontemps*? He had to know that if he told the Dame who he was, she would take him to ransom."

Yes, he'd known. And her father had ordered Andrew to take that option if the need ever arose—but it wasn't supposed to have arisen. *Marco's Terror* should have been the safest ship in the Royal Navy, always surrounded by a fleet, never straying into uncertain waters. Mina didn't know how many letters her father had written or favors he'd asked to make certain that Andrew was assigned to that ship. But they'd all been for naught, and that stupid, *stupid* boy hadn't spoken up and said who he was.

"He knew we couldn't pay the ransom. And he knew what we'd do to raise the money."

"And what is that?"

"Whatever it took. And the most expedient way would be for my mother to break her contract with the Blacksmith, and sell her automata directly instead of through his shops. Andrew knew that— and he knew that the Blacksmith would take her eyes back if we did."

He didn't respond for a long second. "Wouldn't it occur to your family to ask the Blacksmith for a reprieve?"

Was he joking? She looked up at him. He was frowning, his dark gaze serious. She couldn't believe it.

"And warn the Blacksmith of what we planned to do? Why not tear out her eyes ourselves and hand them over?"

His eyes narrowed. "You lived beneath Horde rule for too long."

Her laugh broke from her. Perhaps in another world, it was easy to trust that someone wouldn't hurt them, given the opportunity. Perhaps it was easy to owe someone, despite knowing that the balance of your life rested on that debt.

"You have a talent for understatement, sir."

Smiling, he lowered his arm. "I'll find your cabin and pins, inspector."

He turned to go. She stopped him with, "Who is Hunt?"

His shoulders stiffened. In all of this time, though they'd spoken of almost nothing but the *Terror* and the circumstances in which she'd been taken, he hadn't mentioned Hunt to her, as if avoiding the topic. She was almost afraid to know why, but had to ask.

"Who is he, and what does it mean for the *Terror*'s crew?"

"He was Adams's first lieutenant before the mutiny." His hand curled into a fist at his thigh. "After I killed Adams, I deserted him with the other officers—but I should have killed Hunt, too."

"Why?"

He didn't answer. He said instead, "The ship needs a crew. Hunt will keep those who are useful to him."

But that would be good for Andrew. So why wouldn't he look at her? "Isn't a midshipman useful?"

"Yes. In one way or another."

Dread climbed up her throat. "What does that mean?"

"It means that at the Ivory Market, a fourteen-year-old boy *always* has a use." He looked over his shoulder, and she saw his anger, his hatred—then all were masked by cold detachment. "It only depends on which use Hunt thought would be worth more."

Chapter Eight

Though Mina had half expected that the duke wouldn't let her be after she'd been granted the use of a cabin, he left her alone. She sat on a narrow bed with her boots off, trying not to let her sick worry for Andrew overwhelm her, until the blue skies and white clouds outside the porthole turned to a flat, dull gray.

She went above decks, satisfied that her short coat lay as straight as could be, that she'd scrubbed the smoke from her face and rubbed her boots to a dull shine, that even a hurricane couldn't loosen the coil of hair at her nape. Without her overcoat, the wind immediately set her to shivering. She'd be damned if she'd let it show, though. She nodded to the duke and the airship captain on the quarterdeck, and joined Newberry, who stood with the cluster of boys near the cargo platform, and who formed a sufficient windbreak.

As always, barges and boats crowded the Thames, and the bridges were in full use. From this vantage point, the Southwark slums were a smoking ruin, with only a few buildings left inhabitable. The Horde's tower appeared small and broken—and old Westminster Palace not much better off. The Embankment looked an eyesore. Intended as a new roadway along the north bank of the Thames, the revolution had brought a halt to the Horde project before the construction had been half-finished. Visible girders and struts poked through the foundation, and piles of rubble and muck dotted the bank. But it hadn't been a complete loss. The intended road surface was used as a gravel walk, and trees had been planted along the way to ameliorate the ugliness of it. A few areas had been designated as gardens, featuring lawns and tended flower beds, and provided a pleasant detour whenever Mina had reason to walk in that direction.

The muscles of her neck ached from trying not to shiver, yet she tensed further when Trahaearn drew next to her. The warmth of his breath near her ear only made the rest of her seem colder.

"We're in luck there's no fog," he said. "Yasmeen would be just as likely to dump us in the river as in that garden."

A garden chock-full of people waited. Unless one of them was Superintendent Hale, Mina would not be staying. She would get through them as quickly as possible.

"Yes, Your Grace," she said, and although she felt his gaze upon her, didn't look at him. On the cargo platform, she didn't let him maneuver close, but slipped behind Newberry to stand on the constable's opposite side.

The platform slowly lowered, landing gently on the grass. Young men and parents surged together, blocking easy exit. Sighing, she looked past Newberry to Trahaearn, who did not seem in a hurry to get off—though for once he wasn't staring at her. Mina glanced up.

Lady Corsair had slid down the platform's chains, stopping twenty feet above their heads. Braids dangling, she hung almost upside down and blew a kiss to someone on the ground. A man had joined Trahaearn at the edge of the platform, and he stared up at her laughing, his hand over his heart. Scarsdale, Mina recognized.

"I love you, Yasmeen!"

The mercenary grinned. "Will you marry me, then?"

"Will you come down from the sky?"

"For the likes of you? Never."

Scarsdale laughed again and finally lowered his gaze to the duke's.

Though Trahaearn's didn't speak loudly, his voice carried to Mina well enough. "Hunt has the *Terror*."

The expression that flickered over Scarsdale's face erased the frivolity, left an emotion cold and predatory. It was gone again as he looked up to Lady Corsair. "So we'll be seeing you tomorrow morning, then? It seems we have a ship to catch."

"If you have enough gold, we'll see." She began climbing back up. "You'd all best be off my platform when I reach my lady's decks."

So they would be leaving tomorrow to find the *Terror*. One bright bit of news, to help Mina through the remainder of a day that would surely be hell. She turned to go.

"You're not leaving, inspector."

Unable to ignore that voice, she paused and faced Trahaearn from across the platform. "Yes, Your Grace, I am. I must report to my superior. Thank you for your assistance today. I wish you well on your journey."

His face darkened. Scarsdale glanced at him, at Mina, and rattled the platform chain with a kick of his booted foot.

"I say, captain, Yasmeen will dump you off soon."

The duke's brows came together. He frowned at the other man.

Scarsdale continued with a nod to the crowd. "Look there. That bushy codger in the mustard coat is old Munro, who's been thumbing his nose at your Australian line and sending his cotton out on Harbor's boats. Seeing as you've just rescued his grandson, I say we let his gratitude make the both of us richer men. Can't waste an opportunity like this."

And Trahaearn didn't waste opportunities, Mina remembered.

"I'll leave you to it, sir." With a short nod to them both, Mina turned and slipped through the crowd, avoiding anyone who looked the least bit ragged, anyone with the sharp and hungry eye of a newsman. If Trahaearn came after her, no hope of avoiding them . . . but though her heart pounded, the only giant following her was Newberry.

"That old codger's not one to waste an opportunity, is he?"

Scarsdale's slurred comment didn't require a response. Well

on his way to drunk, he slouched in the steamcoach's bench, still celebrating—and preparing himself for tomorrow morning. The bounder hadn't boarded an airship conscious for years, but with Hunt as their prey, Scarsdale might try. Conscious, but he'd still need to be three sheets to the wind. It'd take him a while to get to that point, however . . . whereas Rhys was trying to shake off the effects of one brandy raised to his honor.

And he'd wasted too many hours on Munro. On the *Terror*, he'd often sailed out of a port on a moment's notice. But even though Rhys had a capable staff under him, he couldn't do the same now. He'd have to work through the night to have everything in order for his departure, and this agreement with Munro had just added another item to the list.

He glanced at the traffic out the window as the steamcoach idled again. Not even past the Banqueting House yet. At this rate, driving out to the island would take another two or three hours, too. *All right.* He could use this time to start making that list, or he could lean his head back, close his eyes, and imagine how his inspector would display her gratitude when he returned with her brother.

She'd only just unbuttoned his breeches when Scarsdale said, "The Admiralty will be out for your blood."

Rhys sighed and opened his eyes, wishing that the bounder prattled when drunk. Then he could have ignored the man and carried on. But although soused, Scarsdale remained sharp as a cutlass.

"They've always been out for it," Rhys said. With good reason. No matter how bad a captain Adams had been, a mutiny couldn't be tolerated. Their failure to recapture *Marco's Terror* had been another blow, as had every piece of cargo Rhys had taken from English ships while captaining her. No one despised his pardon and title more than the Board of Admiralty.

"But they've never had to pretend an alliance with you—and depend on your silence to keep up that pretense."

Rhys had to grin at that. They'd learned from Munro that even before *Lady Corsair* had passed into London, the navy had already been spreading the story that the attack on the Dame's fort had been a joint effort between himself and the Royal Navy. Rhys had led the rescue while they'd bombarded the fort to destroy the weapon.

He hadn't contradicted the story. Never before had the navy been beholden to him, but he hadn't yet decided how they would pay for it. For now, he was simply pleased that the opportunity was there if he wanted to take advantage of it.

Scarsdale tipped his bottle up and grimaced at the small amount in the bottom. A look out of the coach made him groan. "I'll be sober again by the time we—" He broke off, squinting. "I say, isn't that the inspector's man?"

Rhys glanced out. By the light of the gas lamps lining the street, he recognized Newberry's unmistakable bulk seated on the bench of his rattle-trap cart. Parked along the walk not far from police headquarters, but not even idling. No steam wafted from the vents. Waiting then.

For the inspector? It was well past eight o'clock. She ought to have been home. Frowning, Rhys rapped on the ceiling of the coach. Jumping out into traffic was only slightly less harrowing than sprinting through a zombie forest, but Rhys made it to the cart in one piece.

The constable straightened when he saw Rhys's approach. Hope seemed to brighten his expression.

What the hell did he need to hope for?

Rhys glanced toward the headquarters building. "Is the inspector still in there?"

"Yes, Your Grace."

"Then why are you out here?"

"I'm under orders to go home, sir. But my standing orders are not to let her go home unescorted. And so I'm on my way home. I simply stopped for a bit of air."

And was waiting for the inspector to walk by, Rhys realized. "Why wasn't she ordered to go home?"

She'd been bruised, burned. The bugs would heal her, but she'd still be feeling the toll that the escape from the fort had taken on her body. Hell, even Rhys was still feeling it.

"They're still debating whether to strip her of rank for insubordination and for interfering with a naval operation, sir, or to relieve her of duty."

Rhys stilled. Rage spiked through him, cold and hard. Slowly, he met the man's eyes. "Go on home, Newberry. I'll see that she's escorted."

The constable nodded, and for an instant Rhys saw the ferocity beneath the friendly, houndlike features.

"Thank you, sir."

"You allowed a man possessing illegal Horde technology to walk past you and assassinate an admiral of the Royal Navy. You boarded the ship of a known mercenary. You left England's shores and your jurisdiction without waiting for approval from your superiors. You ignored obvious indications that a naval operation was in progress. You displayed gross insubordination resulting in rampant failure across the board, inspector, and you cannot explain yourself to my satisfaction. Do you admit that you failed to apprehend both Jasper Evans and Marguerite Bonnet, and allowed them to escape in a *war* machine?"

England, Mina decided, could use fewer damn dukes shoving their faces into hers and demanding answers. And this one had no greater authority over her than Trahaearn did. The Duke of Dorchester was the Lord High Admiral of England, but he was not her superior, and he would *not* be deciding whether she would be relieved of duty or reprimanded. That decision lay with Superintendent Hale and the police commissioner, Sir John Broyles—both of whom had already heard her report. Repeatedly heard it, now that the Lord High Admiral had arrived at the commissioner's office and demanded to hear it again.

"Yes, Your Grace. Evans escaped in his tree harvester, and although I did not see her, I believe that Bonnet was inside, as well."

Beneath his white hair, Dorchester's dark blue eyes appeared hard as steel. All of him was like steel, thin and sharp-edged as a sword held on end. "Along with the weapon purchased in an Ivory Market auction."

"He didn't have the weapon—"

"Did you see the interior of that tank, inspector?"

"No, sir. An exploding firebomb from the nearby ships damaged the chamber ceiling, and I was not able to venture close to the machine."

She probably shouldn't have mentioned the ships or the firebombs. Dorchester's face turned florid, and he began to cough, which seemed to enrage him further.

Broyles's heavy jowl and bushy dark brows always gave the impression of anger, but Mina recognized the long-suffering expression on the commissioner's features as he put in, "Your Grace, the inspector had been given leave by this office to investigate the matter to its fullest extent, but we do not encourage our officers to put themselves at unnecessary risk. Even armed, she could not have stopped that machine without incredible danger to her person."

Dorchester latched onto one phrase. Never taking his eyes from Mina's face, he said, "You must agree that she took more leave than given, commissioner."

"No, sir. As had been ordered, she sent regular updates to this office. The Metropolitan Police Force has no argument with the steps she took in the progress of her investigation."

Dorchester's gaze narrowed on Mina. "Did you update this office after observing the flotilla headed for Calais?"

"It was impossible to send a gram from the airship, sir—"

"Then you should have turned around and waited for instruction!"

The response from behind Mina came from a voice both familiar and unwelcome. "She wasn't in charge of the airship. I was."

Oh, no. When had the Iron Duke come in? Mina wanted to close her eyes. Perhaps Trahaearn wanted to help, but he couldn't have said anything worse.

Those steely blue eyes flicked away from her face, and registered surprise before hardening again. Trahaearn must have just entered the room if Dorchester was only now noticing him, too.

"Thank you for your input, Anglesey. If you were in command, it clearly demonstrates that she lost control of her investigation."

She would not stand for that. "No, sir. I believe what Anglesey means is that he paid for the use of *Lady Corsair*. I was told to use all avenues available to me in order to identify Haynes's murderers, and apprehending them, if possible. At all times, my objective aligned with the duke's, and I remained in pursuit of the Dame until pursuit became physically impossible. The investigation was never out of my control."

Dorchester's brows rose. "Is this true, Anglesey? You'd have let this inspector order you about?"

Tension gripped her, angry and hot. The bastard. That wasn't at all what she'd said, and he knew it. And no man as arrogant as the Iron Duke would let it be thought that—

"It's true." Amusement filled Trahaearn's response—and infuriated Dorchester, Mina saw. A muscle began to tick in his jaw. "After observing her investigative talents and the speed with which she identified Haynes, I trusted that Inspector Wentworth knew what she was about. I'd have done anything she asked of me."

Oh, sweet heavens. To Mina's ears, that last statement couldn't have possibly sounded more suggestive. Perhaps only to her, however. Mina didn't dare glance at Hale.

Unwilling to let Trahaearn steer him off course, Dorchester zeroed in on Mina again. "And so you *could* have ordered the airship to turn around, inspector."

On this point, Mina would never back down. "No, sir. I could not. Above and beyond my duty to investigate Haynes's murder is my duty to protect English citizens. I knew that the Dame was likely holding eight young men at her fort. When we saw the ships and the steelcoats, I formed the opinion that the marines planned to invade the fort in order to retrieve the Dame's hostages. I received information from the Duke of Anglesey that led me to believe that should an invading force be used, the young men would be murdered by the Dame."

"You assumed that I had ordered the flotilla to recover the hostages?" Blue eyes narrowed. "I see. You did not assume that after the Admiralty learned Haynes's nanoagents had been destroyed, that we might have linked it to a weapons auction in the Ivory Market. Or that when the Dame's ransom demands confirmed that she'd taken *Marco's Terror*, we had reason to be concerned that she'd also brought the auctioned weapon from the Ivory Market, to within spitting distance of this nation's shores. And you did not assume that we had sent the Royal Navy's ships to protect England. You thought we'd attacked like dogs when the merchants whistled."

The quiet anger burning in Dorchester's gaze seemed genuine, and Mina had to admit she'd been wrong. Baxter was not the only admiral who put the interests of England above the merchants.

But although she'd thought exactly what he'd accused her of, sometimes it was prudent to lie.

"No, sir. I assumed that your objective was the same as mine: to protect English citizens. It's true that I lacked information regarding this weapon, information that the Admiralty was obviously in possession of, and so I misinterpreted the flotilla's objective. Now that I understand that your orders to the flotilla had not been to rescue the boys, but to destroy the weapon and the fort, I admit that I assumed wrongly. But I *cannot* regret my decision to continue on to the fort and attempt to save the lives of eight English citizens."

Dorchester's face paled with anger, his nostrils pinched and thin. "And your presumptuous actions demonstrate a dangerous lack of restraint and good judgment, inspector. You needlessly risked the life of a peer and of the constable under your authority. Commissioner Broyles, I *strongly* recommend that the inspector receives the severest disciplinary action."

Broyles nodded. "Your suggestion will be taken under advisement. Be assured that Detective Inspector Wentworth's actions will undergo a rigorous review."

"Very good, sir." With another hard stare at Mina, Dorchester turned his attention to Trahaearn. "And I will remind you, Anglesey, that *Marco's Terror* is His Majesty's ship. Your interest in her situation is neither warranted nor wanted."

Mina's lips parted. Without leave to move from her post in front of Broyles's desk, she couldn't look around to see Trahaearn's reaction—but Hale's said it well enough. The superintendent's alarm and indecision was clear, as if two bulls were about to lock horns in front of her, and she wasn't certain whether to step between them or to get out of their way.

But Trahaearn only said, "I will also take your suggestion under advisement, Dorchester."

If the Lord High Admiral meant to respond, a cough got the better of him. His hacking coughs continued until Mina heard the door close behind him.

Broyles shook his head. "Imperious bloody bounders."

Hale's brows rose. "Sir?"

"No offense to you, Hale."

The wry, thin-lipped smile Hale gave him said that none had been taken, but still managed to chastise him for the comment. Broyles's lips twitched before he looked to Mina.

"Inspector Wentworth, your actions *will* be taken under review, and statements collected from everyone involved. But upon these initial reports already received from Superintendent Hale, the Chatham police, the Admiralty, Constable Newberry, the heads of several prominent families, and the comments from His Grace"—he tipped his head toward Trahaearn—"this office is not dissatisfied with your performance today, inspector."

Even as Mina's throat tightened, some of the tension drained from her muscles. "Thank you, sir."

Leaning back, he steepled his fingers. "And I do not appreciate that the Admiralty is trying to save face at the expense of my officer's. By your account, you'd have apprehended both Evans and Dame Sawtooth had the fort not begun coming down around your head."

"By my account, too," Trahaearn said behind her. "She'd all but convinced Evans that the Dame could be saved with a physician's attention. Given a few more minutes, she'd have had him carrying Dame Sawtooth to the airship himself."

"Thank you, sir." Broyles nodded before looking to Mina again. "And had it not been for your presence at the admiral's residence in Chatham, I believe that his murderer would not only remain unidentified, but would have fled rather than commit suicide. Frankly, inspector, a dead murderer that no one can identify is better than one who remains unidentified and continues walking English streets."

"The credit for that belongs to the duke, sir."

"Take it if you can, inspector, because it is all that you will get. You haven't yet heard, but the official story from the Board of Admiralty is that you were under the command of the Iron Duke, who acted in conjunction with the navy." *Now* Broyles was angry. His jowls shook when his jaw tightened. "And this office has decided it is not worth the bad blood between our agencies if we insist on the truth."

Sickened, Mina looked to Hale for confirmation. The superintendent nodded.

All right, then. She didn't relish the thought of public recognition, anyway. All that mattered was that her superiors knew the truth of it. "Very well, sir."

Broyles leaned forward. "Those within the force will know who brought those boys home, inspector. They'll know why the Dame and Evans aren't in a cell at Newgate. We won't make an issue of it. But we'll know."

"Thank you, sir." She swallowed, then said, "Sir, regarding Baxter's assassin, I must put forth that 'unidentified and dead' is not enough. The device he used suggests that he acted under orders, and so although he pulled the trigger, he was not the admiral's murderer.

If the case is stamped closed, I fear *that* person—or group—will continue to go about unidentified and walking English streets."

"I share your concern, inspector. But without concrete evidence linking Baxter's murder to Haynes's, we don't have justification to take the case out of Chatham's hands. Now that we have evidence of a freezing device, however, we will look more closely at rumors of the Black Guard."

As he spoke, Broyles looked squarely toward the Iron Duke, but whether Trahaearn felt the commissioner's unspoken admonition for having had one of the devices and not bringing it to police attention, Mina didn't know.

After a moment, Broyles's attention returned to Mina. "Your brother is serving on *Marco's Terror*, isn't he? The young one. Not Henry."

This time, the tightening of her throat almost choked her. "Andrew. Yes, sir."

"Then I suppose facing Dorchester was easier than the task before you." With a heavy sigh, he sank a little deeper into his seat. "Go home and tell your parents, inspector."

When the Iron Duke caught up with her on the main floor, Mina was formulating how best to thank him and then dismiss him. He stopped her with, "I promised Newberry that I would escort you home."

And so she was well and trapped. She might as well make the best of it, and discover whether he still planned to pursue the *Terror*. "Has the Lord High Admiral's warning dissuaded you from leaving tomorrow?"

His deep laugh was the only answer he gave—and the one she'd hoped to hear. It continued as they left the building. Across the crush of traffic on Whitehall, light still shone from several windows in the Admiralty building. They were usually all darkened by this time.

Mina started for the familiar steamcoach waiting by the walk.

"Dorchester was furious with me," she said, "but it was only aimed at my investigation. His anger toward you was personal. Do you have a history?"

"I've never met him before, but the mutiny is reason enough. And I've deserted countless naval officers, taken gold and cargo, made fools of them as they escorted merchant ships—"

"Killed them?"

"When a navy ship came up on me looking to sink the *Terror* or to take my crew to hang, I fired back. Men died on both sides." He paused as the driver hopped down from his bench and opened the carriage door. His gaze met hers. "Unlike Broyles, I'm not hobbled by fear of bad blood—there's already plenty of it between me and the Admiralty. And if you want recognition, I'll stir it up."

And probably enjoy stirring it, too. "I'd prefer not to be at the center of it, in truth."

Smiling slightly, he nodded. "Then I'll trade my silence for the *Terror*."

He intended to strong-arm the Admiralty? And he probably could, she realized. The navy's story hinged on the Iron Duke not contradicting them, giving him the perfect opportunity to reclaim his ship.

And yet he'd had given up that opportunity if she'd wanted recognition.

A queer little ache formed in her chest. Not knowing how to respond, she moved out from under that dark gaze, turning to board the steamcoach. As she stepped up, Scarsdale leaned forward from his bench and took Mina's hand, guiding her to the rear-facing seat across from him.

"My apologies for not giving up the prime spot, inspector. If I sit backward, I'll puke."

Judging by the empty bottle next to him, it would be a good amount of liquor that came up. Trahaearn climbed in. He looked to the space next to his friend before prudently choosing the seat beside Mina.

"Leicester Square, Fitzhop!" Scarsdale called through the carriage door, then glanced at Mina. "Number Eight?"

Mina's brows rose. "Yes." When he finished giving the direction to the driver, she said, "You're well-informed, Lord Scarsdale."

"It gives me a purpose, now that the captain has no other use for me." He looked from Mina to Trahaearn, then to Mina again. "So are you coming with us to find the *Terror*, then?"

To see Andrew safe with her own eyes? Yearning speared through her, but Mina shook her head. "It's impossible. And even if it was not, I know nothing of the Ivory Market or locating a ship on the high seas. I wouldn't be of any help to you."

"Of help, no. But it would prove wildly entertaining."

Perhaps, but her family couldn't live on entertainment. And although Hale might give Mina temporary leave to pursue her brother, a salary wouldn't accompany it.

But if money had been no object, she'd have gone. Quietly, Mina said, "I imagine it would be."

Scarsdale frowned at her, then down at his bottle. With a pained expression, he closed his eyes. Aware that the duke watched her again, Mina looked out the window. They'd begun to drive faster, traffic lightening past Anglesey Square. Soon they'd have her home, and each street they crossed wound her stomach into sick knots.

How to tell them? She'd imparted terrible news to so many mothers and fathers. Never before had it been to her own.

"I don't know anything about parents," Trahaearn said abruptly. "But if this will be worse than facing Dorchester, do you want me to tell them with you?"

Mina didn't know who his offer startled more—Scarsdale or her. As she looked round, she saw the other man's widened eyes and an expression that bordered on dismay. And although she fully intended to refuse Trahaearn, realization stopped her.

His presence wouldn't make Mina's task easier. Nothing could. But if Trahaearn confirmed that he was pursuing the *Terror*, her parents might find it easier to believe that Andrew would be returning home.

"Yes," she said. "Thank you."

Trahaearn nodded. Her throat tight, Mina faced the window again. The coach made its way up Dorset Street now. Two hundred years ago, the residences here had been fashionable. Now many of the town houses had been divided into cheap tenements, or stripped and abandoned to the street urchins and the slinking glint of steel and reddened eyes—

A ratcatcher.

Smoking hells. Mina leapt for the carriage door. "Stop! Driver, stop!"

Fitzhop must have, but Mina didn't wait—she jumped out and began running. She heard the squeal of brakes behind her, the heavy pounding of boots that had to be the Iron Duke's. But the shrieks and screams ahead drew her on, through the gaping window of an abandoned town house. Rotted floorboards threatened to crack beneath her as she landed in a crouch. The screams came from deeper inside the house. Mina shouted as she ran past the sagging stairs, praying that the noise would frighten the ratcatcher off, but it never did.

Fifty years before, when a plague had nearly wiped out the Horde, they'd modified common alley cats into large, vicious ratcatchers. After the plague ended, the hound-sized cats were supposed to die off. Now, Mina didn't know what terrified people more—that the ratcatchers would attack anyone with little provocation, or that they'd been able to breed. Unlike the first generation, the teeth and claws hadn't been implanted; the ratcatchers had been born with them. Somehow, the cats' nanoagents replaced bone with steel, and armored plates protected their lithe, quick forms.

An explosion of rotted boards sounded behind her, as if a bull had rammed into the side of the house. Mina didn't dare look back. Through the gutted kitchen wall she could see them, the two writhing bodies on the floor, one screaming child trying to protect his face and belly, the other hissing and growling. Five urchins scrambled around them, attacking the ratcatcher with anything at hand— pipes, broken planks, their fists.

Her opium darts did little good against the ratcatcher's armored body, and she had no shot with her gun. Mina gripped her dagger and jumped in. Pain burst through her arm as one of the urchins aimed for the ratcatcher and pummeled Mina with a pipe instead. She tried to get a grip on the hissing thing, to tear him away from the boy. A big one, its shoulders came to her knees and easily outweighed her. Warm metal slipped through her hands. She couldn't find flesh with her dagger. She kicked its flanks, its legs. The damn thing wouldn't let go of the boy and turn on her.

Another great crash warned her even before Trahaearn shouted, "Move aside!"

Mina grabbed the two urchins beside her and yanked them away. Trahaearn's boot slammed into the ratcatcher's armored side. Yelping, it flew across the room and crashed into the wall—unharmed. It scrambled to its feet, hissing and fixing its eyes on the Iron Duke.

Trahaearn started for it. "Take the boy, inspector."

She'd already scooped up the bleeding boy, his screams quieting into sobs against her neck. She recognized him—Trowel. Not more than twelve years old, he'd been leading this little group of wick-peddlers for half of his life. His forearms had been shredded, and deep tears along his back and shoulders bled faster than his bugs could heal. Holding him against her chest, she ran through the house.

Scarsdale was climbing through the window, Fitzhop just behind him. They both paused when they saw Mina. She sprinted toward them, and almost fell into the gaping hole in the floor that hadn't been there moments before. Recovering, she shoved the boy into Scarsdale's arms.

"To my father!" she panted. "Take him to my father, and hurry!"

Scarsdale nodded. And for a drunk, he could run astonishingly fast. Mina watched through the window just long enough to drag in a breath. The sounds of the urchins cheering, of cursing and hissing told her that the ratcatcher hadn't fled yet.

Then a loud shriek and thud was followed by sudden silence, and she came into the kitchen to see young faces with jaws hanging open. Near the wall, Trahaearn lifted his foot from the remains of the ratcatcher's head.

Mina stared. He'd stomped on the ratcatcher's steel skull and *flattened* it. Her head seemed to spin, bringing her flashes of an uncrowded lift at full capacity, of a rackety tilting steamcoach, of the unexpected hole in rotting floorboards . . . and iron where there should have been bone. She suddenly suspected that all of him had iron in place of bone.

Swallowing to moisten a throat gone dry, she met his eyes. "How much, exactly, do you weigh?"

"More than enough." His grin caught at something in her chest and turned it about. "But don't worry that I'll crush you."

Oh. Well, she hadn't been—No.

Shaking her head, Mina looked to the oldest of the wick-peddlers. Molly, she remembered. With feet wrapped in rags and the rest of her dressed in whatever could be patched or stolen, Molly looked younger than she probably was. All of these children did.

"A friend took Trowel to my father's. You know where that is?" When they nodded, she said, "His physician's parlor is in the rear of our house. Go in through the mews. I'll see if Cook has something leftover while you wait."

And with the promise of food, they'd be less likely to steal her family's chickens. She watched them hurry off before facing the duke—who stood closer than she'd thought, glowering down at her.

Instinctively, she stepped back. "What is it?"

"Don't *ever* do that again."

And *this* was why she preferred driving home with Newberry. She probably gave him an apoplexy every time she leapt from the cart, but he never challenged her.

"Don't do what? Save a child's life?"

Anger sharpened the angles of his face. "You send me in. I'll do it."

"You refused to ransom eight boys. Why would I believe you'd risk your skin for a child?"

His jaw clenched. No, he couldn't argue that . . . but Mina had to admit it wasn't fair. Unlike Trowel, those boys would've been safe if the Iron Duke hadn't paid their ransom. And as soon as it had become clear that the navy's presence endangered them, he hadn't said a word against rescuing them from the Dame—even if their rescue came out of his pocket. She sighed.

"It won't matter, anyway. There will be no reason for us to ride together again." She glanced toward the ratcatcher before looking up at Trahaearn. "I sent Scarsdale on. We have a bit of a walk."

"No." He started for her. "What I have is *you*. Alone."

Oh, no. Her heart thumping, Mina scrambled back and hit a wall. He kept coming.

"Your Grace, don't—"

His big hands caught her hips—and her guns. Too slow, Mina reached for her weapons and grabbed his fingers instead.

Blast. Damn *and blast*. Wary, she looked up at him.

His gaze settled on her mouth. "Have you been kissed before, inspector?"

"Why?" If he wanted virgin lips, she'd claim to have serviced an army.

"If it's your first, I'll do it differently."

"You won't do it at all."

"Yes, I will."

He leaned forward. His left knee pressed into the wall beside her thigh. He braced his right hand beside her shoulder, caging her in between his broad chest and iron limbs.

His hand beside her shoulder . . . Mina's flew to her weapon, found the holster empty. He blocked her grab to his cods by shoving against her, his solid body pushing hers up against the wall. Mina ground her teeth, fingers digging into the heavy muscles of his shoulders. His warmth seemed to burn through her clothing, her armor, forming a layer of fire over her skin and a tight ball of heat in her lower belly.

He cupped her jaw in his left hand, tilting her face to his. Mina stilled. His callused thumb brushed over her bottom lip, and he seemed pleased when her breath shuddered over his skin.

"So you'll try a cigarillo, but won't try a taste of me?" His dark gaze searched her face. "Aren't you curious, inspector? A kiss—and only a kiss."

Only a kiss . . . from someone who wanted *her*. Longing slipped through her, tugging at hopes best kept buried. Yes, Mina wanted to know. But she couldn't afford it.

"No," she said.

He smiled. "Liar."

"You'll take everything from me. You'll ruin me." Frustration boiled up. She tried to twist free, and couldn't budge him. Anger made her voice hard, loud. "You've *seen* how it is! Jade whore, spit on her, don't let her hire your steamcoach. And you'll make it *worse*—"

"No one would *dare* touch you!" Eyebrows snapping together, he put his face to hers. Between clenched teeth, he repeated fiercely, "No one!"

Mina closed her eyes. He couldn't understand. And how could she explain? Anywhere he went, people only saw *him*. The Iron Duke. With Mina, they only saw the Horde.

In a voice suddenly gentle, he said against her mouth, "And I won't just take. I'd give everything you asked of me."

"Trahaearn—"

His lips covered hers—that hard mouth, surprisingly soft. Shock held Mina frozen. For an instant, she absorbed the feel of his kiss, his rough hand cupping her jaw, the heavy weight pressing her into the wall, his tense stomach against hers.

Sense returned. Her eyes flew open.

"Don't." Panic thinned her breath, made the protest weak. She tried again. "Please. Someone might see."

His fingers tightened in her hair. "And know you're mine."

His mouth opened over hers. He tasted the seam of her lips, as if coaxing her open. Mina shut her eyes again, tried not to feel the heat, the gentle pressure, and the unexpected, curling pleasure.

He hadn't understood. He thought that someone seeing them was her only objection, something to be swept away with a wave of his mighty hand—but it was *the* objection.

He lifted his head. Mina opened her mouth to protest, and he dipped low again, *so* quick—and she tasted him, a flavor that she didn't know but that felt right, and hit her like a fist to her chest that didn't pull back after striking but held on, squeezing.

Damn him. *Damn* him. She couldn't have this. And it was nothing like the cigarillo, where the taste hadn't matched the price. This taste—this *feeling*—was worth more.

But she couldn't pay it. She didn't dare try to pay it. If she did, both Mina and her family would pay and pay and pay.

Pain rose up, pain and fear—she could force those away. And so she did, with everything else.

As if sensing her withdrawal, Trahaearn lifted his mouth from hers. "Why—"

"Let me go," she said hoarsely.

He stared down at her for a long second before stepping back.

Throat aching, Mina turned to go. "Are you done with that, then?"

The answer that came after her was everything she feared.

"No."

If she'd just been angry, Rhys wouldn't have let her walk away. But she was afraid. And Rhys needed to take that fear from her, but he couldn't force it away. Right now, she didn't believe he could— or maybe that he *would*—protect her. He'd have to change that.

But hell if he knew when he'd get the chance. A short walk through London streets wouldn't prove anything, not tonight. And she didn't need him for that any other time. She had Newberry.

So he was second to a red giant. No, not second. Rhys didn't even make a showing on her list. For short moments, she seemed to appreciate him, would offer a laugh or a smile. And he'd felt her sexual response before the fear had swallowed it.

And by God, she fascinated him. He admired the hell out of her. But he knew that admiration wasn't returned. Whatever she saw in him, it wasn't enough to overcome her fear. The only thing she needed him for, the only thing she was interested in, and the only thing he had to offer her was the *Terror*, and the possibility of finding her brother.

She had no other use for him. And though it hit at his pride, Rhys couldn't blame her. He'd been a man driven by purpose once—but for nine years, he hadn't had much of one. Nothing to attract a woman who couldn't be bought.

But now he had two things to drive him: finding the *Terror*, and taking away her fear.

He knew the course he'd take for the first. He hoped that walking into her home would give him a better idea of how to accomplish the second.

Leicester Square had obviously seen better days, but its inhabitants seemed determined not to let it go the way of the town houses where they'd battled the ratcatcher. Some had attempted to scrub away the smoke and paint their houses in pale colors. Almost every window pane appeared intact. A few pink blooms poked through the high fence that surrounded the garden at the center of the square.

Number Eight stood five stories tall, with all of the windows on the third and fourth floors shuttered. A simple casement sat over the front entrance, though a pale outline against the yellow stone suggested that it had once featured a pediment and columns—probably having rotted or sold off.

When they arrived, a steamcoach was pulling away from the entrance. Scarsdale met them at the front steps and gestured toward the departing carriage.

"I'm afraid several of the ladies have left. Apparently, it's the height of indecency for a soused bounder to burst through the front entrance carrying a bleeding street urchin."

"Oh, blast." The inspector palmed her forehead and looked to

Rhys with widened eyes. "I forgot the League meeting. Perhaps you shouldn't—"

"I also killed your butler." Scarsdale's mournful confession interrupted her. When both Rhys and the inspector turned to stare at him, he continued quickly, "His fault, I assure you! He didn't come to the door quickly enough, and I caught him full on when I kicked it open. He fell and his head burst to pieces."

"Lovely. Just lovely." With a dismayed shake of her head, she started for the door. "And after Mother worked so hard on him."

Rhys finally caught on. "An automaton?"

"A piece of art, more like." Scarsdale looked at the blood soaking his waistcoat. "I'll wait for you out here."

Christ. Rhys hated gatherings of any sort, but a gathering of ladies seemed pure torture. "Why?"

"I'm not fit company." Scarsdale's voice lowered. "You'll be introduced to them. You've no reason to talk first."

Hopefully he'd have no reason to talk at all. What would he have to say to them?

He joined the inspector in the foyer, where a blond maid knelt on the floor, picking up gears from out of a jumble that might have resembled a man. Her mouth fell open when she saw him.

The inspector smiled, a wry little twist of her lips. "Sally, let me introduce you to the reason you've spent all of today washing the blood out of my skirts."

"It was a pleasure, inspector. My lady." She bobbed her head, staring at Rhys, but not daring to speak to him. "It wasn't nothing at all."

Nothing at all. Bullshit. When Rhys stepped on a ship, he could immediately determine whether the crew was shorthanded or simply lazy by the state of the repairs and cleanliness. A house was no different—and this house was severely understaffed. All the work was done well; there just weren't enough people to do all of it. Adding a blood-stained dress to this woman's daily duties wasn't "nothing at all." It was a burden, and had probably felt like a heavy one.

Rhys looked at the inspector's jacket, soaked through with the urchin's blood. "I'm afraid you'll have more tonight, Sally. My fault, too, for not reaching the boy before the inspector did."

"I cannot wait, Your Grace." The maid made a breathy short sound that ended in a little squeal. "But I don't see how you're at fault, sir. She's awful fast. Too fast, sometimes."

"Yes, she is." She'd outraced him twice.

The inspector glanced at him. He read the gratitude in her expression before she continued down the hallway. Clever woman. She couldn't give the maid more help, but she could give her the Iron Duke's acknowledgment.

But despite her urging him that morning to attend her mother's meeting, she seemed reluctant to show him into the parlor. Hesitating outside the door, she stiffened her shoulders and took a deep breath, as if bracing herself.

Conversation dimmed when she entered the room, then stopped altogether when he followed her.

Seven of them around the parlor, all looking to him. Images crowded into his brain, memories of other women all looking, some with arousal and hunger, others with amusement and disdain, but all expecting to touch. He forced them away. Those women weren't here. The ladies in this parlor were curious and excited, but not one dared to approach him, let alone reach for him.

But for one. A white-haired woman in dark spectacles rushed across the room—but not, Rhys realized, toward him. She was taking in the inspector's appearance, horrified, making certain that the blood on the inspector's jacket wasn't her own.

"Dear heavens, Mina! Are you well?"

Mina. Triumph shot through him. Yes, that fit her. And he'd use it—but not here. Not yet.

She didn't immediately answer the white-haired woman. Hesitating, she glanced at the other women in the parlor before simply saying, "I'm well, Mother. It is only on my clothes."

So the woman was her mother, Lady Rockingham—but Mina

wouldn't be relaying the news about her brother here, he realized. Not until the other ladies left. With luck, that wouldn't be long.

The countess stepped back, looking to a pregnant woman sitting at the edge of a blue chair. "Felicity, dear, will you assist her upstairs?"

Mina seemed ready to protest. Her mother glanced back at her, and the inspector's mouth snapped shut. "Yes, Mother."

The pregnant woman—Felicity—made her way over to them, somehow maneuvering around furniture without ever taking her gaze from his face. When she reached the two ladies, she gave a sharp look to Mina before gesturing to the countess and then to Rhys. When Mina frowned at her, Felicity leaned to hiss something into the inspector's ear.

A moment later, Mina's brows lifted, and she flushed. Awkwardly, she took her mother's hand and pulled her closer to Rhys. "Your Grace, may I introduce you to my mother, the Countess of Rockingham?"

He hated these rules. Apparently so did Mina, if she'd forgotten to introduce them—and even now she winced slightly, as if realizing she'd said something wrong. Rhys could have told her that he couldn't remember the proper response, anyway—Scarsdale's always seemed to be long and effusive, and not worth memorizing—but the inclination of his head and his "Well met, my lady," seemed to do the trick. A brilliant smile lit the countess's small face.

"Your presence delights us, Your Grace. May I introduce you to my friends?"

Blast. And Felicity was drawing Mina away, out of the parlor. He'd rather be heading upstairs to watch her change clothing, but Rhys recognized that he was well and trapped.

With another inclination of his head, he walked with her to the first sofa, and almost stumbled over a table that moved into his path. Christ, the whole room was full of them. Topped with nutcakes and coffee and driven by some of the quietest clockworks he'd ever seen, they waddled in a wide oval that brought them to every sofa and chair on their circuit, and within reach of any lady who desired the refreshment.

Brilliant, and completely nonsensical. Even ladies could get up off their asses and collect food from a table.

"Please pardon the servers, sir." The countess smiled sweetly. "They provide a bit of amusement, and so our meetings are not all about what is bleak and dreary."

Ah, yes. Marriage reform. God help him. Each lady she introduced to him seemed friendly and intelligent enough, but in no time he felt surrounded, bombarded on all sides by their enquiring looks and their well wishes. *Damn Scarsdale.*

Then Mina returned, and he stopped cursing his friend and stared at her, instead. She wore some kind of pale blue frock, and with her hair still tight at her nape, exposed all of her neck and half of her collarbone.

No armor. No buckles. Only a few layers of cotton and ten feet of parlor separated his mouth from her breasts. Without meeting his gaze, she took a seat on an already crowded sofa, and lifted a nutcake from the waddling server. Her pregnant friend sank into the sturdiest chair in the room, leaving Rhys standing beside the fireplace with her mother—who was watching him.

And what had she seen on his face when her daughter had come in? God knew. The Blacksmith could detect a man's lies. Maybe her mother saw just as much from behind those dark lenses.

He couldn't begin to fathom what a mother would *think* of his reaction, though. Such relationships were alien to him. But reading the determined set of her mouth was easy enough—Mina's mouth looked exactly the same.

So it came, the question he'd dreaded—the one he couldn't answer with a single word. The countess turned to him and asked, "And do you support marriage reformation, sir?"

A damned nuisance, not knowing whether he could lie to her. He opted for the truth.

"I know little about marriage or families, and so thoughts of reform occupy little of my time." That wouldn't be enough, he knew. They would want to pick apart every bit he *did* think about. Perhaps he could head them off, however, by offering it wholesale in a form they likely already knew. "But after speaking with Detective Inspector Wentworth this morning, I found that my opinion aligns closely with hers."

Every gaze in the room turned to Mina, who looked back at Rhys in dismay. The countess pursed her lips before saying, "My daughter is famously reluctant to share her views."

Mina sighed. "You are experienced in matters of marriage, Mother. Not I. And very likely, I will never be. Whatever is decided here and put into your bill will hardly affect me, and so I leave it in the hands of those to whom it will matter the most."

Amused, Rhys shook his head. She hadn't been so reluctant to offer her opinion this morning. And she hadn't stopped at her own chances of marriage, but had focused instead on the laborers—women who, thanks to her occupation, she probably met with more often than these ladies ever did.

And if he was to be put on the spot, then he would drag her in with him. "You better know the women this bill will most affect. Yet you don't have any opinions to share?"

She set her jaw. After a brief silence, her pregnant friend came to her defense. "Mina has been the reason behind some of the most important provisions, Your Grace."

He looked to Felicity. She was like another Newberry, he realized, but in a parlor rather than on the streets. So he would need to fulfill this role for Mina, too.

Or better yet, keep them both out of parlors.

But he appreciated the woman for her defense now—especially as it gave him a deeper look beneath the inspector's armor. "How so?"

"The English laws written before the occupation do not protect women. Even the Horde's had more protections. Yet they put those old laws into effect, as if two hundred years hadn't passed." Felicity shook her head. "And Mina would come from her job with shocking stories of women who had been abused and cheated by their husbands. And even more shocking, that nothing could be done according to the laws. We hope to add those protections."

His admiration deepened. He'd put her on the spot, and she came out looking better for it. He wouldn't have.

But that morning, she hadn't seemed satisfied with the steps taken. Curious, he wondered, "And those protections are not enough for you, inspector?"

With another sigh, she looked to her mother. "No," she said quietly.

So she couldn't lie, either. She was trapped, just as he was. *Good.* "Will you tell us what you would change, then?"

Her jaw clenched again. After a short silence, her mother prompted, "Mina?"

Anger filled the look she threw at him, hot and sharp as a poker. "There should be a provision to make it easier for a wife to divorce her husband."

"Mina!" The countess gasped, and was echoed by the other women. Each of them looked at the inspector in horror.

Goddammit. Damn his mouth, and damn Scarsdale for leaving him to cock this up. He'd done this to her. He'd sought payment for his discomfort, and only at this moment did he realize that the price was unequal.

He was only discomfited by having to talk here. But Mina would be affected by what she said.

Even her friend seemed surprised. "You would advocate for divorce in a bill designed to promote marriage?"

"I would advocate for *choice.*" Her back rigid, she stared somewhere over Rhys's shoulder. "My mother is blinded by one privilege that most people do not have."

Her mother's hand flew to her chest as if to cover a wound. In a high, strained voice, she asked, "Mina, did you misunderstand so completely? Marriage is not just for the privileged classes. That is what I am trying to *undo.*"

With a shake of her head, Mina met her mother's eyes, and Rhys realized he'd been forgotten. No longer angry, but earnest . . . as if the countess's wound had become her own, and she wanted to close it.

"No, Mother. The privilege is that you and my father love each other, completely and unconditionally. You hold each other's interests close to your hearts, and you will fight together through any difficulty." She drew a deep breath. "But that is not something everyone will have. Some will marry for convenience, or for love that doesn't last. And when a woman within a marriage finds her interests are unimportant, when her husband's needs completely subsume hers, it is like the Horde overriding thought and feeling—except her thoughts and feelings are overridden by a husband, simply because he has more power. If that happens, a woman should strike for freedom . . . but it should not be so difficult and ruinous to find it."

The countess's face had softened with understanding. Quietly, she said, "Perhaps. But no one would see it as choice, Mina. And the provision would completely undermine the intended reform."

"Which is why I have never suggested it." Mina stood suddenly. She looked to the other ladies, her gaze never touching Rhys's. "Forgive me. I truly believe your reform will make a difference, and for those who wish to marry, the changes to the law will make their lives that much better. And I hope you will please excuse me."

With a swift bow, she left. In the short silence that followed, Rhys stared after her. Christ, he'd made a mess of this. He started for the door.

"Your Grace."

He turned back. The countess's pale cheeks had flushed. Before she could apologize for the scene that he'd caused, Rhys said, "I will let it be known that you have my full support, Lady Rockingham." He started after Mina again, but paused. "Perhaps you should further consider what your daughter has said, however."

She dipped her head. "Of course, sir."

He only needed to ask Sally where the inspector had gone, and the maid showed him to the back of the house. Rockingham's office resembled a library, except for the metal examination table at the near wall. Mina stood beside it, her back to the door. Not much taller than his daughter, the earl wiped blood from the table, his concerned gaze on her face. He was speaking as Rhys entered the room.

". . . I'm sure your mother will survive it, Mina." He glanced up and regarded Rhys with an inscrutable, penetrating gaze. No question where his daughter had inherited it. "I am sorry that I could not welcome you sooner, Your Grace."

He watched Mina's back stiffen. "You had other concerns. Is the boy all right?"

"A few stitches closed up everything the bugs couldn't." His gaze returned to Mina's face as she half turned. "But that is not all, is it?"

She shook her head. "I must tell you, Father. *Marco's Terror* . . . has been taken."

The earl frowned. "Taken?"

"By pirates." As her father's face blanched, she rushed into the rest of it. "Andrew wasn't ransomed, but they'll keep the ship and the crew. A midshipman is useful. He'll have a place."

"Yes, of course," her father murmured, but his shock hadn't faded. His hand gripped Mina's, knuckles white, and he looked to Rhys as if for confirmation.

Although any reassurance could end up a lie, Rhys inclined his head. "It's true."

Mina continued, "The Iron Duke is leaving tomorrow in pursuit of the ship. He'll bring Andrew back."

The older man nodded. He seemed to have difficulty swallowing, but finally said, "Thank you, sir. Thank you so very much."

Rhys didn't want that. He hadn't done anything yet. But he bowed and accepted it, because there was nothing else to do.

Except to add, "I'm the one who ought to be grateful. Your daughter saved my life today."

The earl blinked twice, as if he couldn't follow. Then he looked to Mina with raised brows. "Oh?"

"From zombies." She smiled as shock rendered him speechless again. "I will tell you and mother together."

"Your mother." The earl's voice thickened. "Have you told her?"

"Not yet. I couldn't."

"We will together." Still holding Mina's hand, he turned for the door. "We will see if I can hurry the ladies along."

He didn't need Mina for that. Rhys said, "May I speak with the inspector here, sir?"

The earl glanced at Mina. She nodded. With a sigh, he kissed her forehead and patted her hand again. He left the door wide open behind him.

Rhys had to warn her, "Your brother might not be on the ship."

Her short nod told him that she already feared that. "I know. I'll prepare them."

"And what will you do if he's not?"

"If you find the *Terror* and he is not aboard, my brother Henry and I will be taking a trip to the Ivory Market."

With no money, and no one to guide them. "You'll die."

She inclined her head. "Probably."

Rhys couldn't let that happen. And now he saw why he had nothing to interest her. She was surrounded by people who would die to protect her, and that she would die for in return. He wanted to be one of them. But he needed to take her away from the others, so that she'd see that he *could* be one of them.

And he was in uncharted territory now, needing something that he couldn't take and couldn't buy. The only leverage he had was the *Terror* and her brother.

"Accept my offer and share my bed," he said, "and I'll take you with me to find your brother. And we won't return until we discover his location, whether he's on the *Terror* or not. But only if you come with me."

Her lips parting, she stared up at him. Then shock faded, and the bitter disdain that came into her eyes twisted like a knife in his chest.

But it was the only advantage Rhys had. And he'd be damned if he didn't use it.

"We leave at dawn, so make your decision quickly," he said, and strode for the door. "I'll wait until midnight for your wiregram."

Rhys found Scarsdale standing beside the steamcoach, flirting with the neighbor's maid. *Damn good man.* He'd made himself useful, after all.

He waited until Scarsdale climbed into the coach. "You chatted up the maid?"

"Yes."

"Tell me about them."

"Crazy, the whole lot. Like a French family out of an antebellum salon novel."

That meant nothing to Rhys. "How so?"

"Their title isn't just a privilege. No, they've got the mindset that the peerage's sole duty is to protect those less fortunate—though you won't find many peers less fortunate than the Wentworths. They can't afford their cook or their maids, but they employ as many as they can, and pay the wages even if it means the family goes without. The staff work their arses off in return."

Just as Rhys had thought. "A house full of people with principles."

"Yes." Scarsdale looked out the carriage window. "I told you to let her sail on. You'll ruin them all."

Frowning, Rhys shook his head. He usually found Scarsdale's advice valuable. But this was pure shit. "I'll protect her. No one will dare touch her. And I'll destroy anyone who tries."

"No. They won't come at her like that. Not with fists or guns or even cannons. And even you can't go low enough to touch them."

Bollocks. "They won't touch her. She'll be coming with us."

Scarsdale's face cleared and he nodded. "Good show, captain. The airship would be the only possible place. Certainly not here."

Rhys's frown deepened. That hadn't been what he'd meant.

With a sigh, Scarsdale leaned back into his seat. "How did you manage it?"

"I found her price."

"What price?"

"Her brother."

Scarsdale pinched the bridge of his nose. "Dear God."

"Bad sport?" Rhys didn't need to ask. And he didn't want her this way. He wanted her to come to him on her own. Now, she'd hate him for forcing her—but she was determined to resist him. And he needed some damn time.

"You ought to just hold a gun to her head."

He knew. Blast it all, he knew. "You say the airship is the only place?"

"Maybe the *Terror* on return."

A few weeks. Enough time for Rhys to convince her to carry on with him after they came back to England. "Who could make it so that she comes with us, without force and without ruining her?"

"I know someone. But he'll ask a high price—and I doubt it will be money."

That didn't matter. "Let's visit him, then. And I'll pay it."

The countess of Rockingham couldn't shed tears. But she could still cry, and when devastated, she wept silently. And when Mina and her father sat with her in the front parlor, and told her of the *Terror*, she cried quietly into her hands until Mina's throat felt as if it had been shredded by razors.

After a long time, her mother lifted her head. "But you say that he is still on the ship?"

Her father nodded. "Yes."

"For certain?"

Blast. Mina couldn't lie to her. And though she'd have tried, her mother read her face before a word passed her lips. Determination firmed the countess's mouth.

"I'll repair the butler, then. It will fetch enough." She looked to her husband. "You and Henry will travel to—"

"No, Mother." Mina shook her head. "Henry and I will."

But Mina knew that wouldn't be what happened. She just had to admit it to herself.

Her mother's face crumpled. "And shall I lose you all?"

Mina couldn't answer that, but she was saved from responding by a knock at the front door. They all waited quietly, listening to Sally's voice and the rumble of a stranger's. A few moments later, the maid came to the parlor carrying a thick envelope.

"A messenger has come from the Duke of Anglesey, milord. I've asked him to wait for a response."

With a creased brow, her father took the envelope. He looked inside and blinked very slowly, as if expecting the contents to disappear after the fall of his eyelids. Swallowing hard, he extracted a small note.

"It's from the Earl of Scarsdale. Payment for the butler," he said. "With apologies."

Mina closed her eyes. *No.* It was so that she'd have no reason to stay. She'd told them she couldn't live on entertainment . . . and any amount of money that could make her father blink like that would have to far exceed the salary she'd lose while traveling.

Surprise spread over her mother's face, and almost immediately gave way to dread and fear. "Should I write a letter to Henry, then?"

And shall I lose you all?

"No." Mina stood. "I saved the duke's life today. I believe . . . I believe he will let me accompany him, if I make the request, and help me search for Andrew."

Her mother and father looked to each other. She saw their indecision, their hope, their fear.

"He would protect me from any danger," Mina said. "I know that he would."

And beyond England's shores, he probably could. She believed that—and her parents would, too.

Her father studied her face. "Do you want to go?"

"I want to find Andrew," she said. "More than anything in the world, I want to see him safe."

He nodded, and looked to her mother. She was weeping again, but this time, she made noise. Not just terrified now. Hopeful.

"I'll write the messenger a note," Mina said.

And Mina did, quickly, for she only needed to write two words. Then she went upstairs to pack.

Chapter Nine

Though the messenger must have delivered her note well before midnight, when Mina rose from her bed near dawn, Trahaearn still had not come. She waited in her room, expecting an imperious knock at the front door, expecting an airship to hover above her house at any moment. She heard nothing.

After two hours passed, she realized he must have withdrawn his offer—and feared that she knew the reason why.

She left her valise in her room and came down the stairs to breakfast. Her parents sat at the table, talking quietly, with no newssheet spread between them. Mina looked to the fireplace. The short time they used this big room every morning didn't warrant the expense of heating it, yet ashes lay in the grate.

Silently, she gathered her breakfast from the sideboard, and sat. Though she acknowledged their greetings, she didn't speak until certain that her voice wouldn't emerge as a croak.

Finally, she was able to ask, "Was the caricature so very bad?"

Her mother forced a smile. "You have earned those detective's epaulettes."

"What was it?"

"Nothing worth seeing," her father said shortly. "Just a picture drawn by idiots."

A picture seen by everyone they knew. She couldn't eat. Even expecting that her caricature might appear in the newssheets, she hadn't known it would hurt this much. She wished Andrew sat across from her. He would make her laugh. He would make it easier to bear.

Her father looked up. "Mina, I forbid you from looking at it. If that rag is put into your face, you will close your eyes."

She nodded silently.

His fist struck the table, rattling the plates. "You will close your eyes!"

He never raised his voice. Now, his shout had her mother covering her face, and Mina's heart leaping into her throat and choking her. She fought tears.

"Yes, Father." It was a hoarse whisper.

Her mother gave a shuddering sigh, and tried for another smile. "And you cannot save eight wealthy boys and the Iron Duke every day. So it will only be the once."

If he'd truly withdrawn his offer, then yes—it would only be the once.

Her father nodded. "And by the time you return, no one will remember. When will you be leaving, Mina?"

"I don't know. Perhaps he didn't receive my message." She pushed her egg around. "He said they were departing at dawn."

She glanced up at her mother's gasp of dismay. "And Andrew?"

Her father caught her hand. "Do not panic now, love. We've had a full night to think on this. If Andrew is still on the *Terror*, then he will return with the Iron Duke. If not, we will figure out what to do then."

"Perhaps we will all go after him." Her mother gave a laugh, high and thin. "On the run from the Blacksmith, straight into the Ivory Market. It shall be like an Archimedes Fox adventure."

"Mother—"

With a wave of her hand, her mother cut her off. "I am not panicking, Mina. I am looking forward to our holiday."

Her father smiled and turned to Mina. "Will you be heading in to your job today?"

"Of course," she said, just as a knock at the door sent her heart leaping again. Not letting herself hope, Mina pushed back from the table. "There is Newberry now."

It wasn't Newberry who stood on the step. Cheeks bright and her blond hair wild, Felicity pushed into the foyer, carrying a black overcoat.

"Oh, *Mina*," she said.

Mina stopped her. "If you have the newssheet with you, do not show me. I am forbidden to see it."

"I don't have it. Only this." She held up the overcoat. Mina had given Felicity a summary of the previous days' events while she'd helped Mina dress the night before, and only second to Felicity's questions about the Iron Duke had been the reason he'd stripped off half of her uniform. "It is too big, but the right color. Use it until you have a new one."

"Thank you." Mina slipped on the coat and almost drowned in wool. She looked to Felicity, who watched her with concern. "Was it so terrible?"

"Ah, well. Yes. It's a portrait, of sorts—but not any worse than others we've seen and laughed at."

"I haven't laughed at them." Whenever a caricature of a Horde magistrate appeared in the newssheets, she tried not to even *look* at them.

Felicity arched her brows. "You once sketched a bounder with five missing teeth."

Mina's cheeks heated. So she had. Yet she never would have drawn Hale or Newberry that way.

Now, she wouldn't draw *any* bounder that way.

Felicity blushed, too. "Perhaps that's not the same. It's just so terrible because I *know* you. It must be devastating for your parents, too."

So it was just as degrading and awful as Mina imagined—but it was only bad because it was her.

"And the article was not much better, favoring the Iron Duke's participation over yours, and the navy's most of all."

Mina sighed. "Yes."

"You expected this?"

"Yes."

"Oh." Flustered, Felicity stepped back. "I forgot to tell you—your Newberry is outside."

Relief made her smile. "Thank you."

Suddenly serious, Felicity stopped her. "Mina. I know I don't see things as you do. So I can't imagine . . . I can only tell you, that whatever happens today, your family will be here. I am only next door. And you will have something good to come home to."

Mina knew. And thank the blessed stars for them. She squeezed Felicity's hand and rubbed her big belly, and went out into the square.

It was no different. She received a few extra glances from passing maids, and they whispered a little more than usual, but that was all. She climbed into the rattling cart.

"Good morning, sir," Newberry said.

"Good morning, constable. Let us see if we can avoid both zombies and spoiled brats today, *hmm*?"

With a nod, Newberry threw the drive lever forward. "Yes, sir."

The officers at headquarters were all of a good sort. A few stretched their eyes and loosened their lips, but only to demonstrate how ridiculous the drawing had been. Most were upset that the article had downplayed her participation. What could have been a good mark for the police force had been stolen by the navy, and they took it as an attack on one of their own.

Until today, Mina hadn't known that they considered her one of their own.

And so when she was summoned to Hale's office, Mina climbed the stairs with a light heart. Even the worry in the superintendent's eyes couldn't puncture the fine feelings that her reception into headquarters had engendered.

"You're something of a celebrity this morning, inspector."

"Unfortunately, sir."

"Yes." Hale sighed. "I find myself in a difficult position, and I need you to tell me true: What is the extent of your involvement with Anglesey?"

Mina had expected this. And thank the blue heavens, she didn't need to lie. "Yesterday was the extent of our involvement, sir. With the investigation closed, I believe that will end it."

Hale nodded, but she didn't look completely convinced, and her worry didn't recede. "The constables and inspectors are behind you now. But if this continues, and when the newssheets and the flyers begin looking bad on them simply because you are also an officer, they won't be so friendly. They'll resent being associated with someone who is always painted as a fool—however undeserved."

"I understand, sir." Frankly, it was the reaction she had expected today.

"You are my best, but if you did decide to develop a . . . deeper acquaintance with the duke, I would have to let you go."

"I know, sir. Thank you. But I do not expect our acquaintance to continue." She paused, recalling that the superintendent hadn't just mentioned newssheets. "Flyers, sir? Political flyers?"

"Yes."

"Was there one?" Her heart sank when Hale hesitated before nodding. Mina had promised not to look at the newssheets. But a political flyer would be aimed at her mother or father. "May I see it?"

"Inspector—"

"Please, sir."

With obvious reluctance, Hale slid a sheet across the desk.

Mina stared at the drawing. "I—Well. They have the scale all wrong. If I stood next to Trahaearn's statue, I would not come up to his knee, let alone my mouth to his—"

"Yes."

Sickness rose in her throat. She couldn't swallow it down. "And to hold a picket sign thus, I would have to clench my buttocks very hard, I think, or the 'Ladies Marriage Reform' would too difficult to read. And I'm not certain it could be done with my skirts pulled up so—"

"Inspector!" Hale's face glowed almost crimson.

"I'm sorry, sir. I just need some way to . . ."

Laugh. She couldn't laugh. If only Andrew were here—but no one knew where he was. She fought the burning in her eyes.

Hale's voice gentled. "Yes."

She held out her hand for the flyer, but Mina couldn't stop looking, even when the drawing blurred and splattered with tears. It was the ugliest thing she'd ever seen. And it was of *her.*

"Mina." Hale's use of her name was soft and careful. "This is not something I've asked before, but I've wondered for so long: Is there nowhere you can go? Somewhere you don't need a giant to follow you just so that you are not beaten . . . or worse."

Sucking in a breath, Mina pushed the tears from her face with the palm of her hand. Terrible, to cry here in front of Hale. But better than crying at home. She struggled to find her composure.

"Perhaps I would not be beaten, but even in the New World, they would still stare. They cannot help it, just as people will always look at my mother's eyes, or those from Manhattan City look at a dockworker's prosthetics." She met Hale's gaze. "If they are from England, it is usually hatred. But everyone looks, and at first, they only see the Horde. It changes when they begin to know me—but until then, and if not hatred, there is always the curiosity, the fascination, and they look at me like a bug on a lens, searching out the differences. You know it is the truth. You did so, too. And you glanced away quickly when the bug looked back at you."

Hale flushed. "I didn't realize you noticed."

"I noticed. And your curiosity did not hurt. I only mean that there's nowhere that I will be completely accepted. There's nowhere I can go where I do not draw looks, except for when I'm with the people who know me. And so if I am to be looked at, I might as well be near home."

"I see." Hale smiled faintly. "Then in your place, I don't suppose that I would leave, either."

A scratch at the door was followed by the secretary's announcement. "Duke of Anglesey here to see you, sir."

What? Mina shoved the flyer into her overcoat pocket and hastily wiped her eyes.

Hale waited. "All right, inspector?"

"Yes, sir."

"Then you're dismissed." She raised her voice and called for the secretary to let the duke through.

Heart pounding, Mina walked to the door. It opened before she reached for the latch, and he strode through. He stopped to avoid knocking her over.

"Your Grace."

He didn't meet her eyes. His cold detachment froze her through. "Inspector."

She barely breathed. "Did you receive my message, sir?"

"No." He pushed past her.

Too shocked and numb to respond, Mina left Hale's office, closing the door behind her. She lifted her eyes and met Scarsdale's gaze.

Leaning against the opposite wall, he said, "I think you'll want to wait here with me, inspector. We've just been to your home. I must say, your mother is a lovely woman."

"Sir?"

"She was quite forgiving about the butler. Probably more forgiving than my clumsy entrance deserved."

That was enough. Mina's temper snapped. "Tell me, sir!"

He blinked. "Ah, well. On the advice of His Grace, the Duke of Shrewsbury, and the most discerning of the Lord Regents, the king's regency council has made Trahaearn a special investigator into the matter of the weapon for auction, and they have allowed him to choose his consultants. Due to the display of intelligence and resourcefulness you demonstrated yesterday, you've been conscripted. You have no choice but to accompany us to the Ivory

Market, where we are to determine if that was where Baxter's murderer purchased the device used to freeze you in Chatham, and the status of the auctioned weapon. Moreover, you are to investigate whether the Black Guard is merely a rumor, or something more . . . sinister."

He waggled his brows on the last word. The knot in Mina's chest began easing.

"So I'm to go with you."

"By order of the Lord Regents," he confirmed. "*Lady Corsair* waits outside. May I ask a favor of you?"

She would do anything. "Yes, sir."

"Do you have any opium handy?"

After shooting Scarsdale with an opium dart, Mina left him slumped against the wall and raced down the stairs to find Newberry. Chest heaving, she pulled the constable into an unoccupied corner, and forced him to stoop to her level.

"I have not much time," she said quietly, urgently. "I am leaving for Africa—I can't explain. You'll find out soon enough, and I need you to do this for me while I am away."

"Do what, sir?"

"The *wiregrams*, Newberry. And the freezing device. And Haynes's bugs." Poor man. She was rushing through. Mina tried to back up. "Yesterday, Dorchester said that they'd pursued the weapon after learning that Haynes's bugs had been destroyed. But as I was shooting Scarsdale I realized that *we* did not include that in our updates. Did you?"

"No, sir. I never stated what killed the captain."

"And why kill Baxter at that moment? It makes no sense. Except that Baxter knew why the *Terror* had been sent to the Ivory Market. I believe someone was trying to stop Baxter from telling us about the auction. They knew Trahaearn would pursue the *Terror*. But *no one* knew that the Dame had thrown Haynes on Trahaearn's house, or had reason to believe that Trahaearn would know the *Terror* had been taken. So after we identified Haynes and sent the update, they had to try to beat us to Baxter—which meant someone had to send a wiregram from London to Chatham, to alert their assassin. And there is only one wiregram station in Chatham. Either the clerk or the message runner will know *something*."

Newberry's face cleared. "You want me to find out who sent it?"

"I don't know if we'll be lucky enough to find out *who*. But from *where* it was sent? Yes. But be careful about it, constable. Someone told the Admiralty that Haynes's bugs were destroyed before they sent those ships from Dover. That person is probably connected to the Black Guard."

The constable paled a little. "The Blacksmith, sir?"

"I don't know. Perhaps someone at the Admiralty already knew what had happened during the weapon demonstration. But yes—it could be the Blacksmith." She held his gaze. "And that is why you must be careful, and *only* ask at the Chatham station so that you don't arouse suspicion in London. Find out who sent that gram. Very quietly, and with care. And then keep a lid on it until I return."

"Yes, sir."

Yasmeen had given Rhys the cabin across the passageway from the inspector's, and reconfirmed his belief that her airship was worth every single livre. With Scarsdale a heavy weight over his shoulder, he entered the small cabin long enough to dump the bounder on the forward bunk. When he left, Mina's door was ajar.

An opportunity Rhys wouldn't resist. He pushed open her door. The narrow space had room enough for a bed, a shallow wardrobe, and a tiny writing desk that doubled as a washstand and vanity. Standing over the open valise on her bunk, she glanced at him and raised her brows.

"What did Scarsdale get into?"

"I shot him with an opium dart." She looked past him. "You're sharing a room?"

"Yasmeen already had another contract, and his journey won't interfere with ours. He'll be using the stateroom."

He gestured to the end of the passageway, to the largest cabin on the airship aside from the captain's directly above them.

"Ah, yes. The contract that was already half paid. You must be paying her more. Yet she wouldn't change the cabin arrangements for the Duke of Anglesey?"

"I don't mind. I'm not here to lie in bed." Unless it was Mina's.

She didn't look convinced. Turning back to her valise, she said, "So who rates above you?"

"Archimedes Fox."

With a laugh, she faced him again. "The adventurer?"

A fraud, probably. What little Rhys had heard of the man's escapades sounded ridiculous and implausible. "You've read his stories?"

"Who hasn't? Andrew used to make pennies by reading them to the laborers on the docks."

Resourceful boy. "And so I am not his only inspiration."

"No." She smiled. "You also compete with the Blacksmith."

"But I won out." He watched her gather an armload of clothing from the valise. The cabin door blocked access to the wardrobe. Perfect. He kicked the door closed and moved deeper in the cabin. She had to brush past him to reach the wardrobe, and then frowned when she couldn't open it.

Pushing closer, Rhys showed her how to lift the door before swinging it wide. "So that it won't fling open."

"Thank you." She took a deep breath. "I'm not in my element."

"No."

She smoothed the collar of a white shirt over a hook. "I realize that you have done me a . . . favor. But I intend to perform my duty as instructed."

"Did you expect that you'd have to do something else?"

Of course she had. Folded and tucked in his waistcoat pocket lay a simple message: *I accept. –W.W.*

But if she knew he had the note, no doubt she'd feel an obligation to keep up her end of the bargain. He didn't want her that way. And though he ought to get rid of the message, Rhys knew he would keep it until she accepted all of him. Perhaps beyond that time.

She'd agreed to take him once. That small slip of paper gave him hope that she would again—but without coercion.

"No." She lied well. Not a hint of color tinged her cheeks. "We should compile everything we know about the Black Guard. Will we have a place to work?"

"The officers' mess, or I'll ask Yasmeen for the use of her cabin."

"Either would be sufficient." She paused. "Why an *officers*' mess? This is a private airship."

"Not always."

"Oh." She returned to the bed. "This was a navy airship?"

"Not the Royal Navy's." They tended to be heavier. "It was a French ship. She took it during the Liberé war."

"I see." She frowned and withdrew a small combination box from her valise. "I didn't pack this."

"Your mother brought your case to us."

She dialed in the numbers, and with a clicking of gears, the steel box opened to reveal a silver cross. A soft sigh escaped her. "This. I remember my grandmother would take it out to look at—and she said that *her* mother used to wear it, even though the Horde outlawed all of these old relics. It meant something else to them. I think my mother only looks at it to remind herself of my grandmother." She closed the box, shaking her head. "I suppose she wants me to sell it."

"It would fetch a good price." When she looked up at him, he said, "I used to smuggle relics like these into the Horde territories. Sometimes into the empire itself."

Her eyes widened. "They've outlawed them everywhere?"

"For taxes and peace."

"What?"

"It used to be, after the Horde conquered a region, they let everyone worship whatever they always had—and they didn't tax the clerics. But then rich men started becoming clerics, and hiding their money. In other regions, their *dargas* were squabbling over religious differences. So the Horde eradicated it altogether."

"How do you know that?"

"There are still hidden pockets in the territories. That's where I'd take those relics."

"In the empire?" When he nodded, she asked, "What was it like?"

"Safe. Orderly. The Khan boasts that an old woman carrying a bag of gold could walk from one end of the empire to the other unmolested. And from what I've seen, that's true. You could live there peacefully. *I* could live there peacefully."

"But?"

He had to smile. Of course it couldn't be that ideal. "But if you ever speak out against the *dargas* or the Khan, you'll disappear."

"Lovely." She looked into the valise again and gave a small growl of dismay. *"Mother."*

Rhys reached in. Nestled in a nightgown lay several small, beautifully crafted automata—singing birds, jumping frogs, clockwork bracelets shaped like kraken . . . and a tiny butterfly. Intrigued, he glanced at Mina, wondering if she knew what it was. The butterfly's wire legs were designed to gently fit over a clitoris. When wound, the wings would flutter until the vibration brought the woman to orgasm.

A delicate little device—and nothing like the contraptions at the Blacksmith's. Used for pleasure, rather than to hurt or degrade.

He held the butterfly in his palm. "You say your mother made this?"

Mina barely glanced at it, instead frowning at a thick envelope that she'd taken from the bottom of the case. "Blast it all. They could have used this while I'm gone. These devices would have covered any possible need I might have had."

Rhys recognized the money he'd sent for the butler. "We have to stop in Chatham. I'll wire instructions to my steward, and he'll have the same amount sent to them."

"Thank you." She handed him the packet.

He tucked it into his jacket and looked down at her mother's devices. "And I'll buy all of these from you now."

"Oh." She cast her eye over the collection. "Two livre."

Outrageous, but he could afford to be cheated. "Done. And you'll show me how to use the butterfly later."

Both her faint smile and the color in her cheeks pleased him. "I couldn't use that. My mother made it."

"So?"

She blinked before pursing her lips. "It's difficult to explain to a man from a crèche. Let me put it so: If you had a daughter, would you want her to use a similar device that you made and gave to her?"

Unexpected, instinctive recoil tore through him.

"Just so." With a nod, she closed the empty valise. "Shall we move to the wardroom, then, and begin our work?"

"In a moment." He blocked her access to the door. "You asked if I received your message. What did it say?"

He didn't know what drove him. She didn't look at him with bitter disdain now, or anger—and he shouldn't risk them again. But he had to know how she would explain it, and hope that the lies she chose would reveal as much as the truth.

"Oh. Only, 'Thank you.' For the butler. It was not . . . about your offer."

"I asked too much?"

"Not too much for Andrew. But it promised to be a very high price. Higher than I ever expected." A shadow moved over her face, as if she'd already paid some of it.

He tilted her chin up. "Should I have asked for less? I'm used to taking everything, but I suppose a gentleman should only take in bits. What would have been easier to pay?"

"I don't think a gentleman *takes* anything at all."

"I never said I'd be a good one." When she smiled, he said, "A kiss, then. I should have offered to take you with me for the price of a kiss. Would you have paid it?"

"Yes. But I paid that after the ratcatcher."

So she had. "And to open this cabin door?"

She laughed. And though her hands dropped to her weapons, she rose onto her toes. He dipped his head and her mouth pressed to his sweetly, firmly.

Simple. Nothing. Yet need suddenly raged through him, hardening and heating. Damn her. He'd only meant to play. But it took him over—and not her. Why not her? Was she still so afraid?

She abruptly drew away, her gaze averted, as if she'd stumbled across something that made her uneasy.

And he couldn't play or tease her now. "That's not all that I want. It won't be enough."

She closed her eyes. "Why do you even want it?"

He didn't know. He couldn't account for it. Frustration boiled up, drove him to her. He captured her face between his hands. "I want to possess you. And if I want something, I find a way to have it."

"I see."

His jaw clenched. She didn't see. Neither did he. "This is the first time it's a woman."

She blinked. Rhys lowered his head. Stiffened, her mouth didn't open, but he tasted the sweetness of her lips, the firm line between. His hands circled her waist, carried her up against him. He felt something within her hitch, like the catch of a breath, and her mouth softened against his. Her fingers threaded into the hair at his nape.

Finally. Heart pounding, he delved deeper. The heat of her mouth drew him in, the first glide across her teeth, the hesitant touch of her tongue. She shuddered against his chest and broke away, gasping.

She pushed at his shoulders. "I don't want this."

Bullshit. "You don't enjoy it? Lie to me, if it's easier."

"I don't *want* to enjoy it. That means the same to me."

So she wanted him. She just didn't want to. That was something. And it was enough—for now.

"Set me down."

He did. She stumbled back against the bunk, hands on her weapons.

"Only here," he said. "That's all I want."

"What?"

"You. Me. Until we return to London. There will be no ruin to you or your family. I'll kiss you until we can't breathe. I'll strip you naked and taste every inch of you. Then I'll shag you until neither of us can see straight. And we'll have had enough of each other."

She stared at him, lips parted. A long second passed before she shook her head. "*None* is enough."

He looked her over. Her cheeks had flushed. Her breathing hadn't yet settled. "Are you certain of that, inspector?"

"Yes." She stood. "Let us go now, sir."

Mina climbed up to the main decks with Trahaearn's taste still on her tongue. Trying to ignore the sensation only made her more aware of everything else: her thin chemise, which seemed useless today, protecting the tips of her breasts from the abrasion of her tight armor. The vibration of the engines prevented her from losing herself in her skin; she was constantly always aware of her feet on the decks or her bottom in a seat. The rush of cold air against her cheeks should have brushed away the memory of his heated mouth. She should have scrubbed her lips with the heel of her hand, but she didn't want him to see. So he lingered, and all that she could do was wait for his flavor to pass and for the tingle over her skin to fade.

She paused near the bow to look over the side, drawn by the blue and the white. The airship was headed toward gray, but even rain clouds were different than haze, full of shape and varying shades. Below, pools of sunlight dappled golden fields between the shadows of the clouds, and a breeze sent the grasses rippling like a wave.

Trahaearn stopped beside her. "We're almost to Chatham. We'll wait until Fox boards before heading below again."

"Why?" Though the adventurer piqued Mina's curiosity, the duke hadn't seemed impressed. "You want to meet him, after all?"

He shook his head. "It's not my ship. But I still prefer to know everyone aboard."

"I see." Not his ship, but still every inch the captain. "And what will you learn by looking at him? Are you such a good judge of character?"

That amused him. "No. I don't know whether a man is an enemy until he comes at me with a knife."

"Truly? I think that it's obvious when someone hates you."

"Hate, yes. But how can you know whether they intend to hurt you? I've met men who'd rather shit on my plate than eat with me, but they'll still bend over their tables to make a deal that lines their pockets." He shrugged. "So I treat everyone as if they will stab me in the back until I better know them."

Just like Mina. She almost laughed.

His eyes narrowed. "What is it?"

"I dislike everyone until I know them." Then had to admit, "Some, I continue to dislike even after knowing them."

"I care nothing for like or dislike. It only matters whether they have a use to me."

"Whether they have a use?" Though she shook her head, Mina was not surprised. She'd heard that word from his mouth too many times. "And you make it very easy to continue on as I've started."

His dark brows snapped together. Had she startled him? His gaze searched her face, as if trying to confirm whether Mina meant what she'd said. Would he care if she disliked him? She couldn't be certain.

"Perhaps not everyone according to their use," he finally said. "I would still call Scarsdale a friend."

Mina couldn't imagine anyone who wouldn't like the bounder. "And is he the only one?"

His eyes locked with hers. "No."

She couldn't mistake his implication. That didn't mean she'd believe it. "Ah, but you are also a pirate and a liar, and have a use for me in your bed. I will not trust that you like me, sir."

He grinned. "And your response is why I do."

Her answering smile seemed to grow on its own. She did like him . . . sometimes. When he was not a complete knacker.

They soon came over the Medway River, and then the port at Chatham, where Lady Corsair cut the engines and sailed into position above a boarding house. With the tails of her red kerchief blowing over her shoulders, she left the quarterdeck and approached them, a frown creasing her brow.

"Where is Scarsdale?"

"He'll sleep the day," Trahaearn told her.

"Damn. He is the only one who suffers fools like Fox." She narrowed her eyes at the duke. "He suffers one every day."

Trahaearn gave a bark of laughter. "And he's told me that you read the magazine serials."

"So I do." Yasmeen smiled and lit a cigarillo. "That bounder gave me the first adventure to read. I only follow along now to see when Fox will be killed."

"If he's killed this time, you won't receive your second payment."

"Then perhaps I'll take up writing. As much as he paid me, there must be something in telling ridiculous stories." Turning her head, she called out, "Lower that platform slowly, Ms. Washbourne! I don't trust that our passenger will have brains enough to move out of the way below."

Truly? Mina couldn't yet read the other woman well, but she recognized bravado. And though she wouldn't have wagered her life that the aviator captain had been struck by nerves, Lady Corsair almost seemed like a harder, sharper version of Sally upon meeting the Iron Duke.

When the chains rattled and the platform began rising, Mina glanced up at Trahaearn and saw his narrowed look. Also trying to make out Lady Corsair's strange behavior, perhaps.

The woman sighed and crushed her cigarillo out in her palm.

"Well, I'll have to deal with him, then. There are few men who aren't trying to fight me or to take my ship. I ought to be grateful that this buffoon has money enough to tread my lady's decks."

The platform rose into place alongside the airship. Mina could not be certain if Archimedes Fox was a buffoon, but surely he was an eccentric. He stood beside a large trunk, wearing a gliding contraption with wings strapped to his back, bright green breeches, and a yellow jacket. His shaggy brown hair was streaked with gold and hung over his goggles. Tall and fit, with wide shoulders, narrow hips, and a deep tan, Mina could believe that he was an adventurer. She estimated his age close to hers, but when he pushed up his goggles, he regarded Yasmeen with an eagerness that reminded her of a younger boy.

She was already finding it difficult to hold on to her dislike.

Beside her, Trahaearn went still. "Captain Corsair!"

Yasmeen turned and frowned when she saw his face. She sauntered back toward them, and Trahaearn moved to meet her halfway. Curious, Mina walked with him—and noticed the change that came over Fox when he saw the Iron Duke. All that was young and eager suddenly looked hardened and dangerous.

"That is not Archimedes Fox," Trahaearn told her quietly. "That is Wolfram Gunther-Baptiste."

Yasmeen's lips curled—and then she was gone. Mina gasped. She'd never seen a person move so fast. In a blink, Yasmeen was at the platform, and had Fox on his knees with her fist in his hair and her knife at his throat. He held his hands out wide, as if in surrender.

Trahaearn caught Mina's wrist when she stepped forward to intercede. He gave a small shake of his head. Quietly, he said, "Not here, inspector. Not on her ship."

But they were still over English soil. She could not stand by. With her free hand on her opium gun, she watched—ready to stop them if necessary.

Yasmeen hissed into the man's face. "Are you here to kill me?"

"No. Never."

"I killed your father."

"And I'll thank you for it until I die. He wasn't much of a father." He suddenly grinned, showing white teeth. "Bad enough that I changed my name."

"To Fox?"

"Yes."

"Liar. Get off my ship." With a snarl, Yasmeen shoved her boot into his chest and turned away. He tipped over, landing hard on the platform—and apparently onto his purse. A distinct *ching!* sounded.

Yasmeen's eyes narrowed. She turned back. "Fox?"

He watched her carefully. "It has a nice ring, doesn't it?"

"I haven't changed *my* name. You deliberately sought the services of my ship."

"I wanted to see what sort of woman destroyed him. I'm not disappointed." Slowly, he got to his feet, and his carefree expression fell away again. "We have a contract, Captain Corsair. You've taken my money, and you owe me passage. Don't make a decision you'll regret."

"I don't regret anything, Mr. Fox." Yasmeen sheathed her knife as she approached him again, but to Mina that only made her seem more unpredictable—and more deadly. "The moment you step from this platform onto the deck, never *suggest* a threat to me. Because I'll toss you over the side and won't look back."

"I've been deserted once for less." His boyish grin appeared again, and he looked to Trahaearn. "Isn't that right, captain? Though I've heard you're called something loftier, these days. Have you blown up any towers lately?"

"No. Have you and Bilson?"

"Bilson's dead," he said without a change in his affable expression. "And I had a change of heart . . . in more ways than one."

His gaze returned to Lady Corsair. She stared back at him, her green eyes cold and assessing.

"All right, Mr. Gunther—"

"Fox."

She continued as if he hadn't spoken. "—Baptiste, Mr. Pegg will show you to your cabin. You are free to move about *Lady Corsair*, but I prefer to see you as little as possible."

His jaw hardened. He watched her walk back to the quarterdeck before turning to Trahaearn and Mina. Faint surprise crossed his face. "You must be Detective Inspector Wentworth. I read an account of your insubordination this morning."

The duke frowned. "What account?"

"In the newssheets. They reported the Lord High Admiral's version," Mina said, relief sliding through her. If he hadn't seen the newssheet, he hadn't seen the caricature.

Fox obviously had. His gaze settled on her face. "Yes, they seem to have got a lot of it wrong. Perhaps you'll share the real tale over dinner?"

"I doubt it," Trahaearn said.

With a smile, Fox grabbed hold of his trunk. "Until then, inspector."

A flirt. Mina watched him follow Pegg to the ladder leading below decks. But a flirt who moved lightly, and carried the heavy trunk without any awkwardness.

She looked to Trahaearn. "You deserted him for less than a threat? Why?"

"He and Bilson obtained the explosives I used on the tower, but once they'd boarded the *Terror*, he demanded to know what I wanted to do with them. I didn't know him well enough to gamble that he wouldn't stab me in the back, and I couldn't let him tip anyone off."

"I see. And so?"

"I threw him overboard." When she stared at him, he added, "We weren't far from shore."

"*Which* shore?"

"Galicia—on the northern coast of old Spain."

Which teemed with just as many zombies as France's coast did. Mina shook her head, but found it very hard to criticize him for any action that led up to his destroying the tower. And besides . . .

"That story sounds familiar," she said. Tossed from a pirate ship by a sinister captain, and forced to hike through treacherous forests to stop the pirate from using explosives to demolish the last medieval cathedral still standing in Spain? It *was* familiar—it had been the first serial adventure, *Archimedes Fox and the Blasphemous Marauder*.

Oh, blue skies. Her shoulders began shaking. The pirate captain had been eventually slain, after Fox tricked him into entering a dark cavern where he'd been gored by a zombie boar.

"What story?"

Mina could only shake her head. And it took her twenty minutes more before she could catch her breath long enough to tell him.

Chapter Ten

When Mina left her cabin to join the others for dinner, Scarsdale was waiting in the passageway. He offered her a lovely greeting and his elbow, which she took with a smile. A glance through the open door of his and Trahaearn's cabin didn't reveal the duke . . . but Mina didn't intend to ask.

"Yasmeen's cabin is only one deck up." Scarsdale stared straight ahead as they walked. "If I don't see a porthole and pretend that I don't hear the engines, I can fool myself into thinking I'm on a real ship."

"I could lead you blindfolded, next time."

He gave a short laugh. "I've done that before."

Yasmeen must have known about his fear. The windows of her cabin had all been covered. Mina entered with Scarsdale, and only his forward motion prevented her from stopping to stare. The room could have been lifted from a seraglio painting. Red curtains draped the walls. A small fountain bubbled in the corner, and yellow canaries chirped in a hanging cage. In the center of the room, a round teak table stood only a few inches above a thick woven rug, and was surrounded by tufted ottomans and enormous pillows covered in sapphire and emerald silk.

In billowing shirtsleeves and a blue kerchief, Lady Corsair lounged beside the table, smoke curling from her mouth. Next to her sat Archimedes Fox. The adventurer had traded his yellow coat for peacock blue, and watched the aviator captain with hooded eyes and a set jaw. Whatever conversation had passed between the two before Mina and Scarsdale arrived apparently hadn't been a pleasant one.

A cabin girl took Mina's overcoat, and she sank into the pillows across from Yasmeen, with Scarsdale on her right and Fox on her left.

Scarsdale was all smiles. "Gunther-Baptiste! Fancy seeing you here."

With a curl of her lip, Yasmeen said, "He is Archimedes Fox now."

"Fox? No."

"Yes," Fox said, his expression lightening as Scarsdale laughed until his eyes watered. The adventurer glanced over as Yasmeen nodded to the cabin girls, and they began setting trays on the low table. "But the lady's not pleased."

"Few men please me." Yasmeen smiled at Scarsdale. "Where's Trahaearn?"

Scarsdale shrugged. "You know the captain. A table's for eating, not talking. And he'd rather eat his own hand than sit chatting with . . . and I'm proven wrong."

Mina glanced over her shoulder. Trahaearn stalked into the cabin, his dark eyes sweeping the room. Without a word, Scarsdale moved closer to Yasmeen, and the duke took up all of the pillows next to Mina, and half of hers. She frowned at him. With a half smile, he held her gaze until the absurdity of it all struck her and she had to look away from him.

A girl filled her glass with a deep burgundy wine. Before Mina could say a word, Yasmeen said, "You can be certain that I don't stock wines that are made with sugar."

Grateful that she hadn't needed to ask first, Mina sipped. She closed her eyes in pleasure. The bold flavor was unlike any of the watered honey wines her family sometimes bought during the New Year holidays. This spread through her, warm and spicy, and seemed like it could serve as a meal itself. She took a deeper sip, and had to conceal her delight when one of the cabin girls refilled the glass almost as quickly as she set it on the table.

Scarsdale and Fox carried the conversation around them, with an interjection now and then from Yasmeen. Mina focused on her plate and her wine, savoring every unusual dish that the girls set in front of her: yogurt and cucumber, some kind of beige, garlicky paste, and fluffy round pieces of white bread. But above all, she took her time over the rice. Yellow and fragrant, it was unlike any rice Mina had eaten at home, but she was still glad to see it. Since the Horde's supply ships no longer came into London, rice had become too expensive to buy except for special occasions. And although her family had tossed out many Horde traditions after the revolution, food had not been one of them.

Mina was feeling stuffed, sleepy, and warm when she finally sat back against the pillows, her still-full wineglass in hand. She couldn't contain her sigh of contentment, and it brought Fox to a halt midsentence. With a laugh, he turned to look her over.

"You wear your armor even to dinner, Lady Wilhelmina?"

"Inspector." If he could demand "Fox," then Mina would demand the title she preferred, too. When he nodded, she said, "Of course I wear armor. I am sitting with a pirate, a mercenary, an adventurer, and a bounder. If a shot is not fired tonight, I daresay that your reputations are nothing but lies."

It was a silly thing to say, of course. Her armor wouldn't stop a bullet at this close range. But their laughter seemed to rumble through her, leaving her strangely giddy. She dared a glance at Trahaearn, who wasn't laughing, but watching her with a heated intensity that was really quite attractive. His gold earrings winked at her like cheeky little bastards . . . and his muscular thigh looked the perfect place to lay her head and have a nap.

Blinking rapidly to clear the image from her mind, Mina took another drink. She must have eaten too much. Never before had she been quite this sleepy and fuzzy after a meal.

When the laughter quieted, Scarsdale lifted his glass to Mina before looking to Yasmeen. "I say, where are we headed to? We're flying south by southeast. The Market's a bit more west."

"Braggart," Yasmeen said.

He batted his eyelashes at her. "And handsome, too."

Handsome, yes. But Mina frowned, trying to understand how he was a braggart.

Trahaearn's voice came low near her ear. "You can spin him around in a fog blindfolded, and he'll know the direction he's facing at the end of it."

Ah! "Now that is a fine trick."

Amusement deepened the duke's reply. "And a useful one on a ship."

"And in London, too," Scarsdale said. "But I still am wondering why we've taken a detour."

"After your declarations of love, now you're in a hurry to be off my ship?" Yasmeen nudged Scarsdale's thigh with the toe of her boot. "We're taking Mr. Fox to Venice, first."

"Ah, and he will have another adventure that we shall soon see in the magazines. Which is probably the best way to hear them. It pains me to say it, Fox, but you're much cleverer when you write than when you speak."

"My sister writes them." He looked to Mina, who realized that her mouth had fallen open. "I'm a salvager, not a writer. But if turning my work into a popular adventure allows her a measure of independence, she can continue using my name as long as she likes."

"I see." Her voice sounded deep. Across the table, Yasmeen's eyes had narrowed at Fox, and made Mina wonder if she'd need her armor, after all. "That's very good of you, sir."

"I try." Fox's gaze moved past her to Trahaearn. "So you're continuing on to the Ivory Market? I saw that Haynes was dead. Are you after the *Terror*?"

"Yes."

"I've only read the story in the newssheets. Have you got another version, captain?"

"I don't know their version. I don't read them."

Scarsdale looked up. "I'll tell you how it happened."

Blowing out a mouthful of smoke, Yasmeen rolled her eyes. "You weren't there."

"So I'll make it more exciting. But first, a drink." He lifted his glass. "To Baxter. A damn fine man. I daresay not a one of us would be here if not for him."

How true. Mina would likely still be at home if the admiral hadn't been killed. She drank deep, and noted that although Trahaearn's glass had remained untouched throughout his meal, he drank to his friend.

He hadn't drunk *or* talked much. She liked his quiet. The others always seemed to be laughing and moving and gesturing, but Trahaearn sat, solid and strong and quiet. If the pillows hadn't been here, she could have leaned against him, and not worry at all that she'd be jostled about.

Scarsdale raised his glass again. "And to *Bontemps*. A good airship should never fall into a madwoman's hands, or into the sights of a Royal Navy firebomb squadron."

Yasmeen snorted into her glass, but drank. Trahaearn's face was more solemn as he took his.

"A fine ship," he said.

"And one more to our lovely inspector, for her quick and lovely mind . . . and her opium gun."

This time, Trahaearn smiled as he drank, meeting her gaze over the rim of his glass. Mina grinned at him, suddenly very glad that he'd bribed the Lord Regents.

Fox set his glass back to the table. "Are you married, inspector?"

She laughed. Truly, what an absurd question. "No. I never will be."

His frown smoothed away, and he shook his head. "I forget the English are not Brits. An unmarried lady would never travel without a chaperone in Manhattan City."

Ah, yes. A bounder girl was only worth as much as her virtue. No wonder all of them were prudes. Their dresses only had to lift above their ankles, and they were ruined. "It doesn't matter for us," Mina said. "We're all already compromised."

"By the Frenzies?"

"Yes," Trahaearn said, and the rough note in his voice made her turn to look at him. He stared back at her, with a beat at his temple that said he held himself under rigid control. What for?

"Yes," she echoed.

Behind her, the birds chirped. Mina frowned. The silence that had fallen was thick and uncomfortable. She looked from Fox to Yasmeen to Scarsdale before she realized why. They all knew a Frenzy had come only a few months before the tower had fallen. And nine years ago, she'd been old enough to be affected.

She glanced at Trahaearn again, and something in the way he looked at her made her stomach hot. She stared down into her drink. It was bottomless. Truly, amazingly bottomless. And if she drank enough, it would cool the burning in her gut.

He asked her quietly, "You don't remember, do you?"

Her brows lifted. Why would he think that? "Oh, I *do*," she assured him.

"Dear God, you *asked*." Scarsdale pinched the bridge of his nose. "This is why we dare not attend dinner parties."

No, Mina appreciated it. Trahaearn didn't pretend. He didn't make silly conversation. And when he said something, she didn't always like it, but she liked knowing what was in his head.

He flicked a glance to Scarsdale. "He said your mother didn't remember the Frenzy when you were conceived."

"Oh, well. My mother is very good at not remembering things that she doesn't want to."

"But you do."

Oh, yes, she remembered. The loss of control, the overwhelming need—and the terror of knowing that it wasn't coming from within her, but from the Horde.

"I remember," she said, and sighed. "And my experience was less horrifying than what most buggers went through, I suppose. At least I didn't get with child, and was with someone I knew."

His face darkened. "Who?"

Scarsdale groaned. "I say, inspector, if this isn't something you want to talk about—"

"My friend Felicity."

"Oh." The bounder leaned forward. "Pray, then. Do talk about it."

Yasmeen threw an olive at him. The tension and silence around the table broke into laughter, and Mina laughed with them, glad she was able to. Glad to pretend it didn't matter.

Except when she met Trahaearn's eyes. They said that she didn't fool him.

"That's not why I'm here," she said to him. Out loud. Mina didn't even know what she meant, but he nodded and looked to Fox.

"Have you heard anything of a Black Guard?"

Mina's hand flew to her mouth. "You can't ask him," she hissed. "What if he *is* one?"

The duke shrugged. "Then I'll kill him after he tells us."

Yasmeen shook her head, pulling out another cigarillo. "Not until he's paid me for the remainder of his contract."

"You'll be compensated, captain." Fox leaned toward her, holding a spark lighter. She stared at him as he lit the end, then as he leaned back and lit his own. He looked to Trahaearn. "I'm not Black Guard. But I have had a run-in with one of their men."

Yasmeen smiled faintly. "And which story was that?"

"I didn't let her write it. With people like this, you don't take the chance that they'll recognize themselves in one of those stories, and inadvertently send them your sister's way."

Mina liked him very much for that. "What happened?"

"It was about three years ago. I usually do salvage work, but now and again I'll be hired as a guide. Usually by researchers or scientists. Sometimes people with too much money and not enough sense. This one said he was a historian, and that he'd come across a document detailing the location of da Vinci's clockwork army."

Scarsdale snorted. "You believed him? That legend is as old and as false as my mother's teeth."

"No. But he had money enough for the fee Bilson and I charged, and an airship. But—"

"What airship?"

Fox glanced at Yasmeen. "The *Mary Katherine*."

The captain shook her head. She looked to Scarsdale, who seemed to study her face before slipping his arm around her waist and hauling her into his lap. She settled against his chest with a smile.

Strange, and . . . intimate. Mina tore her gaze away. Fox appeared startled, too, and it seemed with an effort that he turned to Trahaearn again and picked up the thread of his story.

"But once on the airship, we only needed to spend about five minutes with the man before we realized he wasn't a historian. Educated, but not specialized. When I told him that the location he had was farther east than the Habsburg Wall, it didn't mean anything to him."

It didn't mean anything to Mina, either. She knew the Habsburg Wall had stood for almost fifty years as the strongest defense against the Horde's approach into Europe, but the reason why a location farther east meant something kept slipping through her mind.

"What should it have meant?"

"Da Vinci designed his clockwork soldiers after the wall was up. Everything east of Austria was already Horde territory. Even if the legend had merit"—he glanced at Scarsdale, then quickly away—"the army wouldn't have been constructed on that side of the wall. But Pope insisted that we take him to the location he had, regardless. So we flew on."

Mina leaned forward. "What did you find?"

He smiled slightly, reached for his wine. "First, let me tell you about the journey there. It was a two days' flight, and Bilson and I escaped Pope's company for all of thirty minutes. By the second day, I'd have locked myself in the privy if I could."

"Was he so unpleasant?" The member of the Black Guard who'd killed Baxter hadn't been, at first glance.

"Not his manner. Not his physical person." He frowned, drawing on his cigarillo. Finally, he shook his head. "I don't have the

talent for description that my sister does. Just that after every conversation, I felt unwashed—and I'm a man who'll run for a month
through swamps, with my clothes caked in dung and zombie blood,
before I find a bath. Somehow, he always got round to bugs. And
specifically, the control the Horde had had over buggers, and what
sort of acts they were all made to perform. Without ever crossing
what my grandmother would have called polite boundaries, he managed to suggest perversions that were . . . were . . ."

Mina followed his gaze and almost dropped her wine. Scarsdale
had lowered his head to Yasmeen's neck, and was slowly tracing his
tongue up the column of her throat. She arched her back with an
audible purr. Fox stared at them, then looked down into his drink
before throwing the contents back.

Trahaearn didn't appear to notice the display. "What perversions?"

"Incest during the Frenzies. Humans mating with animals and
bearing offspring. Experiments where—" He broke off, shaking
his head. "You've heard them all. And I've heard them before, too.
Had conversations, genuine speculation whether any of it could be
possible, and it didn't turn my stomach like Pope did. And he was
obsessed with the animals. Jesus."

"I like animals." Laughing, Scarsdale glanced up from Yasmeen's throat, then yelped when she dug her fingers into his thigh.
He caught her hand and licked the inside of her wrist. "I like you,
too, love."

"And when we arrived," Fox's voice sounded a little too loud,
but it brought Mina's attention swinging back to him, "we found a
Horde installation. A laboratory, with a package waiting for him."

"Resistance smugglers?"

Fox looked to Trahaearn. "Yes. I recognized it, too. So I asked
what he intended to do with it."

Trahaearn's lips quirked. "Of course you did."

Mina was lost. "What kind of smugglers?"

"Horde resistance," the duke said. "They fund their rebellion by smuggling Horde tech and weapons to the New World. I've picked up dozens of packages the same way."

"But this one wasn't tech," Fox said. "It was a weapon, of sorts—a plague."

"What?" Mina's heart dropped to her stomach. Even Scarsdale and Yasmeen looked up from their pillow.

"Modified from the strain that killed so many of the Horde fifty years ago. Apparently, they wondered how the bugs had resisted it, so they experimented until they found a strain that affected buggers. Not intending to *use* it. Just to know. But the resistance got their hands on it and sold it. And unlike the Horde, Pope intended to use it."

That was much more than they'd ever learned from the assassin in Chatham. "And he told you all of this?"

Fox's grin was sharp and dangerous. "I can be persuasive."

"What else did he say?" Trahaearn asked.

"That even if I killed him, the Black Guard would endure. And that it would never be defeated." Fox shook his head. "It sounded like the type of speech that comes before a man jumps off a cliff. And the next thing, he's running outside, yelling for the zombies. So I shot him."

"Better than the zombies," Scarsdale said.

Yasmeen watched Fox through narrowed eyes. "Except that one didn't deserve the mercy of it."

Maybe not. More importantly—"What of the plague?"

"Bilson and I destroyed it, and flew home." He looked away from Scarsdale and Yasmeen. "I haven't run into others. And I suspect that Pope wasn't running on a full load of coal. But there was money behind him, and someone had contacts inside the Horde."

"And they were looking to kill buggers," Trahaearn said.

"Yes." Fox's gaze darted across the table again. He abruptly stood. "I'm sorry. I must be up early tomorrow. Good night, inspector, Scarsdale. Captain Corsair."

With a stiff bow, he left.

Mina blinked at the sudden change, then realized that Yasmeen was lifting her mouth from Scarsdale's. She lay against the pillow next to him with a sigh. "Thank you, James."

He stroked her hair. "You have to stop hiding."

"I will when you do."

With a laugh, he glanced at the duke. "I doubt I ever will, now. The captain has turned his life around."

"So determined to destroy everything." Though Yasmeen rolled her head to look over at Trahaearn, she still spoke to Scarsdale. "It's unfortunate he stopped before getting to you."

"How true." With a short laugh, Scarsdale picked up his glass. "Shall we raise another to Baxter?"

Trahaearn frowned at them before shaking his head. "I've already had too much to drink."

He stood. And as abruptly as Fox, he left.

Mina stared after him. From across the table, she heard another purr followed by a soft laugh. And she didn't want to be here anymore.

After several attempts to get up, she finally made it to her feet and followed him.

The airship had begun to sway, making it difficult to walk down the passageway without bumping into the bulkheads on either side. Uncertain whether she was seeking air or Trahaearn, Mina climbed the ladder to the main deck and made her way forward. Sharp wind bit into her heated cheeks. Gas lanterns lit her path and threw deep shadows behind stanchions and capstans. Near the bow, a coil of rope knocked into her foot, and she almost tripped against the side. A warm hand caught her wrist and steadied her.

From his seat on the wooden chest—*her* wooden chest!— Trahaearn rose, and somehow managed to link his fingers through hers. His calluses scraped her palm as he locked their hands together.

"You seem to be handling your wine as well as I am," he rumbled against her ear.

Her laugh became a chattering of her teeth. She'd forgotten her over-coat—but Trahaearn had his. Drawing her in front of him, he wrapped the sides of his coat around her front and strapped her in with his arms. His solid form was like a furnace behind her, and she was suddenly, wonderfully warm. She began to relax against him, but then her eyes registered the scene that lay before her, and she jolted up with a gasp.

"Blue heavens! What are those?"

In the distance, moonlight slanted across white peaks and jag-ged black cliffs. And above them shone the moon itself . . . and the *stars*. Heart in her throat, she stared upward at the bright pinpoints of white, white light, feeling like weeping and laughing.

How beautiful. The stars truly must be blessed.

"Those are the Alps."

Her gaze returned to earth again. A mountain range. She'd known that Europe had them, as triangles inked over maps. But she'd never thought of the mountains. Only the cities and the people who'd had to flee from the Horde. She'd never considered that such a sight would have been just as valuable as the buildings and fields they'd all left behind.

She watched the stars and the peaks, and Trahaearn slowly moved behind her. His mouth touched her hair, then her ear. She shouldn't be letting him do this, but couldn't summon the will to stop him. Then his lips found the side of her throat and she felt his tongue on her skin, and she wanted to arch against him and purr. Just like Scarsdale and Yasmeen—though Mina was certain that no woman could possibly make a sound quite like the aviator captain had.

She fought to clear the spinning in her mind. "What happened down there?"

"The Horde took it all."

"No. Not in the mountains. In the cabin. Scarsdale and Captain Corsair aren't . . . they weren't . . . and yet they . . . ?"

"Yasmeen likes to be touched, but she only trusts a few people to do it. Scarsdale's the same."

"Oh." Mina tried to process that. "Are you someone she trusts?"

"I don't know. Even if I was, I wouldn't. I don't like to touch anyone. Or to be touched."

Then why did he stand here now? She felt him all around her. Not skin to skin, yet still touching. "But—"

"I made an exception."

Oh. Her breath came in sharp little pants. His mouth opened against her neck and he bit her, gently. A hot ache formed low in her belly. She shifted her feet against the deck before making herself stand still, arms at her sides.

What had they been talking about? She cast desperately through her memory until she found it. "Everything changed between them when Fox left."

"Ah, well. They were laying it on thick because she wanted him gone."

"Why?"

"He made a fool of her. She didn't know who he was before coming aboard. And he made her uncomfortable. He watched her all through dinner."

"How do you know? You were watching me."

He laughed into the curve of her shoulder. "Yes. And for the same reason. But she wanted to get rid of him, and you . . . you came to me."

Mina didn't want to think of that. "She and Scarsdale have played it before."

"They have an arrangement that benefits them both."

"Because of what they have to hide?"

"You are the inspector. You have to figure out what their secrets are. I won't tell you."

Laughing, she shook her head. She felt his smile against her neck and his palms sliding up over her belly. Confused, she glanced down. To Mina's shock, her short jacket had been unbuckled to her breasts, open in an inverted *V* that he slowly spread wider.

She made a soft noise, and his hands flattened, holding her against him. Heat bloomed between her legs, shortened her breath.

"Mina." His deep voice turned her name into a command.

"No." She trembled against him. "I haven't given you permission to use my name."

"Just like you waited for Hale's permission to cross the Channel? Do you only care for permission when it suits you? No, Mina." He shook his head. His fingers brushed the red band over her sleeve. "Lie, if you must protect yourself. But do not be a hypocrite. I can't tolerate hypocrites."

Then she should list all of her hypocrisies. But the brush of his fingers against her arm resolved into meaning, and stabbed at her pride. "You think this band is a lie?"

"I was in London during the revolution. I saw what happened to every Horde person on the streets. If you had been out there fighting, they wouldn't have cared who your parents were. You'd be dead."

Yes. She would have been. And he must have seen what no one in England ever mentioned now: the murders and the rapes that had nothing to do with the Horde, and the buggers' uncontrollable emotions after being freed. For a few days, they'd been no better than animals.

And it was a collective shame. Most people outside of England didn't know. The revolution had been something to be proud of—but not everything that happened in that time was.

He tensed. "You weren't out there, were you?"

"No. My father locked me in my mother's attic workroom."

"So what happened?"

They didn't speak of this. Yet the words were tumbling out. "I heard my mother scream. I heard a gunshot. And so I used an awl to open the lock."

And she'd still been carrying it when she'd run downstairs. Outside, the city had been screaming and burning, and her own terror had terrified her even more. Uncontrollable, her fear had fed itself, until it had completely consumed her.

Now, it was like a dream. She could remember being afraid. But she couldn't comprehend how much, and hadn't felt anything like it since.

"They were brothers," she said. "They'd lived in the corner house in the square for a few years. They'd offered for me, once. Not for marriage, but to keep as a concubine, and my father turned them down. But that night, they had an airship and were leaving, because all the Horde were being killed . . . and I think they came to save me. To take me with them, where I might be safe."

Trahaearn's arms tightened around her. She took a deep breath.

"So they came for me. They'd shot Henry. And my mother, there'd been the Frenzy, and she and my father . . . She was with child. But she'd tripped, or one of them had pushed her, and there was blood, and my father was trying to help both her and Henry, and Andrew was screaming and trying to fight them off. Then I came downstairs, and the brothers tried to take me outside the house. Tried to take me away from my family. I didn't think. I still had the awl. And so I . . . stabbed. Over and over, until they let me go."

Even now, her hand tightened. Trahaearn was silent behind her.

"And you're correct: I do use the band to protect myself. When buggers see it, sometimes they decide to let me be. But it isn't a lie. I spilled Horde blood. The only lie is that it's supposed to be a celebration." Not a marker of the most horrifying moment of her life.

His lips pressed to her temple. "I'm sorry."

She shuddered, trying to let go of the memory. Trying to return to here, and now, and to the knowledge that she should be pushing him away.

"Yasmeen said that you wanted to destroy everything—and you told me you weren't saving us when you blew up the tower. But is what happened to us what you intended? Did you know we'd become like animals? Like zombies?"

"You were nothing like zombies."

"It felt like it. But instead of hunger, all violence and fear. Did you know it would happen? Is that what you intended?"

"No." His voice was low and rough. "It wasn't."

"Then what did you—" She broke off as he suddenly turned her to face him. "Don't."

"I'm taking advantage of this opportunity." He lowered his mouth, hovering only a breath above hers. "Before you take advantage of me."

Her head swam. "Take advantage of you? How?"

"With an interrogation."

His lips settled over hers. Oh, but he tasted of wine, of warmth and spice. She moaned low in her throat, hands clutching at his shoulders. With a rough sound of need, he carried her forward and the rail pressed into her back. His fingers clenched in the tight roll at her nape. Her pins loosened, giving up her hair to the wind.

She dragged in a breath when he lifted his head. "What did you intend?"

With a smile, he tucked his big hands under her short coat. His palms slid up over her shirt and armor to cup her breasts. His thumbs swept over her nipples. "To suck on these. Then I intend to lick between your legs until you come in my mouth."

Her knees weakened. Mina clenched her thighs together, felt the wetness gathering there . . . with only a kiss and a few words.

She swayed toward him—and the starry skies help her, she lifted her face to his. "Tell me about the tower. What did you intend?"

His jaw hardened and she thought he'd refuse to answer. But he lowered his head and put his mouth to her ear. "I didn't think of the buggers. I didn't think of anyone. I only thought of hitting the Horde as hard as I could. But, yes, if I'd stopped to think—I would have wanted it to burn. I wanted to destroy everything. But I didn't realize what that meant. Not until I saw what I'd done. And so I'm still paying for it."

What? She comprehended most of it, but couldn't fit the last part. "How are you paying for it? Why?"

He kissed her again until she was clinging and breathless. With his hands beneath her bottom, he lifted her against him. She felt the hard press of his erection into her stomach, and the low, melting ache between her thighs. It was all she could do not to open her legs around him and ride that thick ridge of flesh.

He groaned into her neck. "Invite me to your cabin, Mina."

"No."

"You don't have anything to fear here. Not on the airship. Be with me." He lifted his head, met her eyes. "You've thought about it?"

Yes. Again and again. "I don't need to. My answer will always be the same."

Because it was the only sane answer.

He closed his eyes, and let her slide down his body until her feet touched the deck. "Then go. I'll escort you back to your room."

Lifting a lantern from one of the posts, he preceded her on the ladders and steadied her as she climbed down. He followed her along the passageway to her cabin. The faint moonshine through the porthole barely penetrated the darkness of her room, and the only light came from the dim glow of Trahaearn's lantern. She turned back to him.

"I need to find the spark lighter for my lamp."

Trahaearn nodded. Quickly, she searched the small desk for the lighter. The room brightened and the door closed. The light flickered when he set the lantern beside her. Mina froze.

She didn't look up at him. "Have you come in to help me find it?"

"No." His hand curved around her waist. "I'm taking this opportunity to persuade you."

Then she'd see how well her resistance stood. Not long. He *wanted* her. And by the blessed stars, she wanted this.

Deliberately, Mina turned toward him as he drew her in. Lifting her against the solid wall of his chest, he devoured her mouth with another kiss, hungry and wet and hot. So hot. She melted under the onslaught, gripping his shoulders, trying to reach for more, to take him deeper. Her legs wrapped around his hips.

With a heavy groan, he raised his head. His gaze burned into hers, his breathing ragged.

"I won't fuck you," he promised. "Not with both of us drunk. I won't. I'll only taste you."

A taste, yes. He bent toward her, and hot kisses rained down her throat. She made fists in his hair and dragged him to her mouth again. His muscles surged between her legs as he lifted and moved. Her back hit the wall near the porthole. Fire exploded through her as his rigid length ground into the cradle of her thighs. She broke away from his kiss, arching and gasping.

And then dove in for another taste. Blue heavens, she wanted so much. Her hands shoved his overcoat from his broad shoulders. He spread her short coat open, stripped it down her arms, and laughed against her when he found her shirt and her armor. She tried to laugh, but she was hungry for another taste of his mouth, his throat. He denied her both, grabbing the hem of her shirt. Cotton pulled over her head, and the buckles of her armor quickly released beneath his fingers and thudded to the deck. Tugging down the loose neckline of her chemise, he buoyed her small breasts, exposing them to his gaze. Chest heaving, Mina watched the dark need suffuse his face.

His need couldn't be as big as hers. She didn't see any fear in him, and hers was growing huge, frightening.

"Mina," he rasped. His hands lowered to her backside, and she whimpered when he rolled his erection against the core of her, where she felt so wet and hot and swollen. "I'd fill you here. So deep."

Oh, but she needed that. Her head fell back against the wall.

"But not now." His head dipped. "Now I finally taste you."

Lips parted, she watched as his tongue flicked across her nipple. Usually so soft, now they stood hard, like bullets. She cried out when he drew the stiff peak into his mouth, tugging and sucking. Uncontrollable need whipped into her. Her hips rocked. His fingers clenched on her bottom, holding her firm over his thick erection.

Arousal had flushed his cheekbones when he lifted his head. He made a rough noise, as if the sight of her nipple drawn tight and ripe by the suction of his mouth pleased him. He moved to her right breast, sucking and pulling, and Mina almost lost herself again, her fingers digging into his scalp, helpless to the sounds of need and pleasure erupting from her throat.

He returned to her mouth for another hard and hot kiss. The fine wool of his coat abraded her wet nipples. Still dressed, though she was only in her trousers and a chemise that hid nothing at all. And her trousers were loose, unbuttoned, though she didn't know when or how or even if she'd done it herself.

"I need more." His gaze burned into hers. "I want to taste all of you, Mina. I want to drink you up. Are you wet enough?"

She trembled. *I intend to lick between your legs until you come in my mouth.* And she was so slick, ached so much, needed so much.

"Yes." Her breath came in pants. "Yes."

Slowly, Trahaearn kissed his way down her throat. Between her breasts. Her booted feet hit the floor and she braced her shoulders against the wall, watching him sink to one knee in front of her.

He pressed his lips to her belly. His fingers hooked into the waist of her trousers.

Lick between your legs.

Need rushed over her, beyond anything she'd ever felt—except for once. How was he doing this to her? She suddenly couldn't breathe. Fear squeezed her chest and quickly burst into terror. She pushed her hands into his hair to hold him still.

"No more, Trahaearn. Please."

Please.

The word barely penetrated the dull roar in Rhys's head. God, he needed her. He hadn't expected arousal to take him over like this, burning hotter than the wine and the softness in his head. He hadn't known that his need *could* take him over like this.

But only for her. Only for Mina.

"Please," she said again, and this time he detected fear in her voice.

He *would* please her. And show her that he'd take care of her, that she had no reason to be afraid. He dragged her trousers over her hips and halfway down her sleek thighs, and something twisted in his chest. Even by the dim light of the lantern, her short drawstring pants appeared patched and ragged. Pain lashed through his scalp as she pulled at his hair. He kissed her through the threadbare cotton, trying to soothe her fear. And he'd soon give her silk and lace. He smoothed her pants down and groaned.

"Oh, no, no. Please." She yanked at his hair again. "It's too much like the Frenzy. I need it too much."

He could see that. The wisp of black hair covering her sex was no barrier to his gaze, and she *was* wet, and pink, and flushed with her arousal. She tugged again, and he pinned her hands against the wall before she snatched his scalp bloody. No need to urge him on. She needed, and he'd give. He couldn't wait to give. Her musky scent threatened to drive him out of his mind, more heady than any perfume, any wine.

Above him, Mina whimpered on a panicked breath. He understood this fear. Her first time exposed. Her first time so vulnerable. But he wouldn't hurt her.

"Don't be afraid."

"Please, Trahaearn. No more. I can't feel this much, I can't—"

But she could. His mouth covered her sex and her flavor burst over his tongue. He groaned over her thin scream, her electric response. Her hips jerked. Fingers flexing, her nails bit into his hands. Though her wrists were pinned and her trousers bound her thighs, she managed to twist her body. Rhys followed, seeking out every slick drop, licking between her plump lips. She cried out when he suckled on the swollen bud of her clitoris. Her body arched, and she was so wet again, with more for him to lick and taste.

He pushed her relentlessly, relishing every muffled cry, every sobbing moan. She tried to throw him off, as if the pleasure was too much, but he held her still, until she stiffened and convulsed, her flesh pulsing against his tongue.

Triumphant, he tenderly licked until her shudders faded. And though his cock ached, he *wouldn't* carry her to the bed. Hell, he didn't know if he could even stand up, now that the wine had sunk into him with its fuzzy teeth, the wine and the addictive taste of Mina. He was dizzy with it. He'd have done anything for another taste. And her need had been strong. Maybe she could take more.

He looked up and his heart froze.

There was no desire on her face. No ecstasy, no contentment. Only tears. Devastation.

Oh, Christ no. Realization hit him, a sick punch to his gut. Her protests hadn't been what he'd thought. And this hadn't been making love to her.

"Mina." His voice was hoarse. "I thought—"

"Let me go."

Fury boiled through her command. He immediately dropped his hands from her wrists. She lurched for her weapons. He didn't see which one she grabbed. He could have stopped her.

But he had too much to pay for now.

She shoved the barrel against his neck and pulled the trigger.

Numb, Mina watched Trahaearn fall unconscious to the floor. She sank next to him, her back to the wall. She couldn't sob. Couldn't let herself feel anything.

Easier said than done. The room spun. She couldn't think clearly. He hadn't been thinking, either. His shock as he'd looked up at her had been genuine. *Both drunk.* And by the bright stars, she'd been so stupid. She put her head in her hands. Watered honey wine hadn't prepared her for this.

And she couldn't stay here on the floor. Standing, she pulled her trousers up over flesh that was still hot and wet and sensitive. Her fingers shook as she tugged up her chemise and buckled her armor. She had to drag her shirt from beneath his knee, and almost toppled over when she straightened again. Dizzy, she braced her hands on the bed, wondering if she'd soon vomit, but nothing came up.

She looked down at Trahaearn, taking up almost the entire

narrow floor. The deck had been sanded smooth. Perhaps she could drag him to his cabin. Crouching, she slipped her hands below his arms, and tried to lift him up. Even straining, she could hardly move him, and soon she was sick and dizzy again.

She gave up and threw a blanket over him. With his long body stretched out, she could barely open the door without banging it into his head. Turning sideways, she eased through and crossed the passageway.

The duke's cabin was empty—Scarsdale must have still been with Lady Corsair. She recognized the red waistcoat flung over the foot of one bunk. Trahaearn had worn that earlier. Crossing the cabin, she climbed into the Iron Duke's bed.

Probably not how he'd pictured her there.

Not how she'd pictured it, either.

Suddenly exhausted, she closed her eyes. The image of his mouth on her sex floated behind her lids. She squeezed her hand between her legs, trying to suppress the memory of his lips and tongue. Her terror seemed almost like a dream now, leaving only the need . . . and her wish that she could be someone else, someone who could let herself feel.

Footsteps and the flare of a lamp woke her. Her tongue thick and her head aching, Mina opened her eyes and squinted against the light. Scarsdale stood in his breeches on the other side of the cabin, facing away from her. He pulled off his shirt. Mina's breath stopped.

Old scars laddered his back. The white, raised flesh crossed his skin in the distinctive lashes and knots made by a thieves' cat-o'-nine-tails.

Eyes wide, she rose up on her elbow. Scarsdale glanced over his shoulder—then looked again, spinning around and holding his shirt against his chest like a startled matron.

"Inspector!"

She had to force her brain and her tongue to work. "Yes."

He hastily pulled on his shirt again. "Why aren't you in your cabin? Where's the captain?"

"On my floor. I couldn't move him."

"He never drinks that much. I should have—Oh, Christ." Concern and wariness flooded his expression. "Did he . . . ?"

"No. I shot him."

Alarm replaced the concern. "With what?"

"Opium."

"He's fucked, then." He sighed and dragged his hand through his hair. "That will keep him out far into the morning. Between the two of us, we might be able to drag him in here, but we won't get him up to the bed. Shall we leave him?"

"I already did," she said.

He laughed suddenly. "So you have. And pardon me for saying, you look like hell. I don't know that you could stand up, let alone drag anyone anywhere."

She supposed he knew better than most what could and couldn't be done after a drunken binge. "I concur, sir."

With another sigh, he sat on his bed. "Normally I'd offer to sleep in your cabin. But I imagine you left the porthole uncovered?"

"Yes."

He nodded. "Will you be all right with me here?"

"Yes. I'll pretend you're my brother."

His grin flashed and he lay back. "Do you have another opium dart?"

"On the desk in my cabin. Next to the porthole."

"Damn. Not worth it, then."

She stared across the room at him. He turned to blow out the lamp, and caught her looking. A wry expression crossed his features before the room went dark.

"You can ask me what happened to my back," he said.

Blast. "Was I so obvious?"

"Yes. But everyone is. And then they usually make some clever remark about how apt my courtesy title is. *Scars*dale. It wasn't so clever by the third time I heard it, though." She heard his bunk creak as he lay down again. "My first year as navigator on the *Terror*, the captain had me flogged."

"Trahaearn did?" Sickness lodged in her stomach. "Why?"

"I wanted to sail into the Antilles. Captain had plans for Liberé coast, and wouldn't change them. So I gave the helmsmen the wrong heading."

Aghast, she said, "You stole his ship!"

"Yes. And he figured it out quickly enough. He asked me why, and I told him. Then he had me whipped with the cat in front of the crew."

And was fortunate to have *only* been flogged. Trahaearn had told her that a good captain gave second chances, but trying to take a ship from one was a different matter. Scarsdale was lucky he hadn't been hanged.

"Why did you take that chance?"

"I'd heard Hunt was on Antigua. And when I was finally able to walk out of sick bay, I found that the captain had sailed to the island, after all. But Hunt had already left port."

Mina stared up into the dark. Trahaearn had almost slaughtered the Dame when she'd told him she'd given the *Terror* to Hunt. And Scarsdale would have risked death attempting to track Hunt down. What kind of man could provoke such hatred? What kind of man held Andrew's life in his hands now?

"Why were you after him?"

Scarsdale fell quiet, and the only sound in the cabin was the distant huff of the engines. Finally, he said, "You'd probably best wait to hear that after your stomach settles."

Chapter Eleven

When Mina woke again, Scarsdale was still sleeping. She crossed the passageway, bracing herself against the possibility that Trahaearn lay inside, but her cabin was empty.

Relieved, she washed and dressed, then climbed to the main deck. The sun was high, and the deck shadowed by the balloon. She didn't see him. Fox stood alone near the cargo platform, the winged contraption strapped to his back. Mina glanced over the side. They flew over a swamp crisscrossed by sluggish, muddy canals. Green vegetation all but covered crumbling stone ruins. Most likely Venice—or what was left of it.

A bell rang beside her. Mina looked round, where Lady Corsair gestured her over to the quarterdeck. As soon as Mina reached the windbreak, Yasmeen told her, "He's shoveling coal."

Mina frowned, wondering if she'd misheard over the noise of the engine and the wind. "What?"

"You were wondering where the captain is. He's shoveling coal in the engine room."

Oh. But—"Why?"

"Because there's nowhere else to go." As if that was an answer, Yasmeen looked away from her. Her eyes narrowed as Fox approached the quarterdeck.

Wearing a black shirt and breeches now, with leather guards around his neck and shoulders, the adventurer had discarded color in exchange for weapons. He carried a crossbow, and two machetes were tucked beneath his glider's wings. A belt held holsters at both his hips and his back. He'd strapped long knives to each thigh, and four sheathed in his boots. And when the wind lifted his sleeve, she saw that he had two foot-long blades in spring-loaded contraptions along his forearms.

He greeted Mina before nodding to Yasmeen. "Three weeks, captain. I'll be atop that ruin at noon."

Mina looked to where he pointed. The pile of rubble was the highest point in the area. He'd be easy to spot from the air . . . and from the ground.

"Oh, my." With lifted brows, Mina turned back to him. "Good luck to you, sir."

He laughed and bowed, flashing his boyish grin. "Thank you, inspector." Still smiling, he said to Yasmeen, "Don't be late. Those zombies climb fast."

Yasmeen regarded him almost lazily, as if she was deciding whether to be insulted by the suggestion that she might not arrive in time. She must have chosen not to be.

She nodded and said, "I'll be here. And I wish you good luck as well."

Though obviously a farewell, Fox didn't leave. Hesitating, he looked to Mina, then back to Yasmeen.

"Captain Corsair, you must allow me to explain—"

"No!" Yasmeen's snarl cut him off. She slashed her hand through the air, her eyes bright with fury. "I'll be here in three weeks. I'll fly you back to England. You'll pay me the rest of my fee. Money is all that will pass between us, *Mr. Fox*, because I don't care to hear any more of your words."

Jaw tight, he gave an abrupt nod and strode for the side of the ship. Stunned by the sudden change in them both, Mina stared after him as he slung a small knapsack around his waist, jumped up on the gunwale, and leapt off.

Yasmeen drew a ragged breath and called out, "Fire that cannon, Mr. Siegel!"

Eyes wide, Mina looked to the bow, where the rail cannon had been mounted on the gunwale. The engines huffed, and an unholy wail ripped though the air as the electric generator wound up.

She couldn't contain her horror. "You're shooting at Fox?"

"I'm *what*?" Yasmeen whipped around. Brow furrowing, the captain stared at her for a long moment before breaking into laughter. She shook her head. "This is part of our contract. I make noise—"

An explosion from below cut her off. Aviators gathered at the rail began to cheer, laughing and slapping each others' backs. Another explosion followed, and the crew began burrowing into the weapon chests and withdrawing rifles. The rail cannon fired again and again, soundless but for the whine of the generator and the explosions below.

"We make noise to draw the zombies!" Yasmeen shouted between explosions. "Fox glides out as far as he can while they're all running here, so he'll have fewer to deal with when he lands. And it gives my crew a crowd of zombies to use as shooting practice—and fewer of them left in Europe!"

Oh. Mina flushed, and Yasmeen laughed again. Stalking to a chest, she hefted out a rifle and tossed it to Mina.

The captain grinned. "If you hit five, I'll give the stateroom to you instead of to Trahaearn."

The stateroom wasn't as large as the captain's cabin, but had enough space for a full desk and bed, a wardrobe and washstand—and a private privy. It took Mina only a few minutes to move her things. She was tucking her valise beneath the bed when a heavy footstep at the door brought her around.

Trahaearn stood at the entrance, his gaze moving from her valise to the open wardrobe. Coal dust streaked his skin and shirtsleeves. A dark emotion in his eyes burned like a furnace.

"You've moved into my cabin?"

Her heart pounding, Mina shook her head. She almost couldn't speak past the constriction in her chest, and her answer came out thin and high. "The captain gave it to me."

The heat in his eyes flickered out. "I see."

That was all he said. Mina waited for him to barge into the room as he always did, but he didn't come inside. Didn't take advantage of an open door. The silence stretched, and she couldn't bear it.

"Sir?"

"I lost my head last night." His solemn gaze held hers. "I vow to you that I won't drink again. Not while I'm living."

The wine had made her foolish enough that she shouldn't, either. But it wasn't the drink that had made her need him. It wasn't the drink that had overwhelmed her with fear. And wine wasn't the reason she couldn't invite him in now.

She tried not to wish it otherwise. No good came from fighting against something she couldn't change—and her past was immutable. She couldn't take away the Frenzy, or the panic that her need summoned.

Gathering herself, she said briskly, "All of your life? I'm sure that's not necessary. After we find the *Terror*, we'll return to London and won't—"

"It's necessary." His voice was low and implacable. "I'd never have hurt you, or frightened you. I didn't have the head to realize I was. I'm sorry for that."

She wanted to laugh and couldn't. "Just for that?"

"I'm not sorry I had a taste of you." His gaze landed on the bed. A bleak smile touched his mouth. "Though maybe I should be."

Mina wasn't sorry, either. But she didn't say it. He met her eyes again. After another endless silence, he left.

The blue of the Mediterranean had more green to it than the Channel's. Mina watched the Horde's barges crossing the sea far below, carrying harvests from Europe to the ports in the Orient, where they'd be shipped east to the heart of the empire. The sun was setting as they neared the North African coast, and the barges gave way to airships that traveled between the great walled cities of Egypt and Morocco, still under Horde occupation. Though her heart leapt into her throat as she spotted each new vessel, *Lady Corsair* passed over both the sea and the coast unmolested. She watched until the night prevented her from watching anymore.

The duke hardly said a word during dinner. He might have spent it looking at her; Mina wasn't certain. She concentrated on her plate, making her plans to escape the captain's cabin as soon as possible. And so after her dinner was finished, it was with some dismay that she heard Scarsdale say, "Are you ready to hear about Hunt, inspector?"

She glanced up. Trahaearn *had* been watching her, but now he turned to frown at Scarsdale.

Yasmeen groaned. "Again? You tell that story every time you're soused—and you're not even close to it yet."

"I'll make you purr while I tell her, then." Scarsdale pulled her close. Noting the duke's frown, he said, "The inspector saw the scars while she was in your bed last night. I told her where I'd gotten them, and promised to tell her the rest."

That bleak smile touched his mouth again. "I see," he said, and reached across the table for Yasmeen's silver cigarillo case and spark lighter.

Yasmeen watched him with a smirk. "So this time you won't need it?"

"I'm sure I will." Leaning back against an ottoman, he stretched out his left leg and braced his elbow on his cocked right knee. He regarded Mina over the curl of smoke, and his expression cooled into detachment. "But I'll trade one need for another."

With effort, she returned his stare without revealing the hurt squeezing in her chest. How foolish to feel it. She didn't want his attention. But she supposed that no one liked knowing they could be replaced with a roll of tobacco.

She looked back at Scarsdale, and only her determination not to reveal anything of her feelings allowed her to contain her shock. He lay on his side with Yasmeen stretched out on her back in front of him, lazily smoking, her head propped on a pillow. His hand smoothed up and down her stomach *beneath* her untucked shirt. In full view of both Mina and Trahaearn.

Her shock faded into discomfort. She was no Manhattan City miss, but neither was she accustomed to such a display, even one whose aim seemed to be simple physical pleasure rather than sexual. Mina lifted her glass of iced lemon water, wishing that it were wine. Yesterday, she'd felt so content. Today, she could not have felt more out of place among these people to whom wallowing in luxury and sensual indulgence was as normal as breathing.

She could not even relax against a pillow. Spine straight, she prompted, "Hunt?"

"Let's see where to start." Scarsdale's gaze unfocused. "Ah, well. After the captain mutinied and let Hunt escape the *Terror*—"

"Deserted him," Trahaearn interrupted. "If I'd known what he was, I'd have killed him. But there's always a coward ready to do as his superior commands, no matter what the command is—and that's all I thought he was: a coward. I didn't know he was as bad as Adams."

"Worse than Adams, because he's the slippery type with enough powerful friends who owe him favors that he always weasels out of a hanging or prison. That's what he did after the court-martial." Absently, Scarsdale's hand curled around Yasmeen's waist, dislodging the shirt and exposing several inches of olive skin. Mina looked into her glass. "But I didn't know about the mutiny then. No, I was off helping the Liberé fight the damned French."

"I like the French," Yasmeen said.

"You like their money."

"That I do."

Scarsdale laughed before he continued, "I landed in a French war prison in the Antilles. So did Hunt, as part of a group of mercenaries that Colbert had hired to run the place."

Mina glanced up. "On Brimstone Island?"

He nodded. Yasmeen rolled around, pillowing her head on his shoulder and stroking her hand over his chest.

"Everything you've heard about the prison . . . it was a hundred times worse. The money that Colbert provided for food, clothes, and medicine went straight into Hunt's pockets." His mouth twisting, he reached for his drink. "They crowded us in. Twenty thousand men in a prison designed to hold five thousand. Rivers of shit and the dead piled up, rotting. And one little scratch becoming infected until—"

"Skip the maggots, and everything you ate," Yasmeen interrupted. "It's still too soon after dinner."

Scarsdale nodded and took a long drink. He remained silent for a long moment after swallowing, looking down into his glass. "Hunt was also making money on the side. He'd ship prisoners across the Atlantic to Santa Luzia in the Cabo Verde—islands off the west coast of Africa, and just far enough from the Gold Coast that no one cared."

Uncertain what that meant, Mina shook her head and echoed, "No one cared?"

"Even the Gold Coast has rules," Trahaearn said. "Laws that are understood, even if they aren't written down. They don't include throwing prisoners and zombies together on an island, and having rich men pay to hunt them down."

Barbaric. "What sort of men could do that?"

"The sort who didn't think they were killing *men*," Scarsdale said. "So Hunt gave them the Liberé, and the few buggers unlucky enough to end up in the prison. He liked those. Buggers were stronger, so they lasted longer than the others."

"And that's why he sent you there?" Not a bugger, but an infected bounder was just as strong.

Scarsdale smiled slightly. "I wasn't infected then. He sent me for other reasons."

"But . . . he had to know you're set to inherit Halifax's title. When the eldest son of a marquess disappears, it doesn't go unnoticed."

"It might have. The last thing my father said to me was that I was an idiot for risking my life in a war for half men." He shook his head. "But to return—Hunt didn't send me because I was infected. No, I was just foolish enough to be caught kissing a marine captain."

Truly? Mina had thought that the marine corps were still formed only of men—*Oh.*

Startled, she caught Trahaearn's gaze. He regarded her with cool amusement, as if confirming the conclusion she'd drawn.

But . . . ? Surely her conclusion couldn't be right. Even now, Scarsdale was stroking his thumb beneath the curve of Yasmeen's breast . . . though neither of them seemed to notice what he was doing. They simply looked at each other, sharing a quick smile that spoke of a long friendship, before Yasmeen rolled onto her belly and his hand moved to rub her back.

A friendship. And an arrangement between them, because Scarsdale had something to hide.

Mina fought her quick stab of envy. How fortunate that he *could* hide it. That he could pass though society as everyone else did, rather than being hated on sight. She'd have given almost anything to do the same.

"I see," she said softly. "And so you were found out, Hunt decided that you were less than a man, and sent you to the island. The marine captain, too?"

"Yes. They put us in a maze, and the men who paid Hunt were given steelcoats and rifles. They hunted us, the zombies hunted us— but as an extra incentive, the men were refunded their fee if they killed all of the prisoners before the zombies did." His voice thickened. "Thomas's brains were blown out right in front of me."

Yasmeen squeezed his hand. "Better than the zombies."

"Better than the zombies." The hollow echo was followed by another long drink.

"How did you escape?"

He tapped the side of his head. "I can't become lost in a maze, especially one I saw from above while they were flying us in. And those steelcoats aren't fast. I got round behind one, took his rifle, and blew my way past the guard at the maze exit. I hid on the island until nightfall, found a boat, and sailed to the Gold Coast. And as the captain said, there are some rules that can't be broken. As soon as I spread the word, the Ivory Market took care of the island."

"And Hunt was arrested?"

"No." Trahaearn reached for another cigarillo. "There are no police in the Ivory Market. No arrests. The Market czars destroyed the island. Burned it all."

"And Hunt slipped away again," Scarsdale said. "I returned to Brimstone, but Colbert's neglect had already been found out, the prison's condition appalling all of the New World, and the French trying to save face. I met up with the captain shortly thereafter, and assuming that I'd hear where Hunt was sooner or later, I signed on to the *Terror* as navigator."

"You didn't sign on. You were playing parlor games with blindfolds in a rum dive, and I took you because I wanted you on my ship."

Scarsdale lifted his glass to him. "And you still have me, captain. Your finest possession."

For a brief moment, genuine amusement lit Trahaearn's eyes. "Only until I take the *Terror* again."

A possession to whom he'd offered a job instead of a place in his bed. He'd have offered the same to Mina, at first.

Not now. And however determined Trahaearn was to have everything he wanted, he obviously didn't hold on to all of his possessions. He'd given up his ship so that he wouldn't be forced to kill the Dame. Mina had been traded in for a cigarillo. And that was for the best—he obviously didn't take care of what he owned.

"After Scarsdale told you what Hunt had done to him, you still had him flogged?"

The amusement vanished from the duke's eyes. "Yes."

"I'd have killed him," Yasmeen said.

"I should have boarded your ship, instead," Scarsdale said. "Dead looked like a fine option, those days, and whether it was

Hunt or me didn't matter. Sailing on a ship with a captain who was looking to destroy the world seemed the best way to go about it."

Trahaearn gave a faint smile. "I failed you, then."

"Not yet. But I'm starting to lose hope." Scarsdale looked to Mina again. "We didn't see Hunt again until just before the tower, when he threw a zombie off *Josephine* onto the quarterdeck of the *Terror*."

Mina's mouth fell open. "While the crew was aboard? While you were all there?"

Scarsdale nodded and began playing with Yasmeen's hair, winding one of her narrow braids around his fingers. "Right onto the captain, who killed it. After that, blowing up the tower seemed a better way to go out." With a short laugh, he glanced at Trahaearn. "Only you could make a suicide run after being bit by a zombie and end up a duke."

His detached gaze met Mina's astounded one. "Yes."

She stared at him, trying to take it in. He'd been bit. A healthy bugger wouldn't immediately die and become a zombie; it took a few days. But if he'd been bit, he must have been infected when he'd made that suicide run for the tower—and when he'd blown it up, he'd intended to finish the job the diseased nanoagents started. So why wasn't he dead?

"Not the ears!"

The angry hiss tore Mina's gaze from Trahaearn. Across the table, Yasmeen had jerked up to sitting and was pulling the side of her blue kerchief down. Mina had the impression of a tufted point before the blue silk covered the upper half of her ear.

She glared at Scarsdale, who drew her fingers to his mouth for a kiss. "Sorry, love. I was distracted."

Appeased, she settled onto her belly, and Scarsdale began stroking her back. They were almost hypnotic, those lazy circles—and not so shocking now. Instead, Mina was glad for the two of them. The affection between Yasmeen and Scarsdale was warm and unmistakable . . . and for people with something to conceal, and who probably held as little hope for acceptance as Mina did, at least they didn't have to hide from each other.

But Mina still couldn't relax, and now she felt like a voyeur, watching and wishing for something that wouldn't be hers. She needed to leave. She couldn't make herself do it yet.

A rustle beside Mina drew her gaze to Trahaearn. He'd moved close and regarded her with heavy-lidded eyes. Softly, he said, "Do you want that?"

So he'd been watching her watch Scarsdale and Yasmeen. And now she looked at them again, because she didn't want him to read the answer in her eyes. Did she want someone to touch her, not just to arouse but to soothe? Because he cared and wanted to please her? Not just a lover. A friend. Someone who needed her for the same reasons she needed him. The type of man she would marry, if given half a chance.

She'd accepted long ago that chance wouldn't be coming for her. But did she *want* it?

"No," she lied, and finally found the will to go.

Chapter Twelve

Long past dawn, Mina woke to a stifling cabin with her nightshirt twisted around her waist, blinking away a dream of Trahaearn shagging her on the pillows in the captain's cabin while Scarsdale and Lady Corsair watched and laughed. Disturbed, wet from sweat and arousal, she stumbled to the vanity and splashed water on her face.

She dressed to the endless huffing and puffing and rattling of the engines, making certain that the buckles of her armor and her short jacket were perfectly aligned. The damp hair at her nape refused to lie smoothly, until she used double her usual amount of pins and made a coil tight enough to pull at her temples. Above decks was just as hot, but at least the dry air moved past her face. She sat in the bow for most of the day, watching the landscape pass below her. The desert was not just sand, as she'd always imagined. There were flat rocks and cliffs and long stretches of bare, burned earth. All was yellow and brown, except for the patches and rivers of green where water pooled or flowed. She finally stopped sweating about the time that the desert gave way to grasslands that seemed to blur into one infinite field. She didn't see any zombies or people, and the few trees that stood upright against the sun looked so very desolate and alone.

And despite the name it had earned in the New World and England, she could not imagine that anyone who'd actually visited Africa would call it the Dark Continent. As the day wore on, everything seemed to grow brighter and brighter, until even the blue skies hurt her to look at them.

It hurt to look everywhere. Trahaearn passed the day standing at the quarterdeck in his shirtsleeves, cigarillo always in hand and his expression more detached each time she turned around. And so she stopped turning around.

She was tired of the endless huffing engine. Home seemed very far away, and Andrew even farther. She missed them all so very much, and only her will kept her from weeping into her hands. Finally sunset neared, and she had reason to return to her room.

Splashing water against her face again, she found her skin was tender, as if burned. Not something to worry about—the bugs would take care of it. But they could not make her any less tired, or help her find an appetite when a cabin girl appeared at her door carrying a tray of melon and cheeses and a carafe of iced lemon water.

"Captain Corsair says that you'll probably find her cabin too hot. She thought you'd be more comfortable here."

Mina thanked the girl, and told her to thank the captain. Slowly, she changed into her nightshirt, opened the portholes, and climbed into her bed. The engines huffed and puffed. She stared at the orange sky, hot and tired, unable to sleep.

When all outside turned to night, she finally closed her eyes.

The silence woke her. Mina sat up, listening. The airship wasn't moving. She reached for the lamp.

"No lights." Trahaearn's voice came softly out of the darkness. A shadow beside her bed, he touched her mouth. "No talking. Only whisper."

When she nodded, he moved back. She climbed from the bed, her heart thumping wildly. "What's happening?"

His hand found hers. He gave her a moment to pull on a wrap, then led her through the unlit passageway, up to the main deck, where the smooth wood was warm beneath her bare feet. The night lanterns had been extinguished. The sails were furled. Yasmeen waited on the quarterdeck in an untucked shirt and her hair loose, a kerchief covering the tips of her ears. Moonlight revealed only darkness below, darker than the grasslands would have been.

"Is it another airship?" she whispered when they reached the quarterdeck. "Pirates?"

"Worse." He gave to her a spyglass, and pointed to the east, where the moon shone full. "Believers."

She couldn't make sense of the shape silhouetted in the dark sky. It looked like a cluster of grapes sitting upon a plate.

"William Bushke calls it New Eden—a city made of airships tied together. If he sees *Lady Corsair*, he'll bring her in. Us, too. And there's no ransom from New Eden."

With narrowed eyes, Yasmeen was studying the distant floating city. "What's Bushke doing so far west?"

"I can't imagine."

Mina lowered the spyglass. "Where is he usually?"

"He claims all of the Indian Ocean as his territory," Trahaearn said. "He circles from Australia around north to Horde territory, and sometimes as far west as Madagascar. And he'll take any airship he encounters."

"Why?"

"He adds it to his city. They use the upper decks for gardens, the lower decks to live. He promises a paradise, and all that everyone does is attend the church services, work the soil, and live in peace . . . and Bushke doesn't let them go."

Almost like the Horde. "How can he capture an airship peacefully?"

"That's the exception to his 'peace.' There are those he's forced aboard, but he also has his devoted followers. And he has steam-powered flyers and firepower to back them up. They fly out, circle an airship like wolves, and keep it in place until the city arrives. The only choice is to abandon the ship or be taken."

If given that same choice, Mina would abandon ship, no question. "If no one escapes, how do you know what the city is like?"

He smiled a little. "Because he promised me a fortune to smuggle relics out of Italy. Scarsdale and I used an autogyro to deliver them. And Bushke didn't let us go."

She looked at him doubtfully. "You're here now."

"Well, there is one way off—to jump. Between the worshipping and weeding, we made a glider out of the junk we found in the city."

Yasmeen slipped a cigarillo out of her case, then scrunched her eyebrows together in annoyance, as if realizing she didn't dare light it. "And that was the last time Scarsdale could climb any higher than he can jump without sucking on a bottle first."

"Oh." So that was it. Mina bit her lip in sympathy. "Was he hurt?"

"No. The glider began tearing apart halfway down, but we made it to shore," Trahaearn told her. "Watching pieces of the wings come off as we flew in was enough to do it to him. Me, I was just glad we made it in to land. I sink like a stone."

So would Mina, but only because she couldn't swim. She didn't have iron for bones. "And yet you're a pirate captain?"

"As long as the *Terror* floats, I don't need to."

His grin flipped her stomach about, drew out her own smile. Where had his detachment gone? It wasn't here now—and Mina no longer felt tired and sick and alone. Perhaps one had nothing to do with the other. She didn't know. But she didn't want to return to the stateroom yet.

Yasmeen looked through the spyglass again before lowering it. "He's heading east now, but we'll wait until dawn before we fire up the engines again. Our exhaust trail is too easy to spot in the moonlight."

Mina glanced up at the white envelope. "And the balloon isn't?"

"If we were south of him, or between him and the moon, we'd be easier to see. But there's a few clouds, so we ought to be all right." Despite that assurance, Yasmeen apparently wouldn't leave it to chance. To Trahaearn, she said, "I'm ragged for sleep. You'll watch her?"

He nodded. "I'll take care of her."

"I've put three of the crew on watch, two in New Eden's direction." She waved toward the aviators standing at the side rail. "They'll give a shout. But if they close their eyes to do anything but blink, throw them over. I've got crew bedded down by the engines. If Bushke changes heading, yell down the pipes to them before you wake me. Then try to outrun the flyers."

"Aye, captain," he said.

Her laugh turned into a yawn. "I'm off, then."

And Trahaearn was, too, making a round of the deck and speaking with the aviators on watch—and checking the weapons stations, she noted. Mina took her seat at the bow, curling her toes against the deck. For the first time, she didn't need her goggles. The night was warm, and only a faint breeze stirred the air as the airship hovered over the dark below.

She listened to the murmur of the aviators, Trahaearn's low voice. Heavy steps marked his approach. Mina wasn't used to hearing anything on this ship but the engines and the wind. Now, she only heard those footsteps and the pounding of her heart.

He stopped beside Mina's wooden chest, his dark eyes shadowed. "At dinner, Yasmeen's girl said you were sunsick."

Sunsick. She'd never heard of such a thing, but she must have been. "I'm fine now."

"Yes. But I watched you all damn day. I should have—"

"I'm well." Strange, that she had to reassure him. But here she was.

Nodding, he sat beside her. She followed his gaze to the airship city. Without a spyglass, it only appeared like a speck of darkness beneath the moon.

"What happens if they come? Do we use the emergency gliders?" She'd seen them all over the airship, folded and tacked against the bulkheads.

"Yasmeen wouldn't leave her," he said. "She'd blow it all to hell first. And we're over the Niger River marshes. If we took the gliders, we might live two minutes after landing."

A chill ran through her. "Zombies?"

"Not as bad as the Congo, but still thick as fleas. Farther west and south—at least some of the people made it aboard the rescue ships to South America. Not here." He fell silent for a moment. Then, "If Bushke comes, I'll protect you. And I'll make a better glider for our escape."

"I'll stay close to you, then." She tilted her head back, looked up at the balloon. "If they come, why not just fire on their balloons with the rail cannon?"

"Three thousand people live in New Eden. Children, women."

"Oh." And all of them killed if it came crashing down. "Yes. Better to make a glider."

"Yes." Beside her, Trahaearn's weight shifted as he withdrew a small folded paper from his watch pocket. He pressed it into her hand. "I want you to have this."

Even before she unfolded the note, Mina knew what it was. Her neat writing stared up at her.

I accept.—W.W.

She swallowed past the unbearable ache in her throat. "You lied about receiving it."

"You lied about sending it."

"And now? I haven't . . . *performed* as you liked, so you will bring this back between us to find my brother? What should I do first, Your Grace? Should I be on my knees?"

He captured her face between callused palms, made her look at him. Dark emotion burned in his eyes. "No. I showed this to you so that you'd know I didn't want that. I *could* have had it. I could have let the acceptance in this note stand. But I don't want you to come to me like that. Not forced. I didn't mean to force you two nights ago. I won't now."

Her heart thudded, pounding against her ears. "I know you won't."

"Two nights ago, you wanted me." His hands tightened. "Have I destroyed that?"

No. She closed her eyes, but he must have read her face. Relief seemed to pour through him. His voice softened.

"Was it so much like the Frenzy?"

"Yes," she said, but thought: He'd wanted *her*. She thought that she didn't want to return to her room alone. That she didn't want to return to London without knowing, without *trying* to change the damage the Horde had done with their tower. And that she didn't want to be afraid. So she admitted, "But not all of it. Just at the end."

"Mina . . ." His gaze searched her face. "Tell me straight out."

So he wouldn't make an assumption. She took a deep breath. "You said that we could be together on the airship and the *Terror.* I want that. To try, at least."

"Try me." His thumb stroked down her cheek. "And I'll stop when you're frightened."

"Yes."

"Good." He dropped a kiss to her mouth, hard and brief. Before Mina could react, he lifted and settled her over his lap, his shoulders braced against the rail. "You control it."

Here? Now? "But—"

"I told the aviators not to look this way or I'd burn their eyes out. Kiss me, Mina. Hold me down, make me pay for forcing you. We'll start this off equal."

She had to laugh. "That's hardly punishment."

The darkness that flickered across his expression stopped her laughter. "If I'm restrained, you'll have your payment."

Mina didn't know if she wanted that. But she wanted *him*.

Rising and lifting her hem, she turned to straddle him, her knees on the wooden chest and his hard thighs between hers. His hands found her hips and he tilted his head back against the gunwale, offering his mouth to her . . . or his throat. Mina bent her head. His lips softened under hers, and she parted them with a thrust of her tongue.

He moaned with her, his fingers tightening, and she deepened the kiss. Only two days had passed, yet how she'd missed this. The hot stroke of his tongue. The taste of him. His stubble-roughened jaw abraded her chin and her lips as she trailed kisses from the corner of his mouth to his ear. She pushed her fingers through his hair, exposing those tiny rings.

He shuddered when she flicked them with her tongue, and he laughed softly, as if surprised by his reaction.

She drew back. "Why these rings?"

He hesitated before he said, "I didn't like where they were. So I put them where I wanted them."

Her gaze narrowed on the faint scars in his lobes. Faint . . . and ragged.

"Did you rip them out? Or did someone else?"

"I did."

Six of them. "Where else?"

Eyes never leaving her face, he brought her hands to his chest. His nipples, she realized, and instinctively cringed. "You ripped them out *here*?"

"Yes."

And two more. "Where else?"

His fingers curled into her palms as he drew her hands between them. Then lower, until she cupped his hard length through his breeches, and he ran her thumb over the wide tip of his erection. She stared at him in horror. The corner of his mouth ticked up.

"Or I lied so that I'd have your hands on my cock."

She barely stopped the loud laugh that rose up through her. Catching herself, she whispered, "But truly?"

He nodded, drawing her hands up to his shoulders and smoothing his palms down her sides to her hips. "I paid for these rings. But I didn't like where they'd put them."

So matter-of-fact. Her heart seemed to slow, but every beat struck harder and harder inside her ribs. He'd said there was always a use for a boy of fourteen at the Ivory Market—and she'd seen too many broken children in London not to guess that there'd been a use for a boy of eight, too. But only eight years later, he'd been sold to the Americas, bound for a coal mine. Her fingers traced his face. Despite being so handsome.

"You must have been uncontrollable for them to have sold you again. Were you of iron, even then? And as strong?"

Whatever sort of nanoagents he had, they'd done more than help graft metal prosthetics to flesh, as they did to most buggers. She couldn't even lift him. Yet they'd made him strong enough to move, run, jump—despite the heavy weight of his bones.

"I've always had the iron. The strength grew with it."

But not quickly enough, she thought. No need to break a boy's bones when he had flesh. With enough pain or threat, they could still have controlled him. And he wouldn't have reached his full strength until he'd been full grown. Still, whatever he'd possessed at sixteen must have been enough that he hadn't been worth the risk of keeping.

When she said so, he nodded. "They decided I was too dangerous to use anymore. But I was worth more sold than dead."

Too dangerous to use. "You killed them. Some of those who used you."

"Sometimes *while* they were using me." His lips twisted. "And afterward, that meant I fetched a higher price."

Because the danger meant excitement. The thrill of restraining something so strong, and then to take him. Yes. She could see why it would fetch a high price. And she saw more.

"And so now, you don't force women." Something was growing in her chest, light and airy, leaving her almost giddy. "And if Hunt had sold Andrew, you wouldn't have left him to that. You'd have found him even if he wasn't on the *Terror*."

"Along with any other boy sold off my ship." His fingers tightened on her hips. "But don't be mistaken, Mina. I don't crusade on principles. I just protect what's mine. They were on the *Terror*, so they're mine. And when I found Andrew, I wanted your gratitude."

"I will be grateful. But I'm not doing *this* for that. This is for me."

His eyes challenged her. "You aren't doing much of it."

Smiling, she kissed him again. The warm breeze slipped around them, tangling her hair, catching the collar of his shirt, and cooled the perspiration on her face, her neck. Tugging at his shirt, she smoothed her hands beneath. His abdomen contracted beneath her fingers, and she slipped up over hardened muscle and crisp hair. He stiffened when her fingers brushed the small hardened nubs on his chest.

She froze. "It still hurts?"

"No."

Good. The memory of his head at her breast made her ache. She'd lick him, too. "The same as mine?"

"I like it. But they're not the same."

Oh. "I loved your mouth on mine."

Stark hunger scraped across his features. "Then let me taste you again."

Suddenly trembling, she lifted to his mouth and pulled down her neckline, baring one breast. Slowly, softly, he circled the hardened peak with his tongue before drawing her into his mouth. Her fingers dug into his hair. With a groan, he shifted his body down, and instead of straddling his thighs, her legs were spread over his hips. He pressed her down until his erection formed a thick pressure against her burning core.

She rocked against him and had to bite her lip, stifling the need to whimper, to cry out. Aching, needing him inside her, she kissed him deep—and then lifted herself again, up and down, rubbing that hard ridge against her sex. His face darkened, cheekbones flushed. His ragged breaths urged her on, his hands on her hips helping her move.

And it was too much for her. Too much. Need that had been building slowly began a rapid, uncontrollable rise. Gasping, Mina scooted back down his thighs and cut off his groan of denial with a kiss. Her lips explored his mouth, his jaw. Her hands traveled down the muscled planes of his chest to his stomach, until she found the edge of his breeches. Her cheeks heated. The material stretched over his cock was soaked with her need.

So wet. And he'd barely touched her, yet she wanted and ached.

She'd been afraid that as soon as he touched her, she'd lose control. But she'd lose control without it.

She wondered if he would, too. Her fingers moved to the front placket of his breeches.

He caught her hands at the first button. "Mina. This is for you."

"It was too much. So just . . . let me." She stilled. "Unless you don't like it?"

With a short laugh, he pushed his erection against her hand. "Then let me."

He released her, fisting his hands beside her knees, his gaze fixed on the shadows between them as her fingers unfastened his breeches and loosened the tie of his drawers. Though barely able to see, Mina could feel. Hot, hard—and so thick that her fingertips didn't meet when she closed her hand around him.

At her touch, his breath hissed through his teeth. At her first stroke, he jerked upward, thrusting through her grip. Marveling at his reaction, she fisted him in both hands and pumped his length again.

"Mina. God!"

His head fell back against the rail, the tendons in his neck straining. Impulsively, she leaned forward and put her mouth to his throat, sucking and licking. He jerked again, and her palm slipped over the wet tip of him, a slick drop that eased her way back down. A harsh sound came from his chest. He bucked, and she realized the moisture had done it, made the sensation that much better. There wasn't enough.

"Help me." She panted against his neck. "Help me make you wet."

His chest heaving, he brought her hands to his mouth and licked a wet stripe up the center of each palm, through the sensitive crease between her middle fingers. She shivered.

"I was wrong, Mina." His gaze burned into hers as he lowered her hands to his cock again. "You couldn't punish me with restraints. Only if you stop."

He'd already paid when she'd shot him. He'd paid with his horror when he'd realized what he'd done, with his regret and apology. He didn't need to pay more now.

She closed her fingers around him—and the moisture was soon gone. He reached for her hands again, but her body was wet. So wet. Shifting forward, she rocked her sex against him.

He choked back a guttural moan. Heart racing, Mina grabbed onto the gunwale and held on as she rode over his thick length, each long stroke tying the knot burning at the apex of her sex tighter and tighter, every thrust through her slick folds digging a deeper ache within her. Need and panic began screaming together, but she wanted to see him to the end, wanted to see him when he came apart. Wanted to see what it was to come without fear.

His hands suddenly grasped her hips, forcing her to stop. His muscles turned to steel and he shook beneath her, and she felt the pulsing of his heavy flesh, the spurt against her belly. Gasping, she remained still, watching as the orgasm contorted his features, looking so much like pain but it was ecstasy, pleasure—and her own so strong that she poised at the precipice, where a tiny movement would tip over into terror, and she'd shatter.

Then his was done, his body unlocking, his muscles no longer so rigid. A tremor ripped through her when he sank back against the side of the ship. He opened his eyes—and froze, staring up into her face. "Mina?"

She had to answer. She whispered, "That's all I can do."

"Mina, God." The tightening of his hands on her hips made her whimper. He stilled again. "You're so close. Do it yourself. Your fingers, like my tongue."

Trembling, she shook her head.

He held her, not moving, waiting until her need eased and he could bring her in to lie against his chest. Then longer, until she yawned against his neck.

"To bed, Mina," he said softly.

"And you?"

"I have to stay until dawn. Let me come to you then. To lay with you."

"To take advantage of me when I wake up?"

"No." She felt his smile against her hair. "I'll begin when you're asleep."

Rhys hesitated at the side of her bed. Mina lay in the center of the white sheets, the thin nightshirt twisted around her legs, a sheen of perspiration on her skin. He'd disturb her when he lay down—heavy as he was, a sagging mattress was a given, but he'd broken more than one bed. And if he woke her, anxiety might keep her from sleeping again. Even though she'd agreed to share his bed until they returned to London, this was still new.

To him, too. But he was already certain the airship and the *Terror* wouldn't be enough. Why had she trusted him when he'd said they would be? She knew he was a pirate, and a liar—but perhaps she truly believed that he'd be done with her before they reached London. Perhaps it was what *she* wanted.

He'd wait until he'd had her. Then she'd learn differently.

The engines started, shattering the silence that had lasted through the night. Mina stirred. Her eyes opened and widened at his appearance. He searched her face for fear when she realized that he only wore his drawers. He didn't see any.

All right. The bed creaked as he got in. She rolled toward him with a startled laugh, coming to a rest against his side. He lifted her over him, tucking his arm around her waist. Christ, she was a small thing. Her shoulders were barely the width of half of his chest. He could feel her toes at his shins, and the top of her head tucked beneath his chin.

The fingers of her right hand skimmed over his pectoral, as if hesitant to touch him, testing his reaction. He lay still, and finally her hand rested against him.

Sleepily, she said, "I hate that blasted engine."

Rhys did, too. He preferred the quiet of the *Terror*—though he didn't know if she'd find it quiet. There was always creaking, the cawing of the seabirds, the roar of the waves, the voices and footsteps of the crew.

"London is loud," he said.

"But with different noises. Not just one. I thought one would be easier to ignore, but it just becomes louder and louder. It becomes everything."

It struck him that he'd thought that his first time on an airship, too—that the engine would drive him mad. Then a few days later, he didn't notice it anymore. "It'll be better soon. The heat, too."

He felt her nod. Then she said, "It will soon be too hot to sleep like this."

"Do you care?" He didn't.

She seemed to think it over. "No."

Good. He closed his eyes.

When Rhys woke up, she was sitting cross-legged at the head of the bed, watching him. The cotton nightshirt stretched over her knees, blocking his view between her legs. So he'd have to get under there. But first, he wanted to look some more.

Her black hair fell smoothly from the part at the center of her head, framing her round face. A damned pretty face, he realized with some surprise. Driven by his need to possess her, he hadn't thought much about how her features came together—he'd already liked all of them. But now, with his need still urgent but soothed by the promise of soon having her, he could truly see her. And she wasn't just pretty. Her face contained everything. Her features could be soft and hard, cool and hot. They gave him her laughter and anger, insight and confusion.

Now, she was studying him with her keen inspector's gaze, patient and razor-sharp, as if she was preparing to peel him apart.

All right. But only if he could peel away something from her in trade.

Rhys turned onto his side. "Take off your nightgown," he said.

Her eyes widened. "Why?"

"Because you have small tits and big nipples." Both the perfect size for his mouth. "I want them now."

She still hadn't recovered from her confusion and surprise. She glanced at the sun streaming through the portholes. "Now? But—"

In a quick movement, he rolled over onto his stomach, his elbows alongside her knees, his palms cupping her hips. All he had to do was shove her nightshirt up and lower his head, and he could bury his face in the crevice of her thighs. Her fragrance penetrated the cotton, warm and earthy, the musk of sweat and woman. His cock ached. To take the edge off, he rocked his hips into the mattress.

"You're about to interrogate me. I'll answer. But I intend to suck on your nipples while I do." His gaze dropped. "And when you're done, I'll spread your legs and fuck you with my tongue."

"Oh, blue." On a gasp, she twisted away. He caught her knee with his right hand and ran his left up the inside of her thigh. She quivered and looked back over her shoulder.

His fingers found moisture, heat. She wasn't wet. Not yet. He slipped through her folds and circled her clit.

Her teeth dug into her bottom lip. Her head bowed. "Stop that."

He didn't. The little bud was swelling beneath his fingertips, stiff and slick. "Because there's daylight outside? Because it's difficult to interrogate me like this? Or because you're afraid?"

He'd stop for the last. Only for the last.

"Because I can't think."

Good. He dragged her beneath him and onto her back. Her nightgown rode up on her waist. She was naked beneath. He came down between her parted thighs, his weight on his elbows, pinning her hips with his. Letting her feel him through his drawers. She was hot now—and so wet, soaking the linen through to his cock.

"Ask what you want to know," he said, lifting his hand to his mouth. Her lips parted in shock as he licked her flavor from his fingers.

"I—he—Scarsdale." She closed her eyes. Her throat worked, and she continued with slow deliberation, "Scarsdale said that Hunt threw a zombie off an airship onto the *Terror* and it bit you."

"It did." He angled his forearm until she could see the scar. "A big chunk."

And the feel of her beneath him was doing a lot to keep that memory at bay. But not for her. Horror had filled her eyes, as if she was imagining it. And still not understanding.

"But how—?"

"Am I still alive?" He shook his head. "I don't know."

Her brow furrowed when she frowned up at him. Rhys kissed the frown away, but had to admit he wouldn't last long like this. And she seemed determined.

So he'd let the lady have her way.

He rolled over and off the bed, glad he'd visited the privy before he'd fallen asleep and had no need for it now. His erection was so hard, he'd either break his cock bending it the right direction or piss in his own face.

The cabin girls had already been in. Coffee, grapes, and melon waited on the small table, along with bowls of the yogurt and honey that Yasmeen favored. Aviators were lucky bastards. Traveling short routes and stopping often enough, they could load up on fresh food and supplies as needed. Never down to hardtack and picking worms out of it.

Coffee in hand, Rhys glanced around at Mina. Her gaze wasn't on his face, but fixed somewhere on his chest and stomach, and hungry— as if she wanted to take a bite of him, too. He resisted the urge to find a breeches and shirt. If she liked it, he'd let her look.

Though he sure as hell couldn't understand it, any more than he understood Scarsdale, or what any woman saw in a man when he was all but naked. In the Market, they'd tried to keep him shaved and oiled up after he reached puberty. Probably for good reason. Twenty years later, he was nothing but hair. Hairy chest. Hairy legs. A jaw that was rough five hours after he scraped a razor over it. But even with all the hair gone, there were just harsh angles and rough muscle. Hands coarse and callused. The jut of his cock against his drawers was ridiculous, and uncovered, was nothing but a blunt ugly tool. But Mina . . . God, look at her. Even on the thin side, she was soft and curvy, with every part of her made to fit his hands, his mouth.

But still thin. Frowning, he glanced down at the plate. There was enough here for two, but he knew himself well enough that he could polish this off without a second thought. And so would she. At dinner, she ate with concentration, and though she never asked for seconds, she never left a crumb, either.

He did that, too. He had too many memories of plates that weren't full to waste what was put in front of him. He pulled out a chair. "Get over here and eat this with me."

She did. Unable to turn down a meal, even when he ordered her around like a sailor. Christ, that twisted at him. She pulled her blue wrap on over the nightshirt and sat. Taking her coffee, she said, "You must have some idea why you survived."

"My bugs are different."

He said it without thinking, and immediately wished he hadn't. He might run her off before they reached the Ivory Market tonight. Of course, as quick as her mind was, she might have already figured it out. He didn't see any surprise on her face. Instead, she popped a grape into her mouth and arched her brows, waiting for him to continue.

"But I don't know if that's why. Might have been that I shoved my arm in a boiling pot right after. Maybe that killed the diseased ones." And had hurt enough, had felt like it'd almost killed him. "I might just be that lucky. Whatever the reason, I'm not looking to get bit again."

"Animals don't become zombies."

His lips quirked. "I'm not an animal."

Though some would say he wasn't entirely human, either—even less human than other buggers. Hell, if they knew it, some buggers would think so, too.

"I didn't mean—Just that ratcatchers . . ." She flushed a little and pressed her lips together. "The Horde tried to control them with the tower, too. To lock them down, to freeze their bugs. They couldn't. The first ones, the ones they made, yes. But not the second generation."

So she *had* figured it out. "They must have used the wrong frequencies," he said.

She stared at him. Maybe searching out the differences. Carefully, she said, "Were your parents born with their nanoagents, too?"

"I don't know. I doubt it. There was a Frenzy nine months before I was taken to the crèche."

"So they must have been affected by the towers," she murmured.

"Yes."

"And if you have children?"

"I wouldn't know. And I don't know if I ever will." That depended on whether she'd want to have children off a man who'd been born with iron bones and bugs that hadn't replicated, but had become something new. And he wouldn't ask her now. He'd wait until they returned to London—but since he'd be sharing Mina's bed before that, he realized he ought to tell her, "I'll use a sheath when I'm inside you."

He watched her reaction, but he didn't see the relief he expected. He saw understanding, instead.

With a sad little twist of her lips, she looked down at her plate. "I don't know if I will, either," she said quietly. "I'd like to. But my children would be . . . It would be difficult for them. And I don't know if I could watch it happen."

He frowned at the top of her head. The reasons for her uncertainty weren't anything like his. And by God—she must be thinking of children that came from another man. No child of theirs would be left unprotected, any more than he'd allow her to be hurt. But reassuring her meant asking her *now* to bear his children.

After her confession, however, he had no doubt that they'd raise children, even if they weren't from his seed. Blood didn't matter to him. What Rhys called his *was* his, and Mina wanted to be a mother—so he'd make certain she was, in one way or another.

"There are always children in the crèches."

Her head jerked up. She stared at him, her face slowly brightening. A smile broke from her, then a wondering half laugh. "Yes. I don't know why I didn't—*Yes*. That would be the perfect solution."

Good. He didn't know a thing about families, but he'd damn well get theirs right.

Her gaze unfocused, and she continued eating with a soft expression on her face. Perhaps thinking of future children. But it wasn't long before her attention returned to him, and that keen look entered her eyes.

"So you didn't know that the zombie's bite wouldn't kill you."

"No, I didn't."

"And thought you were dead. So you loaded up the *Terror* with explosives and made a run for the tower."

"I did."

"Why?"

That was a big question for such a little word. But boiled down, the answer was simple enough. "Dying pissed me off. Worse, that I'd come back a zombie."

"So you struck at the Horde for making them?"

He nodded. "I couldn't get to Hunt. So I got to the tower. And they had so few guards, the Horde might as well have invited me in."

"Because the radio signal wouldn't let the rest of us come near it." She was staring at him, her brows slightly pinched together. Still not satisfied with his answer, he realized, even before she said, "And that's it? It wasn't because you wanted to destroy every government, every institution?—And why did you want *that*?"

For the same reason. "Because I was pissed off."

She looked baffled. "At what?"

"At how fucking useless they all were." He frowned back at her. "Why weren't you pissed off?"

She blinked. Her shock melted into wry humor. "The Horde wouldn't let us become that angry."

That was true enough. But that wasn't what he meant. "No. I'm talking about afterward. I strolled into that tower with a few members of my crew who weren't infected with bugs, and brought the damn thing down. And for two hundred years, Manhattan City was full of men without a nanoagent between them. The navy was, too. They *ought* to have been saving you. All bloody fucking cowards."

Something flickered in her eyes. Anger, yes. But resignation, too. "One: They thought we weren't worth saving. Two: Bugs and the Horde terrify them. Three: They thought they couldn't defeat the Horde. Did you know you'd be able to stroll in? When you served on Baxter's ship, did you tell him he ought to sail up the Thames so that you could walk in? Did you know one tower would affect *so* much?"

He clenched his jaw, but had to admit, "No."

"Was Baxter a coward? Was he useless?"

His inspector was ruthless. Evenly, he said, "Not a coward. But useless? Yes. Before that tower came down, yes. All of them were. The Khan, who can't stop his *dargas* from earning extra money on the side by selling eight-year-old boys to the skin trade. The Lusitanian parliament that forbids buggers from crossing their borders, but won't stop the mines from bringing in slave ships full of men with pulverizing hammers and drills grafted to their bodies. I could spend an hour naming them. From the moment I was chained on a ship heading to the Ivory Market, I began making lists of every government and institution that was useless or run by hypocrites, and by the time I killed Adams and took the *Terror*, the whole fucking world was going to pay."

She regarded him quietly. He tried to read her expression, but she'd retreated into that penetrating, inscrutable look. Christ. He didn't know what she thought of that. He couldn't change his past, wouldn't be ashamed of it, didn't need to defend it. And he couldn't regret anything he'd done. But her opinion mattered.

After a long moment, she only observed, "You *were* angry."

"Ah, well." He shrugged. "I was young. And then I grew out of it."

"The revolution?"

"Yes. I've seen worse in my time. But I hadn't been the one to do it. And I'd never been so careless that I destroyed more than I intended."

"We aren't sorry."

"I know." He smiled slightly. "But all of the English are mad."

Her eyes lit with laughter. "That, from a Welshman?"

"Born in Caerwys doesn't make me Welsh."

His inspector appeared ready to argue before she shook her head. "What does it make you?"

"What would you say?"

Her lips pursed. "You sound like a sailor: French, Lusitanian, and a dockworker all combined. And a bit of a bounder in there, too."

Someone who didn't quite belong anywhere, except for a ship. He nodded. "That's about right."

"Even with the title? That ties you to both England and Wales."

"Yes. But that's something else."

"Paying for the revolution?"

So she remembered their conversation up on deck two nights before, even though she'd been three sheets to the wind. "Yes," he said. "And I've Baxter to thank for it."

"Not the king or his council?"

She didn't let up. Holding back his laugh, Rhys finished his coffee. He usually didn't like interrupting eating with talking, but he was enjoying the hell out of breakfast with the inspector. Her every response fascinated him, the challenge of trying to predict her next question and the direction her thoughts would take. He could easily imagine beginning every day like this—and ending them the same way, too. Maybe even reading newssheets, just to hear her reaction to every report.

But she was waiting to hear his answer. "The title meant nothing to me, except that it represented something that I'd hated for almost twenty years. And I'd have left—until Baxter told me what it meant. I had people and holdings to take care of, and they were mine now."

"And you protect what's yours," she murmured. "But how is that paying?"

"That's not paying anything. That's what I do. But a duke?" He shook his head. "Baxter said it was what I deserved, though. For my arrogance, for my recklessness, for my selfish anarchism."

"His words?"

Rhys had to laugh. "His words, yes. But he wasn't wrong. So I agreed to pay, to take on a duke's responsibilities, and to build what I could."

"And?"

"And it's not any different than captaining a ship."

She narrowed her eyes and slowly repeated, " 'Not any different than captaining a ship?' "

"Yes. Instead of a crew I have staff, tenants, my docks, shipping fleets . . ." Too much to name now, especially when he could feel her temper rising. Hoping to push it higher, to see if she'd reveal what had sparked it, he summed up with, "Basically, a much bigger ship. And I take care of it."

"A big ship." Sitting back, she stared at him in disbelief. "And your duty is only to the people on that ship?"

He frowned. Her tone suggested he'd shirked his responsibilities, hadn't taken on enough. "It's a good number of people."

"But your duty isn't just to *your* people."

"Who, then?"

"All of us. Oh, I know—" She waved carelessly in the air, as if brushing away an imagined response. "You don't care. You haven't cared for anyone but those you call yours from the day of the tower. Fine, then. You don't do it for that reason. You do it because if you take care of everyone, that will keep *your* people happy and safe. You think a title and a seat in Parliament is just duty for my father? *Everything* he does, every letter he writes, is so that we'll be safe and happy. Because that can only happen when the people around us are taken care of, too—whether they are his tenants or his staff or not."

He'd never thought her an idealist. And she far overestimated the scope of his power. "No matter what I do, life can never be perfect for everyone."

"No. But it can be *better*." She sat back. "There's a rope factory in Leeds where the owners decided to cut wages. They said the buggers put in less effort, because they're stronger than men who aren't infected—and because the Horde installed more efficient machines than in New World roperies. And the buggers were barely getting by before, but they can't find a position anywhere else, so they've no choice but to stay, working twice as long for half the money. What do you think of that?"

He thought the ropery owner was full of shit. And she might have been pleased to know that it sparked anger in his chest. But he wanted to push hers and see where she took it. "It sounds like the buggers should hang the fucking owner."

Her eyes flashed. "And then see all of them killed? Other factory owners—bounders *and* buggers—are making the same wage cuts, citing the same reasons. It's disgusting. And I'll tell you why you should care. Those goods you're shipping in? The buggers can't buy them. You make less money. And the people on your lands? The buggers can't buy anything they produce. And yet your ships are paying the same amount for rope that costs half the price to make, with all of the profit going into the pockets of some bastard who won't pay his people. And the buggers are tired, and hungry, and they'll make mistakes while they're producing your rope, and you'll lose a sail, or a ship, and a significant amount of money when your cargo sinks. And before long, all of England falls again because a factory owner wouldn't pay his workers what they deserve."

Rhys stared at her. She was brilliant. Magnificent. But he wasn't yet certain what she was getting at. "What are you asking me to do?"

"That's your duty! To take care of the people. To take care of all of us. You've got a voice big enough for the White Chamber. Yet you sit in your house counting your money and your fleets and your tenants."

So that was it. Parliament. "I hire people to count the money for me," he said. "And I'll be in the White Chamber come the session following the election."

She blinked. "What?"

With a grin, he lifted her out of her chair, carrying her against his chest. "That was my agreement with the Lord Regents. To bring you with me without force, without affecting your career, and without ruining you, I agreed that I'd take my seat."

Her lips parted. He wasn't sure what shocked her more: his agreement, or why. He laid her on the bed.

As the mattress sagged under his weight, she narrowed her eyes at him. "You aren't Free Party, are you?"

"No. I lean toward Lug. Now take off your nightgown. I plan to finish my meal."

Though her cheeks flushed and her breath shuddered, she bit her lip, as if uncertain.

"I won't shag you. Not today. I didn't bring a sheath in with me, and I'm not leaving this cabin until we reach the Ivory Market tonight." He pushed her hair back over her shoulder, and leaned in to press his lips there. "But I'll try to make you come, Mina. I'll stop when there's too much fear—but then I'll try again. And I'll keep trying until you can need without thinking of the Frenzy. Even if it takes all day. Even if it takes several weeks. Because I don't want you afraid when I'm finally inside you."

"I don't want to be afraid." She hesitated. "Did it take you a long time . . . after the Ivory Market?"

"No. Because I didn't want anyone. I didn't even try. I pushed everything I had into the *Terror.*" His mouth stilled on her throat. With a wry grin, he lifted his head and looked down at her. "Perhaps that means it *did* take me a long time."

She smiled faintly. "And since the *Terror*?"

Since the *Terror*? There'd been plenty of opportunities, but few he wanted to take. He hadn't had many women—and he still hadn't liked being touched. Every time, it hadn't been about wanting them, but proving that the Ivory Market hadn't broken him. When he'd simply wanted physical release, his imagination and his hand provided both.

But then came Mina, and the flare of lust that had burned through him when he'd taken her glove. He rarely felt anything like that . . . and never like the need that drove him now. Even his imaginings were better with Mina featured in them.

"I put everything I had into being a duke," he finally told her. "Sitting in my manor house counting money takes a lot of effort."

Her laugh was soft and easy, without a hint of fear. *Good.*

Because from this point, Rhys was putting everything he had into her.

Chapter Thirteen

Cutting *Lady Corsair*'s engines the previous night had delayed them. It was nearing midnight before Mina climbed above decks in anticipation of her first glimpse of the Market, prudently leaving her short uniform coat behind in favor of a less conspicuous black waistcoat that buckled tightly over her shirtsleeves and armor. Trahaearn had already joined Yasmeen at the quarterdeck, and she knew they were discussing whether to wait until morning before attempting to find Colbert. That decision was made for them, however, when the notorious settlement finally came into view as an unmistakable orange glow against the dark sky.

The Ivory Market was burning.

Though the spyglass, Mina could only see flames and gray smoke. "What happened?"

Beside her, Trahaearn shook his head.

Lady Corsair's approach seemed endless, and from a distance, the extent of the fire impossible to determine. Trahaearn's grim expression reflected the captain's and the crew's, and they waited, their eyes on the horizon.

They passed the spyglass between them, and the orange glow slowly resolved into detail. Mina watched through the lens, astounded by the size of the Market. She'd pictured a larger version of the carnival near Chatham, not a city that sprawled along the edge of the coast. By the orange light, she could make out the market proper—an enormous collections of tents and stalls that formed a wide swath at the city center. But it was flanked by large houses of stone and wood, pockets of shantytowns, and rookeries that Trahaearn told her were as dangerous as the worst in London. Not all of them were burning.

He took the spyglass again. "The fire is centered in the French quarter."

Where Colbert's residence and his auction house would be. Though the Market included more than four distinct sections, each one was known as a quarter—including the Horde quarter, populated by refugees who'd escaped the empire. As soon as Trahaearn pointed it out, Mina trained the glass on the terraced roofs with reluctant fascination. What would it be like to walk through those streets? To look like everyone else? She couldn't imagine.

"Eighty ships in the harbor," Trahaearn continued. "None of them the *Terror*. Twenty, perhaps twenty-five airships."

"*Josephine*?" Yasmeen named Hunt's skyrunner.

"I don't see her. Either Hunt has given her up, or she's flying along with the *Terror*."

"I'll make a round of the harbor to be certain."

Trahaearn shook his head. "Take us into the French quarter first. The auction house is of stone, and secure. It won't be long before the looting starts—if it hasn't already—and Colbert would escape the fire there. So we'll find him."

With a nod, Yasmeen looked back out over the city. "I'll send teams of runners down. They'll ask around, find out what happened. I have five men to send with you, and I'll return to the French quarter and wait as soon as I've had a look at the harbor."

"And Scarsdale?" Mina wondered. "Will he be able to ride down the platform with us?"

The duke glanced at her, faint humor in his eyes. "Yes."

But not on his own. White-faced and shaking, Scarsdale made it up to the main deck. One look over the bow sent him scrambling for the ladder again, retching with fear. Trahaearn stepped into his path, barked his name. Scarsdale stopped. Bracing his feet, he faced the duke. Trahaearn's fist shot out and the other man crumpled to the deck.

With a sigh, Trahaearn hauled the dazed man up over his shoulder and joined Mina at the platform.

Chaos reigned below. Carts sped through the lanes, rattling over the ruts in the baked earth. A man led two horses who snorted and pranced, necks arched and heads high. Arms loaded with children and clothing, families ran together down the walks, ducking through the sparks and burning ash. Some spotted the descending platform and rushed toward it, screaming and waving. One of Yasmeen's crew struck the chain, and the platform jerked to a halt eight feet above the street. Mina leapt down and rushed out of Trahaearn's way. A faint vibration shook up through her boots when he landed.

The air shimmered with heat. Backing to a stone wall off the street, Mina helped carry Scarsdale to the ground and patted him awake while Trahaearn stood over them. As soon as Scarsdale blinked, the duke hauled him to his feet by his coat.

"Ready?"

Gaze quickly sharpening, Scarsdale nodded. Trahaearn pushed a gun harness into Scarsdale's grip and grabbed Mina's hand.

Led by Scarsdale and trailed by Yasmeen's men, they ran into the street, past a long vehicle that clipped along on dozens of narrow legs like a centipede, the seats loaded with children and guarded by hard-eyed nuns armed with scimitars. Mina had only a second to gawk before they rounded a corner. The sounds of shattering glass and cracking wood came from every direction. Shots and shouts rang out. Not just the panic of the fire, Mina realized. Ahead, a team of three men tossed a chair through the window of a house before climbing in. A blunderbuss boomed nearby. A robed woman crying in the seat of an abandoned rickshaw shrieked and covered her ears. Scarsdale slowed, pointing to the crater caving in the side of a large stone house. Mina's eyes widened.

Firebombed. The French quarter had been *firebombed*.

They didn't take time to look. Turning down a narrow lane, Scarsdale led them to a large iron gate set into a high wall of white block stone. It protected a columned marble building topped by a pilastered dome. Behind the gates, two men armed with rifles stepped forward—and quickly took aim through the iron bars as Trahaearn reached into his coat.

Their shouts of warning died when the duke withdrew a purse.

Little wonder that he assumed that everyone was for sale, Mina thought moments later, racing through the gates to the auction house entrance. Most people he encountered *were*—and this time, she had to appreciate it. Paying those men had been easier than shooting their way in.

Scarsdale was grinning when they paused at the doors and Trahaearn bent to the locks. "If Colbert paid a man what he's worth, we'd have holes in us by now."

"If he'd invested in a bar for this door, we'd be climbing in through the dome," Trahaearn observed as he pushed the door open. "But he didn't."

Inside the thick walls, the building was cool and dark. Two pink damask sofas inhabited the small parlor to the left of the grand foyer—perhaps a waiting room. On the right, a wide marble staircase wound up toward the dome. The auctions were conducted upstairs, Trahaearn had told her. But the merchandise was secured underground and on the main level, and carried to the auction floor by lift. They listened. No sounds came from upstairs. One of Yasmeen's men ran up the steps, confirmed that the dome floor was empty. Toward the back, then.

A locked door across the foyer opened to a narrow passageway. From deeper within the building came the hiss of hydraulics, the rattle of chains, the squeal of metal bearing too much weight. Trahaearn moved to the front, followed by Scarsdale and Mina, holding her pistol at ready. Opium wouldn't stop an uninfected man as quickly as it would a bugger. They passed empty rooms, stopping to check each one. As Trahaearn stepped into the next corridor, metal glinted in the dark to his left.

Mina opened her mouth to call a warning, but Trahaearn had already pivoted around and charged into the dark. A quick scuffle was followed by a thud and the sharp clatter of a blade hitting the floor. Trahaearn dragged a man back into the passageway, his forearm across the man's throat.

"Is Colbert that way?"

Colbert's man shook his head, wheezing and pulling at the duke's wrist.

The muscles in Trahaearn's arm flexed. His voice flattened, cold and deadly. "Are you certain?"

Eyes bulging, the man pointed down the corridor.

"Good man," Trahaearn said. His arm tightened. The man struggled and slowly weakened, his eyes rolling back. The duke dropped him to the floor—just unconscious, Mina saw with relief. Not dead. She didn't want to think that he'd have killed a restrained, unarmed man.

Scarsdale must have read her expression. As they followed Trahaearn, he said softly, "That man is just crew. And you don't kill crew unless they're a threat."

Mina understood. This wasn't a ship. But since no law ruled this place, they used the law they knew.

And that also meant his treatment of Colbert—who wasn't crew—would be guided by a different set of rules.

A harsher set, Mina guessed. Colbert obviously didn't take care of his own well. That man proved to be the only guard they met, and the secured chamber opened easily. Inside, steel cages housed hissing zombies. Others contained a lion, a small gray elephant, and a sad-eyed antelope with a delicately boned face and legs. Almost a dozen men worked the levers of a lift and packed items into crates. Everyone busy, no one watching the door. And when Trahaearn and Scarsdale entered the chamber with guns drawn and backed up by Yasmeen's men, no one was ready to shoot back.

"Colbert!" Trahaearn's voice froze everyone in place.

Though it was easy for Mina to guess who was Liberé or native to the Gold Coast, she didn't know how many of the paler men were French. Picking out Colbert wasn't difficult, however. Although his buff trousers and white shirt were streaked with dirt and sweat, they'd been fashioned at obvious expense. His brown beard didn't quite hide the softness of his jaw. Thick gold rings studded with rubies bedecked his fingers.

Slowly, Colbert propped a painting wrapped in cloth against a crate. He faced the door. "Trahaearn. You've come looking for the *Terror*?"

"Yes."

Mopping his brow with a handkerchief, he looked to the nearest man. "Finish with these crates. I want them ready for the airship in twenty minutes. Looters," Colbert explained as he approached the door. His pale blue eyes flicked uneasily from Trahaearn's guns to Scarsdale's. "Waiting this madness out is best done above. Your weapons aren't needed, Your Grace. I'll tell you now: The *Terror* isn't here."

Trahaearn didn't holster his pistols. "I know. Hunt has her. Where?"

"South. They weighed anchor two days ago."

"He's had the *Terror* for ten days, and there's an English fleet nearby. Why risk waiting so long to leave?"

"There was a sickness among a few of the crew. It took him time to secure more hands."

Mina's heart jumped. Only a few? "What kind of sickness? Bug fever?"

"I don't know what kind of sickness." Colbert's gaze settled on her, seemed to weigh and measure. She wondered what price he'd set. His attention returned to the duke when Trahaearn asked, "Did he sell any boys through you?"

"No."

Mina's relief billowed through her. That meant Andrew was probably still on the ship. Sick, perhaps. Not sold. But her relief was short-lived.

"Men line up at the harbor looking for work," Trahaearn said. "Why did it take so long to find a crew?"

Scarsdale said softly, "Perhaps his reputation finally caught up with him."

"No." Colbert gestured to the cages. Disgust curled his mouth. "He bought zombies and took them aboard—shipping them to Australia, for a new game he's set up. A rotten business, if there ever was one."

Mina stared at him. *Zombies* aboard Andrew's ship. With just one faulty lock, one little misstep, the entire crew could be destroyed— and the bug fever would have been a mercy in comparison.

"You sold him the zombies?" Scarsdale's face had hardened into a smooth, dangerous mask.

Trahaearn's gaze was sharp and cold, an icy razor that would have flayed Mina to the bone. Colbert seemed oblivious to it.

"I only provide the merchandise. I don't dictate how it's used. I'm not a tyrant." Looking slyly pleased with himself, he patted sweat from his neck and brow. "And it matters little what he's bought if you will be chasing after the *Terror*. I daresay Hunt will finally get what is coming to him, will he not?"

Revolting. That Colbert hated Hunt was clear—as was his reluctance to stop the man himself. But he'd happily send Trahaearn to do it. *Coward.*

Whether Trahaearn was just as disgusted, she couldn't tell. And he couldn't act on it yet, anyway. They still needed to know more.

"The weapon that was demonstrated," Trahaearn said. "Has the auction taken place yet?"

Colbert laughed and lifted his hands. "The firebombing outside? That is my unhappy patron."

"You auctioned firebombs?"

"No, no. That is Bushke. He wanted the Horde's weapon to create a new place on the ground, you see? But yesterday during the auction, he was outbid. And so the wrath of New Eden rained down upon us."

Trahaearn frowned. "Bushke did this?"

"Yes. He accused me of cheating, of setting up the auction for my family to win. But even they were outbid."

"Then who bought the weapon?"

Colbert laughed, mopping his brow again. "And risk more of this? No. Bushke was enough. Now you will threaten to kill me if I do not tell you—but if you do kill me, still you won't know. And so go on, Your Grace. Find your boat and leave us be."

Colbert was too afraid to tell them who'd purchased the weapon? Not too afraid of Trahaearn, Mina realized—he was too afraid of the buyer's retaliation. Who had that much power?

But whoever it was, Colbert had chosen to fear the wrong one. His triumph when Trahaearn holstered his guns transformed to sick fear when he glanced up at the duke's face. In one quick stride, Trahaearn fisted his hand in Colbert's brown hair and yanked the man forward, deeper into the cargo chamber.

Screaming in French, Colbert tried to dig his heels in. Trahaearn was relentless, dragging him toward the cages. The men all looked up from the crates and the merchandise. Not a single one moved for a weapon, though Colbert continued screaming—for help, she guessed by the high, desperate pitch, though she didn't comprehend a word of it.

Trahaearn shoved him toward the zombie cage. Inside, the thing raged and reached through the bars, filthy fingers only inches from Colbert's throat.

"Who bought the weapon?"

Colbert screamed and babbled, but he must not have given the answer. Trahaearn pushed the man closer to the zombie's grasping claws. Long bleeding furrows opened on Colbert's neck.

"Who bought it?"

This time, Colbert's frenzied babbling held a placating note. Mina didn't understand it, but Scarsdale's reaction to the man's answer was clear.

"Fuck," he spat.

Trahaearn's shoulders had gone rigid, and Mina realized he was deciding whether to throw Colbert closer to the cage, anyway. She couldn't let him. Although the man might deserve it, a diseased Colbert would endanger everyone.

After an endless second, he pulled the man away from the zombie's claws and drew a revolver. In low French, Trahaearn asked another question. Colbert answered, sobbing. Trahaearn nodded, and Mina almost jumped out of her skin when he suddenly fired at the zombie. Then into the second zombie's cage, and another, until only the animals were left, wild-eyed and panicked by the noise.

Trahaearn glanced over his shoulder at Scarsdale. "Do you want him?"

"To pay for Brimstone?" Scarsdale shook his head. "He's too pathetic. I'll wait for Hunt."

That seemed to satisfy Trahaearn. Pushing Colbert to his knees, he booted the man into a small empty cage and locked it. He looked to the workers watching them with flat eyes. "You'll make more money selling these items than you'll ever earn from him—and he's too much of a coward to take revenge."

The men looked to each other. By the time Trahaearn reached the corridor, they were already gathering up items, breaking down crates. On his knees within the cage, Colbert began shouting. No one stopped.

Mina was glad when the chamber door closed behind them. "Will he be let out?"

"These men will let the animals out before they will him," Trahaearn said. "But he'll eventually be found."

Satisfaction stamped Scarsdale's features. "And everyone will know he's a coward. He'll never hold on to anything again."

The duke nodded. "He'll pay."

Outside the entrance, the quarter still burned. They had a few moments of relative quiet between the building and the gates. Mina didn't waste them.

"Who bought the weapon?"

Trahaearn's jaw tightened. "The Black Guard."

Shock held her silent almost until they reached the gate. Jasper Evans had said the weapon's price began at twenty-five thousand livre. That kind of money couldn't have come just from the sale of slaves. There must have been other sources. *Many* other sources, each contributing enormous amounts . . . and the Black Guard must be much bigger and more powerful that she'd imagined.

"Did he know where they took it?"

"It's on a ship. It *is* a ship—*Endeavour*, an old English collier. The engines and electrical generators that the weapon needs were too big for an airship, and too big to transfer to another vessel. So he sold the whole damn thing."

"Where is it headed?" But Mina feared she knew. At least one member of the Black Guard wanted to kill buggers. And they'd purchased a weapon designed to destroy nanoagents. A sick dread rose through her chest. "England?"

He met her eyes. The set of his mouth was grim. "Yes."

Mina shot Scarsdale with an opium dart as he boarded the platform. She helped Trahaearn stow the unconscious bounder in his cabin, then returned above decks to meet with Yasmeen.

"Is the English fleet in the harbor? We have to tell them about the ship."

The aviator captain looked from Mina to Trahaearn. When he nodded, Yasmeen shook her head. "The fleet has gone. My runners reported that they weighed anchor yesterday."

Just as Baxter had told them. The fleet had been scheduled to return to England. But it wouldn't be difficult to catch up to them.

Lady Corsair's engines fired. Yasmeen raised her brows toward Trahaearn. "Where to now, captain?"

"South," Trahaearn said. "I'll be damned if Hunt sees another sunset on the *Terror*."

South . . . while the Black Guard took the device to England. "No," Mina said. "We can't. We have to fly north."

Yasmeen paused with her cigarillo halfway to her mouth, lips parted. She glanced at Trahaearn.

His face had set. Taking Mina's hand, he pulled her along with him to the bow. Should she be glad he didn't drag her by the hair? Would she suffer a lashing for contradicting him? She was too heart-sick to care.

But when he touched her, his hand was gentle, cupping her jaw. "And your brother?"

"Don't ask me that." She fought to keep her voice from break-ing. Andrew might be alive. But if that weapon reached England, the rest of her family wouldn't be. "Please don't. That device will kill everyone within a two hundred mile radius. And it'll be so easy. They'll sail up the Thames. Then London will be gone. Almost all of England. Do you care?"

Did he at all? Or did he just care for the *Terror*? For his possessions. "I care."

"And you're not lying?" She couldn't tell. And hoping he spoke true wouldn't make it so.

"No. Trust me." His thumb smoothed over her cheek. "But even if you don't believe it, Mina—my people are in London, too. You believe I care about that? That I'd take care of them?"

Swallowing past the ache in her throat, Mina nodded.

"All right. Now, listen. If Hunt weighed anchor two days ago, *Lady Corsair* will catch up to him within a day. And *Marco's Ter-ror* is a fine ship. Fast. We'll find her, we'll head north, and we'll overtake *Endeavour*."

"And we'd still be four days behind."

"I'll catch her. I'll have her before she sees Europe—and she's behind the fleet, who'll give us the firepower we need. As soon as we've found the *Terror*, Yasmeen can scout ahead and find *Endeav-our*, then fly on north to warn the fleet. But we'll find the *Terror* and your brother first."

Indecision warred through her, feeling as if it might tear her apart. She wanted to believe that it would happen as he said. Oh, how she wanted it. But to gamble *so* much? She didn't know.

"Trust me, Mina. I know these waters. I know my ship. And

I know what an old collier like *Endeavour* can do. She's wide-bottomed, heavy, and square-rigged. This time of year, the winds from the east will favor fore-and-aft sails, and the *Terror*'s canvas is rigged to run. We'll catch her. Trust me."

Did she? She must. With a shuddering breath and a nod, she said, "All right, then. South."

He kissed her. As if that were a signal to Yasmeen, bells rang around them. The propellers began to spin, thrusting the airship forward.

Trahaearn lifted his head. "We'll spend tomorrow searching the water, and we'll find them, Mina. So come with me now, to sleep. We can't look for them if we can't keep our eyes open."

Sleep wouldn't come. Mina lay against Trahaearn's chest, listening to the slow, heavy beat of his heart. She'd returned to her stateroom nothing like she'd left it. Then, she'd been content, warm. The day they'd spent here had been punctuated by fear as he'd taken her close to orgasm, over and over—but there hadn't been frustration. Just need, and laughter, and then she'd dozed in his arms through the heat of the afternoon.

Now, it was almost just as hot, and she couldn't doze. And instead of contentment, terror lurked close. She could only think of Andrew, on a ship with zombies and a cruel master in Hunt. Could only think of *Endeavour* bringing death closer and closer to everything she knew and loved and had sworn to protect.

She spoke into the dark. "What if we miss seeing the *Terror* in the night?"

"Yasmeen won't."

He sounded so certain of it. If Mina had been standing over a dead body, she might have spoken with as much confidence. She knew her job. Now she had to trust that he knew his.

Trust me.

He'd been right, all those days ago, when he'd said that she'd

lived beneath the Horde for too long. It was difficult to trust that
someone with the power to hurt her would choose not to.

But there were those she did trust: her family, and the friends
she'd come to know. Did she know him well enough?

He held her now. And though he knew her emotions were in tur-
moil, he wasn't taking advantage of her; he was taking care of her.
She couldn't understand all that drove him, but Mina knew that for
certain: He took care of what was his.

She *was* his. Maybe not always. For now. And so she turned
to him.

Resting, Trahaearn had closed his eyes, but at her movement he
opened them. His steady gaze met hers—patient, but not indifferent.
His hunger burned, a man who'd wait for a taste of what lay before
him . . . but anticipating every bite.

Mina slipped her leg over his abdomen until she lay atop him, her
thighs alongside his flanks. He met her kiss, letting her lead but not
letting her go, his hands delving into her hair. Coils of heat began to
wind through her. She drew away before they screwed deep.

His face sharp with need, Trahaearn watched her again. When
she moved off the bed, he sat up, his stomach flexing. "Mina—"

"Where are the sheaths?"

She turned toward the bureau. His things had been brought in
from the cabin he and Scarsdale had shared, but she had no idea
where something like that would be stowed.

After a silence, his answer came from a voice gone low and
rough. "In the wardrobe. On the shelf."

Nerves made her fumble with the wardrobe's door, but she
finally opened it. No mistaking the purpose of the small ebony box
tucked behind her pants and stockings; the black wood was inlaid
with carved ivory figures that would have put roses in the cheeks of
a Manhattan City miss. Clutching it tightly to conceal the unsteadiness of her hands, Mina brought it to the bed and stopped beside it.
Wearing only his drawers, Trahaearn was sitting up with his back
against the headboard. Not making a move toward her.

Letting her take control, she realized. He'd done so earlier that day, too—urged her to touch herself, to take control of her need, to be its source. But this would be taking control of *him*. Would it be difficult for him? How many women had straddled him, used him? Mina didn't want to be one of them. Not to prove something.

He didn't miss her hesitation. "What is it that you're thinking?"

If she told him, he'd say that it wouldn't matter. That it wouldn't affect him. Lie or not, she wouldn't know—but she didn't want to use him, anyway. And so she gave him motive, not truth.

"Earlier today, when we were . . . I didn't want to panic. So when it became too much, I tried to stop feeling everything."

"That didn't work." Amusement deepened his voice. "Not when my tongue was inside you."

Her face warmed. No, it hadn't worked. She'd felt that. Could *still* feel it, the memory moving through her like liquid heat. "I thought now that I'd just take you inside me. Because that's what I want. When you're touching me, I ache. And I thought: I could have you before I feel too much, before I ache . . . before I panic."

"You can have me like that, Mina. But you wouldn't enjoy having me inside you without needing it, too."

"Yes. I know." Despite the panic, so much pleasure came from that ache, that need. Without it, she might as well be sitting on her billy club, or using the contraptions sold by the Blacksmith. Feeling lost, she stared down at him, her fingers tracing the ivory carvings. "I couldn't fight the Horde then. So I tried to fight what they were making me feel. And I still am—except I'm fighting myself instead of them. I don't want to."

His dark gaze searched her face. "Then fight me."

"What?"

"You couldn't fight the Horde, so you fought what they did to you." With a predatory smile, he rose from the bed. He slowly stalked her. "But I'm making you feel it now. So fight me, instead. Hit me, push me away. But don't stop yourself from feeling. Let that happen."

Uncertain, Mina backed toward the wardrobe. "I don't want to fight you."

"But you do anyway, because you're trapped into fighting yourself. So you panic and push me away. This time, you'll control it from the first."

"And immediately fail. You wouldn't force me. As soon as I hit you, you'd stop."

"No. I often trade one need for another. You need to fight; you need to be fucked. You panic now because you couldn't fight during the Frenzy. Maybe you'll separate them, put that panic where it belongs when you fight me. If you can do that, Mina, I'll take anything that you lay on me. Because *I* need to fuck you, but more than that—I need to see that you're not afraid. And even if you hit me, I'll know you want me inside you. So I'd only stop if you're truly afraid."

He was right. It wouldn't be force, no matter how hard she pushed him away. "If I'm fighting you, how would you know if I'm truly afraid?"

"Use the Horde language."

She frowned her displeasure. "I never speak that."

"Then I'll know it's real."

Real. And inescapable, these emotions. Mina stared at him, the ebony box clutched over her heart like a shield. "From the very first, I knew you'd be dangerous to me. I should have run."

"I'd have caught you." He did, swinging her up and letting her feel him, thick and hard against her belly. When she gasped, he said, "I can still just put my cock inside you."

Laughing, she shook her head. *Far too late for that.* She was already aching for him, a need that burned hotter as his lips took hers. His tongue stroked and she moaned, kissing him deeper. Trahaearn's arms tightened around her waist. Without lifting his head, he carried her to the bedside and set her feet on the floor. With efficient tugs, he stripped the nightshirt over her shoulders, down her hips.

He took the ebony box and tossed it onto the mattress. "Lie back and spread your legs."

Her lips parted. Anticipation slipped through her like rivulets of fire. She sank back onto the mattress and let her knees fall wide open.

His gaze was hot and amused. "That's not fighting me."

"I know," she said on a laugh, feeling light and breathless—and panic very far away. She didn't know why it was. Maybe because she trusted him. Maybe by knowing that she *could* fight him, she didn't need to. Mina couldn't be certain. But she wouldn't fight the ease with which she could offer herself to him.

"Good." He braced his hands beside her hips, and bent his head between her legs. "Because I want this."

He covered her sex all at once, open-mouthed and hungry. Mina cried out, stiffening, and let herself feel it all. Each hot lick. The scratch of his jaw against her inner thighs, and his hoarse groans of pleasure. His grip on her knee as he pushed her open wider, his fingers tightening as he savored her flesh. Her hips writhed. The flick of his tongue whipped her into a frenzy, and she screamed, clawing the sheets, letting it shatter through her.

When she came back together and looked down, Trahaearn was staring up at her with astonishment. It slowly transformed into heated intent.

He moved up, kissing her belly, her nipples, her jaw. Settling beside her, he cupped his hand between her thighs, his middle finger sliding through her wet folds. His gaze on her face, he pushed inside her. Bigger, thicker than his tongue—and unyielding. Mina bit her lip, moving against him, trying to ease the pain of his intrusion.

He closed his eyes. "You're tight. Gripping me. I'll hurt you."

Yes. But she couldn't avoid that. And if they did it right, she'd only hurt the once. With a deep breath, she tried to focus past the need. Not denying it. Trying to separate it from the coming pain.

"Mina, I can feel . . . you're still a virgin."

"No." She'd been with Felicity. "But I'm still intact—and if you rupture my hymen now, it'll be easier for me than with your penis. But we'll have to wait afterward, or the nanoagents will heal me, and I'll tear again when I take you inside."

Whether her dispassionate speech amused him, she couldn't tell. He looked at her for a long moment before nodding. Mina braced herself, trying not to tremble as he slipped another finger inside. Swiftly, he scissored them apart. Stiffening against the tearing pain, she fought not to cry. He murmured an apology and kissed her temple before resting his forehead against hers, his fingers still inside her.

The pain faded to a faint stinging, and the intrusion of his fingers became an intriguing fullness. Mina wanted to move on him, to squeeze tighter around him, but forced herself to wait. She cast her mind about for a distraction.

"Once, I assisted my father on a surgical visit—a woman whose husband finished so quickly that she always healed afterward. So she tried to rupture her hymen with a candlestick and then wait, so that it wouldn't tear every time. But the candlestick was metal—pewter, I think—and the bugs treated it like a prosthetic tool. And so when she bled, they began grafting the candlestick inside of her, and she couldn't pull it out."

Trahaearn's big body was shaking against her. The corners of his mouth were tight, as if he were struggling hard not to laugh. He lifted his head.

"This is what you think of when you're with me?"

She grinned, and then he dove and his mouth captured her nipple. She arched up with a gasp. *Oh, blue heavens.* Biting her lip, her hands fisting in linen, she turned her head to the side. The box of sheaths lay beside her, and on its face, a woman of ivory knelt in front of a man.

Imagining the same with Trahaearn came easily. "Would you like me to do that to you?"

Releasing her nipple, he moved to her right breast. "Do what?"

"Like shown in this picture—I could shag you with my mouth."

He lifted his head, eyes narrowing on the image. "Yes. Later."

Pleased, she turned the box over, and had to tell him, "This one shows a woman with two men. We could invite Scarsdale in later, too."

"No good. I'd hate to kill him for ignoring you."

"Oh, and this one has two women . . . on a box for male sheaths." She frowned. "How odd. What use would a sheath have then?"

Laughing against her neck, Trahaearn didn't—or couldn't—answer.

"I could ask Yasmeen to join me," Mina suggested. "But I suppose she bites."

With a sudden growl, Trahaearn snatched the box and pulled out a handful of square parchment envelopes before tossing it aside.

"That box gives you too many ideas that don't include me." He dropped the sheaths to the mattress. His gaze returned to her face, and his fingers pumped gently inside her. Her laugh became a gasp. No pain now. Only pleasure, only need. "Are you all right, then?"

With a soft moan, she lifted her hips and pushed against his hand. He bent and kissed her, openmouthed and hot, his tongue thrusting and his fingers moving deep inside her until she was wet and aching, her breaths coming in ragged pants. His lips left her then, and she shook her head, trying to draw him down to her again. Resisting, he sat back on his heels, knees spread and digging into the mattress.

Hands lowering to his waist, he began loosening his drawers. His gaze moved from her face to the spill of sheaths beside her.

"Do you want to put it on me?"

She did. Heart pounding, Mina picked up the crinkling parchment and broke the red wax seal. Inside, the lambskin sheath was thin and pliable—and slippery, prepared with light oil.

And his cock was nothing like a billy club. Though thick and blunt, his smooth, heated skin felt delicate under her hands. He guided her, showed her how the sheath worked, groaning as she rolled it down over his length. Small strings secured the sheath at the base of his shaft, above the full hang of his cods. Mina's knuckles pressed into the heavy sac as she fastened the ties, and she looked up as he hissed an indrawn breath.

"Too tight?"

"No." He spoke through gritted teeth. "Come here now."

With his hands beneath her bottom, he hefted her against his chest until she was spread wide against him, sitting almost cross-legged around him. Her inner thighs clenched his sides, feeling the hard muscle over his ribs. She twined her arms around his neck, her face just above level with his. His kiss was soft and slow as he lowered her, until the thick tip of him lodged against her entrance.

Shuddering, she broke the kiss. "Now. Please, now."

Trahaearn didn't have to move. He slowly released her weight and pressure built just inside her. Mina whimpered and tried to swivel her hips, tried to ease it. But it only grew, pushing deeper and deeper. Gasping, she looked down. Inside her. He was *inside* her. But only half his length. She wanted him all.

But his hands were at her lower back now, supporting her without holding her up. Her weight wasn't enough. And she didn't have any leverage.

She kissed his mouth, his jaw. "Help me. Help me take you in."

"Mina." Her name was strained, raw. His big hands covered her hips and pressed down. A wild noise broke from her. She buried her face in his throat, feeling nothing but his thick length embedded deep within, the wide stretch of her thighs, the burning knot in between. She'd die if she moved.

She'd die if she didn't.

A shiver ran over her skin when his hands smoothed up her spine. His arm tightened around her waist. With a harsh groan, he rocked upward and the thrust pushed through her like a wave. Mina's head fell back, her hands clutching at his shoulders, and suddenly she was moving all over, rubbing that burning knot against his ridged abdomen until his hair-roughened skin was as wet and slick as hers. She looked down between them, watching the thick slide of his cock into her—two pieces that shouldn't have fit but worked together beautifully.

And it was ratcheting her tighter again, a need so big that it frightened, but she felt no terror this time. Just Trahaearn—*Rhys*—his strength and his relentless driving thrusts. Watching her, she knew, for any hint of fear. Holding back his need for hers, until she shuddered and cried out, her inner muscles convulsing around him.

A guttural moan tore from his chest and he stroked hard, deep—and then held utterly still. Almost sobbing with the pleasure of it, she felt the pulse of his flesh, and the answering clench of her own.

Chest heaving, Mina lay her head against his shoulder. Still inside her, Rhys laid her back on the mattress and came down over her, his weight on his elbows and knees. He rocked slowly into her, watching her face.

"Again, Mina."

She'd thought she was done. But with each leisurely stroke she was rising, softly, gently, until the orgasm crested through her. Rhys finished her off with a kiss before leaving the bed and dragging off the sheath.

When he returned and lay down, Mina rolled against his side, feeling slightly giddy—almost drunk with triumph, with pleasure, with contentment.

"You didn't fight me," he said, stroking his hand over her hair.

"I didn't need to." Though she didn't know why. Perhaps trust. Perhaps more.

But the thought of that "more" was too frightening to dwell on now. Heartache lay in that direction. London lay in that direction.

"You inspired me," she said instead. "You didn't have to fight when you destroyed the Horde. So I decided to make your tower explode."

His stroking fingers stilled. He seemed speechless, then laughed and pulled her over to lie atop his broad chest.

And it was there that she slept.

Chapter Fourteen

The faint crackle of parchment invaded her slumber. Mina stirred, squinting through heavy lids. Faint light marked the coming dawn. Still too early, and she was too content, lying on her side with Rhys behind her, in the crater his body made of the mattress. She closed her eyes again, searching for sleep, but welcomed the rough hands stroking her side, her bottom, lifting her leg up and back over a heavy thigh.

"Are you all right, Mina? Or sore?"

"*Mmmm*" was all that she could manage.

She was still only half awake when he pushed inside her.

Gasping, she opened her eyes—and was rolled onto her stomach. Rhys came over her, his knees wide between her spread legs. With an unyielding grip, he dragged her up by her hips, her bottom angled up and her weight on her knees and chest. His palms flattened in the mattress above her shoulders.

His voice was low and rough in her ear. "I was a gentleman. I only took a little."

Not a little, though just the head of his cock was inside her; it felt like a small fist. Trembling, Mina twisted her hands in the sheets. She understood this. He'd been a gentleman before, letting her take him.

Now he was taking *her*.

"I'm waiting." His whiskered jaw scraped her neck, was followed by a quick, sharp bite. "As soon as you're wet . . . *God*, Mina."

With a single deep stroke, he buried his cock to the hilt. Devastating pleasure exploded beneath her skin, and Mina screamed into the sheet. He filled her completely, his cods pushing tight up against her most sensitive flesh. She gripped his forearms, straining on either side of her head and caging her in, preventing her from jolting forward with each powerful thrust. His heavy sac buffeted her clitoris with each annihilating stroke, until she was writhing and crying out, and still he pounded into her. Then his hand moved to her sex, callused fingers stroking, and she shattered, tears hot against her cheeks. Her name tore from him in a harsh, exultant groan. He gripped her hips and slammed forward, as if stamping his mark on her flesh.

Mina shuddered again as he came, but his release didn't let her go. No. He had her. He'd plundered, and laid waste to her every defense.

Not a gentleman, but the pirate captain, His Bastard Grace, the Iron Duke. It didn't matter which.

He knew exactly what he was about.

Mina didn't seem to regret being with him. When Rhys had woken, certain that she'd try to pull away, he'd been driven by the need to take her again. But he hadn't been able to go easy on her. After he'd fucked her so roughly, he expected hesitation, uncertainty . . . but there was none. Over breakfast, she interrogated his politics in a way that told him just as much about hers, and fascinated him with every word until he had to have her again, making a feast of her body on the small table.

He'd never needed anything as much as he needed her. Self-preservation warned him to push her away. He couldn't stand the thought of it, only wanted to bring her in closer. But if she didn't come to need him in return, then away or close, it wouldn't matter—either one would destroy him.

And she didn't regret shagging him, but he didn't think she needed him yet, either. At least she'd come around to liking him a bit.

She sat with him in the bow, sharing a spyglass between them while they searched the sea for the *Terror*. The wind made it difficult to talk, but he didn't mind. When she faced away from him, he liked looking at the curve of her cheek and the thin stripe of skin between her armor and her jaw. A few strands of her black hair had come loose from the severe roll at her nape and escaped the goggles' strap, flicking against his face and neck. Last night, this morning, he'd had her hair unbound and spilling everywhere: over the backs of his hands as he'd held her waist, watching it part over her shoulders as he'd driven his cock into her. Tonight it'd be the *Terror*. He'd never had a woman in his cabin, but there was no question that she belonged with him—and when he wasn't looking through the spyglass at the endless blue, he was imagining all of the ways he'd have her.

Not long after noon, he saw her stiffen with the telescope to her eye, no longer sweeping the horizon. Without a word, he took it from her. Hot triumph shot through him. There she was. *Marco's Terror*. Just the masts were visible, but he knew their shape. He could have stood blindfolded on a pier, and recognized her sound when she sailed past him.

Mina watched his face, waiting for confirmation. When he nodded, she waved to Yasmeen. A bell rang behind him, but he didn't look around, keeping the spyglass trained on the masts.

The *Terror*'s canvas was furled. In this low wind and calm water, she'd need to be under full sail to move at any speed. Had they dropped anchor? No reason to in this stretch of water, unless they were tethered to an airship.

Frowning, he searched the sky for *Josephine*. No sign of the skyrunner against the thin clouds, and they didn't provide enough cover to hide in. He turned to Yasmeen, gestured for her to cut the engines.

They'd sail in, quiet. *Lady Corsair* didn't need the propellers to catch an anchored ship.

He saw Yasmeen's brow furrow as she lowered the spyglass, and he shook his head when she cast him an inquiring glance. He couldn't explain why the *Terror* wasn't under full sail. And he didn't want to mention them and worry Mina yet.

But soon enough, he didn't need to say anything. *Josephine* came into view, her white balloon almost completely deflated and floating next to the Terror. She'd been tethered, and something had brought her down. Wooden wreckage floated nearby, but the bulk of the skyrunner was still under the balloon.

Mina's mouth dropped open. "Is that the airship?"

"Yes."

"But how . . . ?"

"I don't know."

"Why is the *Terror* still tethered . . . and not moving." She seemed to realize the significance of the furled sails. "Have they stopped to salvage the airship?"

Rhys shook his head. "We'd see crew."

"Deserted." Mina sucked in a breath, peering intently at the *Terror*'s empty deck. "Just like the Dame's fort."

"Including zombies," he said. "We'll see soon enough if they broke out of their cages. Hunt wouldn't have kept them in the hold. He'd have wanted an eye on them all the time."

And Hunt would like seeing their effect on his crew all the time.

"If they broke the locks, is there somewhere for the crew to go?"

"The cargo hold. The interior of the *Terror*'s hull is reinforced with steel ribs and plates." Unlike kraken, whose tentacles damaged the timbers and could pull the ship so far off keel that she capsized, megalodons rammed their armored bodies into the hull and ripped up the rudder and wood with their massive jaws. "I added more to the entry of the hold to keep the cargo secure, too. The crew could wait there."

"For how long? They wouldn't have food or water."

Not long, but that wouldn't matter here. "At most, they've been down there a day."

Nodding, she handed him the spyglass. He trained the lens on the decks. *Goddammit.* "Three cages are sitting on the foredeck. One is open."

Mina rubbed her arms, as if a chill shivered through her. She looked to the floating wreck. "Could the zombie have gotten onto the airship?"

"It couldn't puncture the envelope." Steel mesh strengthened the balloon's airtight fabric. Even someone armed with a sharp knife would have difficulty stabbing through it; a zombie's ragged finger-nails would just scrape off.

It must have been a puncture; a burn would have meant the whole thing blowing. But even a puncture wouldn't usually cause this much damage, unless an enormous hole had been ripped through the envelope. Usually, a puncture meant a slow leak, which wouldn't have left that wreckage. Rhys could climb up *Lady Corsair's* balloon with a harpoon in hand, and it'd take hours before she slowly settled onto the water.

His guess was that *Josephine* had been wrecked while tethered to the *Terror*—and in the confusion on board, the zombie's cage had taken a knock, and the lock broken. But he'd find out for certain after descending to the *Terror's* decks.

He stood, slinging on a shoulder harness. Next to him, Mina began checking her weapons.

"Not you," he said.

"But—"

"No. Cover me with a rifle, if you want. But you're not heading down with us. I won't risk it."

Her lips firmed and jaw tightened, as if she wanted to argue. She must have realized it wouldn't do any good. He'd have Yasmeen's aviators lock her in *Lady Corsair's* hold rather than let her step foot on his ship before he secured it.

Finally, she nodded. "I'll cover you."

*   *   *

When Scarsdale came up from his cabin, he was white-
faced, but fighting through the fear. Rhys knew it wouldn't happen
again, but this time was for Hunt.

He waited until the bounder shrugged into his harness. Scarsdale preferred swords over machetes, but they both backed up their
weapons with guns that would finish any job. "Ready, then?"

At Scarsdale's nod, the aviators dropped two ropes over the side
to dangle above the *Terror*'s quarterdeck. Rhys kissed Mina hard
and threw himself over, slowing just enough that he wouldn't slam
into the boards. Scarsdale landed lightly beside him.

He listened, holding his machetes at ready. Beneath the hisses
and wild growls of the zombies in the cages, he only heard the hull
creaking with the gentle rock of the waves, the slap of water against
the *Terror*'s sides. All else was quiet.

God, it felt good to have these decks beneath his feet again.

"They've been keeping her tidy," Scarsdale said.

For the most part. There was some recent slipshod work, but
they'd been short on crew—might be even shorter now. Rhys hoped
to hell they had enough men left to sail back, or they'd be making
another stop at the Ivory Market.

All was still quiet as he made his way to the foredeck—but that
would soon change. Drawing his revolver, he shot the zombies in
their cages. Only one had escaped, but that didn't mean there was
only one zombie left. Their bite took time to kill a bugger, but not all
of the crew would have nanoagents. And as soon as a bugger died,
he'd turn into one. A zombie tearing a man's neck out had a way of
hurrying that death along.

The gunfire brought more noise. Garbled hisses. Running feet.
Five or six of them, all below decks. So they'd chased the crew
down there, but probably weren't clever enough to know the way
back up.

He returned amidships and stood over the ladder leading below. "Lantern?"

Scarsdale had already taken one from the posts and sparked the lighter. Rhys didn't bother with the ladder. He dropped through the hatch, landing heavily on the next deck. Nothing came at him from the dim passageways or from behind the launch. The captain's cabin lay aft. Scarsdale followed him with the lantern, but he didn't need it for the cabin. Sunlight streamed through the gallery windows.

The navy had kept his desk and his table. Everything else was new—and a mess. Christ. Hunt was a pig. Clothes piled on the trunks, wet and torn papers strewn across the deck. He'd burn the fucking bed before he took Mina on it.

He called out, listened for any human response. Nothing. He turned back toward the passageway.

Wood splintered behind him. He pivoted, machete ready, and caught a glimpse of Hunt, wild-eyed and naked, wielding a pistol. Scarsdale's blunderbuss boomed. Hunt's chest caved in. He staggered and dropped.

"Hiding in the goddamn privy." Scarsdale shook his head and reloaded. "I wish I'd killed him in there."

If Scarsdale hadn't, diseased nanoagents would have. Rhys eyed the scratches on the man's face, the chunks of flesh missing from his arm. "Had he already turned?"

Hunt's eyes popped open. He lurched up to sitting. Rhys leapt out of Scarsdale's way. The bounder fired again, took off the top of the bastard's skull.

Ears ringing, Rhys watched Hunt drop back to the deck. "We run into any more, you shoot it in the head the *first* time."

Scarsdale grinned. "But now, I killed him twice."

Probably still not as many times as Hunt deserved. They cleared the rest of the deck, moved farther below. On the tables off the galley, that morning's breakfast still filled the tin plates.

"They left in a hurry. I've never seen a sailor run from a table without taking the bread to eat on the way." Scarsdale checked the mugs. "Or throwing back the last of his grog. And I say, with all of this shooting, your inspector is probably mad with worry by now."

His inspector. "Quickly, then."

Later, Rhys would make up a better story than Scarsdale standing over a ladder and banging a pair of pots together, with Rhys shooting the zombies as soon as they appeared on the deck below. He'd say that a few chased him along dark passageways, that a few more jumped out of storerooms. But in truth, the day he ran scared on the *Terror* was the day he'd hand her over to Dorchester and the Admiralty. Both the crew trapped in the hold and the *Terror* herself deserved a better captain than one that cowered in a privy— or one that cowered anywhere else on the ship.

The decks clear, he and Scarsdale made their way below. The crew had blocked access to the cargo hold from the inside. Pounding on the door, Rhys raised his voice and ordered them open. They did, and his gaze met shocked faces, a disbelieving crew—and a look deeper into the hold confirmed that most of them had survived.

The cheers began, one hundred and twenty men stomping their feet. In colder waters, that would risk bringing a megalodon or a kraken, but he allowed them this. He looked the crew over, counting eight boys that might have been Mina's brother.

Rhys barked over the noise. "Andrew Wentworth! Are you present?"

There. As silence fell over the crew, a white-haired, gangly boy froze in place. Eyes wide, he called out, "Aye, captain."

"You will join me on the quarterdeck, Mr. Wentworth."

Brows rose. Heads turned. Pink to his ears, Wentworth said, "Yes, sir."

With a sharp nod, Rhys cast his gaze over the others. "I want every able-bodied man on deck, and the *Terror* cleaned up and ready to sail within an hour. Those zombies that were crew will be prepared for burial. The others—including Hunt—I want tossed over the side before I climb above decks. Warrant officers and mates, you'd best be ready to report on status and crew in the wardroom in half an hour." He wanted to know what the hell had happened on this ship—and to *Josephine*. "Haul to."

Men began filing out of the hold. Some navy, some new. Rhys recognized more than a few of them from his crew.

He stopped one. The engine master had been with him during the mutiny, though he'd been a ship's blacksmith, then. Almost twenty years on the *Terror*, and he had the leathered skin and steel prosthetic arm to show for it.

"Still with her, Mr. Smiegel? How's her engine?"

The old man straightened shoulders that were all but permanently stooped from ducking beneath low decks. "She still has the finest engine that's never fired, captain."

"You've taken care of her."

"That we have, and she's taken good care of us in return." His eyes gleamed with emotion. "And we knew you'd come for us, sir. Even those navy boys knew it."

Rhys had to grin at that. Still his ship, even in the eyes of a naval crew. And as soon as they returned to London, she'd be his by law again, too. No chance in hell was the Royal Navy going to keep her.

Smiegel hesitated. Recognizing that the man was reluctant to speak out of turn, Rhys nodded for him to say his piece.

"If you've come aboard, then you must have . . . Has the kraken gone, sir?"

"Kraken?" The echo came from behind him. Scarsdale stared at the old man, his face pale. Rhys could feel the blood draining from his own, his gut tightening with dread. "Not in these waters."

No, not in these waters. Not that Rhys had ever seen. And the sea around the *Terror* had been clear. But something had brought that airship down . . . and could have been hidden under it, using the balloon for shade. *God*.

He turned and sprinted for the ladders.

* * *

Too much time had passed since the last round of gunfire. Several minutes, at least.

Her fingers clenched on the rifle, Mina stared down though the *Terror*'s web of crisscrossing lines and timbers, willing Rhys to return. The ship's upper deck remained empty. All was quiet, until a deep rolling rumble sounded, as if hundreds of horses trotted across a wooden bridge.

What was that? She looked at the aviators, saw their puzzled expressions. Frowning, Yasmeen left the quarterdeck, approaching the rail.

Mina glanced back down, then to *Josephine* when movement under the deflated balloon caught her eye. Beside her, an aviator called out, "Captain!"

Yasmeen joined them, bracing her forearms against the gunwale and looking over. Between the *Terror* and the airship wreckage, a dark shadow was gliding deep beneath the water. A *big* dark shadow. The captain's face stilled, her lips parting. Horror, Mina recognized.

"Captain?" she said, her heart pounding.

"It should be too warm," Yasmeen murmured. "It must have been carried up on the cold current that runs northward along the coast, maybe hit a storm . . ." She shook her head. "I've never seen one so far north."

Oh, blue heavens. The giant armored sea creatures the Horde had created were well known to inhabit the colder waters: the megalodon sharks in the north and south, and the kraken in the south. But not so close to the equator.

The shadow became a shape, a bulbous head and thick tentacles, a monstrous iron-plated cephalopod. The two arms trailing behind were longer than the *Terror*.

"No," Mina whispered. But denial wouldn't make it true.

"They just need to keep quiet and sail out of here," Yasmeen said. She looked along the rail. "Mr. Pessinger, please fire up the engines and the generator."

For the rail cannon, Mina realized. "Can we lower the platform?"

Yasmeen nodded to the floating wreckage. "That's probably what they did. With their engines firing."

As *Lady Corsair*'s engines would need to be in order for the generators to power the rail gun. And the noise would have attracted the kraken . . . which had destroyed the skyrunner.

Astounded, Mina stared at *Josephine*'s balloon. How could a kraken pluck it out of the sky? "They have that great of a reach?"

"It's long, no doubt. But if it wraps those tentacles around a cargo platform, it can drag the whole ship down."

With a shudder, *Lady Corsair*'s engines started up, huffing and bellowing. The generator whined. Below, a plated form surfaced and dove beneath the *Terror*. Too quick.

"Mr. Pessinger, do you have a shot?"

"No, sir. Not without hitting the *Terror*."

"Fuck." Yasmeen breathed the curse before shouting, "Mr. Pegg, Ms. Washbourne, mount that rapid-fire gun! Pepper the water over there. See if we can't draw it away. The rest of you, haul out the harpoons!"

She was shaking her head, even as she called the orders. Catching Mina's gaze, she said, "Kraken aren't zombies, investigating every new noise. They fixate."

Noise from below had them both looking over again. Men were running onto the *Terror*'s deck. Rhys was with them, sprinting to the side and looking over. He turned. Mina couldn't hear the shouts over the airship's engines, but knew he was yelling orders.

"They'll man the axes," Yasmeen said, her pointing finger tracing the path of several men racing toward the weapon stations. She nodded to the men climbing into the rigging. "They'll drop the canvas."

And sail away. *Josephine*'s tether line had already been cut from the *Terror*'s stern. Everyone was in motion, except . . . Mina's heart leapt. A pale-haired boy stood on the quarterdeck with an axe in hand—Andrew.

The *Terror*'s bow lurched to the side. Thick tentacles curled up around the front of the ship, just beneath the jutting bowsprit and the figurehead lifting her face to the sky. Armed with axes, men rushed to the foredeck, crowding into the point of the bow. The tentacles were too low for them to strike.

Sick with fear, Mina couldn't look away. "Can they kill it?"

"Not with that armor. Not unless they're lucky and get a shot at the eye. They just hope to hurt it enough that it'll let go."

"Can we make that shot?"

"It's impossible at this angle, or anywhere more than ten or twenty feet over the surface. And even if the kraken floated into open water, the rail cannon's penetration into the water isn't deep. The best chance is using one of the harpoons." She gestured to the men lined up along *Lady Corsair*'s side, each holding a speargun. "They'll be watching for that chance."

Mina looked at her rifle. Yasmeen pointed to the quarterdeck.

"You'll find a harpoon in my weapon chest."

Even at her fastest, she couldn't run quickly enough. Mina returned to the rail, speargun ready—and with nothing to shoot. The tentacles crawled up the *Terror*'s sides, as if an enormous, monstrous hand was taking hold of the ship from below.

Yasmeen was right. They had absolutely no angle. They wouldn't from any direction, not from this height. And so they waited—for the best, or the worst. And the worst would be dropping ropes and saving who they could.

Or drop a rope now. She turned to Yasmeen. "Why not lower a man on a rope beside the *Terror*? He'd have a shot."

"I don't pay my men enough to commit suicide."

"Then me," Mina said. "If the kraken takes hold of the rope, you can cut it. It won't drag you down."

"I'm not interested in suicide, either, and Trahaearn would kill me." She flicked a glance at Mina's harpoon. "Try to take a shot with that, if you must do something. But you're not heading down."

And Yasmeen would physically prevent her, if necessary. Mina remembered Newberry, and the six aviators who'd taken him down. Just three of them could handle Mina . . . unless she didn't give them the chance.

With determination washing away fear, Mina took her place on the rail, near the ropes Rhys and Scarsdale had used to descend to the *Terror*. They were coiled up again, but the ends were still secured to the steel anchoring loops embedded in *Lady Corsair's* decks. Directly below lay the blue strip of water between the *Terror's* side and the skyrunner's balloon.

She kept a firm grip on the harpoon. Below, the *Terror* began to tip sideways, the masts no longer vertical, but swinging toward the water at a sickening angle. The kraken clung to the *Terror* . . . and its enormous body would slowly be exposed against the ship's bottom as it keeled over. No choice, then.

Mina grabbed the rope and tossed herself over, sliding rapidly down the line with one hand. Friction burned her palm. Her stomach dropped faster than she did, the wind pulling tears. Shouts from above rang out—and then below. Rhys's unmistakable voice, roaring an order to stop.

So sorry, Your Grace. It was too late for no.

She stopped ten feet above the water, with not much rope left dangling. The side of the *Terror* was rising above her, and she was too low to see the decks, the angle too steep. The undulating and constricting tentacles were dark gray and slick, and as thick as a railcar where the arms attached to the body. The undersides were covered with plate-sized suckers, pink flesh that pulsed and contracted against the *Terror's* wooden hull in a manner as obscene as it was horrifying.

Near the base of the bulging, armored body, the lidless black eye was big enough to drive a lorry through, and stared at her through the clear water. Seeing her? Mina didn't know. And she couldn't wait.

A swipe of her face against her shoulder wiped away the blur of tears. She breathed deep. Hanging on to the rope with her burned and bleeding hand, she looped the dangling end around her foot, creating a sling step that could take her weight, and secured it by trapping the rope end between her sole and her ankle. She would have one shot, and she needed to be steady, needed to remember that the water would distort the angle.

She aimed low and fired.

The speargun pierced the bottom center of the creature's eye. Black liquid spewed. The tentacles bulged and the ship's hull shrieked, then the *Terror* was rolling toward her, bottom crashing back into the sea. Tentacles thrashed the water. Mina reached up, ready to climb, but something struck the rope and whipped her about, ripping the line from her shredded palm.

She fell—and jerked to a halt with a tearing pain through her knee. Mina cried out, dropping the harpoon. Swinging upside down, dangling with her head two feet above the water, she stared at the rope around her foot through a haze of disbelief and pain and tears.

Blessed stars. Slowly, she crunched the muscles in her stomach and began to roll up.

"Mina!"

Rhys's shout cut through every other noise, made her glance over. The *Terror* was nearing—Yasmeen must have been bringing the airship closer to its side. Men at the rail were leaning over with fishing gaffs, trying to catch the line and bring her in. Relief burst through her, and turned to horror when she felt the unmistakable sensation of her foot sliding from her boot.

Oh, blue.

She dropped, splashing into the water. Shocking warmth enveloped her, and a strange, swirling silence. The dark shape of the kraken floated below, no longer thrashing or moving. The sun was above. She tried to turn, flipping her hands. She couldn't swim. But how difficult could it be? Just splashing and kicking.

Her eyes burned. She clawed at the water, kicked her legs though her knee screamed. Her lungs screamed. The sun seemed farther away, the wavering shadow of the airship. She just needed to kick *harder*.

She couldn't. She couldn't.

A dark figure torpedoed through the water. Rhys—who sank like a stone. He grabbed for her, hauled her against him, and the tightness of his grip hurt more than not breathing. They'd both go down, now. He shouldn't have come for her.

But they were dragged up. Mina's head broke the surface and she coughed, throwing up water and sucking in more. The cargo platform floated beside them. Rhys shoved her onto it and hauled himself up, dripping all around them. A thick rope circled his waist, attached to what must have been half the *Terror*'s crew. The platform lifted with a rattle and slowly swung them to the *Terror*'s rail.

Mina coughed again. Her wet stocking slipped on the deck when she stepped aboard, and her knee collapsed. Rhys caught her. All around her, men were cheering. Not Rhys. His face was dark, forbidding. Above them, the airship's engines cut off. Quiet suddenly fell as Rhys barked an order to tether *Lady Corsair* to the *Terror*'s stern.

Lifting Mina against his chest, he carried her to the quarterdeck and set her down. Bracing her weight on one leg and her hand against the rail, she said, "Don't let Captain Corsair come down here. She might kill me."

"I might, too," Rhys said grimly, but he didn't—he looked to someone behind her and nodded.

And then Andrew was there. Thin, but strong. Not sick. He threw his arms around her waist. She held him tight.

"If you're lucky, they *will* kill you," he said. "Because that will be nothing compared to what Mother will do when she hears that you lost a good boot."

Chapter Fifteen

Mina wasn't killed, if only by virtue of there being too much work for both captains to waste time with her. She stood out of the way as zombies were thrown overboard, followed by Hunt's belongings—and the captain's bed. Heat bloomed through her cheeks as the mattress from the stateroom and her valise came into view on the cargo platform. And because she'd rather tell Andrew that she'd be sharing the Iron Duke's bed than have him learn from a sailor, she limped across the quarterdeck to ask Rhys for her brother's help unpacking her things and tidying up the captain's cabin.

Without glancing away from the men climbing the rigging, he said, "If your brother helps, you'll stir up trouble between him and the cabin boy."

Oh. Yes, she supposed the men would be territorial in their duties. "Will you ask him to help me down the ladder, then—and perhaps write a letter to my mother, so that my family knows I'm shagging the captain?"

His gaze flew to her face, brows raised. Understanding and amusement flickered across his expression. "I see. Take him down, then, and tell him."

"Thank you."

He looked her over. "Do you need one of Yasmeen's cabin girls?"

"Yes." Her clothes were soaked through, and without help, she wasn't certain whether yanking off her remaining boot would be possible. "This one time. I ought to be all right on my own once I'm dry. Do I have your permission to look through Haynes's logs? Perhaps I'll find information regarding his journey and when the *Terror* was taken."

He nodded. "And that is what your brother will help you do—sort through the logs and find the relevant cylinders. Until your knee heals, you only sit."

Which suited Mina perfectly well. After Yasmeen's girl was done with her, she'd have happily curled up on the bed and slept the afternoon away, but she sat at the captain's desk instead. A large phonograph had been fastened to the mahogany surface, its tulip-shaped mouthpiece bent to accommodate the height of the captain who should have been sitting in Mina's chair. Andrew joined her, carrying a collection of wax cylinders that the cabin boy had found scattered about the decks. He dragged up a chair from the table, his thin face solemn and worried.

Bending his head close to hers, he spoke quietly. "Is this what you had to pay to come for me?"

"No." Mina saw that he wasn't convinced. "Coming for you gave me this opportunity. I couldn't have had it anywhere else—and it won't continue after I return to London," she added, to be certain that he didn't form any expectations about his sister and the Iron Duke.

His pale concern gave way to pink cheeks. "Do you expect me to bend prude?"

"No. I wanted to prepare you. The talk amongst the crew might be difficult to hear. Your sister is the captain's jade wh—"

"Don't." He sat back. "You *saved* us, Mina. The crew is ready to kiss your feet if you let them." His grin pushed little apples into his thin cheeks. "In truth, they might confront the captain for not continuing with you after London, because they wouldn't under-stand why."

But Andrew did. And it was a stab through her heart that at only fourteen, he understood why she couldn't be with the duke, knew the cost of her blood. He'd paid it in small ways before. He'd have been paying it now if she hadn't slain the kraken. Perhaps only sly digs at first, but continuing and growing bolder with each day, and whether he fought them or ignored them, there would have been no winning.

He was watching her face. "Do you wish you could?"

"Don't ask me." Her throat suddenly tight, she shook her head. "That was never a part of it."

"So you'll be giving it up." With a sigh, he looked out the cabin's windows, to the blue sea and sky beyond. "I think I know."

Perhaps he did. At fourteen, she hadn't felt deeply. But without the Horde's control, Andrew would. The sea might very well seem to encompass all of his heart.

She pushed away her troubles and focused on him. His flat midshipman's hat and blue uniform coat fit him well, but still managed to look oversized on his gangly frame. He'd tanned in the past few months, and freckles had popped out across the bridge of his nose. She would tease him about them later.

Retrieving one of the wax cylinders, she glanced at the end for the date. Too early. "Do you like it, then?"

"Yes. Though it's difficult proving that I'm not aboard just because I'm the son of an earl."

"You *are* aboard because you're the son of an earl."

He took offense. His brows rose and temper flushed his skin. But being Andrew, it quickly dissolved into acknowledgement and humor. "That's how I secured the position. But I have to work twice as hard for the men to think me worthy of it."

"And by the time you become a lieutenant or captain, they'll think twice as much of you. They'll know you aren't here because of your father, but that you've earned it. And they'll trust you." She cast him a wry look. "Of course, you'll have to earn it again with every new ship and crew."

His tortured groan made her laugh. Picking up another cylinder, she nodded to the phonograph barrel drum and mouthpiece. "This is set up to record. We will need it to play the acoustics on these cylinders, instead."

Andrew bent over the machine to make the adjustments. "Did you work twice as hard for Hale?"

"Twice as hard? I'm a woman and Horde-blooded, to boot. So double that again." And she ought to be working a little more now. "What happened when the Dame took the *Terror*?"

He told her, giving her almost the same story that the boys held for ransom had, except most of the *Terror*'s crew had been put in the hold during the demonstration. She looked up from the cylinders when he described the crew who'd remained above contracting bug fever—and all of them dying from it—while the others only suffered minor symptoms. Nor had they felt a thump through their chests, but something that Andrew described as a pressure in his ears, quickly gone.

Protected, Mina thought. Whether because they'd been beneath the waterline or surrounded by steel in the hold, she didn't know—but the weapon hadn't hit them as hard.

He hesitated before adding, "They had people watching from *Bontemps*. We saw them before we were taken down into the hold."

The potential buyers watching the demonstration. Mina nodded. "Yes."

"I knew one of them—Hale's airship man, the one who builds the big dreadnoughts for the navy. Sheffield."

Sheffield? No. Mina's heart stuttered. She was convinced that the industrialist loved Superintendent Hale. *Surely* he wouldn't betray her. "Are you certain?"

"Yes."

She didn't want to believe it. Her first instinct was to name it impossible—she'd *seen* him the night Haynes had been dropped onto Rhys's steps, and he'd just returned by airship from Manhattan City. But that might have been a lie; he could have just come from the demonstration on the Gold Coast. And although his presence in London meant that Sheffield couldn't have attended the auction, a member of the Black Guard could have acted as his proxy in the Ivory Market.

And he hadn't known that it was Haynes's murder she'd been investigating that night—but had he been with Hale when she'd received Mina's wiregram updates, identifying the captain? Had he been the one to contact the assassin in Chatham, and to tell Dorchester that Haynes's bugs had been destroyed? Through his dreadnought contracts with the Royal Navy, the man had connections with the Admiralty, and if he was Black Guard, reason to hide news of the auction until it was too late for everyone in England.

Sickness roiled in her gut. It wasn't too late to catch *Endeavour* and stop the weapon, but they were still four weeks out from England. Four weeks until she could warn Hale. Four weeks for Sheffield to escape back to Manhattan City.

Lady Corsair, however, would collect Fox from Venice and return to Chatham in a little more than a fortnight. Mina could leave for England with the aviators . . . though that would cut her time with Rhys short. Would a message to Hale suffice?

Mina knew it wouldn't. Sickness became a deep ache.

Pumping his foot against the treadle, Andrew began winding the phonograph's clockwork drive. "It should be—" The grating of gears cut him off. Brows drawn, he peered into the base of the phonograph. "Ah, blast. The turnstile mechanism has been bumped out of alignment."

Probably while Hunt had been throwing off his clothes and knocking things about the cabin. "Can you fix it?"

Like their mother, Andrew was mechanically inclined. Mina would just make the problem worse. He hesitated before nodding slowly. "I'll need access to the machine room."

Oh. "I'll ask the captain to tell you to fix it."

"Yes."

And too many special projects and assignments might be interpreted as the captain's favoritism. For any other boy, that might have been something to embrace. Not for an earl's son who was trying to fit in with the other midshipmen. "I don't suppose we'll be able to meet like this often."

"No. If I was already a lieutenant . . ." With a shrug, he sighed. "I'm not."

"It's all right." She understood.

Perhaps too well.

In ten days, the Dame and Hunt had made Rhys's return to the *Terror*'s decks as difficult as possible without actually destroying the crew or the ship. The navy's food stores had been sold in the Ivory Market and replaced with rat-infested shit. Though Rhys had almost a full complement of seamen and warrant officers, the master and two of his senior mates had died of bug fever. With no lieutenants, that left no one who could be put in command of the ship during the night watches.

He left the wardroom and started for his cabin, wishing he could kill Hunt all over again. The food, he could replace quickly enough. All but one days' worth of Yasmeen's stores would be brought down to the *Terror*, and he'd send her north to the Ivory Market to replenish *Lady Corsair*'s hold and bring back enough for the *Terror*'s return to England.

And Scarsdale would have to take up a few of the watches. He'd trod the quarterdeck often enough to have a feel for it, and he'd know whether they strayed off course. Although the bounder was a damn fine navigator, however, Rhys wouldn't be able to leave her in Scarsdale's hands for long. The *Terror* needed more than someone pointing her in the right direction, but someone who knew the individual sails and lines, who understood the roles played by every member of her crew, who anticipated her response to every wave and breeze. To catch *Endeavour*, to carry them home, she had to be steady and strong . . . and Rhys couldn't give her any less than he asked, though it would mean devoting less time to Mina than he wanted to.

And he hadn't given the *Terror* as much as Mina almost had.

Christ. Even a zombie biting into his arm hadn't matched the horror of watching her slide down that rope, harpoon in hand. And even that had been dwarfed by the sick terror of watching her drop into the water. He'd have traded every man and the ship for her life. He'd have traded his own. But he'd been helpless to make that offer—helpless to do anything but watch her fall.

Decades had passed since he'd felt anything close to helplessness. He didn't like it any more now than he had then.

Before he reached his cabin, the boy—Andrew—came through the door into the passageway, eyes widening when he saw Rhys. Quickly, he lifted his hat in salute. "Sir."

"Mr. Wentworth."

His acknowledgement brought Andrew to a halt, waiting for an order. Rhys looked the boy over—the boy that Mina had risked everything to save. What hold did he have on her? Not just blood. Scarsdale hated his family. Yet something about this boy made her love him enough to jump from an airship. Rhys wanted that from her.

But he also wanted to strangle her for jumping, no matter that she'd saved them all. He *would* strangle her if she ever risked her life for him.

Blast it all. She'd made him helpless, irrational—and jealous of a boy.

A boy who was growing red and uncomfortable under his stare. Hell, no wonder. The uniforms might be all right farther north and south, but in the tropics they were ridiculous, hot, and constricting.

"This isn't a navy ship, Mr. Wentworth. No need to salute or wear that uniform."

"Yes, sir. I understand that we're a pirate ship, now."

His earnestness almost startled Rhys into laughter. What tales did these boys pass around? The reality of a pirate ship should have inspired dread, not excitement.

"No. She's in my fleet, which makes her a merchant ship."

The boy's disappointment showed in the same twist of his mouth that Mina made. "Of course, sir."

Rhys moved on down the passageway. "Don't stomp on your hat too quickly, Mr. Wentworth. We'll be back to England in four weeks. If your work and your lessons aren't up to snuff, I'll boot you off, and you'll be looking for another ship in Chatham."

"Yes, sir!" Andrew called after him. "I'll do my best, sir."

"Go on, then."

Inside, Mina sat at his desk, arranging wax cylinders. Her hair was loose and dry. Still dripping, her wet coat and trousers had been hung over the front of the wardrobe. She'd changed into a blue frock, her ankles peeking out from beneath the skirt hem, her bare feet tucked neatly beneath the chair.

The image of her falling into the water flared behind his eyes again, her shock and fear as the boot gave way. He wanted to pick her up, hold her close. Afraid of crushing her, he walked to the windows and held on to rigid control, instead.

Outside, the sea was calm. The *Terror* would soon be cutting smoothly through those waters. "We're about to weigh anchor. Do you want to come above decks to see her underway?"

"Yes. Thank you." A reply as serene as the sea.

He watched a wavelet break at the crest, boiling over with white. "And you'll never do anything like that fool stunt again."

"Shooting a kraken in the eye? No, I can't imagine that I'll have reason to."

He swung round. "No. Don't risk your life again."

She met his gaze squarely. "You must imagine that I'm someone else. *I* couldn't stand by and do nothing while every man on this ship died."

His jaw tightened. How could he tell her what not to be? She wasn't part of his crew, to be ordered around. And he hadn't been there to stop her, to protect her. Short of chaining her down, he had to accept this.

How could he accept it? When she risked her life, she stole his.

"And despite the zombies, *you* risked coming down to the ship."

Rhys frowned. "That's not the same."

"How?"

"My ship. My responsibility."

She couldn't seem to dispute that. But she wasn't done. "You sink, yet you dove over to catch me."

"I had a rope." Though he'd have gone over without one, if necessary.

"So did I, to begin," she said, and her brows arched up while her mouth curved into a smile, and he was lost. Arguing with her became impossible.

"I lied on the airship," he told her instead. "It won't be enough, only having you until we return to England. I won't tire of shagging you."

His statement left her frozen, except that her smile fell and her eyes closed and she shook her head. He'd never seen any woman seem so still while offering a denial that moved every visible part of her.

And it rattled him, threatened to tear him loose from his moorings. He wanted to take her, to pin her down. To demand that she stay. But he steadied himself. She *was* in his cabin. She didn't have to be. They'd found her brother, and now there was nothing Rhys possessed that might hold sway over her. She could have remained aboard *Lady Corsair*. No one would have forced her onto one ship or the other.

But she'd come here, though every man on his ship—six times Yasmeen's crew—would know that he'd have her in his bed. And four weeks remained for him to convince her to stay there.

So he had time yet. The knowledge gave him some ease. And now his only need was to take away the tension that his declaration had left in her, the fear that had tightened her lips and stiffened her shoulders.

"All right," he said with the calm that came with lies. "Then I'll shag you often enough that it won't be necessary. Shall we go up, then?"

Nodding, Mina stood. Her lips parted. Apparently realizing that nothing lay between the deck and her bare feet, she looked at the toes peeking out from beneath her hem as if she'd never seen them before.

"It won't matter," he told her. "Most of the crew goes barefoot. It gives better grip on the decks and the ropes."

"Oh. Will that be necessary for me?"

Probably not. "I've asked Yasmeen to fetch you new boots from the Ivory Market," he said.

She replied with a thank-you as she stepped forward, exposing all of her foot but the heel—but he could picture it clearly, tucked beneath the chair, the tough little mound that curved into a delicate arch. He could picture her heels digging into his back, into his ass.

In two long strides, he swept her up. She didn't seem surprised, perhaps thinking that he was carrying her because of her bare feet or her injured knee, but when he steered toward the bed, she began laughing against his neck.

"Aren't we weighing anchor?"

"We've still a few minutes." A man starving, he rucked her skirts up to her waist. "Enough time for this."

Four weeks never would be.

After the first day and night on the *Terror*, Mina didn't wonder that he'd thought a month wouldn't be enough. On the airship, they'd been able to spend a full day in bed. Here, stealing more than a few minutes during the day was all but impossible. Though the crew changed shifts several times, Rhys stood over them from before dawn until well after midnight. He broke to eat dinner with Mina and Scarsdale, but even then he worked, describing the upcoming stretches of water to the navigator, relaying what the crew needed to accomplish during their shifts, and poring over maps and ledgers.

His dedication was beyond admirable. And perhaps she shouldn't have judged him so harshly for comparing the management of a dukedom to captaining a ship—one he considered a very big ship. If Rhys put even half the effort into his holdings and his shipping interests, he still worked harder, and his decisions affected more lives than any other peer she knew. Taking his seat in the White Chamber would add another heavy burden.

He'd had to know that. Yet he'd agree to take his seat in order to possess her. And now that he'd had her, he claimed that he'd be done with her in weeks.

Parliament seemed a lot to pay for so little—and if she'd learned one thing about the Iron Duke, it was that he always demanded equal return. So he'd probably lied about letting her go after they reached London.

Mina didn't even let herself dream of staying with him. Whatever he intended, she only had the *Terror*.

So she spent almost all of her time above decks, standing in the salty spray and the heat, just to be with him. Each night she fell asleep before he came into the cabin, but eagerly turned to him when he arrived, clung to him. And each night he took her, every kiss heated and hungry, each caress seeming to draw out forever, as if he refused to let the day exact its toll before he'd had her. And Mina found herself needing every moment, painfully aware that four weeks simply weren't enough.

And soon, she only had three.

Though the day was warm, a downpour forced Mina below decks. Oppressive gray clouds and the rain battering the boards over her head made the cabin seem smaller, isolated from the sounds of the ship. With some reluctance, she sat at the neglected phonograph. They'd been underway for a few days before Andrew had found the time to fix the recorder, and Mina had spent every spare minute with Rhys.

Both he and Scarsdale had known *of* Sheffield and his dreadnoughts better than they'd known the man, and so they'd had little to offer but impressions—and with *Endeavour* in front of them and Sheffield still weeks away, they'd spent little time discussing him.

Mina had tried to push thoughts of Sheffield away, but had still mentally composed her report to Hale hundreds of times, rephrasing and rewording in hopes of softening the blow of his betrayal.

If she'd listened to Haynes's cylinders earlier, she wouldn't have needed to expend all of that effort. In concise reports, the captain detailed his last days aboard the *Terror*.

And then, in a much longer recitation, his last morning.

The downpour had ended by the time Mina made her way back to the quarterdeck. The sky had already cleared to a deep blue, and the clouds formed a faint smudge to the east. The sun gleamed off the wet deck. She looked up at Rhys's profile rather than squint against the glare.

"The Dame locked Haynes in his cabin before he was taken out in the boat for the demonstration," she said. "He spent most of it at the phonographic recorder. Sheffield isn't Black Guard. He's the man who met Baxter in Port Fallow and told him about the auction."

Rhys frowned and looked over the bow, his gaze unfocused as if he was reordering his thoughts. "Why in Port Fallow? That's not Sheffield's type of port."

"I suspect that's why they chose to meet there. Sheffield had Colbert's invitation but didn't plan to use it—until he was approached by the Black Guard, who hadn't received one."

"They probably heard about the weapon through their Horde resistance contacts," he said softly. "So they blackmailed Sheffield? How?"

"Haynes didn't say. What I know of Sheffield, however, I suspect they either threatened Hale or his purse."

"His purse—His dreadnought contracts with the navy?"

"Yes."

His gaze sharpened. "Anyone could threaten Hale. But for him to take the other seriously, it would have to be someone that actually *could* threaten those contracts."

"And if it was someone with power in the Royal Navy, that would give him and Baxter reason to meet in secret."

"Yes." He studied her face. "You have more to tell me."

"Sheffield came to the demonstration." And although he might not have known that Haynes would die, he'd watched it happen—and hadn't said a word of it after returning to London. So the Black Guard still had a hold over him. "But he wasn't alone. Haynes recognized the man with him: Admiral Burnett, of the Gold Coast fleet."

The edges of Rhys's mouth whitened—with shock, dismay, or anger, she wasn't certain. But she'd felt all of them when Haynes had first named the admiral.

"We're chasing that fleet. Yasmeen's scouting ahead to contact them now. He's in command?"

"Yes." With a deep breath, she said, "The fleet left the Ivory Market almost at the same time as *Endeavour*."

"And a Black Guard admiral is protecting the weapon during the journey back to England. Christ." His face was bleak, his laugh short and bitter. "While the weapon turns up in the hands of one of Dorchester's admirals. Instead of firebombing us at the Dame's fort, he should have been protecting England from his own men."

"Not all of them," Mina said. "It can't be all of them."

"No. Most will fire a cannon when an admiral tells them to, though. And I could take two ships, Mina. Maybe three. But a fleet will outgun me thirty cannons to one."

But they still had to try. She gripped his sleeve. "It doesn't have to be another suicide run."

"I hope you're right," he said, but the grim set of his mouth betrayed his doubt.

Lady Corsair didn't slow as she approached the *Terror* later that afternoon. As the airship passed directly overhead, Yasmeen leapt into the rigging and slid down the ropes. To her back she'd strapped a leather tube containing rolled maps and diagrams. With

Mina, Rhys, and Scarsdale gathered round, she spread them out on the captain's table.

She bent over the first map, depicting Morocco's coast. "*Endeavour* isn't behind the fleet. She's—"

"With the fleet," Rhys said. "We know."

Yasmeen's brows arched at his interruption, and she stepped back. "Ah, well. Since you don't need me, I'll just—"

Scarsdale grinned and pulled her up to the table again. "Show us."

Mina looked with amazement at the amount of information Lady Corsair had gathered. Not only maps, but the names of each ship and number of guns they carried, their heading and speed, the formation of the squadrons.

"The fleet contains twelve ships aside from *Endeavour*," she said. "Plus two dreadnoughts, and a skyrunner. Six are ships of the line, with two fifth-rates. The rest are gun brigs and cutters. The firebomb squadron is at the center."

Rhys nodded. "Where's the admiral's ship?"

"His flag is flying on a first-rate in the center squadron—one hundred and twenty eight guns on three decks. *Endeavour* is nearest him. And they're slow enough, you can catch up to them in a week."

"But when we do . . ." Scarsdale shook his head. "Christ."

His jaw tight, Rhys stared hard at the formations, as if willing them to change on the paper.

Mina frowned at them. "Are you planning to *attack* the fleet? Why? You're on an English ship—"

"No."

She should have anticipated that response from the Iron Duke. A response that completely missed the point. "*They* consider it an English ship. Famously so. And you're under order of King Edward's regency council to investigate the matter of this weapon."

Mina watched in amazement as all three blinked and looked at each other.

Blue heavens. "You'd forgotten?"

Rhys didn't answer—or couldn't. His hands braced on the table, he stood with his shoulders shaking and mouth compressed into a tight line.

Scarsdale began to laugh. "I believe the captain would say that it wasn't forgotten, but that it never figured. He was never acting under the Crown's power—only his own. That investigation bit with the council was just to allow you to come with us."

"Well, then." Flushing deep, Mina said, "Run up your flags . . . or whatever it is that sailors do."

Regaining control, Rhys straightened and studied the fleet's formations again. "Burnett might suspect that he's caught when he sees the *Terror*. If he follows the Black Guard's pattern, he'll kill as many of us as possible before committing suicide. And this time, he has a first-rate ship as his weapon . . . and a fleet behind him."

"It's bad sport for a ship of the line to fire on a frigate like the *Terror*," Scarsdale said. "He won't do it; he'll lose too much face."

Yasmeen gave him a doubtful look. "And you're certain he'll care about that?"

"If it looks like he's moving in to attack, we'll strike colors and run up the white flag." Rhys tapped his forefinger against the diagram. "But hopefully we'll avoid him by signaling to this rear squadron first. Which is the commanding ship?"

Yasmeen pointed. "A second-rate, *Bellerophon*, was flying a rear admiral's flag."

"All right. Gather the crew. See if any of them have served under Burnett or in *Bellerophon*. I want to know what sort of ships they run."

And if all went well, the admiral wouldn't overreact when he saw them. But there was one other ship that needed to be accounted for. The Black Guard committed suicide rather than allowing themselves to be caught. No doubt they'd take as many others as possible along with them.

"What if *Endeavour* sees us coming, and fires up before we contact the fleet?" Mina asked.

"Then we fire on her, and take our chances against the fleet's guns." Rhys met her eyes. "That weapon can kill every nanoagent within two hundred miles. If it detonates, we're all dead anyway."

Never would Rhys have imagined that he'd soon resent his ship. But as another week passed and the *Terror*'s demands prevented him from lying with Mina every night, his frustration mounted. She remained at his side throughout the day, but her nearness only increased his need. Finally he ordered Scarsdale to begin taking his meals with the warrant officers and sat with her alone, waiting until she'd eaten her meal before tossing her onto the bed and finishing his own. Afterward, she joined him again at the beginning of first watch, standing with him on the quarterdeck in her coat and trousers, the lanterns casting a soft glow over her features.

They would meet with the fleet tomorrow. A thousand times, Rhys considered whether to order her aboard Yasmeen's ship, but if they fell under attack, *Lady Corsair* wouldn't be any safer than the *Terror*. And he wanted Mina where she'd been the past two weeks— by his side. For almost a decade, he'd commanded this ship alone. Now he could hardly imagine standing on this deck without her.

He'd put half again the number of crew on each watch, and they were still hurrying about, readying the ship, checking every weapon. She observed them quietly.

"It's more work than I ever imagined." She glanced at him. "And you're tired."

To his bones. But there was work, and it had to be done. "Does that matter?"

"I suppose not." With a sigh that he'd begun to recognize was her signal that she'd soon be heading to bed, she said, "Tonight, when you come to the cabin . . . just sleep."

"I can't. I have to shag you," he said baldly.

Even by gaslight, he could detect the pink in her cheeks, and her sudden resolve. "Then I'll take you. You rest."

And long after midnight, she did, pushing him onto his back and climbing over him—but there was no rest. With her lips, she explored, and wrecked him with the heat of her mouth and the stroke of her tongue. She kissed him into desperate need, until they were both rigid and panting. And when her fingers smoothed the sheath over his cock, when her thighs parted over him, when she took him deep into her wet passage, the tightness and the friction held him in a mad grip. Insensate with pleasure, but not resting, no—she moved upon him, and he met her with heavy upward thrusts, seeking oblivion within her hot depths. But there was only exquisite awareness, of her every sigh and gasp as she rode him. Of the warmth and softness of her hands and mouth. Of Mina taking him all, kissing, biting, and losing control as he finally came deep inside her. Stiffening, she breathed his name on a shudder, then again on a hoarse cry.

Rhys. He was to no one else. Only her. Whereas she was Mina to many, and inspector to more.

But no matter what name she went by, she was his. With her cheek pillowed on his chest, Rhys held her. He said into the dark, "Another fortnight won't be enough."

Aside from a hitch in her breath, only silence answered him. And after a long moment, the shake of her head.

"It has to be."

Chapter Sixteen

The next morning, Mina went above decks early, her uniform coat brushed and her new boots at a high shine. She read the tension among the men, stiff in their uniforms and hats, but also among the seamen in their everyday slops. For the first time in two weeks, the captain wore a blue waistcoat and jacket over his shirt, topped by a neckcloth knotted so high it looked ready to choke him. The white ensign had been hoisted to the masthead, declaring that *Marco's Terror* was a Royal Navy ship. Aside from His Majesty's jack, Mina didn't know the significance of the flags that flew beneath it, but hoped they'd make all the difference.

The fleet was already in view, the rear squadron visible even without the spyglass. Peering through it, Mina's breath almost stopped. The stern of *Bellerophon* appeared enormous, twice as wide as the *Terror*, and with three more decks above the waterline. Some of her sails had been reefed—the squadron was slowing to obtain a better look at the *Terror*, Rhys told her—but Mina imagined that they must comprise acres of canvas when full.

She looked to Rhys, aghast. "Burnett's *Vitruvian* is larger than that?"

"Yes."

Though she looked, Mina still couldn't see anything other than a mast—her view blocked by a ship in the rear squadron. High above them, the dreadnoughts floated like great fat beetles. Though far ahead of the fleet when she'd first come above decks, the skyrunner had turned around, begun flying south.

"When will we be close enough to signal?"

"We have been." He nodded to the colorful pennants hoisted on a halyard. "Those tell them we're here by order of the king, and that we've requested communications with the fleet. Now that we're close enough to read, we'll soon have a response."

It was an endless wait. Her heart pounding, she watched the other ship. Why hadn't they responded? "What do you think is happening?"

"They're relaying our signal to Burnett in the center squadron."

And he must have responded. The dreadnoughts changed heading, as if intending to come round in a wide, slow circle. She spotted a flash of color from *Bellerophon*.

"We've been asked to hold our position while they verify our papers." Rhys lowered the spyglass. "The skyrunner is coming."

Not as quickly as *Lady Corsair* would have. Rhys called for the men to prepare the *Terror* for tethering to the airship. They raced about hoisting sails and dropping sea anchor, and then waited, ready, for an endless time. Finally, a young aviator captain came down with a small escort, all in blue coats and white breeches, and backed up by redcoats. They stayed on the cargo platform until Rhys invited them aboard; the marines remained topside and visible from the other ships while Mina accompanied Rhys and the aviators to the cabin.

Slightly plump and red-faced, with a short blond beard, Captain Seymour seemed the type who tried for severity, but whose amiable nature thwarted him. He read the regency council's decree and carefully inspected the seal, lips firmed and nodding.

"This looks in order," he declared in a flat bounder's accent. "But I say, Your Grace, this is highly unusual. What of Captain Haynes?"

"He was killed and dumped from an airship onto my house."

Mina read the man's dismay. Not just surprise, she thought, but sincere grief. "Haynes was a friend of yours?"

"Yes." Still staggered, he looked to Rhys. "What happened, sir?"

"Haynes was headed to the Gold Coast to meet up with the fleet. Dame Sawtooth found him first, and used him in a weapon demonstration. After he was taken to London, *Lady Corsair* brought us to the Gold Coast in search of *Marco's Terror*."

"I've just made the same run, though in both directions," Seymour murmured, as if steadying himself with routine thoughts. He read the regency council document again. "He was killed by the weapon mentioned in this decree?"

"The same sort of weapon. Admiral Baxter was assassinated shortly thereafter—by a different party. And that is the Black Guard we're pursuing." Rhys stopped. "We'll have Haynes tell you himself."

Seymour kept firm as the wax cylinder began playing, except to verify that the voice was Haynes's—but at the mention of Sheffield and Admiral Burnett, horror and disbelief passed over his face, and was mirrored by his lieutenants.

Recognizing that he was lost for words, Mina told him, "*Endeavour* is the auctioned weapon. And it is headed for England, where it will destroy everyone infected with nanoagents."

Seymour shook his head. "Burnett's always been zealous in his protection of England—sometimes uncomfortably so." His lieutenants were nodding, as if they'd also experienced the admiral's passion firsthand and too close. "He wouldn't do this. Captain Haynes must have been mistaken."

"And so we might be," Rhys said. "And that is why we must speak with him."

With an abrupt jerk of a nod, Seymour said, "Yes, well. Everything here is in order. And so I will signal to the fleet."

Before he could turn to go, Mina asked, "Captain Seymour. The run you recently made between London and the Ivory Market— were you carrying a civilian passenger? Mr. Sheffield, perhaps?"

Seymour didn't answer. His face pale, he bowed stiffly to her, and took proper leave of the captain. Mina exchanged a glance with Rhys; he'd also thought Seymour's nonanswer was confirmation enough. And it wasn't difficult to guess that Admiral Burnett had ordered the skyrunner to carry the man back to England.

They followed the aviators topside, where Seymour had halted beside Scarsdale on the quarterdeck, both men looking out over the bow.

"The admiral's ship is coming round." Seymour frowned and glanced at Rhys. "Perhaps concerned by my having taken so long listening to Haynes's recording. I'll scramble, sir."

Yes, scramble, Mina thought, watching the ship. Rather than directly approaching the *Terror*, the wind forced the vessel to come round on an arc, cutting through the calm seas at speed and displaying a stomach-dropping view of the enormous ship's decks and gunports. Smoking hells, the *Terror* couldn't stand against that—Mina would have more luck trying to take a hit from the Iron Duke.

"She's moving into position to fire," Scarsdale said.

Rhys's gaze rose to Seymour's airship. "He's signaling now—telling Burnett that all was in order."

That didn't bring Mina any relief. "Then why are *Vitruvian*'s gunports opening?"

Seymour shouted over the airship's side. "Sir! Hold fast! We're signaling again!"

Rhys nodded—but apparently he had little confidence that the signal would do any good. He called to an older man standing amidships. "Mr. Smiegel, is the furnace burning?"

"Yes, sir. Low, as you said."

"Stoke her up, then. Be ready to fire the engines on my signal."

"Yes, sir." But he paused, as if uncertain whether he'd misheard. "Fire them, sir?"

"Yes."

Smiegel gave a tight nod. "Right, sir."

He vanished down the ladder. Rhys caught Mina's gaze. As if to reassure her, he said, "It's too warm for kraken or megalodon."

"So was the Gold Coast," Scarsdale said in an undertone that wouldn't carry past their ears. "And the sharks in these waters are big enough."

"Yes. But we'll have to take that risk." Rhys's mouth tightened as he marked *Vitruvian*'s progress. The sea smashed into white plumes against the onslaught of her heavy bow. "Mr. Charles!"

The gun captain who ran up to the quarterdeck couldn't have been much older than eighteen, but years under the sun had already leathered his face. "Sir?"

"How quickly can your men mount the full complement of rail cannons?"

The gun captain's chest filled up. "They're ready to fire in forty-five seconds, sir."

A time that must have been worthy of the man's obvious pride. Rhys smiled a little, nodding. "All right. Have your men ready and standing by for my orders. Forty-five seconds later, I want *Vitruvian*'s waterline looking like a sieve."

"Yes, sir."

Charles left the quarterdeck. Mina tried to catch her breath. The rail cannons had a greater range than a traditional cannon, but were usually used as a last resort rather than the first option. But if Rhys was planning to fire them against *Vitruvian*, to stop the great ship from coming within range, then the rail cannons must be their *only* option.

Scarsdale looked uneasy. "If you fire first, captain, then the whole fleet will have no choice but to—"

"I know." He raised the spyglass. "She's coming around broadside."

To fire on the *Terror* full on with more than sixty cannons. Mina squeezed her fingers together as Rhys shouted to the men in the rigging. Two sails dropped and filled, and the ship began to drift around the sea anchor, keeping the bow pointed toward *Vitruvian*—preventing them from using the *Terror*'s side as a target. Looking at the number of gunports, Mina doubted that it would matter. From the front or the side, they'd still be blown apart.

Her nails dug into her palms as the *Terror* began a different motion beneath her feet, a deep side-to-side rather than the forward up-and-down that had grown so familiar the past two weeks, the low waves moving against their side instead of their bow.

If the waves had been any larger, the alignment could threaten to capsize them. But even the low swells had the crew tense. The captain, too.

And *Vitruvian* had appeared enormous from a distance. As she closed in, the ship was simply terrifying. "Has the admiral's ship given any signal at all?"

"No."

Then what was the admiral waiting for? Mina stared at the ship, trying to imagine. She had no mental picture of the man, couldn't guess whether Burnett stood on *Vitruvian*'s quarterdeck, anticipating their demise with manic glee, grim determination and duty, or without any emotion at all, as if they were nothing but bugs. What went through such a man's mind as he bore down on a threat, intending to crush it?

Finally, colors flew from *Vitruvian*'s bow as they hoisted the signal pennants. But the starkness of Rhys's face told her that it wasn't the response they'd hoped for. "What is it?"

Almost drowned by the sudden whine of the airship's generator, Scarsdale called to her, "He ordered Seymour to fire on us!"

Boots pounding the deck, Rhys raced to the stern, where the airship hovered thirty yards behind the ship. He roared over the noise. "Stand down, Seymour!"

Mina's hands flew to her mouth. The aviator captain himself had manned the airship's rail cannon. The long barrel swung down, aimed for the *Terror*.

She was jerked off her feet as Scarsdale yanked her against him, crouched over her, shielding her with his body. An explosion of splintering wood sounded to her right. Scarsdale's grip loosened. She looked up, heard his disbelief.

"He only clipped the rail. He *missed*. Impossible from that distance."

"He saved our ass." Striding across the deck, Rhys hauled Mina up. "We've been fired on. We're justified firing back. Mr. Smiegel! Mr. Charles! Now!"

His shout had barely faded when the rumble of engines shook the boards beneath her feet. Generators screamed to life. Men raced to mount the rail cannons.

With no recoil, no sound, she couldn't tell when they fired them—except for the implosions in *Vitruvian*'s hull. Timber exploded in a rough pattern along the waterline, shattered wood splintering and flying into the sea. Smoke puffed from the first-rate's gunports. Geysers erupted between the *Terror* and the admiral's ship, cannonballs falling far short of their mark. *Vitruvian* faltered as she took on water through her shattered hull, slowly tipping to port.

"Another round to her engine deck!" Rhys ordered.

Mina looked to him with wide eyes. Was that necessary? The ship was doomed.

Scarsdale must have read her face. "She'll go down slow. The captain can't allow them time to fire up their own rail cannons. So he'll take them out. Their only option left is abandoning ship."

"Sharks coming in astern!" The shout came from the crow's nest.

Mina spun around, and her heart dropped through to her knees. Three metal-plated, razor-edged fins knifed through the water, each half as tall as the captain. Beneath the surface, sleek shadows arrowed toward the *Terror* at shocking speed.

Rhys didn't look. "How big?"

"Thirty-five feet!"

He shook his head. "She'll survive them. Another round at her engines, Charles!"

More timbers shattered—and that must have been enough. Rhys ordered the engines off. *Vitruvian* sat low in the water, the waterline almost at her second deck. Her men poured into small boats.

Seymour's skyrunner fired its propellers, lowering its platforms and ropes as he flew toward the men abandoning ship.

"Strike the colors!" Rhys shouted. "The rest of the fleet will know we're done."

Mina glanced astern, looking for the sharks. Red water seemed to boil almost two hundred yards away—and there were far more than three sharks now.

"Yasmeen took one out with her rail cannon," Scarsdale said from beside her.

And the blood had started a frenzy. She watched in horrified fascination, until a shout from the crow's nest sent ice sliding down her spine.

"*Endeavour*'s firing her engines, sir!" The man pointed toward a column of steam rising from the center of the fleet. Mina turned, stomach trembling. No generator's whine, not yet.

"She's out of our range," Scarsdale said.

"But not theirs." Rhys strode to the rail, calling orders to the crew. "Get on those flags, signal to Seymour! And tell the fleet to blow her out of the water."

Mina would liked to have seen the dreadnoughts destroying the ship, but the Iron Duke ordered every bugger on the *Terror* into the steel-plated cargo hold—including her and Scarsdale. They waited there until Rhys came down to tell them that *Endeavour* was nothing but a few floating planks barely visible through the clouds of gunpowder smoke.

Sitting by Andrew, she threw her arms around him before running to Rhys and letting him sweep her up into a sweet, victorious kiss. The giddy relief lasted through endless questions as *Bellerophon*'s rear admiral and the van squadron's vice admiral boarded the ship. *Vitruvian* was lost, and although much of her crew had been rescued, Mina wasn't surprised to learn that Burnett had gone down with the ship. But even with a king's decree in hand, an admiral's death couldn't be pardoned without rigorous examination. When the admirals opted to continue their questioning on *Bellerophon*, Rhys left with them on Seymour's airship. Mina spent the rest of the afternoon writing out a long report to Hale. At sunset, Yasmeen and Scarsdale joined her for dinner at the captain's table—and as they'd made an early start on their celebratory drinking, Mina was well entertained until midnight approached, and Rhys finally returned.

With him were Captain Seymour, several lieutenants, and warrant officers who would fill the positions of the men the Dame had executed. While the officers left to claim their quarters, Rhys and Seymour came into the cabin. With a greeting to the airship captain, Yasmeen stood and stretched in a long sinuous arch. Seymour returned her greeting, his face deeper red than usual.

She grinned and looked to Mina. "I'm leaving for Venice in the morning. I could have you back in England within five days."

Aware of Rhys's sharp gaze, Mina shook her head. "I'll stay on the *Terror* for the remainder of the journey. But if you would deliver a report to Hale, and a message to my parents? It would relieve them to know that my brother has been found."

Yasmeen nodded, but Seymour spoke up. "I say, I could deliver them within two days. I'm flying ahead to take the vice-admiral's report to the Admiralty Board, and to inform them that *Vitruvian* has been lost."

Two days was even better, and Yasmeen didn't look put out at being passed over as messenger. Almost dizzy with relief and happiness, Mina handed over the envelopes. She smiled and nodded as they all took their leave, and spun to face Rhys as soon as they were alone.

He stood in the middle of the cabin, watching her with a lazy grin. "So you'll stay?"

"Yes," she said, and gasped out a laugh as he hefted her up against his chest, until their eyes were on level.

"Two more weeks won't be enough for you, either."

Sudden sorrow squeezed the laughter in her throat to nothing. He was right. But it hardly mattered. "It has to be," she said.

"Why? How can I ruin you, your family?" His dark brows lowered over his searching gaze. "I *will* protect you both. And a connection to me can only raise their status—politically, socially, financially."

Her heart hurt. "No. It won't."

Setting her heavily to her feet, he pushed away to stare out the gallery windows. "Why won't you try?"

"You always attract the notice of the newssheets and the public. If I'm with you, then so will I, and *that* will ruin us."

"So you said." Frustration hardened his jaw. "Why assume that?"

"Because I've already seen it." And she didn't want to show him. But she braced herself, and dug the flyer from the bottom of her valise.

He frowned when she passed it over to him. "What is this rubbish?"

"That's me."

"The *hell* it is!"

His gaze shot to hers, burning with sudden fury. Tears started to her eyes. She turned away before they spilled over.

She'd imagined many reactions, had seen them all, from laughter to horror to a shrug of dismissal, as if the drawing shouldn't matter. But anger didn't seek to smooth or dismiss hurt feelings, as if she'd simply been a victim of a thoughtless joke. His anger said that she'd been *wronged*.

And she loved him for it.

But his fury also said that someone needed to pay . . . and that he didn't understand that there was no *one* to do it. He thought that this wrong could be righted with a sweep of his mighty iron hand. And so he wouldn't understand that she couldn't be protected from this—or why, no matter how much she wanted to stay with him after they reached London, she couldn't.

His voice came from behind her, low and dangerous. "Who did it?"

Mina lifted her hands. "Most likely one of the ladies at the meeting. Not that she intended *this*. But she probably mentioned to her husband or to her brother that you'd accompanied me home, and he mentioned it to another man at a club, and by the morning these flyers were being passed out on the streets."

"*Who* passed them out?"

"Street urchins. Do you want to know who drew it? I don't know. Do you want to know who asked him to draw it? I don't know. Do you want the name of the man with the printing press? I don't have that, either. And what if I did? Would you burn down the printing shop? Ruin every man who had a finger on that flyer?"

"I'd do a hell of a lot more than that."

She believed him. But he still didn't understand. "And the newssheets, too?"

Like a cold razor, rage passed over his expression again. "This was in the newssheets?"

"Not that. But there was another caricature. There would be almost every day."

"No. There wouldn't." A statement of determination, ground out through clenched teeth.

"How will you force them to stop? Will you control what rubbish they write, what they report? If you do that, whatever sway you have over them will disappear, along with the power of your name. Because by forcing them, by censoring them, you'll be no better than the Horde."

He apparently couldn't refute that. So he took a different tack. "If it's rubbish, why do you care? They constantly print rubbish about me."

"And it's easy for you not to care! My friends will be outraged. But that won't protect my job. It won't protect my family. People who know us will cry out against it at first, but then there will only be embarrassment. And eventually, they won't want to associate with us. Not with someone who is *that*."

She flung her hand at the flyer. He crushed it in his fist, face darkening.

"You're not this. Don't *ever* say you're this."

"I know! But no one else will. *That* will be what they see when they see *me*. They will already think that they know me. All they will know is that hideous . . . thing."

He raised his fist to his temple, as if struggling for control, and let it drop to his side again. "And that is why you won't continue with me?"

"Yes."

"So you're afraid of these people who mean nothing to you. You're caring about what people think, even if they'll turn from you for this rubbish. You're running in fear from the stupidity of people who aren't worth your time." His face closed up, hardened. "You're a coward."

Coward. The word struck like spit on her face. She stared at him with bile in her throat and a knife through her heart. "You don't tell everyone that you were born with nanoagents."

"Because it's not their concern! I don't fear their reaction."

"And what concern is it of theirs that the Horde raped my mother? But everyone sees the evidence of it. Everyone has an opinion of it, judges us for it. Unlike you, I don't have the privilege of hiding that I'm something everyone hates and fears. And so for all of my life, that rubbish is what will be said of me. And if I am with you, it will be said *every* day, by practically *everyone* in England!"

"And I won't let—"

"You can't! You can't control what they *think*!" She approached a scream. Chest heaving, she battled the rage and pain and frustration. She tried again, though still not completely steady. She tried to tell him in a way he could understand. "If I stay with you, Your Grace, you'll have your possession. But *I'm* the one who will pay for it."

But she couldn't pay any more tonight. While he stared at her, Mina turned her back on him and walked out of the cabin—and made it to the ladder before she began to cry.

Rhys slammed into Scarsdale's berth and shoved the flyer into the bounder's face. "What is this?" he demanded.

In his bunk, Scarsdale weaved up to sitting. When he focused on the flyer, dismay and resignation closed his eyes again. "Where did you get this?"

"Mina. It came out the morning we left London."

He put a hand to his head. "Good Christ, they're faster than the newssheets."

"You saw the newssheet?"

"Everyone does."

Everyone but Rhys. *Jesus.* All these weeks, everyone had carried around a disgusting image of Mina in their brains, and he hadn't known to rattle it out. "How do I stop it?"

Brow furrowed, Scarsdale shook his head. "Come again?"

"Who do I pay? Who do I kill?"

The bounder stared at him. "Every bugger in England? You were too quick to destroy *Endeavour* today."

Christ. Rhys ripped his hands through his hair. Slammed the flat of his palms against the bulkhead. Nothing helped.

"Captain, you could marry the bearded lady out of a carnival tent. You could pull a woman out of a brothel with warts on her face to match the ones on her arse. Liberé, Lusitanian, *me.* And in the newssheets, they'd make us look beautiful. Not the inspector. They'll only see the Horde, and a jade whore. Hell, they'll applaud you for screwing one, because it'll mean that you're still fucking them over. But if she's a nobody—"

"An earl's daughter isn't a nobody."

Mina wasn't. Born in a crèche, she still wouldn't be a nobody. She was everything.

"She's near enough to one. London society isn't like Manhattan City. If she's no one, she can get by—and just coping with what she faces every day is surely more than anyone should have to."

Every day. He knew that. Yet he'd called her a coward.

He couldn't reply. He couldn't think.

But if he didn't think of something soon, he was going to lose her.

Looking at the flyer again, Scarsdale sighed. "But this . . . This wouldn't just come from the people she meets. And those, at least she can change. They can come to know her, or they'll pass on by and forget her. But the people she doesn't meet, she can't change—and those people will see her every day, and they'll see her like *this*. And soon her family and everything they work for becomes a joke."

And that would destroy her.

Rhys closed his eyes. "Is there nothing?"

"Maybe she'll think you're worth it. Does she love you?"

No. But he fought bleak truth with the memory of how she always turned to him. Of how she slept, wrapped around him. "She needs me."

"Ah, yes. Because she hasn't gotten along for almost thirty years with a family and friends who adore her—and who'd die for her." Shaking his head, Scarsdale passed the flyer to Rhys. "Even if it was true and she needed you, do you want to make her pay *that*?"

He looked at the paper, but didn't see the caricature. He saw the ink, smudged and splattered with dried tears. This thing had hurt her. It didn't matter that the drawing was rubbish. It had still torn her apart.

Rhys wouldn't let it happen again. On one flyer, or from the people she met every damn day.

"She said I can't control how they think. So I'll change it."

Scarsdale tilted his head consideringly, as if Rhys had made a suggestion rather than stating how it would be. Slowly, he nodded. "As the memory of the Horde fades. And you've a big voice. You could persuade them that this would be an unacceptable depiction of *anyone*—not just someone with Horde blood—and do it without singling her out."

"How long will it take?"

Scarsdale's sigh said that it would be too long. So Rhys couldn't have her now. And he wouldn't stop until he could. But he had to let her go until then.

"I'll have the men signal Yasmeen." Rhys opened the door. "She'll take Mina aboard."

Taken aback, the bounder said, "I say, captain—you don't have to send her away *now*."

"Yes, I do." Or he wouldn't be able to.

As it was, stopping himself from begging her to stay would take every bit of control he had.

The salty mist wafting up from the bow cooled Mina's face, washed away the damage the storm of her tears had left. Feeling empty, she stared out over the water, watching the silvery path of reflected moonlight without seeing it.

She wanted so much. She almost hated him for bringing it within reach. For asking her to take it. No—for *telling* her to take it, when she'd never even let herself imagine having him.

Now, imagining it was all that she could do.

The public reaction would be a terrible blow to her parents. And they'd already withstood so much. Yet if Mina chose to stay with Rhys, they'd fight every whisper, every caricature, everything that caused her pain. They'd fight together and stand firm, because they loved her . . . and because she loved him.

And every day would be difficult. But if Rhys loved her, they could fight together, too. Everything she gained would be worth the pain.

But if she was only a possession, only someone he loved shagging . . .

She couldn't guess. She needed to find out.

With a shuddering breath, she wiped her eyes and stood. At the other end of the ship, the crew worked by the light of the lanterns, tethering *Lady Corsair* to the *Terror*'s stern. Mina climbed down the ladder, bracing herself with every step toward the captain's cabin—and so was almost prepared when she pushed through the door and saw her valise on the bed, already packed. Rhys, pulling a cigarillo out of a silver case. The awful detachment in his expression.

Mina had plenty of experience pushing away pain. She hadn't known it could grow so enormous that it pushed away everything else. No room for grief. No room for denial. No room for anything. So big, it left her numb.

She wondered how long it would take to recede. And when it did, how much everything else she felt would begin to hurt, too.

Lifting her gaze from the valise, she said, "So I'm to return on *Lady Corsair*?"

"Yes. I'm done with you." His gaze raked over her, landing on her face. Thank the blessed stars she couldn't feel anything—she wouldn't give anything away. "As you've said, continuing into London wouldn't be worth it. So we'll end it now."

"I see." She forced her reply past an aching throat.

Done with her. Not forced to part in two weeks by something Mina couldn't fight, by something that even the Iron Duke couldn't overcome. Not leaving him, yet holding on to the sweet, impossible knowledge that he still wanted her. Just . . . done with her.

His lids lowered, and he exhaled on a cloud of smoke that made his voice sound hollow and rough. "Unless you've changed your mind?"

She'd come so close to doing exactly that, though it would hurt so many people she loved—one of the most difficult decisions of her life. But this hadn't been difficult for him. He just had to exchange one need for another, and he was rid of her . . . and looking as if he didn't care whether she lived or died.

She had her answer, then.

Unable to speak, she simply shook her head and collected her valise. His heavy steps sounded behind her as she left the cabin. She was glad he was behind her. The pain wasn't receding. But other emotions were filling her up now, too, overflowing past ragged edges, as if she'd been ripped up the center. And with one look at her face, he would see them.

Head down, she remained ahead, passing Scarsdale as she walked to the stern. Rhys's boots went silent on the quarterdeck. Not even escorting her to the platform. Just watching her leave from a distance.

Her head came up at the sound of quick steps, chasing after her. Not heavy enough to be his.

"Mina! Bevins said that you're—" Andrew broke off when he caught sight of her. "Mina? Are you—"

"Don't ask." She barely heard her own hoarse whisper.

Though his face was blurring, she saw his grin. "All right, then, you slatternly wench! Go on back home where you belong, having babies and singing the praises of marriage reform!"

Mina choked. Not a laugh, not a sob. Both. She stepped onto the platform.

"That's right! We don't need your type around here. Any *decent* jade would be wearing a skirt . . . so that the crew could have a look as the platform goes up."

Mina managed a smile for that one, shaking her head. Her smile lasted only as long as the platform rested on the *Terror*'s decks. Lady Corsair met her at the side of the airship, frowning.

She studied Mina for a long second, then sighed. "This is what happens when you go soft. Do you want opium or wine?"

Not soft, Mina thought. A jagged stone existed where her heart had been. And she didn't want to feel it. Didn't want to feel anything, all the way back to London.

"Wine," she said.

Rhys saw her laugh, saw her smile. Leaving hadn't touched her—or the relief of not being forced to stay with him after they reached London had been stronger than her regret. The platform lifted. The boy turned, his face as stricken as Rhys felt. Andrew's eyes met his. Rhys recognized the anger and hatred in them. Her brother wanted to kill him for making her leave early.

Too late. By making her leave, Rhys had killed himself.

Scarsdale's gaze followed the rise of the platform. "I'm damned sorry, captain."

Him, too. And he couldn't watch her go. With a shake of his

head, he tossed away the cigarillo. It wasn't any kind of substitute. Now, the only thing that drove him was having her back—and he'd do that by taking away the fear that she lived under every day. "When we return, I want the name of every man in Parliament. I want to know what he believes, why he believes it. The newsmen, too."

"You'll have it." Scarsdale paused as the clank of the platform docking sounded through the night air. "It might take all of your life."

That didn't matter. He didn't have much of one without her.

Chapter Seventeen

Mina was still in a warm, spicy haze when they stopped in Venice three days later, hovering over the tall ruins. Noon arrived.

Fox didn't.

Near the bow where Mina was sitting, Yasmeen looked over the side, tapping her fingers against the rail . . . though the aviator's fingers were more like claws when she bent her fingers just so.

Minutes passed. Mina drank out of a bottle. After what seemed a long while, Mr. Pegg said, "Your orders, captain?"

"To wait!" Yasmeen snapped. "He's just late. And he owes me too much to leave him behind."

What a bloody liar, Mina thought, and set the bottle aside. It wasn't helping. She wasn't Yasmeen. She didn't want to pretend to feel something else—and she didn't want to hold her emotions at bay anymore.

Throughout the afternoon, Yasmeen paced the decks, smoking. Night fell to eerie growls below, from zombies drawn by the lanterns. Mina refused her wine over dinner. Yasmeen seemed in good spirits, and they'd spent enough time together of late that the occasional silences were no longer awkward. After she'd finished eating, Yasmeen pulled out a tattered magazine and settled into the pillows to read.

She caught Mina's look and said, "If he survived the damn zombies in the Egyptian tombs, he can survive Venice."

"No doubt." Though after observing the number of zombies below, Mina wasn't so certain. "Have you seen the tombs?"

"Not those underground, but I've flown over the pyramids several times. New Worlders will pay almost anything to see them. The only route that makes more is smuggling pilgrims into Mecca." She narrowed her eyes at Mina and let the magazine fall against her chest. "Where would you go, if it could be anywhere?"

Back to the *Terror*. But unless she stopped imagining herself with him, the pain would never fade. "The Ivory Market," she said. "The Horde quarter. So that I could see what it's like to walk down a street without being stared at."

"They would anyway. So small and pretty, and yet you look like a police inspector even when you aren't wearing your uniform." She pursed her lips. "I don't want to return to the Ivory Market, but I know of another city where people wouldn't care what you are. After we've picked up Fox, how does a week in Port Fallow strike you?"

A week where nobody cared what she was—before she returned to London, where people cared so much that she couldn't have what she most wanted.

"I couldn't pay—"

Yasmeen waved that off. "Trahaearn paid enough."

Twenty-five livre for one day, and that was only to Calais. Mina couldn't imagine the amount Lady Corsair had made on this journey.

"How much is Fox paying you?"

"Five livre." Her hard stare dared Mina to say anything.

Prudently, Mina didn't.

Burnett couldn't have sent the wiregram to Chatham.

Mina woke, staring into the ceiling of the narrow cabin. From giddiness to devastation, then muzzled by wine—but for the first time in several days, her mind was sharp.

And she was clearly an idiot.

Through the porthole, she heard the growls and hisses from below. Fox still hadn't shown or signaled to the airship. She hauled on her overcoat, buckling it over her nightshirt as she left the cabin.

Sheffield wasn't Black Guard. He wouldn't have sent the order to the assassin. Burnett *couldn't* have—he'd been on a ship near the Ivory Market. She'd missed someone.

Arriving at the captain's cabin, she knocked softly. Yasmeen opened the door wearing a crimson silk wrapper that clung to her breasts. She'd uncovered her hair. Her ears poked through the narrow braids, revealing the black, tufted points.

The sweet, sickly smell emanating from the darkened cabin was unmistakable.

Blissed on opium, Yasmeen's pupils were dilated as she looked Mina over. She smiled slowly, and asked with a purr, "Yes, inspector?"

"Burnett didn't order Baxter's assassination. We have to return to London, so that I can discover who did."

"Yes, I suppose you should. Do you have five livre?"

Of course she didn't. "No."

Yasmeen shut the door in her face.

When the aviators' shouts sounded above decks a week later, Mina was pacing her cabin like a woman crazed, and trying to convince herself that she'd have no better luck returning home if she jumped from the airship and took her chances with the zombies all across Europe.

She climbed up into the glow of the deck lanterns. At the side of the airship, Yasmeen was ordering the rope ladder tossed over. Rifles cracked as the aviators shot into the dark at the zombies below.

Fox climbed over the gunwale, dirt encrusted over his skin, clothes hanging off his frame, his mouth hidden in a month's growth of beard. He set down his glider—folded now into some other contraption, Mina saw—and looked up at Yasmeen. His face held none of the eagerness he'd displayed the first time he'd boarded. His features were hard, dangerous.

"Take me to the Ivory Market now," he told her.

Mina couldn't see the captain's face, but the aviators around them went suddenly still.

Yasmeen's voice was pleasant. "Our agreement was that I'd return you to Chatham, Mr. Fox."

"I'm changing it." Withdrawing a heavy purse from his belt, he tossed it at her feet. "The Market. Now."

"By way of Chatham. I've another passenger, Mr. Fox. I cannot kidnap her."

Jaw setting, he pulled his revolver and aimed it at the captain. Mina's hand went to her own weapons, but she wondered if shooting him would be necessary. Beneath his determination lay obvious and severe exhaustion. He might simply drop where he stood within another moment.

Yasmeen lifted her hands out to her sides. Her voice softened to a purr. "Put that away now, Mr. Fox, and we'll both pretend that four weeks of running from zombies has muddled your head. You'll sleep—and wake up alive. But only if you put it away *now*."

Without lowering the gun, he glanced at an aviator. "Set the course for—" He broke off, his gaze searching the spot where Yasmeen had been. His head turned.

She came up from behind him, as if she climbed up the outside of the ship's hull. Her forearm snagged around his throat and yanked him back over the rail. Both disappeared.

Heart racing, Mina sprinted forward. Before she reached the side, Yasmeen flipped back up, landing in a crouch on the gunwale.

Gingerly, she hopped to the deck. "Pull that ladder up, Mr. Pegg. Ms. Khouri, fire the engines. Take us the hell out of here."

Blue heavens. "And Fox?"

With the toe of her boot, Yasmeen flicked his purse up to her hand, and continued on. "I threw him over. Will you arrest me, inspector?"

No. He'd tried to take her ship at gunpoint. Even over English soil, Mina wouldn't have arrested her. But she was still shocked by the suddenness of it—and saddened by the stupidity of it all. She hadn't known Fox very long, but what she had known, she'd liked well enough.

She watched the captain drop through the hatch to the lower deck and moved back the rail. There was only darkness below. Only the hisses and growls of the zombies. Fox must be one of them now.

What had possessed him to do something so foolish? What possible motive could he have had for immediately heading to the Ivory Market? Not just exhaustion or insanity.

She glanced down at his glider.

Mina found Yasmeen in her cabin, downing a snifter of green absinthe. Feathers floated in the air—she'd torn the pillows to pieces. She looked at Mina as if nothing were out of the ordinary.

"What's that?"

Mina held up his glider. "It transforms into a reinforced carrier."

"Oh? For what?"

Kneeling beside the low table in a pile of feathers and shredded silk, Mina opened the carrier. Yasmeen sucked in a breath.

Between carefully cushioned plates of glass lay a small sketch, the paper yellow and fragile, the ink faded to brown. A study of a wing skeleton, paired with a mechanical counterpart created of a wooden frame manipulated by pulleys and strings—a glider contraption, perhaps.

The captain stopped with her fingers hovering above the glass, as if not daring to touch even that. "Is it real?"

Mina's gaze slipped over the neat, backward script. Though she couldn't read it, the shape of Leonardo da Vinci's handwriting was as familiar to Mina as her own—as it was to everyone in England and the New World. If this was genuine, it would be worth thousands of livre. Tens of thousands.

And because it might be genuine, she gently closed the contraption again.

"I'll find his sister," Yasmeen said.

"To give her this?"

She grinned. "No. To tell her that I killed him. If I gave her this, she'd have no reason to write."

"She won't have anything to write about now, anyway."

"I suppose not. The stupid bastard. Why do they always try to control *everything*? Why can't they just let us be?"

Men? Mina shook her head. Her experience with them had obviously been different than Yasmeen's. "I don't know," she said.

Yasmeen sighed before sliding her a wry, sideways glance. "To England, then?"

To England, and back to the gray. Clouds blanketed London—not the yellow fog that often came at night, yet still low enough that Yasmeen could sail in during the afternoon without drawing much notice. Mina had said to drop her in Chatham, but the aviator captain had only looked at her for a long moment, and Mina had decided not to argue. As they flew closer, following the path of the Thames, she was glad for Yasmeen's stubbornness.

London was burning in patches.

Across the river from the Isle of Dogs, the navy docks had caught fire. To avoid the thick column of smoke, Yasmeen sailed over the island—and the Iron Duke's docks hadn't been touched. Mina's breath caught painfully in her throat when she recognized the *Terror*, her sails furled and decks empty. Though she'd been trying to avoid looking at it, her gaze flew to his house. Was Rhys home now? How long ago had they arrived? Had he tried to contact her—and what had he thought when he'd learned that *Lady Corsair* hadn't returned to England yet?

But the airship sailed on, and unless she followed the rail to the stern with spyglass in hand, she had to let that small glimpse of him go. With an ache in her throat, she looked forward again. They flew past the tower and its ruined wall, and the grounds that no one had built on in nine years.

"Inspector!" Yasmeen came to the rail. "Look there. My men spotted steelcoats. Near the prison, they said."

In the city? Revulsion turned in her stomach. Perhaps they were necessary on navy ships, for protection on the seas and abroad, but nothing in London wanted or warranted the use of that much force. If not for the ratcatchers, the police wouldn't even carry guns with bullets—just the opium darts.

She found the steelcoats through the spyglass, dozens upon dozens of them. In their great hulking suits, the marines formed a solid line in front of Newgate prison, apparently guarding the entrance from—

"There's a mob!" Astonished, she strained to see. "They're packed solid from Ludgate to the meat market!"

Great blue heavens. What had happened? Had the police called in the navy's steelcoats to help manage it? Mina simply couldn't imagine Commissioner Broyles doing anything of the sort.

She glanced up the river toward headquarters and froze. Where was *that* smoke coming from? "Is Scotland Yard on fire?"

Yasmeen signaled to her men. "We'll soon see."

Within a few minutes, the source of the fire came into view—not headquarters, but the Admiralty building across the street. Yasmeen ordered the sails furled, and she climbed down the rope ladder with Mina. Despite the fire, the street was all but deserted. A pair of constables rushed out of headquarters as they approached the entrance, not even pausing to gawp at Yasmeen's tall boots, shirtsleeves, or the pistols and knives studding her person.

"Constables!" They stopped at Mina's voice. "What's happened?"

"The Iron Duke's been arrested, sir! He's set to hang at sunset!"

She couldn't comprehend it. "Arrested by whom?"

"The Lord High Admiral, sir, as *Marco's Terror* came into dock this morning. The duke's at Newgate now—as we've been ordered to be." Without waiting for dismissal, they began to move on at a fast clip. "Your man's upstairs with Hale, inspector. They're coming right after us."

Headquarters' first level was as empty of people as the street. Mina ran up the stairs, followed by Yasmeen. She almost collided with Newberry on the stair landing.

"Sir?" He stepped back into the hallway, his eyes wide with shock and relief. "Thank God, sir! We thought you were on the ship—and in Newgate with the others now."

"*All* of the crew was arrested?" Had everyone in London gone completely mad? "Why?"

"Because the Iron Duke destroyed the Black Guard's weapon." Hale joined them in the hall. Her gaze flicked to Yasmeen. "Captain Corsair. Thank you for bringing her home."

Yasmeen smiled, showing her sharp teeth. "Is that a dismissal?"

"Not if the Iron Duke is a friend of yours." Hale looked to Mina again. "Your report arrived."

And had detailed Sheffield's involvement in this. "Sir, I'm sor—"

Hale held up her hand. "Mr. Sheffield confessed all to me the day you left—including that it was the Duke of Dorchester who approached him, asking for the invitation to the auction in return for my safety."

Smoking hells. The same man who'd arrested Rhys. "The Lord High Admiral, sir?"

"Yes. As you can imagine, that put me in a delicate position. My involvement—my *former* involvement—with Mr. Sheffield immediately made my investigation into Dorchester's activities . . . problematic, and anyone would have regarded Sheffield's confession as suspect. I lacked evidence of any sort. Your Newberry provided me with the first bit."

"That wiregram came from Dorchester's office, sir," Newberry said.

And they couldn't have arrested the highest ranking member

of the Royal Navy on so little evidence: Sheffield's word, and the memory of a clerk in Chatham.

"But your report told me that I only had to wait for the *Terror* to return, and I would have Haynes's recording, and testimony from the men on the *Terror* and in the fleet."

"None of it named Dorchester, sir."

"Not yet," Hale said. "But we'd have found enough, and that would have led to more, and finally tightened the noose. Dorchester beat me to it."

And took Rhys and the crew. "But how is the Iron Duke in Newgate?"

"Dorchester was waiting at his docks this morning, with his steelcoats lined up, and under naval authority, charged him with piracy, treason, and murder." Hale shook her head. "Of course, he underestimated the public's reaction. Now Dorchester has dug his heels in and taken over Newgate. He has his steelcoats guarding the gallows outside the entrance, where he insists the hanging will take place."

Mina couldn't dredge up a dram of fear. A hanging simply wouldn't happen. If he brought the Iron Duke up to that gallows scaffolding, the crowd would surge—steelcoats or not. "Is he mad?"

"I don't know what he's thinking. But I won't assume that he's mad." She held Mina's gaze. "*All* of the crew is in Newgate, charged with piracy. Your mother and father left for the prison earlier, hoping to apply for your brother's release. I don't know if they've returned since the mob has formed."

They'd be all right. They'd take care of each other. "How do we stop a mob?"

"I don't mean to stop them—just to keep them at Newgate and from burning the rest of London. And if we cannot stop this hanging, then I hope to God that *they* do."

"So we're off to Newgate, then." Mina turned to Yasmeen. "And you?"

"I can't be known to associate with London coppers." Though she grinned, her gaze was serious. "I'll pay a visit to the Blacksmith. If I ask nicely, he'll bring more against the steelcoats than your opium darts. Perhaps he already is."

Mina frowned. "What?"

"Come now. You don't think he's just been building mechanical whores?"

She looked to Hale. After the Horde's occupation, most of London's citizenry thought it bad enough that the police carried guns. If the Metropolitan Police ever used anything like steelcoats, the outcry would have been long and loud. There was simply too much fear that so much power in the hands of a single entity would be used to suppress them.

But they viewed the Blacksmith differently. And even those who feared his appearance never seemed to fear that he'd crush them, any more than they feared that the Iron Duke would.

"We'll accept all of the help we can get—especially if it means that fewer people in that mob will die," Hale said, and turned to regard Yasmeen. "Will you take me to him?"

"I say, when they built this new prison, I didn't expect the accommodations to be so fine. Much finer than the last prison I was in, to be certain."

Scarsdale had to raise his voice over the hiss of the steelcoat's boiler. Seated in a chair beside Rhys, the bounder wore irons around his wrists, and was forced to lean forward with his elbows on his knees to accommodate the chain that fastened his irons to the steel loop set into the floor with mortar.

The warden's reply was just as loud, but less cheerful. In apologetic tones, he said, "Thank you, my lord. We try to make certain that our more esteemed guests can stay in relative comfort. Without a doubt, you are both our *most* esteemed thus far."

After a pause, the warden added, "Your Grace, are you certain that you would not like my men to find a bench for you?"

Crouching on the stone floor, Rhys looked up from his own chains, his own steel loop. His chair's legs had splintered out from beneath him when they'd brought him and Scarsdale to the warden's office ten minutes before, but he didn't mind the floor. He'd have more leverage when he finally decided to stand.

"No," he said.

Sweating, the warden looked over Rhys's shoulder to the steel-coat guarding the door. Anger flashed across the man's expression, but he remained behind his desk.

Good man. There was courage, and there was stupidity. An unarmed man attacking a steelcoat only qualified for one of those descriptions. Rhys had made a similar decision when they'd come into dock, and found Dorchester and his steelcoats waiting for him. He could have ordered his men to fight their way through, but the cost of their lives would have been too high of a price to pay.

And Dorchester wasn't worth dying for. They'd take him down and leave this prison another way—not with the blood of a warden on their hands.

The warden *or* his crew.

"Where are my men?"

"In the yard, sir. There wasn't room in the cells," he said.

And he must not expect them to stay here long. Rhys didn't expect that they would, either.

As if discomforted by the silence, the warden cleared his throat. "Is there anything that I can have brought to you while we wait for the Lord High Admiral? We dine modestly here, but—"

"Absinthe?" Scarsdale looked hopeful.

"I don't think so, my lord. Nothing stronger than wine."

"Wine will do."

"And for Your Grace?"

"Water," Rhys said.

"Yes, yes." He could hear Scarsdale's grin. "A big mug of water. A man of his size possesses a burning thirst, and needs an awful lot to douse it."

Looking grateful to be of some use, the warden went to the door and called for a tray. He stopped by the window returning to his desk. Rhys didn't need to see outside to know what was happening.

Neither did Scarsdale. In a low voice, he said, "The mob's quite loud now, isn't it?"

"Yes."

"Do you imagine that your inspector is out there with them?"

Mina had best not be. For now, the crowd had focused on him, but as Newgate remained closed and they became frustrated, they might turn on each other. She'd be the first target.

So he needed to escape from here soon.

The door opened, and a secretary brought in their drinks. Rhys set the water in front of him. Scarsdale's chains wouldn't let him raise the wineglass to his lips.

He heaved a sigh. "I say, warden. Will you release my chain from that loop?"

The warden hesitated, looking toward the door.

As if he'd forgotten the steelcoat was there, Scarsdale swiveled around as far as he could. Shaking his head, he looked to the warden again. "Bother, man. I'll still be in irons and chains—and you've got nothing to fear from me, regardless. I'm just a navigator, and a drunk to boot." He jerked his chin toward Rhys. "It's *him* you have to worry about. And look, he can put a glass to his mouth without bending over so far that he could see up his own arse. No need to release him."

"All right." Keys in hand, the warden came around the desk, muttering, "You can't do much with that lumbering sack of metal watching over you."

"Quite right," Scarsdale agreed.

Soon the heavy steps of another lumbering sack of metal sounded from the hall—but this steelcoat didn't come in, waiting outside the door. An escort, then. So the lighter steps would be Dorchester's.

About damn time.

Even using Newberry's bulk as a wedge to push through the crowd, it was almost an hour before Mina forged close enough to *see* the prison at the corner of Old Bailey and Newgate. The few windows built into the gray stone didn't weaken its imposing face, but revealed the walls' impenetrable thickness. When Mina stood on her toes, she could see the gallows platform and the steelcoats' thick, rounded helmets. The prison's arched portcullis gate stood behind them, visible through the smoke rising from their boiler packs.

The shouts from the crowd had raised in volume, become more regular—almost a chant. They suddenly swelled, and a small surge moved through the mob near the prison's southwestern corner. The steelcoats' rifles fired. Screams followed, and the shouts began again, cacophonous, deafening.

Her father would be there—up at the steelcoat line on Old Bailey, with the worst of the wounded. Mina shouted for Newberry to begin pushing along the buildings containing the mob. Circling to the side of the prison and finding a narrow space to cross would be easier than fighting through the enormous crowd gathered in front.

For fifteen minutes, she followed him, almost clinging to his back through the roughest spots. All around them, people were climbing up steps, onto windowsills, onto carts and coaches, all hoping for a better view. Every crate had been turned over and supported at least two men.

Mina stopped. Wearing welding goggles and a hat, a small girl was clinging to a lamppost, looking over the crowd. A tinker's tattoo circled her wrist.

"Anne!" Mina's shout brought Newberry to a halt, but the girl didn't hear. She tried again. *"Tinker Anne!"*

The girl looked round, pushing up her goggles. Her eyes widened. *Oh, blue heavens.* "Newberry! Bring that girl here."

He didn't need to. Anne scrambled down from the post and wriggled through bodies and legs like an eel. Mina drew her behind an abandoned lorry topped by thirty men and women, and with almost as many urchins huddled beneath.

The noise of the crowd forced her to shout. "What are you thinking, tinker? This is no place for you!"

The girl's smile wavered. "The Blacksmith's coming, inspector! I wanted to see his walker up against the old suits!"

So did Mina. But she shook her head. "You have to go, Anne. If this mob riots, you'll be taken down first. Do you understand? Some will care that you're a girl, and you're young. But there's too many that won't!"

"*You're* here."

"It's my job to be here. Go home, Anne, so that I know you're safe!"

An apologetic cough came from beside her. "Through these streets alone, sir?"

Mina looked to Newberry. Damn it all. He was right—running alone through London wouldn't be any safer than remaining here. All right, then. "Newberry, turn your back to us. Unbuckle your overcoat and spread it open."

As soon as he did, Mina hauled off her own coats and untucked her shirt before unbuckling her armor. It was too big for the girl, but would do the job. Within moments, she had the girl covered and her jackets refastened.

Newberry, bless him, survived the experience.

She bent toward Anne again. "Now, you stay with us—but especially with Newberry. If we're separated, if the mob comes at you, you run. And if you can't run, try to hide beneath something, like this lorry. Roll into a ball and protect your head and belly. All right?"

Face pale, the girl nodded.

"Good." Mina smiled to reassure her, then abruptly straightened when a noise began penetrating the clamor of the crowd.

Heavy, like steelcoats, but not in rigid formation. And intermittently, a thunderous boom—accompanied by a tremor.

The crowd quieted. Still loud, but many of them turning their heads, murmuring and wondering instead of shouting. Mina looked to Newberry. From his great height, he could better see over the mob.

"What is it?"

He shook his head. "I don't see anything yet, sir."

"Inspector." Anne tugged on Mina's sleeve, her eyes bright. "That's the Blacksmith."

Though the man had charged Rhys with piracy, treason, and murder—despite his having acted under the regency council's order—Dorchester wasn't insane. Rhys had briefly wondered so at the docks, but the emotion burning in the man's eyes wasn't madness. Dorchester was furious.

Rhys could allow him that—and was why he allowed the man *this*. He'd killed an admiral and had blown a first-rate to pieces, both on what must seem to be little evidence that Burnett had been Black Guard. And the proof of *Endeavour* was gone, as well.

He'd struck the Royal Navy and the High Lord Admiral a severe blow. The man obviously meant to strike one back by bringing him and his crew here, but Rhys cared little if he spent time in a prison.

He did care that Mina was probably in a mob outside—and that the people who formed it would be hurt on his behalf, simply because a man couldn't manage his temper.

Or his arrogance. Dorchester came in carrying one of the Horde's freezing devices, but otherwise unarmed. He must have felt safe with Rhys crouching low on the floor, practically on his knees.

Rhys remembered many men who'd thought that position gave them power. They'd forgotten that Rhys had teeth.

With a drunken grin, Scarsdale showed his own teeth. "Quite a snappy jacket, Your Grace. You must be furious that we sunk your ship—expensive, aren't they?—and that your Black Guard admiral went down with it, but all of England is better off for it. So let us go on, then."

"Better off?" Dorchester seemed to taste the words. "No."

"Well, to be sure, the Royal Navy's fleet isn't better off with a first-rate at the bottom of the ocean. But in England, yes—everybody's better off *not* dead. You realize that's what *Endeavour* and Burnett would have done?"

"Not everybody," Dorchester said. "Just the infected."

Fuck. Rhys didn't glance at Scarsdale, but he knew by the bounder's sudden silence that he'd had the same realization: Dorchester wasn't just furious. He was Black Guard.

Did Mina know? She undoubtedly did. Returning to London more than a week ago after picking up Fox, she'd have delved straight back into the investigation, tying up loose ends . . . no doubt she'd have followed one of those to Dorchester.

So she'd know who had him now. Not just an angry man, but one who would kill himself and everyone around him to avoid discovery. Well, Dorchester had all but announced himself now. So Rhys assumed he planned to act soon.

That suited Rhys. It'd give Mina something more to arrest him with.

Dorchester must have recognized the silence for the realization that it was. "Do you not wonder why?"

He wanted them to say it aloud? To show fear? *Bah.*

"He probably only wonders what your son's political leanings are," Scarsdale said. "I imagine that the boy will take your seat in Parliament soon."

As soon as the man was dead.

Rhys suppressed his grin. And though he knew Scarsdale had intended for his response to increase Dorchester's fury, to bring him to careless rage so that the man wouldn't be careful with his words, the admiral's anger cooled and hardened.

"Parliament *is* the problem. They fight, they argue, they say their decisions are for the good of England. Whether the infected should inherit, whether they should be a judge. But they ignore that infection itself is the danger—and will be our downfall."

"Is that so?" Scarsdale downed his wine. With shaking hands, the warden refilled his glass.

"You can be controlled. It would only take one of our enemies to create the right signal, and all of England burns. I have heard what happened in the revolution—and that was damage done when the infected were under no one's control. Under the control of our enemies, the infected could destroy the country this quickly." He snapped his fingers. "So the Black Guard fights for the security of England—and we will accomplish what the politicians don't have the will and the courage to do."

"Kill everyone!" Scarsdale nodded and lifted his glass to the man. "Quite right."

"*Protect* England by eradicating the infection."

"Yes, yes! Protect England by killing Englishmen! Sound logic, sir."

"The infected *aren't* Englishmen. They're something the Horde has created. Controlled. They're a dormant disease, waiting for something else to control them. England can't afford the risk of having such creations on English soil."

The warden's face had reddened. "Sir, I must object to this—"

Dorchester touched the base of the freezing device, cutting the warden off. Scarsdale sat frozen with his wine filling his open mouth—overflowing onto his jacket. Rhys remained still.

With another touch, Dorchester released them. The warden heaved in a long breath, devastation weighing on his features. Scarsdale blinked.

"I say, did I spill? Sorry about the mess, warden."

The man didn't answer. He stared at the Lord High Admiral—hating him, Rhys knew, with every fiber in his body. Just as Mina would have. As everyone who'd lived beneath the Horde would have.

"You're not men," Dorchester said. "You're windups. Automatons. Men use machinery. You *are* machinery. And some of the infected are worse, not machines but *animals*. We won't let that infection spread to England, too. And there is still *another* threat, as you breed. Shall England be populated by men who are like rat-catchers? Shall children be born with armor and razor teeth? No, it *shall not be*."

Passion reddened Dorchester's cheeks. Carelessly, Scarsdale blotted his jacket with a handkerchief.

"That seems a waste," he said. "Within a few generations, this might be a country full of strong men with iron bones—and bugs that can't be controlled. Wouldn't that make the Horde or anyone else think twice before trying to destroy us again?"

"They would be monsters who destroy *true* men. The whole world would be filled with them, stomping out all that is human."

"I think men like that would prefer stomping on admirals who overstep their power." Scarsdale paused, looked up—still cheerful, but not the least bit soused. "So why is it that you're hanging us, then?"

Dorchester looked to Rhys. "First, him—the symbol of England's freedom from the Horde. But there was no freedom. The country is still infected, and still under the Horde's threat. So I'll take that illusion away. I'll quarantine the infected and give them a choice between Europe or eradication—and those who resist us will be put down. And finally, the Black Guard will take England back from the Horde."

"And you'll save your own life." Rhys spoke for the first time since Dorchester had entered the warden's office, startling the admiral.

"What?"

"You bought a weapon for over twenty-five thousand livre. The

Black Guard wouldn't have that in their coffers, not just from selling slaves. So the other members must have entrusted enormous
amounts of their personal money to you." Rhys watched Dorchester's face tighten. The man controlled himself well, but this fear
didn't lurk deep. "You must have promised results, assured them of
success—and yet you lost the weapon."

And now, it was not just anger that drove Dorchester. Not just his
belief in the Black Guard's cause. That he'd resorted to such a drastic
and self-destructive plan told Rhys that a great deal of desperation
lay behind it—much like a frigate captain watching a first-rate bearing down on his ship, and ordering his men to fire the engines.

But Dorchester was all but done. And Rhys wanted to know who
to go after next.

"Even now, those members of the Black Guard must be hearing
the news that the weapon was sunk. Men to whom you promised
an England free of buggers. So you're still trying to give them one,
because they'll make you pay if you fail again. Who are they?"

Face pale, Dorchester shook his head. Gesturing to the steelcoat
behind Rhys, he said, "It's time to escort His Grace outside. Warden, take his chain from that loop."

With the hiss of hydraulics and the clank of gears, the steelcoat
moved behind him. Scarsdale gave a pitying snort and leaned close
to Rhys, holding out his wine, chains swinging from the irons on
his wrists.

"A last sip of the good stuff, captain?" When Rhys shook his
head, Scarsdale lifted the mug. "Of water, then?"

"No."

Scarsdale sighed and backed out of the way, glass and mug in
hand. "It's no use fighting, captain," he said. "These steelcoats
aren't fast, but they'll flatten you with a single blow."

"So I've heard," Rhys said.

Dorchester was losing patience. "Warden?"

As the man reluctantly came around his desk, Scarsdale prattled on, "I once sat and drank Jasper Evans under the table in Port

Fallow. Dreadful conversationalist. All he talked about was losing the steelcoat contract to Morgan. Evans's were a bit faster, you
know. Morgan changed the boiler and made adjustments to the
overall design to prove that he wasn't stealing Evans's—but they all
added up to a slower suit."

Keys shaking in his hands, the warden bent in front of him.
Rhys gripped the chain and met the man's gaze. The warden's eyes
widened—then narrowed in fierce satisfaction. He stepped back.

With a powerful surge, Rhys stood. The steel loop tore from the
stone in a shower of mortar. From behind him, he heard a great hiss
of steam, and a low gurgle. Dorchester stared at them, flabbergasted.

Scarsdale continued, "He also told me about Morgan's design
flaw—how he left the exhaust tube from the furnace wide open,
so the coals were easy to douse. So easy that a single glass of water
does the trick. And I say, your marine is trapped inside all of that
metal, isn't he? Another member of the Black Guard, I suppose, if
you trusted him to watch over us." He rapped his knuckles against
the chest plate and shook his head over the hollow echo. "The navy
ought to have paid the extra money for Evans's design. 'Always pay
a man what he's worth,' that's the captain's—"

Dorchester reached for the Horde's device, freezing Scarsdale
midrap. Chains dangling from his wrists, Rhys stepped forward,
towering over the man.

Resignation swept over Dorchester's face, followed by stiff determination. He lifted his chin. "You may kill me, but you'll never stop
the Black Gua—"

"Pipe down, admiral!"

Christ. Rhys could stand to listen to nonsense—hell, Scarsdale
had inured him to that—but he couldn't tolerate the shit Dorchester
spewed. He knocked the freezing device to the stone floor. The spike
broke. Scarsdale continued rapping.

The warden came forward, relief loosening everything from his
gait to his expression. "Shall I remove your wrist irons, Your Grace?"

Mina had once told him that people might be inspired by such an image—and he still had to face all of those waiting outside. He owed them that, owed all of those who'd come for him. He might not have made all of them his, but they'd obviously made him *theirs*. So he'd see them off, and make certain as few as possible were hurt for having come to help him.

"No," he told the warden. "But remove Scarsdale's, and put them on the admiral. Behind his back, so that he can't easily kill himself."

As soon as that was done, Rhys grabbed the admiral's hair, began dragging him to the door.

"I say, it's a good thing you rarely come up against bald men. God knows what's crawling through the hair you'd have to steer them around by." Scarsdale listened at the door, pointed in the direction of the steelcoat waiting outside. "What now?"

"We give the crowd what they want." And his inspector an arrest.

He strode into the hall. The steelcoat raised his rifle—and dropped it as soon as Rhys twisted the admiral's head, making the threat clear. Scarsdale collected the weapon and they moved on. The warden joined them, and soon his prison guards.

"There will be more steelcoats outside," Scarsdale said. "Surely not all Black Guard, but still under his command."

"And the admiral will order them to stand down."

"Never," Dorchester said.

Rhys looked to the window as a faint tremble shook through the prison's floor, then met Scarsdale's eyes.

The bounder grinned. "Then again, perhaps we won't need him to."

Clinging to the side of the lorry, using the tire as a step, Mina looked over the crowd. Apparently half-spider, Anne climbed up to the top and forced herself into a tiny crevice between two men.

A ripple started through the mob on Newgate Street, pushing and spreading the crowd apart. The Blacksmith's name swept along with it, carried south along Old Bailey to Mina's ears. Marching single file, his steelcoats came into view. Lighter than the clunky marine steelcoats, they moved more easily, and the steam and smoke coming from their boiler packs rose in wisps rather than clouds.

But what threat would they pose? Mina shook her head. "His steelcoats aren't carrying any weapons."

"He calls them his metalmen, not steelcoats. And they don't have to carry weapons," Anne said. "The weapons are built into the arms. They just have to"—the tinker cocked her wrist and gave it a flip—"and the gun mechanisms fold out. Or this"—she pulled her elbow back before throwing her hand forward, palm flat—"for the flame jets."

Astounded, Mina looked to them again. The crowd had moved back, and the metalmen had lined up across from the steelcoats. The marines held their formation.

"If *they* are metalmen, what is a walker?"

The tinker pointed. Around them, a great cry rose up. Not terror, but an astonishment that echoed Mina's as the machine stepped into view.

A walker, yes. On enormous steel legs constructed of pneumatic pistons and gears, it stood almost as tall as the prison walls. Steam rose from the boiler, a giant pipe cylinder that formed the walker's body. At the base of the body, still fifteen feet off the ground, the Blacksmith occupied the pilot seat, his skin gleaming in the dull afternoon light. Standing behind his seat was Hale, clinging to a stabilizing rod with one hand and her hat with the other.

The Blacksmith reached for an item near his feet—a speaking trumpet designed to amplify sounds, which he gave to Hale. She put it to her mouth.

"ROYAL—"

Her voice exploded over the crowd, shocking all to silence. Hale jerked the trumpet down, staring at the Blacksmith. He gestured for her to continue.

"Royal Marines, on the authority of the Metropolitan Police Force, I'm ordering you to stand down! Your siege on this prison is unlawful and unwarranted."

Newberry shook his head. "They won't do it. Not on her authority."

Hale must have realized the same. She addressed the crowd, instead. "Clear a path to the prison gate—in an orderly fashion, if you please!"

The response wasn't immediate. Then the huge machine let out a great huff and one of the legs moved forward. The loosely woven path that the metalmen had left suddenly widened, and the mob seemed to move outward, squeezing and expanding like a compression wave.

Mina hopped to the ground. "Newberry, we need to be closer."

The constable looked doubtfully over the crowd. "I don't see how we'll—"

Shouts erupted around them. Cries of "At the gate!" and "The Iron Duke!" rang through the mob.

Mina's heart constricted. Was Dorchester daring to bring Rhys out to hang? Truly?

"What's happening, constable?"

He shook his head. "I can't see the gate, sir."

"Newberry, please!"

The men and women on the lorry began to jump and yell, rocking the vehicle from side to side. Anne scrambled down. Mina grabbed her hand as Newberry pushed a path farther into the crowd, battling for every inch. Mina fought her despair. Reaching the front line would be impossible.

Cheers sounded from the lorry behind them—and from the front of the mob. Mina couldn't see anything but the constable's back. Red-faced, Newberry turned to her.

"Try this, sir."

Giant hands circling her waist, he hauled her up, and suddenly she was seated on his broad shoulder. Mina swallowed her surprise and narrowed her gaze on the gallows scaffolding, trying to make sense of the scene on the platform.

Rhys was in his shirtsleeves, chains hanging from his wrists. In

front of him stood Dorchester, head held high—and in irons. Even
over the cheers, Mina heard the Iron Duke's command.

"Lord High Admiral, order your men to lay down their weapons." The line of steelcoats seemed to waver as several marines
turned to look. "This is over, Dorchester. You'll soon be under arrest
for conspiring with the Black Guard. Don't make these marines pay
for your crimes against England."

Yes. Mina clenched her fists, tempted to cheer along with the
others. But she needed to focus on a way to that scaffolding and
make the arrest. This mob wanted Dorchester's blood, they wanted
to see him swinging in the Iron Duke's place, but Rhys had told
them an arrest would be enough. So they needed *that*, at least.

She looked to the Blacksmith's walker. Hale was nearer to Dorchester, but she likely wouldn't be jumping down from that thing soon.

So Mina needed to get up there. But how would she—

Something hit her head. Mina instinctively ducked, almost
throwing Newberry off balance. Suddenly furious, she grabbed for
the thing that was *still on her*, and . . . found a rope. She looked up.

Lady Corsair hovered quietly overhead, her engines silent. Yasmeen peered over the rail and lifted her hands in a clear *What are
you waiting for?*

"Watch Anne!" Mina shouted to Newberry, and hauled herself up.

Yasmeen didn't wait for her to climb more than a few feet. Mina's
stomach swooped as the airship flew forward. Clinging to the rope,
she sailed over the mob toward the scaffolding.

Her gaze met the Iron Duke's, and the connection seemed to
guide her in. *Rhys.* The pain of him sending her away had gone. At
this moment, all that remained was the sheer relief of seeing him
unharmed. She dropped lightly to the gallows platform, and he
was there to steady her with a firm grip on her hand. Loss speared
through her when he let go.

"Detective Inspector Wentworth."

"Your Grace." Because it seemed appropriate, she executed a
short bow.

That amused him. "The Lord High Admiral has confessed to being a member of the Black Guard, and part of a plot to kill every bugger in England . . . which would include the king."

With a short nod, Mina turned to Dorchester. "Your Grace, I am placing you under arrest for treason, conspiracy to commit mass murder, and for ordering the assassination of Admiral Baxter." That was for the mob; more formal charges would be made later, Mina was certain. Her gaze searched the nearby crowd and found a bowler hat. "Constable! Please secure this man, and prepare to take him to headquarters for questioning."

She wished it had been Newberry. But she would make up for it, somehow.

Though the constable looked uncertain as he approached the lines of metalmen and steelcoats, he walked through them without incident. Almost all of the marines faced the gallows now. Through their helmets' eye slits, Mina saw dismay, anger, disbelief.

Dorchester waited, tall and dignified. His chest puffed up as he drew in a deep breath.

"Marines!" he shouted. "Open fire on the Iron Duke!"

Mina's blood froze. But though the remaining steelcoats turned to face them, no one raised their weapon.

"Fire! If you love England, fire!"

Several shook their heads, setting down their guns. Mina began to nod her satisfaction—but from the corner of her eye, she saw one barrel swing up.

A member of the Black Guard—or simply someone who always followed orders, no matter the manner of man they came from.

Rhys saw it, too. He began to turn.

But he wasn't as fast as she was.

Mina slammed into his chest. Holding her tight, Rhys pivoted to take the shot at his back. The echoing crack of the rifle faded. He gave an astonished laugh.

They hadn't been hit. Only a few yards away, and the idiot had missed. From behind him came a clamor as steelcoats or metalmen downed the shooter. Something burned in his ribs, probably jabbed by a part of Mina's uniform as she'd thrown herself at him. He felt her relief, as the tension slowly left her rigid form, leaving her limp.

Too limp. She almost slipped out of his arms. Rhys hauled her back up, trying to comprehend her closed eyes, the slackness of her body. The blood, soaking into his shirt.

So he'd been shot after all; the bullet had hit a rib. And—

Shot *through* Mina.

No. He shook her. "Mina?"

Her head fell back. Her chest separated from his.

Blood gushed down her front.

"Mina? No. *Mina!*" Roaring her name, he hauled her close again. His hands found blood at her back. No, no. Dropping to his knees, he lay her down, ripped off his shirt and pressed it to her chest. Blood pooled beneath her. "Help me! Ah, God. *Help me!*"

The hissing of boilers answered him, silence from the crowd. Feet pounded across the gallows platform. Scarsdale dropped to the boards beside him, tearing his shirtsleeves away. Rhys shoved them beneath her, trying to stop the bleeding at her back.

God help him—he didn't know if it was.

Raggedly shouting her name, he pulled her up to half-sitting and dragged her between his legs, cloth clamped to her chest, pushing her back hard against his thigh. She convulsed, coughing up a bubble of blood.

"No, Mina. No, no." Rhys held her tight. He bent his head to hers. "Please. *Please!*"

A hand on his arm brought his head up. With bleak eyes, he stared at the white-faced man kneeling beside him. Realization snapped through him.

Father. Surgeon.

"Help her," he whispered hoarsely. "Help her."

The man nodded, leaning forward. A woman in a billowing blue skirt fell to the platform next to him. Rhys recognized the white hair, disheveled and falling over her shoulder, the tinted lenses.

Mother.

"William?" Devastation lined her delicate face. "William? Can you—"

"Trahaearn, keep pressure here and here." The father's hands covered Rhys's at Mina's front and back. "If you value her life, don't let up."

Rhys pressed hard. He didn't think she'd be able to take a breath, he pressed so hard.

But he didn't think she could breathe, anyway.

The father looked to the mother. "The bugs are helping, Cecily, but they can't do it alone. I need a heart. A pump like you made for Beatrice Addle. Do you remember?"

She glanced at her empty hands. "But I don't—"

"Look, Cecily. *Look.*"

Her mouth firmed. Nodding, she stood, her gaze sweeping the crowd. She pointed.

"You! Come here. You! And you! All of you, up here. You! The dockworker! You two steelcoats. The rest of you, make way for them. And *run*, damn you all." She spun around again, grabbed Scarsdale. "You, help me. We'll hold them down and rip the pieces off, if we must."

They hurried off, but Rhys didn't watch where they went. Only Mina. The father withdrew her opium gun and shot a dart into her neck. Rhys held onto her, faintly aware of the murmurs from the crowd, the cries from the mother, Scarsdale's cajoling voice. Faintly aware that the woman was taking parts from prosthetics and putting them together.

"Hurry, Cecily!"

Another convulsion ripped through Mina's small frame. Drifting away, and taking Rhys's life with him. He buried his face in her hair, whispered her name over and over. Trying to give her a line to hold on to. Trying to give her an anchor.

His was slipping, and her name was no longer a whisper, but a cry through clenched teeth.

The mother rushed up, winding a pump made of pistons within a tin canister. Narrow rubber tubes capped with steel valves projected from each side. "It's dirty. I couldn't—"

"It doesn't matter," the father said sharply. "The bugs will clean it."

"And she'll rip it off. The moment she wakes up. She wouldn't want this."

"Let that be *her* choice, Cecily! Now, which tube is the intake—?" His voice broke. His wife tucked the right tube into his palm, and clasped her fingers over his. His hand stopped trembling. "Yes. Thank you, my love. Be my eyes, now. Hold her still, Trahaearn."

He pushed Rhys's hand from Mina's chest. The mother and father bent over her. He had to look away when he saw Mina's dagger in the father's hand.

If he saw what the man did with it, Rhys feared he would kill the only man who could save her. Even the Blacksmith couldn't graft a mechanical heart more quickly.

Saving her . . . He pictured the mechanism that would be her heart—a crude pump. He'd heard of others who'd been saved the same way. The clockwork pump only had one speed, and so it was too dangerous to be excited. Too dangerous to move around. Even climbing the stairs could overtax the windup heart. Mina would be stuck in a single room. Trapped, for the rest of her life.

But that was only if she survived. With an injury like this, bug fever became a certainty.

The mother's breath hitched. "They're grafting it on," she said.

Scarsdale's shout rang out beside them. "The bugs are grafting on her new heart!"

Stomps and cheers rose over the steam from the steelcoats and the mechanical clicking of Mina's heart. Rhys watched her blood surge through the tubes. He pressed his lips to her black hair, just above her ear, and said the words he needed to say. The words he'd tell her again, the moment she opened her eyes.

He looked up as heavy steps shook the boards beneath them. The Blacksmith crouched beside the father, studying the mechanical heart.

"You've done good work."

The mother's small hands fisted, and she said fiercely, "We will pay you anything. *Anything.*"

Rhys met the Blacksmith's eyes. There'd be no payment from them. *Not ever.*

"She's already paid enough," the Blacksmith said. "Take her home, Rockingham, and keep her quiet and still. If she survives the bug fever, I'll come to you. Do you have enough ice and opium?"

Tears leaked over the father's cheeks. "I have some. I'll need more."

"I'll see that you get it."

The Blacksmith stepped back, making room for two prison guards carrying a stretcher. He gestured to someone above—Yasmeen, Rhys realized, when the cargo platform lowered to the gallows.

Though it almost killed him, he laid Mina on the stretcher. The heart lay on her chest, subtly rocking as it clicked and pumped. Carefully, the two guards lifted her and carried her onto the platform. The mother followed.

The father stopped Rhys from boarding with them.

"Sir. Thank you for all of your help. But there is nothing left for you to do, and I must insist that you let her recuperate in solitude and privacy, surrounded by those she loves."

That had to include him. Feeling scraped and raw through to his heart, Rhys told him, "She jumped in front of me. She saved my life."

Though sudden pity warmed the other man's eyes, Rockingham shook his head. "My Mina would have done that for anyone. Now, if you care for her, leave her be for now. She can have no stress or excitement—and both seem to follow you about."

Mina would have done that for anyone.

It was true. Stricken, Rhys stared at him. But he stepped back. His gaze fell to Mina's still face, and remained there until he couldn't see her anymore. He'd wait. And if she loved him, she'd come for him.

She might come for him, anyway. His inspector went where the dead bodies were. Without her, that was all that Rhys would be.

And until then, Rhys still needed to make certain that when she finally came, that she could stay. He looked to the crowd. They'd all cheered for her. They hadn't seen the Horde, but a woman who'd risked everything to save someone that belonged to them—the Iron Duke. He wouldn't let them return to seeing her as they had.

So he would give them *Mina*.

Chapter Eighteen

Snow came two weeks before the New Year, the flakes fat and pale gray. Huddled within her overcoat at the foot of the statue in Anglesey Square, Mina watched them come down, sticking to the wet pavers before melting away. By evening, perhaps it would be cold enough for them to stay.

Mina hoped not. As lovely as the snow was, the cold always brought more death—and London already gave Mina quite enough. No need to add freezing temperatures into the mix. Outside the square, traffic seemed to immediately snarl, as if snowflakes hit the carts and steamcoaches like cannonballs. A stalled steamcoach driver stood on his bench to shake his fist at a spider-rickshaw pedaler. Drivers who had installed horns were merrily using them. A shouting match broke out between two lorry drivers, drawing as many glances from the people walking through the busy square as Mina did. A few men and women peered up at the sky in dread, as if expecting the gray to open up and dump piles of snow around them.

But others were enjoying it. Three children who'd been playing knucklebones on the nearby steps while Mina ate her noodles were racing about now, mouths open to catch the flakes on their tongues. One stopped to stare at something beyond the statue.

Mina followed that awed look, and her belly dropped through to the pavers. *Rhys.* Striding across the square—striding toward *her.* The brim of his top hat shielded his eyes from her, but not the determined set of his jaw.

In the street behind him, his steamcoach stood with the carriage door open, and the driver looking after him with surprise.

Her fingers tightened around her bowl. He'd seen her, then. Had jumped from his steamcoach with the intention of speaking with her.

Three months had passed since she'd been shot on the gallows, and they hadn't met in all of that time. She had no idea what he'd say now. What *she* would say.

He stopped before her, sweeping off his hat. His gaze burned into hers, his voice like a rasp over iron. "Are you well, Mina?"

"Yes, Your Grace." She began to rise, but he abruptly stepped forward, hand outstretched.

"Don't. Finish what you've—" He gestured to her bowl. His hand dropped to his side, and this time his gaze moved over her, soft and searching as the first time he'd kissed her—and she felt it, just as much. "May I sit?"

Struggling for breath, she simply nodded. Three months had passed, and yet it still hurt to look at him.

It hurt *not* to, and so she drank in the sight of him. The rough shadow of his jaw, the glint of gold at his ears. The thick lashes that intensified the darkness of his eyes, the penetration of his gaze.

But whatever he saw in her didn't please him. He frowned. "You're thinner."

Ah, well. "It is not an easy thing to first have a clockwork heart grafted to one's chest, and then have it replaced by a heart made of mechanical flesh."

His face whitened. That brim of his hat crushed in his hand. "But you *are* healed?"

"Yes." Stronger, faster—and with extraordinary endurance.

"And you have returned to your job." His gaze fell to the epaulettes sewn into the shoulders of her new overcoat. "I've seen mention of it in the newssheets."

Yes, there had been *many* mentions of it. And the caricatures accompanying them must have been drawn from some of Newberry's ferrotype photographs, each feature true to Mina's own. They had not even tried to dress her up, rounding her eyes or narrowing her face and nose.

"They were kind," she said. "I have you to thank for it."

Her investigation into Haynes's murder and everything that had occurred afterwards had been well covered by the newsmen. And though they'd had many sources, piecing the story together, Mina knew that Rhys had been a significant one—and Scarsdale, too.

"No. I only told them the truth of what happened. The rest they saw for themselves at Newgate. I have you to thank for *that*."

She smiled. "I think we might be even, then."

"No. The accounting does not come close to even," he said, and his fierce stare bored into her until she nodded. His expression lightened, and he gave his own nod, as if satisfied. "I heard a boy from the Crèche reading the kraken account to the laborers in the Narrow yesterday."

Mina had to laugh. "I think they like to reprint that and the Newgate story, simply to include drawings of me clinging to a rope."

His eyes flattened. "Better than drawings of what happened after."

"Yes." She had heard many accounts of those terrible minutes up on the gallows. They had given her enough of a picture. Shaking it away, she studied his clothes, his top hat. "And you've just come from Parliament? How are you finding that?"

"It's much like piracy. You tell your enemies that if they don't fall in line, you'll leave them to die." His gaze narrowed and fell to her grin. "But you know very well."

She laughed. Indeed, she did. Not only her father's accounts, but the newssheets and the political flyers, too. Everyone Mina knew had been abuzz when the Iron Duke had announced that he was taking his spot in the White Chamber, but as the first days passed and he'd remained quiet and seated, simply listening and watching the proceedings, a pall of disappointment had seemed to join her mother and father to dinner—until the day the leader of the Free Party had been speaking, and Rhys had stood and declared him full of more shit than the Thames.

Their meals had been quite lively since then.

"Yes," she admitted.

"And?"

Another laugh burst from her on a puff of cold air. Yes, he knew her well. "And I cannot believe you are *already* talking of giving more power to the Commons! First, you must—"

"Clear out the rotten boroughs, yes. I remember."

His voice had deepened. *I remember.* Mina did, too, every conversation they'd had over breakfast, and it made her heart ache. Such a strange thing, that she could still feel pain in an organ made up of nanoagents and metal.

She suddenly couldn't laugh anymore.

"Where's Newberry, Mina?"

Her empty bowl stared up at her. "Waiting for me to return to headquarters. I left a body for him to examine. I ought to head back and see how he's done."

"But why is he not with you?"

"Oh." She met his frown with a half-hearted smile. Soon she'd have to stand up, to walk away. "Since Newgate, and the newssheets . . . it's not the same. Not as bad."

A fire lit behind his eyes. "What does that mean?"

It meant that she only heard "jade whore" a few times a day—and that people she didn't know would take the speaker to task for insulting her. That in the month since she'd been up and about with her new heart, she'd only been spat at once. That no one had tried to hit her.

"It's better," she said.

"Already?" Something bleak moved through his expression. "But you didn't come to me."

"Come to you?" She stared at him, trying to read his face. Bleakness was quickly turning to detachment. "For what?"

A bitter smile touched his mouth. "So that I could renew my offer to you. My bed, and you will have anything that you want. I'll take you anywhere you desire to go."

Until he was done with her again.

"No," she said.

His jaw hardened. Looking out over the square, he asked, "Do you have another man, then?"

Another man? That assumed that she had one to begin. "No."

His gaze met hers again, burning fiercely. "Then have you been lying, and you truly *aren't* healed?"

Stunned, she shook her head. "I'm well."

"Then why—" He suddenly crouched in front of her, eyes searching her face. "No. *No.*"

His hands shot to her waist, hauled her to him. The bowl flew from her grip, shattering against the steps. Around them, peopled cried out in surprise.

"Rhys!" Mina struggled, but he held her fast, cradled against his chest. "Let me down!"

No one tried to stop him as he crossed the square. He started for his steamcoach—and made an abrupt left turn and entered the nearest building, instead. An office of some sort. He kicked open a door. Three scriveners looked up, mouths dropping open.

Rhys roared. "Get out!"

He slammed the door behind them, pushed Mina up against it. Holding her wrists over her head with one hand, he found and tossed her weapons. His fingers ripped at the buttons to her trousers.

"Rhys—"

"Tell me no, Mina."

She should. She couldn't. Heart pounding, she said, "Let my hands go."

"No." His denial was hoarse. "I can't let any of you go. Not now that I've seen you. Not now that I live again."

He shoved trousers and pants to her knees, until they were stopped by the tops of her boots. His hand worked at the front of his breeches. He rose up, pushing her thighs as wide as her trousers allowed, and Mina cried out as he was suddenly inside her, filling her. Deeper, lifting her against the door, driving his thick length home.

He levered his torso back. Pinned against the door by his cock, held motionless by his hand circling her wrists, Mina called his name on a ragged breath. Relentless, he unbuckled her jacket, ripped aside her shirt, unfastened her armor.

His fingers traced the edges of the livid palm-sized scar beside her breast and along the soft inner curve.

"It's healed," she said, panting.

His gaze lifted to hers again. "Completely?"

"Yes!"

"Good." His hand skimmed down to her bottom, fingers digging into her cheek, holding her hips still as his thick length slid from her body. "I'll shag you now."

She expected—anticipated—a hard thrust, ramming deep. Instead he came into her with an excruciating slowness that left her gasping, writhing. Again, and again, until both ecstasy and frustration had her sobbing his name.

"God, Mina. At least there is this." He buried his face in her neck. "At least you love this."

He released her wrists, and for a terrible, shattering moment, Mina thought he was letting her go. But he gripped her bottom in both hands and began hammering into her with hard, devastating strokes. Her fingers fisted in his hair. Her mouth found his and he kissed her, hot and wet, tasting her deep and then swallowing her cries as she came, shuddering and lifting against him.

With a tortured groan, he pulled away.

No sheath, Mina realized. She reached down, intending to finish him, but he set her on the floor and backed against a desk. He sat for a moment, watching her, his chest heaving. Then his gaze cooled. Pain tore through her chest, and Mina spun toward the door, using her overcoat as concealment as she hauled up her trousers.

Rhys stood and shoved his cock into his breeches. In his detached voice, he said, "We'll continue on, then, as we were on the *Terror*."

What? That wasn't going to happen. And she wouldn't leave until he understood that. She dropped her hand from the door latch and faced him.

"No," she said.

"Why? You love fucking me. The only objection you had was the hatred you'd face in the newssheets. That's not a concern now."

"You said you were done with me," she reminded him.

"I'm also a pirate and a liar. You can't trust my word. So we'll continue as we left off, with you in my bed—or me in yours."

Mina stared at him. How *dare* he offer this to her again? When it was all she could do to get by every day without dreaming of it?

"Damn you," she whispered. "No!"

He came up off the desk, stalking her. "Why? *Why?* Nothing holds us apart now—"

"Until the next time you're done with me!"

"I'll never be done with you!" His palms slammed to the door on either side of her head. Teeth clenched, he pushed his face to hers. "I'll never be done—"

He broke off, eyes widening. His gaze searched her face, settled on her trembling lips.

Softly, he said, "Why would you care, Mina? Why would you care if I'm done with you? Why does that frighten you?"

She closed her eyes. His palm cupped her cheek, and Mina knew he felt her shaking. "Let me go."

"I can't." Warm lips caressed her temple. "I can't."

"You did before."

"No. Even then, I didn't. I was only waiting to take you back." He drew back, and she knew that he was studying her face again, watching her. Feeling like a coward, she opened her eyes, met his wondering gaze. "But now you're afraid that I will let you go. What happened, Mina? These three months, have you realized . . . Have you come to care for me?"

His features blurred in front of her. His thumb tenderly stroked her cheek.

"Come live with me, Mina. Love me. And let me—"

"I can't." It burst out on a sob. Her tears spilled over. "When you're finished with me . . . I can't go through that pain again."

His hand stilled. Face white, he stared down at her.

"No." His voice was ragged. "Mina, no. You didn't—when I sent you away? *No.*"

She couldn't answer. The agony of it broke over her again. She buried her face in her hands, her tears and tattered breaths hot on her skin. His arms came around her, holding her to him, his mouth against her ear.

As her sobs eased, he said fiercely, "I wouldn't have hurt you, Mina. I'd *never* hurt you. But I didn't know you cared. And I sure as hell didn't dream that you would." He gave a gruff laugh. "That's all I've been doing since. I used to imagine shagging you. But since you've left the *Terror*, I've only imagined seeing you again. That you'd come to my home. That I'd run into you on the street. That I'd look up, and you'd be there, and you'd be *well* . . . and I'd tell you that I love you."

He offered her this, too? She wanted it so *much*. She only had to trust that it was true.

"Mina?" So much emotion filled her name, she had to answer.

"I didn't let myself dream anything like that." Her fingers curled into his jacket. Turning her head, resting her cheek over his heart, she held on to him. Her breaths came in hiccups. "I didn't let myself hope. I can barely hope now."

"You *can*," he said, as if saying made it so, and she had to laugh.

He cupped her face in his hands, made her meet his gaze. Solemnly, he said, "I heard you say that when two people love each other, they fight through everything together. Every doubt, every challenge, every pain. *Fight with me, Mina.* Please. You are the only one for me, for as long as I live. And if you love me, fight with me."

Her heart filled. Overwhelmed, she battled tears again. "I do."

"Say it."

"I love you."

His mouth came down over hers, hard, searching. Sealing this agreement between them—a bond as unbreakable as he was.

He lifted his head. "Do you want marriage?"

She knew the vow he'd just spoken had been the same for him. And it was for her—but if she was to have him, she wanted him all.

"Yes," she said.

"It will be done. But if we pass that marriage bill, don't ever imagine that you'll need that divorce clause. I'll tear all of England down before I let you have one."

"I won't want one." She grinned up at him. "And I should tell you—I come with a little girl."

"A girl?" Ragged wonder suffused his features, as if he was torn between fear and joy. He dropped to his knees, kissed her belly. "My baby?"

"No." Almost in tears again, she pushed her hands into his hair, held him to her. They would have that, one day. "A girl, Anne. The tinker girl. I gave her my armor at Newgate—"

His head snapped back, eyes blazing on hers.

"It wouldn't have mattered!" she hastened to tell him. "That armor is best against knives, not bullets—and it was at such close range, the bullet would have gone through, anyway. But Anne felt guilty, and she came to my house that night, and slept outside until my mother brought her in. And she's been with us ever since. With *me*. Though she's still the Blacksmith's tinker, and continues training at his smithy."

"Then she'll be mine, too."

"Thank you." Relieved, she drew him up again, kissed him. "I do love you."

"And our own children?"

"One day."

He nodded. "When we've made this place better for them. And when you're in Hale's position, behind a desk. I'll not have you clinging to ropes while you're pregnant. The caricatures would be—"

Her burst of laughter cut him off until he kissed her again.

And when he lifted his head, he promised, "We'll do this, then. You can hope for this, Mina. The Horde tore into us, I burnt it down, but we'll build it into something better. I swear to you."

Tears filling her eyes, she nodded. "We'll do it, then."

"And whenever we need to leave it behind, I'll take you anywhere you want to go."

He pressed his lips to hers to seal the vow, but it wouldn't be difficult to keep. He'd just have to take her in his arms, and Mina would be exactly where she wanted to be.

Right here.